BATTLETECH:
LEGACY

EDITED BY JOHN HELFERS AND PHILIP A. LEE

BATTLETECH: LEGACY
Edited by John Helfers and Philip A. Lee
Cover art by Des Hanley
Interior art by Franz Vohwinkel
Design by Matt Heerdt & David Kerber
Special thanks to: Matt Fredericksen, Mike "Cray" Miller, Andreas Rudolph, & Chris "Chinless" Wheeler

Published by Catalyst Game Labs,
an imprint of InMediaRes Productions, LLC
7108 S. Pheasant Ridge Dr. • Spokane, WA 99224

CONTENTS

FOREWORD
PHILIP A. LEE

In the 30th century, life is cheap, but BattleMechs aren't.
—*BattleTech* slogan, 1985

Since the inception of the *BattleTech* universe, one of the common threads has been the idea that many of the giant war machines known as BattleMechs have been around in some form or another for hundreds of years. A single 'Mech would often be passed down from one generation to another, like a family heirloom. Regardless of whether a 'Mech remained in the same family over the course of its lifetime, or was claimed as battlefield salvage and reassigned to a Dispossessed MechWarrior, these veritable walking tanks would always be repaired over and over again unless there was literally nothing left to repair or the vital parts were simply impossible to acquire or manufacture. 'Mechs would be salvaged from battlefields, rebuilt to the best of their techs' abilities, and pressed back into service, no matter who piloted them, no matter how much damage they had sustained in previous battles, simply because they were too expensive to replace outright. So as long as a 'Mech could walk out of a 'Mech bay, it would be fixed up to fight again.

But if you replace nearly every part of a 'Mech over the years, do you still have the original, or over time, does it slowly become something else entirely?

Across the history of *BattleTech* fiction, we've seen countless instances of the same MechWarrior changing their 'Mech for various reasons, but in those stories, the *pilot* remains the constant anchor of the narrative, never the 'Mech itself. In *Legacy*, we've flipped that script: each story in this collection showcases a different peek at the life of a single GHR-5H *Grasshopper*, from its birth as a Lantren Corporation prototype and all the way to its eventual fate after nearly three full centuries of combat across the Inner Sphere.

A common question regarding this collection will undoubtedly be, why a *Grasshopper*? Why not something more iconic to the *BattleTech* universe, such as a *Warhammer* or a *BattleMaster*? The answer to that question is simple: though not as heavy or flashy as an *Atlas* or *Marauder*, the *Grasshopper* is first and foremost a survivor. It is a solid workhorse capable of outlasting and outmaneuvering heavier models, and it lacks the ammunition dependency of many other 'Mechs in its weight class. And, most importantly, it gets the job done and (usually) lives to tell the tale. But not even workhorses are invulnerable. They sometimes fall, only to be rebuilt again for the next owner.

This collection features a total of thirteen stories. Veteran *BattleTech* author Kevin Killiany's "What's in a Name?" kicks off this anthology by showcasing an unsung hero involved in the *Grasshopper*'s creation during the latter days of Stephan Amaris's tyrannical rule over the Star League. From there, you can follow the 'Mech's fortunes and misfortunes across an incredible cross section of *BattleTech* history: the devastation of the early Succession Wars; the tireless grind of the Third Succession War; the short-lived War of 3039; the blitzkrieg of the Clan Invasion; the vengeance of Operation Guerrero; the resolve of Task Force Serpent; the brutality of the FedCom Civil War; and all the way to the nuclear fires of the Word of Blake Jihad, which culminates in Craig A. Reed, Jr.'s "End of the Road," followed by the epitaph, "Where Legends Come to Rest."

When you read through this large swath of *BattleTech* history as seen through the cockpit of a single 'Mech and the many different men and women that pilot it, take a moment and ask yourself: What legacy will *you* leave behind?

WHAT'S IN A NAME?
KEVIN KILLIANY

LANTREN DEVELOPMENTAL LABORATORIES
APOPKA, BRYANT
27 MARCH 2779,
0049 HOURS

Lucia Cavaletta cursed and caught her safety glasses before they hit the bench.

They'd slipped off the end of her nose. Again. The one-size-fits-most frames were designed for people with adult-sized heads and something more than cute-but-otherwise-useless button noses. Lucia set the grinder aside to settle the frame firmly against her eyebrows and press in on the temples in a futile effort to make them fit more tightly.

Her goggles—built to scale and complete with retention strap— were on the disassembly table sixteen steps to her left. Right next to the actuator from Prototype One she'd cannibalized. Too far away to be worth the trip.

She felt no guilt about gutting the one-of-a-kind unit, handcrafted for the original GHR prototype. She'd built it herself— its housing was the first she'd autographed. (In theory techs were required to etch their names on every part they fabricated. This helped the engineers keep track of who did what—important in puzzling out which variation had been responsible for what test result. So every part had a name, but only the work a tech was particularly pleased with got an autograph.) She'd needed a tensioner subassembly and had been in no mood to wait seven or eight hours for someone in supply to come on duty and—no doubt after their second cuppa—notice her parts request. She was on a roll.

Or had been.

Lucia leaned her butt against the edge of the stool placed for the convenience of average-sized people using the workbench and looked around. At something past midnight, her task light and the light she hadn't turned off over the disassembly table were the only bright spots in the hangar-*cum*-lab. Not that the cavernous space was dark, but Lantren was all about saving energy (money) and general lighting was cut to 25 percent during off hours. Helpful LEDs outlined the steps up to the catwalk that ran along the near wall to the heavy steel personnel door. Ground level to the outside world.

Behind her, rows on rows of shelves—scaled to hold everything from microcircuits to missile racks—covered most of the soccer field-wide chamber, with the colony of test benches and work stations at one end and the BattleMech bay at the other. The bare metal skeleton of GHR's fifth iteration stood in a clear area. Free of the mobile scaffoldings and devoid of armor—devoid of just about everything except the reactor and gyro—Prototype Five towered like a surreal titan surveying a field of ruins.

My name is Ozymandias...

Actually the GHR didn't have a name as such—just the production designation. The Lantren brass would make that decision—the final choice traditionally a riff on the production code heavily informed by the Marketing Division—but there was (of course) a betting pool among the engineers and design techs.

In the early days, when they were still trying to incorporate stealth technology, *Ghost Hunter* had been a favorite until the spectacular failure of Prototype Two prompted Lantren to abandon stealth tech altogether. The name was still on the odds board above the repeater screen array, but with stealth out of the mix, "ghost" and its variants were clustered at the bottom of the list.

The current top contender for Prototype Five was *Grim Reaper*, with *Harvester* a close second. While both names incorporated Bryant's agricultural heritage and addressed the hunter-killer role Lantren envisioned for their first BattleMech, Lucia thought the martial names lacked imagination. She'd suggested *Grasshopper*— secretly a little joke (the only kind she told) apparent to anyone who spoke Italian. The deceptively fragile but almost impossible to kill insect was the bane of every farm on Bryant. Or had been before Amaris forces destroyed the weather control satellites.

(Bryant would flourish again, she had no doubt. The Star League had retaken the world, and despite the growing storm cycles, most of the farmland was still viable or salvageable. Once Amaris was put down, the League would restore the network of storm suppressors.) She'd championed the *Grasshopper* name on the grounds that it captured the spirit of what they were trying to accomplish. No one realized how dangerous a grasshopper is, she'd said, until their fields were barren dust. *Grasshopper* was at the bottom of the pool, but still a contender.

Lucia resettled the glasses, which had slipped again while she'd sat admiring her domain, and leaned back into the job. She left the grinder where it lay—hand filing and fitting from here on out. Multistage fluidics, replacing sequential hydraulic actuators with a self-contained unit *senza* potentially problematic moving parts, had made perfect sense—particularly at the projected workload of the actuator. But until now it had been one of those brilliant-in-theory-impossible-in-practice ideas that convinced engineers that designers were out to get them.

Heat was the issue. Add heat to a fluid system and you either lose density or gain pressure, depending on how or if the fluid's contained. Solutions considered in the case of a transfer system that hugged the large laser's chamber had been either a convoluted and expensive rerouting of just about everything, or a staggered series of hydraulic units working separately or in concert as pressure demanded. One was guaranteed to cause more problems than it solved and the other was finicky.

But what if heat wasn't the problem? What if thermal energy were part of the solution?

Sixteen hours and forty-seven minutes after asking that question, Lucia had the answer in her hands. Well, on her workbench. At sixteen kilos, she'd let someone else pick it up.

In the morning—later today—the control interface would be bench tested to confirm she'd done what she thought she'd done. Then it would be taken apart—every component documented, diagrammed, recorded, and replicated right down to the file marks—before being reassembled and assigned a place of honor (or ignominy, depending on field trials) on the numbered racks surrounding GHR Prototype Five.

Safety glasses off, Lucia turned her creation under the light, giving it one last critical evaluation. If anything wasn't perfect, she couldn't see it. Satisfied, she slid her files into their sheaths, racked the grinder, and dropped the polishing cloths in the waste. The laser etcher—not engraver, cutting too deep risked compromising the housing integrity—was hot before she remembered to put the safety glasses back on.

I remember Cavaletta. The one who blinded herself with vanity, right?

She only needed one hand for the etcher, the other held the glasses in place. Small *l* for Lucia, small *a* for Angelina, and a small *c* to begin Cavaletta. Her "official" autograph signature was part homage to her mother's favorite Terran poet and part little joke of her own.

The steel door at the head of the catwalk slammed open.

Lucia jumped, her involuntary jerk mangling the autograph's final *a*.

"Run!"

It was Jennings, night security, leaning drunkenly over the railing.

No. Not drunk. Hurt.

"Run..." His voice was weak. He slumped, his legs folding as he clung to the rail.

Training saved Lucia from frozen immobility. She set the etcher in its rest, doused her task light, and pulled off her glasses and gloves in the time it took Jennings to settle to the floor. By the time figures appeared in the doorway she was crouched, lower than the tables, and working her way toward the deeper shadows of heavy component storage.

"He warned someone. There's an active workstation."

He meant the cannibalized component on the disassembly bench. She hadn't been able to shut off that task light.

"Jammers are up and lines are cut," someone answered. "He's not going anywhere, and he can't call for help."

"Concise summary of the obvious." A third voice. "But whoever he is can help us cut through the crap and get the data we need. Find him."

"Yes, sir," said three male voices—the first two and a new one.

At least four intruders.

Lucia had no doubt the smallest of them had twice her mass, probably all muscle, and seeing Jennings fall told her they were willing and able to kill when it suited them. On her knees behind the last workstation, she shed her lab coat and draped it over the stool. Maybe it would look like it'd been casually left at end of shift and not belatedly abandoned by someone who forgot they were wearing white while hiding in shadows. Good thing the overhead lights were on timers—she wouldn't be hiding at all if the invaders could get the hangar fully lit.

She crabbed to the shelves on toes and fingertips, then rose to a crouch to scurry—glad of her crepe-soled lab shoes—toward the racks of armor plating. The men's voices were indistinct behind her. Conversational. They were making no effort at stealth as they quartered the work area trying to flush their quarry. If their relaxed and casual tone was meant to unnerve her, it worked beautifully.

Lucia found some hope in the fact they didn't have thermal or other sensors—if they'd had, they would have found her already. On the other hand, there were only so many places to hide, and she had no idea how long it would be before security mounted a rescue.

"Gryphon," someone said loudly, then laughed. "Legal would be all over them on trademark."

"Gray Hawk," said another voice.

They were reading the remotely potential 'Mech names on the odds board.

"Grendel," said the first. "Someone read a book."

"Ghost Hunter." The leader. "Confirmation, if we needed it, that we're in the right place."

A curved section of shoulder plate was the perfect hiding spot. Lucia forced as much air as she could from her lungs, flattening herself to wriggle under the reinforced ceramic. The metal shelf grid cut into her back, but the dome above her—centimeters from her nose—was so shallow no one would imagine it could hide a person.

She could still hear the voices, though the words were again indistinct. Relaxed, like they had no cares and were in no hurry.

Where was security? Dead.

The certainty chilled her. Jennings. Ricco. Ericson, just back from having her twins. Wallace. The Star League Defense Force had some sort of garrison around the plant—she passed through it, scanned and recorded as she signed in and out, twice each day. But Lantren ran its own security inside the plant. Good people, the ones she knew, and good at their jobs because Lantren shaved pennies on lights, not security. But they were good people, good at their jobs, who hadn't expected any trouble at all inside a solid ring of SLDF security. Nguyen. Pace. What's her name—Evers?—with the red hair. They'd stood no chance against spies—assassins—good enough to outsmart the SLDF. They were all dead.

An angry buzz. Brief. Then a moment of silence. No voices. Again. Maybe a bit louder?

Lucia strained to hear, to identify the noise.

Again. Definitely a shade louder. Again. Louder. Closer?

She thought she heard a crackling sound, faint, and something like a hum beneath the coarse buzz.

Ag—

Lucia shrieked. She threw herself helplessly against the half-ton of armor above her—pounding, clawing to escape the metal grid burning into her flesh.

The agony stopped.

Hands grabbed her ankles and yanked. She was dragged roughly into the open—scraping her back, her arms, banging her face on the edge of the armor—and stood her on her feet.

"It's a kid!"

Two men, big, one holding her the other holding two leads connected to a heavy generator strapped to a dolly. They'd been running current through the metal shelves, one at a time—letting electricity shock their prey into breaking cover. Easier than peering into every cranny.

"Scratch that," said the man with the leads, facing her. He was talking into a headset, she realized. "One adult female. One-forty-five—"

"One-forty-seven," Lucia corrected, habit momentarily victorious over terror.

"Hundred and forty-seven centimeters, maybe forty kilos soaking wet."

"That would be..." The voice of the leader, tinny through the headset speaker, paused. No doubt he was consulting data. "Control System Design Specialist Lucia Cavaletta."

His pronunciation was Deutsch, or maybe English. It ignored the lilt and roll of her name, rendering a flat *Kav-el-etta* instead of the musical *Kah-vah-LAY-tah*. Lucia felt no urge to correct him.

"One of the artists responsible for all these beautiful originals," the leader was saying. "Bring her."

Her mind was clearing. Intellectually she knew her back was probably not the torn and bloody mess her nerves insisted it was, but that was no consolation. She still needed the huge hand crushing her biceps to stand, much less walk. Running was out of the question.

Two more men were waiting for them by the workstation with the actuator she'd dismantled. She assumed the one with his hip on the table was the leader. He didn't look like an evil mastermind—none of the men looked like anything. There wasn't a distinguishing feature among them. Nondescript. Unremarkable. Deliberately and meticulously forgettable.

And relaxed. Men with all the time in the world. Her faint hope of rescue died.

The bright task light had been shifted away from the table to glare down on a chair where the stool had been. From the break area, she recognized. The computer terminal was on but not connected. They apparently had copies of personnel files, but not the protocols to access the system.

She did not resist as they secured her ankles to the legs of the chair, her wrists to its arms. There was a row of tools on the bench, between the terminal's keypad and the very first casing she'd been proud enough to autograph. Pliers, of course, and various blades; a soldering iron on its rest and, leaning against it, a steel wire already glowing cherry hot.

The leader was speaking. Threats, no doubt. Or promises of reward for cooperation. She ignored him, willing her mind not to comprehend his words. She didn't know if her captors served Amaris or Steiner or Liao, and she didn't care. They were here to steal a weapon of war—a weapon they would turn on her world, use to kill her people.

And she was the only one who could stop them.

0917 HOURS

Lantren Industries Research Operations Supervisor Aaron Bosworth flattened himself against the wall, giving the forensics techs as much room to pass as the catwalk allowed. They carried a stretcher between them. A stretcher bearing the shape of a pitifully small body wrapped in sheets. Wrapped in bloody sheets. Aaron averted his gaze.

"Dr. Bosworth?" A man in SLDF Army greens greeted him at the bottom of the stairs.

"Mister," Bosworth corrected. "I administer, I don't science." He cringed at his habitual disclaimer. Not the right thing to say at all.

"Captain Scarlatti," the officer introduced himself. Bosworth didn't recognize the patch on his shoulder. Constabulary, he supposed, or maybe counterespionage. "Thank you for coming."

"Not at—my God!"

Blood. So much blood soaked into the chair, spilled on the floor, spattered on the workstation. Technicians, masked and gloved, were carefully—almost reverently—collecting tiny bits of, bits of...

Bosworth shuddered and looked away.

"Sorry," Scarlatti said. "I should have warned you."

"No warning could prepare a man for *that*."

"True," Scarlatti agreed. "Would you care to sit down."

"Not here. Perhaps we could move, um, this way?"

"Of course."

The SLDF officer matched Bosworth's pace, letting the administrator pull himself together.

"Lucia was tortured?" he asked unnecessarily. Scarlatti nodded. "Without going into detail—"

"Please don't."

"Yes, she was tortured. For more than an hour, quite likely two."

Bosworth swayed against an assembly bench. Scarlatti put a stool by him and he sat.

"Who would do such a thing?"

"Evidence indicates Defiance Industries, acting on its own," Scarlatti said. "Which could mean another House is trying to implicate Steiner. More likely it was Steiner trying to establish plausible deniability."

"Two hours."

"That is excessive," Scarlatti mistook Bosworth's horror for a question. "It would have been quicker to breach the system—but they evidently didn't realize that until it was too late, and they had no choice but to continue. They'd wasted too much time thinking they had plenty of time."

"What's remarkable isn't how long they took, but how long she—Lucia?—held out."

Bosworth said nothing.

"Tell me about this BattleMech she worked so hard to protect." Bosworth looked up at the odds board—the techs' and specialists' silly naming game.

"It's just a BattleMech," he said. "Something different, but not too—a hunter, a survivor, a heavy that can go alone."

Scarlatti followed Bosworth's gaze to the odds board. "Sounds impressive." He paused, waiting for Bosworth to look at him. "I need you to override her codes. We need to know what she gave them."

"You said she fought them."

"She put up a hell of a fight, for longer than most people could," Scarlatti confirmed. "But her fingerprints, in her blood, are on the keyboard. She gave them something."

Bosworth blinked.

"We need to know how bad this is," Scarlatti prompted. "And we need to know who to go after."

"Of course," Bosworth gathered himself. "Who the hell to go after."

He pulled the terminal to life and tapped in a rapid series of codes. He didn't care the SLDF officer could see his every keystroke. Lucia's avengers would have every tool he could give them. Her lockouts surrendered to his admin code. Her files opened. In three taps he had her activity log—

"*Ghost Hunter*."

"What?"

"*Ghost Hunter*," Bosworth repeated, double checking the data. "She gave them *Ghost Hunter*."

"What is *Ghost Hunter*?"

"GHR Prototype One," Bosworth said. "Stealth technology."

"She gave them a hunter-killer heavy with stealth technology?"

"Yes. No. Yes." Bosworth waved the confusion away. "We didn't develop stealth technology, but we wanted our first BattleMech to be something special. Dominate the market and establish our name right out of the box. *Ghost Hunter* incorporated an aggressive stealth technology that we'd acquired from—someone we thought we could trust. The stealth system's matchup with our sensor and targeting arrays looked beautiful on paper. Elegant, our people called it, only a few inconsequential variances kept it from being perfect."

"Surely you didn't keep the plans for this acquired technology here, in your test lab?"

"It streamlined integration," Bosworth shrugged. "And we knew everything would be perfectly safe with..." His voice trailed off. "We thought we were safe."

Scarlatti did not respond.

"But their calculations completely underestimated the danger," Bosworth said. "Powering up triggered an a-synchronic feedback loop that heterodyned catastrophically in milliseconds."

"She gave them a hunter-killer heavy with stealth technology that doesn't work?"

Bosworth nodded.

"The plans look perfect, the computer modeling is flawless." He pointed at the screen as if Scarlatti could see the truth in the file list. "That's what she gave them. But she didn't give them the live test data."

"And if they do their own live test based on the files she gave them?"

"They'll fry their testbed mainframe before they realize there's a problem," Bosworth said. "At the very least. We lost a year cleaning up that mess. Why would she go through torture to protect useless information?"

"Because she was *coraggoisa*," Scarlatti said. "Courageous. Magnificently so."

"What?"

"She sold it," Scarlatti's voice was rough. "She knew they wouldn't believe anything she gave up too early. She knew they had to break her, she knew they wouldn't believe a word she said until they hurt her so bad she was begging them to kill her.

"So she fought them with everything she had. She fought them 'til they broke her." Scarlatti paused, blinking. "And then she took them down."

Bosworth blinked against the sting in his own eyes.

"I didn't know her personally. No more than to nod to," he said. "But saw her performance reviews, signed off on all her raises.

"We all knew Cavaletta was something special."

"Cavaletta?"

"Her," Bosworth motioned at the screen. "Lucia Cavaletta."

Scarlatti stared at him for a moment, then looked up at the odds board. He cleared his throat.

"If I might suggest?"

PORT PAIX, LE BLANC
DRACONIS MARCH, FEDERATED SUNS
13 APRIL 2830

"Hey, Rossi!"

Tony Rossi jumped, not quite dropping his calipers. Looking between his feet, he saw McGuire's mottled, grinning face haloed in a cloud of red curls had been thrust through the access hatch at the foot of the ladder.

"Check this out!" The head disappeared.

Rossi sighed. In the six months since hiring McGuire, he'd learned that level of excitement meant the kid had no idea what he was talking about.

Give him an armature to true or a circuit gremlin to hunt down and McGuire was a genius. Ask him to predict which horizon the sun would rise over and he'd be stumped. His talents for fixing anything he set is mind to was second only to his talents for losing every cent he earned. Sucker bets and magic charms were his specialty.

He'd sent the kid to pick up some gray market parts Wong had promised. Not to pay for—he wasn't that stupid—but it would be just like that *lestofante* to conveniently "forget" Rossi had instructed her, repeatedly, not to extend his credit to his employees. Rossi mentally prepared himself for whatever well-intentioned mayhem the kid had wrought as he eased out of the *Centurion*'s leg.

"What?" He tried to make it a question, not a demand. No need to hurt the kid's feelings until he knew the extent of the damage.

McGuire waved an arm grandly—he had an eight-year-old's sense of showmanship—and indicated a burnished metal component displayed in the center of a hastily cleared cutting table.

What Rossi didn't see immediately was the cart of parts he'd sent McGuire to collect. Before he could ask, Caufmann whistled and waved—he and Reynolds had taken possession of the materiel and were wheeling it toward the vehicle bays. Reassured, he spared the unwanted piece of expensive-looking equipment a second glance then gave McGuire his full attention.

"What?" he repeated, still inquiring. "It's a fluidic control actuator."

"I see that."

There was a moment of silence while McGuire figured out Rossi wanted more information.

"It's for a *Grasshopper*."

"I recognize the configuration." The second pause was shorter.

"It can replace that control module that's giving us fits." McGuire waved toward the shadowy shape of the *Grasshopper* in the far corner of the hangar. "If we can get that heavy running, we can make some real money."

Rossi recognized his own words being parroted back at him. A reputation for selling properly refurbished BattleMechs, not salvage, is what drew mercenaries willing to pay for quality to Tony Rossi's. A credo he drilled into every new hire's head. But the fact it was fresh in his newest hire's head did not mean his newest hire understood what it meant. Case in point:

"We only make real money from a rebuilt 'Mech if we can avoid spending too much real money rebuilding the 'Mech," he explained. "If we spend too much, we end up losing more real money than the real money we make. And if that happens too often, I won't be able to afford so many people working for me."

McGuire nodded at the wisdom of Rossi's words, completely missing the message.

"It's a custom job," he said. "All materials exceed specs and everything is hand fitted. Mrs. Wong said it's a masterpiece, a one-off handcrafted at least a hundred years ago, maybe even two. She said it came from an antique BattleMech used by the Draconis Combine's elite kamikaze warriors."

Rossi looked over at the *Grasshopper*—anywhere except at the shining innocence in front of him. He could just see Wong piling absurdity on absurdity, waiting for the kid to tumble to the fact she was spinning lies. Had she been amused or appalled that he never had? Amused, definitely. No wonder she'd extended him credit on the pricey hardware.

"A Kurita never gave anything as good as a *Grasshopper* to those pathetic convict 'kamikazes' he threw at random worlds," he said. "Two, the *Grasshopper* design is only fifty years old, so there are no two hundred-year-old parts. And gamma, you had no business telling that *chiacchierone* Wong we've got an eighty percent-operational *Grasshopper*. A BattleMech at a hundred percent is worth twice what it is at eighty. We want this machine pristine before prospective buyers start nosing around."

"Well, yeah, but..." McGuire stared at the piece on the cutting table. "But it *is* handcrafted. It's perfect. You don't get joins like that on an assembly line."

The kid was right, Rossi gave him that. Even at this distance the seams on any component housing should have been visible, but this piece looked like a polished ingot. Real craftsmanship. When it came to mechanics, McGuire's instincts were golden.

"And Mrs. Wong said it was better than new. Smoothest she's ever seen."

"And you believed her."

The kid surprised him: "No. I made her run a bench test with me watching."

"And?"

"Energy transfer twelve percent above optimal, response sensitivity above test parameters," McGuire said. "Drop-off and flux were both good—not up to the other numbers, but at spec."

"Really?"

"Really." McGuire proffered a folded hardcopy. The numbers were everything he'd promised. "It's from Lantren on Bryant. The folks who invented the *Grasshopper*."

"You should have led with this, kid." Rossi said. "What I'm not seeing is a price."

"Yeah there is. At the top."

"I was hoping that was a serial number."

"No, that's—" McGuire's hand stopped mid-motion. He'd recognized the joke a half second before pointing to the serial number in its clearly marked box.

Rossi liked the kid. Seeing signs he was developing a brain gave him hope.

"But it's worth that," McGuire insisted. "Especially if it brings the *Grasshopper* up to a hundred percent. Even if it doesn't, this is a bona fried work of art."

"'Bona fried' I believe."

"I'm serious," McGuire insisted. "The guy who turned this out was a real artist. He even signed his pieces. Only the top machinists signed their pieces, and only their best work. A signed piece is the best available—better than anything standard issue."

"Signed, you say?" That was a new one.

"Yeah, etched. It's pretty small, but you can read it clear."

Interested despite himself, Rossi examined the actuator closely. There were tool marks, but exceedingly fine. Just enough to verify it had been assembled by a craftsman and not a magician. Nose almost to the metal, he found a slight misalignment. The actuator had been taken apart and reassembled at least once—but the bench test told him it had been put back together right. Nothing wrong with McGuire's instincts, this was some of the best work he'd seen.

"Where's the signature?"

"Here," McGuire pointed out the discrete line of fine script, then read aloud helpfully: "*La cavaletts*."

Rossi laughed.

"What?"

"That's not a signature," Rossi said. "No capital letters, no periods—what made you think that was a signature?"

"I've seen people not use periods in their signatures," McGuire said. "And Mrs. Wong said many artists don't capitalize their names because they think their work is what's important."

"I'll give you the periods," Rossi said. "And that no-capitals thing is better than most of the crap Wong makes up. But this still isn't a signature."

"What is it?"

"A label," Rossi said. "A fancy one, fanciest I've seen, but it's just a label all the same."

"What?"

"That *s* on the end is really a botched *a*—like the guy's hand jerked—but all this does is tell you where the part belongs."

McGuire looked stubborn. He clearly wasn't buying a word Rossi was saying. He liked having an artist-autographed actuator.

"It's Italian," Rossi explained—gently, because he really liked the kid. "It says *la cavaletta*: the grasshopper."

SWORDS
OF LIGHT AND DARKNESS
TRAVIS HEERMANN

**KENTARES IV
DRACONIS MARCH,
FEDERATED SUNS
17 APRIL 2797**

Benevolence

Benevolence and mercy, love, affection for other human beings, sympathy, nobility–these are the highest attributes of the soul. Just as water subdues fire, benevolence and mercy bring under their sway whatever hinders their power.
—The Tenets of Bushido

Sam Tanaka, *tai-i* of Gamma Company, Third Battalion, Sixth Sword of Light Regiment, decorated war hero, leaned against the trash collection bin, squeezing his palms into his eyes to hold in the horrors embedded there.

He huddled among the rubble of this nameless alley, amid seared and smashed hulks of buildings, ribs of steel spearing from shattered concrete, on a night so black it seemed that daylight would never come again. A searchlight from the regimental compound a kilometer distant swept blinding bright over the devastation. In the distance, the crunching footsteps of 'Mechs on patrol sounded like pile drivers.

Despair clawed at him, chewed at everything he thought he knew. The coarse, jagged grit of pulverized concrete covering everything dug into his buttocks, but pain was the purifier, pain was the only constant in a universe fallen into madness, pain was the truth.

Then a quiet scuffling, shifting, shuffling inside the trash collection cube pulled him back into the moment. Whatever it was, it was bigger than a rat. Other mammalian life in this razed suburb had long since fled.

He jumped up and faced the bin. His right hand went to his hip, where his sidearm should have been, but wasn't. "Who's there?"

The shuffling ceased. "Show yourself!"

He snatched up a jagged chunk of ferrocrete the size of two fists and flung open the lid of the bin.

It was empty. No, not empty.

In the sweep of the searchlight, he glimpsed a doll's head with one eye burned black, the other open and staring. A filthy, handsewn blanket. A half-empty bottle of murky water. Unrecognizable bits of paper and rags. Bits of wrapping from DCMS rations. A ragged hole in the back wall of the bin led into blackness under the rubble. More scuffling away. A rat trying to escape the predator.

A large laser, a sword, a jagged chunk of ferrocrete, any of these could end a rat's miserable life. Kentares IV was a planet full of rats to exterminate, vermin.

Oh, but he was a skillful exterminator. His kill numbers could no longer be tallied. The decorations had multiplied across the breast of his dress uniform. He could feel their weight now as if pinned to his very flesh with serrated talons.

Then nausea washed through him again. His breath was ragged, thick, the same choking air that had driven him from his quarters out into the open night. His skin felt cooked, like he'd just run his 'Mech to the edge of heat shutdown. The chunk of brick fell from his fingers.

He clutched the back of his head, trying to breathe.

The crunch of 50-ton feet clumped nearer, and he dropped down again, out of sight. He carried his identification, but he was out of uniform, wearing only exercise gear. He had told the gate guards he was going out for a late night run. His rank and status had cowed the guards. For months, the Sixth Sword of Light had been shooting first—everything on the planet was considered a hostile target—and not bothering to ask questions later. Their campaign of extermination had been incredibly successful. No centers of enemy population remained within easy striking distance. They had become lords of the lifeless rubble of Kentares IV.

All hail the Dragon.

Even out here in the dark, he could not escape the images that denied him sleep, that had driven him from his quarters.

With the rest of the galaxy obscured in the night sky by thick clouds—hiding the crimes committed here—he could imagine that he was just one man struggling with the tenets drilled into him from boyhood, the tenets of Bushido. That the ancient Japanese from a land—a planet—he had never visited could carry so much power a millennium after the samurai had ceased to exist...

Another movement caught his attention in the darkness. The panning searchlight turned the night into rotating splashes of blinding white and cave darkness.

"You're too close," said a small voice in a barely audible whisper.

The darkness yielded no sight of the speaker. He said, "What do you mean?"

"You're too close to the monsters. They always find big people this close to their house." A shadow shifted, a suggestion of presence.

"Who are you?"

"Nobody."

Just another rat, waiting for its turn to be exterminated. But the extermination had paused when Jinjiro Kurita, son of the assassinated Coordinator, left Kentares IV a few weeks ago. It was then that commanders had scaled back the extermination efforts, drawing down, citing "more pressing duties" than killing every man, woman, and child on Kentares IV. It had become a game of diminishing returns, with 90 percent of the population already neutralized. No one spoke of what had happened. Jinjiro Kurita's absence gave them an excuse to sheath the headsmen's swords.

Sam's *Grasshopper*, along with the rest of the Sixth Sword of Light regiment, had been called to maintenance. Not in stages, as normal, but the entire regiment. And the rats he had killed, personally, untold thousands, gnawed at his mind whenever sleep was near.

"Who are you?" said the rat.

"Nobody."

"You look hungry."

"I haven't eaten in a couple of days." It was true, such was the plague upon his mind.

The shadow darted out. She was small, this rat, emaciated, with hair the color of mud, cheeks sunken and eyes hollow and furtive, in a filthy shift and leggings of gray rags.

"Here." She held out her hand, holding something out to him. He did not reach for it.

"*Here*." She edged nearer.

A shard of blue candy, the wrapper half-untwisted, dusted with grit and pocket lint.

Candy from a starving rat.

He slapped it out of her hand.

**KENTARES IV
DRACONIS MARCH
FEDERATED SUNS
11 SEPTEMBER 2796**

Loyalty

Loyalty and affection are ever in conflict. In the Way of the Warrior, loyalty must never waver. It is the highest ideal, requiring even the shedding of one's own blood to uphold.
—The Tenets of Bushido

"The Coordinator is down! Repeat, the Coordinator is down!"

Memory of those words echoed down the corridors of Sam's mind, driving other thoughts into hiding. The unthinkable had happened. The Coordinator had been shot in the back by a sniper. The entirety of the Draconis Combine's forces had held their breath until confirmation came planetwide an hour or so later. And then, for two days, until the arrival of Jinjiro Kurita, the entire planet held its breath with anger and fear.

Smooth as new silk, his *Grasshopper* had moved through the streets of Carinda City, a town of perhaps fifty thousand in the center of an agricultural bread basket. There was little industry in this part of Kentares IV, but it fed much of the planet. The Sixth had seized this province about three weeks ago, and with the help of the Seventeenth Pesht Infantry, had kept it suitably pacified.

Over his exterior public address system, he kept repeating the words he had been given. "All civilians are ordered to report to city center immediately."

Among one- and two-story homes and apartment blocks, the 'Mechs of the Sixth Sword of Light Regiment walked the streets. The troops went from house to house, clearing them of occupants, forcing everyone to the city center, an open, green park surrounded by children's playgrounds and burbling brooks.

The mass of civilians flowed ahead of the *Grasshopper*'s feet, huddled masses shuffling forward, glancing furtively over their shoulders at the armored behemoths herding them on.

Even after two days, Sam's thoughts felt unmoored, flailing.

The supreme leader of the Draconis Combine was dead.

A private comm channel beeped a request for transmission. "Sam, it's Errol."

Sam accepted the transmission. "A private channel? Comm discipline—"

"Screw comm discipline. We're not under fire right now." Errol Ishibashi, *tai-i* of Beta Company, sounded shaken, his voice quavering.

"Hold it together, my friend," Sam said. "It's a difficult day, but we'll get through it."

Anticipation of retribution simmered in Sam's gullet like bitter tea. The Davions were giving them a fight, but it was only a matter of time. The defenders were outmatched, overpowered, and soon to be exterminated, leaving Kentares IV in the hands of the Dragon. The Coordinator's son, Jinjiro, had just arrived. Was he strong enough to take over leadership of the Combine now? Or would the Dragon bite its own neck to determine the next succession? And how would the rest of the Inner Sphere—

"No, what are we going to do?" Errol said.

"Go on about our—"

"No, dammit! Is your brain online? Why are we herding an entire population into one place? Haven't you thought about that?"

In truth, Sam had not. He was simply following the last order he'd been given to assist in rounding up all the civilians in Carinda City. "I would imagine they'll be screened for infiltrators and insurgents."

Errol's voice relaxed, but only slightly. "Maybe you're right. I hope you are. But there are better ways to do it than lumping them all in one place."

After several hours of clearing neighborhoods, the entire population of Carinda City was now gathered in the city center.

The 'Mechs of the Sixth Sword of Light took positions at the major streets, blocking any exit. Squads of infantry were still bringing small groups, families with hands on heads into the park, shoving them forward.

The afternoon sun's light beamed down like a searchlight, too bright, too stark, too harsh. Comm chatter buzzed around him as the infantry formed ranks around the BattleMechs.

Across the city center, *Sho-sa* Kait-linn Wong's 100-ton *Atlas* stood over the treetops, surveying the throngs. The battalion commander's Death's head cockpit gleamed like polished bone, an armored skull with a gleaming scarlet eye. Her voice came over the comms. "Second Battalion, energy weapons free. Target the civilians. Fire."

The deadly moment hung silent. Fifty-one BattleMechs raised their weapons. Screams of rising terror rose across the park.

Errol's voice came over the command channel, "Request clarification, *Sho-sa*."

Sho-sa Wong's voice was as sharp and bitter as a sword edge across bone. "Target the civilians, Ishibashi. Our orders from the Coordinator's son are to 'kill them all.'"

Sam's fingers hesitated over the firing studs. His *Grasshopper's* large laser and four medium lasers were charged and ready.

"I will not comply with this illegal and immoral order." Errol's voice trembled, thick but steadfast.

Sam whispered, "No, Errol!" Errol was closer to him than his brother, rising with him through the ranks for the Sixth Sword of Light, the Pillar of Ivory, of Righteousness, the most loyal of the Coordinator's forces, second only to the palace household guard.

Sho-sa Wong's voice went quiet and deadly. "Then you are relieved, *Tai-i* Ishibashi. *Tai-i* Tanaka, you are in temporary command of Beta Company."

"*Hai, Sho-sa*," Sam said, a lump of cold lead forming in his belly. His throat so tight he could barely speak.

Errol's voice choked out, "But—!"

Wong's voice was a hissing slash. "Do not dishonor yourself further nor endanger your comrades. You are relieved. And you are under arrest. Power down immediately!"

Two blocks away, the arms of Errol's *Grasshopper* went slack as it powered down. Errol would await his fate imprisoned in his own cockpit.

"All forces!" *Sho-sa* Wong shouted. "Open fire now! These vermin must pay with their lives for the Coordinator!"

Sam's voice felt like sand in his throat. "Gamma Company, Beta Company, open fire. Energy weapons only." Then he squeezed his firing studs and burned three clumps of rats into smoking chunks.

Chaos exploded as the rats realized their fate. They charged the infantry lines and were cut to pieces. They tried to slip between the feet of the 'Mechs and were ground into pulp.

Sam's hands were slick with sweat. Fires blazed across the greensward, with every slice of laser and every PPC blast adding pools of charred, molten hell to the conflagration. Flesh and foliage set ablaze. His aim deteriorated. It must have been the sweat on his hands or the smoke from the fires.

When the ceasefire order came, the interior of the *Grasshopper* was a sauna from its steady torrent of laser fire, even though it had been designed with plenty of heat management.

The park was a flame-licked, smoking wasteland of craters and laser scars. Bulldozers were already moving in to clean up the remains of fifty thousand dead rats. The fires whipped up gusts of hot wind, billowing ash and scorched detritus.

Something small and flaccid slapped against *Grasshopper*'s cockpit window. A tiny, charred sock clung there for a moment, its hand-knitted rainbow eyes fixed upon him. Then it slid out of sight.

KENTARES IV
DRACONIS MARCH
FEDERATED SUNS
12 JULY 2796

Character

A warrior's first lesson is to build his character. Prudence, intelligence, and reason are all qualities to be esteemed, but should never supersede readiness for action—or inaction, as circumstance requires. Warriors must first master themselves because from there it is but a short leap to mastery of all.
—The Tenets of Bushido

Chu-i Sam Tanaka, commander of Bravo Lance, Beta Company—the Stomping BBs, as they called themselves—throttled forward, heading for a high outcropping of rocks that would offer cover from which to rain missiles onto the incoming FedRat 'Mechs.

Tai-i Gibbons's voice came over the comms. "Devil Lance reports a full company inbound. Assault, heavy, and light lances. Target the assaults with all available LRMs. Lance Commanders, concentrate your fire."

At the mention of a full lance of assault 'Mechs, Sam stopped breathing. Beta Company had only lights, mediums, and heavies. The incoming enemy boasted half again as much firepower. Devil Lance was Beta Company's recon unit of *Javelins* and *Firestarters*, light 'Mechs all custom refitted with Guardian ECM systems. They were doing an admirable job of pacing the incoming enemy, relaying telemetry and movements to Beta Company while keeping themselves out of range or line of fire.

"Acknowledged," Sam said, forcing himself to breathe again, using the moment to review the incoming targeting data. The enemy assault lance looked like a *Stalker*, a *Banshee*, an *Atlas*, and a *King Crab*. With the lightest armor of the four, the *Stalker* represented the easiest way to rob the assault lance of one-fourth its fighting strength; plus, the *Stalker* was deadlier at long range than close. "Bravo Lance, target incoming *Stalker* variant. Looks like it's packing LRM-20s."

"Six kilometers and closing," *Tai-i* Gibbons said.

The 70-ton *Grasshopper*'s paltry LRM-5 was nothing compared to the thunderous rain of an LRM-20. Its strength lay in the constant peppering of a long approach—troublesome, but easy to overlook as it chipped divots out of the target's armor—until the massive punch of concentrated heavier weapons at close range administered an unexpected *coup de grâce*.

Since taking command of this *Grasshopper*, Sam had come to relish that final, devastating punch. This was already a machine with history, with character of its own, character he could feel in its gait, in the sounds it made. Every time he went into battle, his purpose was to do honor to his weapon.

The enemy assault lance moved in and out of target-lock as it approached through the dense, rugged forest. Massive boulders heaved up among the thick trunks of forty-meter trees.

In this terrain, the *Grasshopper*'s jump jets made it much more mobile, even for a heavy 'Mech. The ground pounders had to pick their routes carefully, lest they find themselves unable to maneuver at a critical moment.

"Charlie Lance engaging heavies." Errol's voice came over the comms. The thunder of autocannons and PPCs echoed among the boles. The strobing flashes of explosions shook the ground. Leaves fluttered down, even here, two kilometers from the engagement.

Bravo Lance took its perch high on an outcropping. The enemy assault lance picked its way through the forest. "Two kilometers and closing," Sam said. "Commence LRMs at maximum range."

Truc Corlis took the highest point of Bravo Lance's position to give her *Orion*'s autocannon the greatest field of fire. She leaned into the crook of two massive boulders to steady her aim.

"Corlis, weapons free," Sam said. "Fire at opportunity."

"Copy that," said Corlis with that tone in her voice that said she was already seeking a target.

Bert Oda said, "*Chu-i*, did you see that?" His *Catapult* was positioned fifty meters to Sam's flank, poised to unleash his LRM racks.

"See what?" Sam said, his attention focused on the assaults' approach. His lance of heavies would be outgunned, but they had the advantage of terrain and mobility. They would withdraw and attempt to lure the enemy assault lance into range of Beta Company's other heavy lance; against two heavy lances, even behemoths would be cut to pieces.

"Movement bearing two-six-zero, range approximately four hundred meters. Nothing on the scope, but I'm sure I saw something." Oda was not a man to invent shadows.

Sam turned the *Grasshopper*'s torso and zoomed his visuals onto that bearing, scanning the dappled forest undergrowth. His targeting scope was also clear in that direction, but what if the FedRats had set a pincer trap? "Hold position. I'll check it out."

"You're going alone?" Oda said. A lone 'Mech was a vulnerable target. But so was a flanked lance with its rear armor exposed, and he wasn't about to withdraw from a superior firing position without good reason.

"Two hundred meters," Sam said. "I'll be back before those assaults are in LRM range."

Sam turned his legs toward the area, a downhill slope thick with massive boulders in a dry creek bed. He jumped down from his perch to the forest floor. Without the rest of his lance around him, his belly tightened, his breath quickened. *Just a quick dash out to check...*

Using his jump jets to leap over and around fallen trees and boulders, he throttled up to full speed, feeling the thrill of moving 70 tons as light as a feather. He had piloted 'Mechs of various sizes, but he'd never encountered one that moved so smoothly, with an almost organic grace. Most heavy 'Mechs felt like driving a tractor, but this one moved like a sports car.

At 250 meters from his lance, he paused to scan the downhill. He cycled his view through thermal imaging, light enhancement, and EM signatures.

There.

He flipped back to the thermal imaging.

A line of footprints, cooling in the detritus of the forest floor. Two lines. Three. All of the trails snaked out of sight behind a massive deadfall centered upon a bend in the creek bed.

Sam called with growing alarm, "Beta Company, Beta Company, possible enemy presence in Grid Six-Juliet."

"No one's in that grid," Gibbons said. "Can you confirm?"

"Visual on three 'Mech trails—"

Missiles sprayed into his armored torso, sending crackling shudders through the 'Mech's frame, filling his cockpit window with flame and smoke.

His voice went low and calm. "Contact. Under fire. Repeat, under fire." He jammed the throttle forward to present his unseen enemies with a moving target. But he had to get a look at the shooters. Finally, his targeting system back-tracked the incoming missiles. Two *Javelins* had nosed around the massive deadfall and unleashed a furious salvo of short range missiles.

Almost as if anticipating his wishes, the *Grasshopper's* jump jets blazed, thrusting him skyward over the deadfall. Hiding behind it were two more light 'Mechs. In the moment he hung at his jump's zenith, time stretched until he seemed to have full minutes to choose his target. Center crosshairs on the nearest *Javelin's* cockpit. One green and four blue needles gouged blackened furrows across the *Javelin's* head. Sparks snapped out, and the 'Mech's legs collapsed under it.

Sam's heat meter surged into the caution zone. A shutdown alarm sounded, but he kept the jump jets blazing, changing his vector in midair to drop beside the deadfall, out of the line of enemy fire.

Gibbons was on the comms. "Bravo Lance, fall back and engage those lights."

"We're coming, Boss!" Corlis shouted. "Hold on!"

The air in Sam's cockpit rippled with heat. Sweat slicked his palms and soaked his uniform.

The three remaining enemy lights erupted from around the deadfall, raining fire onto the *Grasshopper*. With no option left to him but to die beneath the lethal hail, he slammed his feet on the jump jet controls, lifting him away from slicing lasers and autocannon shells. But the locked SRMs followed him, raking his 'Mech's legs with detonations. His thermal shutdown warning emitted a high-pitched whine.

The camouflage on the light 'Mechs' armor looked wrong. Or maybe it was the armor that looked wrong. Even this close, Sam's targeting systems would not easily lock on them.

Alarm klaxons for incoming missiles sounded. The incoming assault lance had reached LRM range.

Was that how the enemy had sneaked up so close? Some sort of stealth armor? He'd read about such things from the old Star League, but that kind of tech was rare.

The *Grasshopper* pirouetted in midair. A quick vector shift, cut the jets, drop, slam the feet down into the other *Javelin*'s head. A 30-ton *Javelin* could not withstand the sheer impact of a 70-ton 'Mech slamming down on it. Up through the actuators and myomer fibers vibrated a tremendous metallic *snap* and *crunch*. Before the crushed 'Mech could bring down the *Grasshopper* in a deadly tangle of armor and limbs, another blast from the jump jets carried it aside onto level ground. The *Javelin*'s cockpit looked like a crushed egg, and flame boiled from a gigantic rent in its shoulder.

An enemy *Commando* surged toward him, peppering his torso with short range missiles. Armor integrity warnings flashed. Another blast like that would bring the *Grasshopper* down.

Suddenly, the deadfall exploded with splinters and bark. The shell from Corlis's autocannon shot a hole clean through ten meters of deadfall, but missed its nimble target. The incoming heavies of Bravo Lance loosed a storm of death at the only target in sight, staggering the *Commando*.

At this range, Sam could not miss. He spun and blasted through one of its legs with the large laser. The crippled *Commando* limped to a halt. A moment later, Corlis's next autocannon round punched through the *Commando*'s center armor into its fusion engine. Sparks and plasma erupted in a blinding flash, then it collapsed onto its side. The last light 'Mech, a *Commando*, backed away, seeking cover behind the deadfall.

Sam charged around the deadfall from the other direction, hoping the enemy would lose lock on him, hoping that the respite from jump jets and weapons fire would give his 'Mech the moments it needed to sink the *Grasshopper*'s heat level out of the red zone. The deadfall screened both him and the enemy from view of the rest of Bravo Lance.

"We're taking fire from those assaults!" came Oda's voice.

"Take cover and return fire of opportunity. This one is mine," Sam said.

The *Commando* had turned tail, maxed the throttle, and was picking up speed as it plunged down the slope. In a few seconds, it would be out of range.

Sam drew careful aim. One shot. Alpha strike.

Five laser beams pierced the *Commando*'s armor across its torso in a shower of sparks and coruscating flame. The *Commando* twisted and sagged sideways in a way that bespoke a liquefied gyro, then it stumbled and fell.

**KENTARES IV
DRACONIS MARCH
FEDERATED SUNS
17 JULY 2796**

Honor

Dishonor is rot in the heart of a tree. It weakens the tree from inside out. Consciousness of one's personal dignity and worth is ever at the forefront of the warrior's mind. A warrior must never be short-tempered, because he is bred to the privilege of his profession and thus bears the burden of greater power than any other. The warrior must be able to bear the unbearable.

—The Tenets of Bushido

"For bravery and initiative under fire," said *Tai-sa* Evan Watanabe, commander of the Sixth Sword of Light Regiment, "for singlehandedly neutralizing an unexpected attack, for exemplary leadership that saved your command from almost certain destruction, I hereby award you the Bushido Blade."

Sam stood at attention in full dress uniform beside the podium before the two hundred-odd MechWarriors of the Sixth Sword of Light, plus several hundred more technicians and support personnel. His heart swelled against the breast of his crimson-trimmed, snow-white coat. His body was as light as a puff of down.

Tai-sa Watanabe stepped forward and pinned the five-centimeter scarlet disc with a black katana crossing the center to Sam's left breast. Then he stepped back they bowed to each other.

"May Bushido live forever in your heart," said *Tai-sa* Watanabe. "May you serve as an inspiration to your command, to your comrades, and uphold the highest ideals of the Sword of Light. May the Coordinator himself look upon you and your family with favor. May the light of divine righteousness burn forever within you."

Tears filled Sam's vision.

He then turned toward the three other MechWarriors on the dais with him. Errol winked at him from that line. Errol and two others had also earned commendations over the last week of heavy fighting. He had held off an entire medium lance, allowing two of his severely damaged comrades to retreat under their own power, and scoring two kills in the bargain.

The Sixth Sword of Light had finally driven the Federated Suns forces into retreat, giving themselves a brief respite.

As Errol stood up to accept his award, fresh pride surged in Sam's chest, and he held his chin high. He felt taller, stronger, for counting such a brave man among his lifelong friends. Sam and Errol had come up through the rigors the Sun Zhang Academy Cadre together, had shared live-fire training, had helped each other through physical and academic ordeals, and found themselves together in the most prestigious regiment in the DCMS. They had drunk together, fought scorching battles together, and fully expected to rise together through the ranks until they both commanded regiments themselves.

Tonight they would drink together again, celebrate their victory, and Sam would tell him how he owed his commendation to his 'Mech. It was as if the *Grasshopper* knew what it wanted, reacting smoothly, effortlessly, to his commands. He never had to wrestle it.

Errol would tell him that sometimes man and machine simply click together and combine into the perfect warrior.

And they would clink their saké cups.
Brothers in arms to the end.

KENTARES IV
DRACONIS MARCH, FEDERATED SUNS
11 SEPTEMBER 2796

Courage

*Courage is a virtue only in the cause of righteousness.
Death for an unworthy cause is a dog's death. True courage
knows when it is right to live, and when it is right to die.*
                                    —The Tenets of Bushido

Military Police removed Errol Ishibashi from his 'Mech and dragged
him away in handcuffs.

It was the katana Sam had received upon graduation from Sun
Zhang Academy Cadre that, at sunset, he raised above Errol's head.
Sam had accepted the duty of *kaishakunin* as Errol bared his belly
to commit *seppuku*. Sam begged his hands not to tremble, not to
waver, not to *miss*.

Neither of them could meet the other's gaze. Errol's face was
a Noh mask.

It was as if from a distance that Sam watched Errol and four
other MechWarriors stab their dagger blades deep and drag them
through their entrails. It was if someone else wielded the sword
that severed Errol's head. It was as if watching a holovid drama that
he saw fourteen infantry soldiers summarily beheaded for refusing
to fire on unarmed civilians.

They were traitors. They were disloyal. They were not worthy
of the uniform.

That was the last day that Sam Tanaka slept a full night.

KENTARES IV
DRACONIS MARCH, FEDERATED SUNS
16 OCTOBER 2796

Truthfulness

*Dishonesty is cowardly, a dishonorable thing. A warrior
never needs to make an oath. The simple act of speaking it*

means it shall be done. The surest way to cultivate sincerity is to encourage thrift, frugality, and abstinence from excess. Luxury is the greatest menace to honesty; it erodes strength of will.

—The Tenets of Bushido

Destroying or disabling every facet of the civilian long-distance communication networks made the planet-wide extermination possible. If the little rats had known how many of their warrens had been utterly destroyed, how many rats had been excised from the galaxy, how ruthless their exterminators, they might not have gone so meekly before the rat catchers.

Infantry units were sent to round them up like docile, little pets. The soldiers were not to shoot them. Rats were a waste of ammunition. There was not enough ammunition in all of the DCMS's on-world depots to exterminate 58 million rats.

So the infantry commanders took to using swords to systematically behead all the rats they could find.

But sword arms eventually wearied. Blades eventually dulled. The hearts of warriors withered under the onslaught of death, even the death of rats.

The triumph of finally driving the last of the Federated Suns forces from the face of Kentares IV, the resounding victory the Sixth Sword of Light had sought for so long, had turned ashen, bleak, and empty.

The 'Mechs of the Sixth Sword of Light, also known as the Ivory Dragon, representing the pinnacle of the Bushido Code, razed towns, villages, farms, scoured suburbs and city blocks for any signs of rat infestation. Every day, they turned in their tally of rats.

Today, Sam sat in the cockpit of his *Grasshopper.* It stood, powered down, in the 'Mech bay alongside his brethren from Gamma Company. Technicians moved among the shadows deepened by the setting of Kentares's star. One by one, floodlights came alive around the 'Mech bay, and still Sam sat unmoving in his cockpit. His hands, numb after all this time, gripped the control sticks as if glued there by the blood on them. His feet on the control pedals returned to his awareness, but somehow these small physical movements felt like a disconnection from himself.

The hatch beside him sprung open.

"Oh!" said a voice. "Apologies, *Tai-i,* I didn't realize you were still here. Are you all right?"

"Fine," Sam said.

"They called for officers' chow over an hour ago..." The speaker was Sergeant Saru, the *Grasshopper*'s lead tech.

Sam couldn't imagine eating ever again.

"If you want to stay put, that's all right, sir," Saru said. "I was just going to run up the gyros and targeting system and check the calibrations..."

"Very well, Sergeant. I was just...finishing up a few things."

He unstrapped himself, flexed his limbs to reinvigorate the feeling in them, then climbed out. At the base of the rolling stairs, his boots splashed in crimson liquid flowing toward a drain grate ten meters away.

Another tech was scouring thick, rust-red stains from the *Grasshopper*'s feet and ankles with a high-pressure sprayer. A cloying, coppery stench hung in the air.

Paint. It was red paint.

So much of it, though. Splattered all the way to the 'Mech's ankle actuators. Matted with...

He couldn't bear to look closer. It was just paint.

He stood in a crimson river, flowing toward the drain.

KENTARES IV
DRACONIS MARCH
FEDERATED SUNS
1 JANUARY 2797

Rectitude

Righteousness is the bone that gives strength to the arm of justice. The warrior must know right from wrong without thinking about right and wrong. It must be in his bones. Without bones, justice cannot walk, cannot see, cannot strike. Without righteousness, the seeker will never walk the Warrior's Way.

—The Tenets of Bushido

"It's awfully nice of you, *Tai-i*, to host our little soiree," said Rai Sakaguchi with a smirk. A tall man, peppered at the temples, with deep lines carved into his forehead and cheeks, *Chu-sa* Sakaguchi commanded Second Battalion, but tonight he carried a case of

Kentaran wine under one long arm. "Two days of liberty and we can't afford to waste it, can we?"

Sam stepped aside and gestured him in. Behind him came a lean, hard-looking woman with a chiseled face like the planes of a 'Mech's armor. She introduced herself as Krinda Ueda, a *tai-i* like Sam by the blue kanji on her collar.

"You understand this is to remain utterly discreet, Tanaka," Sakaguchi said.

Sam could not very well disobey a superior officer, so he bowed. "*Hai*, of course."

Behind Ueda came four bedraggled women and two men—all rats—followed by two armed guards. The rats looked terrified, as if just dragged out of their warrens into the sunlight.

"Where did you find them?" Sam said. "I thought we had cleared this sector."

"An unnamed acquaintance spotted these lovelies and saved them. They agreed to come on the promise that we'd spare them." The look in Sakaguchi's eyes suggested he intended no such thing.

They were pretty, females and males, even haunted as they were by terror and hunger and besmirched with grime.

One of the males, a large muscular one, carried a crate, which Sakaguchi directed him to place in the center of the room on a thick, hand-made carpet of intricate floral patterns.

"Mighty nice quarters you have here, Tanaka," said Ueda. She gazed around at the elegant paintings that crammed the walls of Sam's quarters, frame to frame. A full set of beautiful, crystal-and-gold goblets awaited the wine. The pair of bejeweled platinum rapiers hung crossed above his hardwood dining table and gleamed in the light of the exquisite crystal lamp in the corner. Rubies and opals splintered the light.

"Lovely taste in prizes." Sakaguchi nodded his appreciation, apparently heedless that such opulence in anyone's quarters was strictly against Sword of Light regulations.

"Thank you, sir." Sam bowed. "I'm glad you...approve."

"We must find comfort where we can in these heinous times, yes?" Sakaguchi said.

The guards forced the rats to sit on the floor near the case. One of the guards said to Sam, "You worried about the carpet, sir?"

"No, Sergeant," Sam said. If the guards opened fire, he would just find another carpet. They had an entire, depopulated world at their disposal.

"You may open the case," Sakaguchi said to the rats.

The male unsnapped the buckles and opened the lid, revealing a delectable mound of fresh fruit, vegetables, bread, and containers of delicacies grilled, steamed, and fried. The spacious crate contained more than enough for the entire party.

The rats' eyes nearly bugged out of their faces, mouths falling open, licking their lips.

"We must show kindness to our guests, yes?" Sakaguchi said. To the rats, he said, "You may eat."

"And I'll pour!" said Ueda, who opened a bottle of deep-red wine and began to fill the goblets.

And so the party began. The wine flowed, a vintage sumptuous and rich; the food disappeared, the rats admirably restraining themselves from gobbling. On equipment Sam had taken from an abandoned recording studio, he played audiovisual recordings of symphonies from around the Draconis Combine, rousing martial marches, clever operettas. As much as he tried to enjoy himself, as much as the music should have uplifted his spirits, he found the black emptiness within him growing stronger and stronger.

After sufficient wine, the night fell apart into disjointed pieces. Raucous laughter that was too loud and too long. Thinly veiled sneers directed at their captive rats, which they bore with averted eyes and false joviality.

At one point, Sakaguchi lurched upright, half naked. "Sergeant, your sidearm."

Unease shot a hole through Sam's armor of inebriation.

The sergeant pulled his laser pistol and offered it with both hands to the *chu-sa*, grip first.

Sakaguchi took it with an unsteady hand.

The rats cowered and edged closer to one another.

He pointed it at the metal ceiling of Sam's quarters, took careful aim, tongue poking from the corner of his mouth, and fired, sweeping the beam across the ceiling. It left a blackened furrow in the steel. He laughed unsteadily, maniacally. A few more sweeps, and a crude caricature of the House Kurita emblem, a writhing dragon within a circle, had been engraved on the ceiling of Sam's quarters.

The laser pistol swept toward the rats, who cowered away. "Zap!" he said, and they flinched. Fresh laughter poured out of him.

Sam drank until he had no choice but to fall asleep, and did so with a trembling rat in his arms.

In the morning, he awoke to a headache that made him want to stare into the emission lens of his laser pistol and pull the trigger.

Everyone was gone, and he never saw any of the rats again.

KENTARES IV
DRACONIS MARCH
FEDERATED SUNS
17 APRIL 2797

Respect

Politeness is but a dismal virtue if it is actuated only by a fear of offending good taste. Rather it should blaze like the corona of a star from a sympathetic regard for the feeling of others. The highest form of respect is love.

—The Tenets of Bushido

The little rat fell back onto her haunches and began to cry. "Why are you so mean?" She scuttled toward where the candy had fallen, snatched it up, and brushed it off.

"Why are you still here?" he said.

She huddled there in the shadows, hugging her knees. "Because I haven't talked to anyone in a long time."

The searchlight swept across them again, and in that light, he recognized her face, even though he had never seen it before.

"No," he said, "I mean, why haven't you fled this area? It's dangerous for you here."

"I'm waiting for my mom to come back. She said to wait right here. She said she was coming back."

"She's not coming back."

"How do you know?"

Because he had seen her. That night in his quarters. He had... "I just know."

She squeezed herself into a tighter ball.

"What's your name?" he said.

"Why should I tell you? You're mean."

"You're right." He leaned his head back and clunked it again and again on the concrete wall. "Thank you for offering me your candy. I shouldn't have done that."

An alarm klaxon sounded from the compound. She flinched and ducked deeper into the shadows.

Distant PA speakers blared: "All personnel report to duty stations. Repeat, all personnel..."

At this time of night, it could only mean one thing. Enemies had just jumped into the Kentaran system. The Federated Suns had come for reprisal. Did they know about the 52 million slaughtered civilians? No matter; the enemy would be repulsed without quarter.

The urge rose up in him to run to his *Grasshopper*, to embed himself in the cockpit, to join with the only thing in the universe where some shred of his honor remained. Something deep within him stirred awake, something that had been driven into hiding.

There was nowhere for this child to go. A few small enclaves of Kentaran civilians still existed, but the nearest of those was hundreds of kilometers away. There was nothing here for her, only 'Mechs, infantry patrols, and rubble wasteland. Perhaps she was stealing into the base's rubbish bins at night to find food. Soon the DropShips would come to relocate the Sixth Sword of Light to the next battlefield.

Certainty of this little girl's fate filled the void in his belly with cold ashes. She would die. And there was nothing he could do about that. Once the Sixth departed, there would be no food for her to scavenge within ten kilometers. If he took her with him, they would both be executed, she as a rat and he for treason.

For a long time, he thought about it, ignoring the distant summons.

He thought about it until the mechanical pounding of moving 'Mechs carried over the distance. The Sixth was mobilizing. He was reporting late—in effect he was AWOL—but dull lassitude pervaded the Sixth at every level of command. Those who noticed his tardiness would simply shrug it off.

The girl was going to die. But perhaps he could give her a few days of relative comfort before someone noticed her. Perhaps in the meantime he could find a place for her. The *Grasshopper*'s cockpit was spacious enough for her to hide for a while, with food stores and sanitation facilities. Such was the disgraceful state of the entire Sixth Sword of Light that the gate guards were unlikely even to question his bringing a little girl onto the base.

And if command discovered his treason? Better to open his belly than to add the blood of any more civilians to his hands.

"Do you want to live?" he asked.

She nodded.

"I was mean to you, and I'm sorry. But I want to help you now. I don't want you to get hurt." He offered his hand.

She held her place, looking at him, eyes wide and fearful.

"Please," he said. The dark, grimy sight of her blurred through his own tears.

She took his hand.

FATES AND FORTUNES
DARRELL MYERS

CAPELLAN CURASSIERS HEADQUARTERS
PHACT
CAPELLAN CONFEDERATION
11 OCTOBER 2840

Footsteps echoed across the ornate tiles lining the hallways of the Capellan Curassiers' headquarters. Carved with images of the unit's founding members, the frieze's symbolism was important, a fact Carl Lipetsk was reminded of almost continually as he had completed his indoctrination two years ago. As he strolled slowly down the hallway, the intricacies of the imagery were truly a tribute to the units' original founders, selected from across the Confederation and forged in the same mold as the First St. Ives Lancers.

With a history dating back to the Terran Hegemony, the Curassiers had endured more combat that most other Capellan units, providing artisans plenty of material from which to draw inspiration. Carl's eyes swept over the intricate carvings depicting Capellan BattleMechs assaulting Hegemony worlds during the Amaris Coup, defending Ibstock against House Marik raiding forces, and most recently, conducting a daring orbital assault that wiped out Marik-aligned mercenaries on Gomeisa.

Regardless of the intrinsic beauty laid out before him, a tinge of disappointment always accompanied Carl on these sojourns. No matter which memorial hallway he chose, the tiles chronicled only one part of the Curassiers—its MechWarriors. Surely the cavalry and infantry units supporting the unit had made great sacrifices along with the MechJocks. Without a single tile dedicated to the unit's armor and infantry elements, Carl knew there would *never* be a tile dedicated to the one of the most important components of any modern combat formation—the technical staff. Without highly trained technicians keeping the units operational, no amount of hotshot pilots would make a difference.

The oversight was typical of modern combat units. The MechWarriors were elite, untouchable—godlike. They were the pinnacle of the warrior class—afforded privileges and status unknown to all but those in the Chancellor's inner circle. Everyone else was beneath them. *Typical MechWarrior arrogance.* Shaking his head in dismay, Carl turned and headed to his technical bay to prepare his team for the day.

Fifteen minutes later, as he sorted through the deluge of communiqués awaiting his attention, Carl's eyes were drawn to one in particular. A verigraphed message from the Lantren Corporation, addressed directly to him. Opening the message, he began reading.

> *Mr. Lipetsk:*
>
> *Thank you for your recent inquiry about the unique workmanship of your GHR-5H model Grasshopper. After a bit of research, we have determined that you may be in possession of one of the original production run. Our records are somewhat limited, but it appears that your particular unit has never returned to Bryant for a full factory refit.*
>
> *As you may know, in addition to producing new builds, we are also able to restore war-worn units to full factory specifications. In exchange for the opportunity to analyze how an early production unit has fared in the heavy warfare of the last century and take a look at your unique fluidic actuators, Lantren would like to offer you a full factory restoration of your GHR-5H at no cost to your organization. Given your location on Phact, the full duration you would be without your Grasshopper is estimated at less than one standard Terran year.*
>
> *If you are interested, please contact me at your earliest convenience so that we may arrange the appropriate transportation.*
>
> *Regards,*
> *Jansen Rivetti, Senior Refit Manager*
> *Lantren Corporation*

Rising from his terminal, Carl debated his next step. His first inkling was to call the tech staff together and figure out who the wise guy was, but the inclusion of a verigraph stopped him cold in his tracks. No one in his office had the deep pockets needed to afford a verigraph, and besides, it would have to be a phony, something that a verigraph, by its very nature, could not be.

"Andrea, get in here ASAP," he called, starting the wheels rolling as his path became clear.

"What do you need, boss?" came the reply as his undeniably attractive assistant appeared in the doorway.

"Assemble as much maintenance information as you have on Bravo Lance's 'Hopper, then meet me in the senior tech's office in twelve minutes. You are not going to believe what I just read..."

Carl glanced ruefully at the battered behemoth parked in bay seventeen, thinking he was certainly on the winning end of this deal—if he could make leadership sign off on it.

UNION-CLASS DROPSHIP SILENT SWORD
HADARI INTERSTELLAR SPACEPORT
PHACT
CAPELLAN CONFEDERATION
27 OCTOBER 2840

"Whoa, whoa, *whoa!*" Carl bellowed into his communicator as Andrea tried to walk the *Grasshopper* into the *Silent Sword*'s maintenance bay. Her first attempt nearly took out an adjoining bay along with her own. Cute she might be, but there was still so much to learn about how to maneuver a BattleMech, even just for maintenance purposes.

"Take your time. She's a tired mass of parts held together with baling wire and good wishes, Andrea. You need to give her gentle commands. Now let's try again." Carl watched her back up and, gently this time, maneuver the massive war machine into its transport cradle. After the pneumatic attachments hissed into place and Andrea vacated the *Grasshopper*'s cockpit, they stepped down the ramp together, clearing the area for the ship's boost to orbit.

Moments later, Carl was safely behind cover when he felt it. A low rumble vibrated the ground as the *Sword*'s fusion engines shot superheated plasma into the launch pit. After a short hesitation, the vessel rose into the darkening evening sky, shrinking in size to a bright dot as it headed for Phact's zenith jump point. Following a seven-day transit, the DropShip would dock with a waiting JumpShip and nearly instantaneously "jump" to a system thirty light years away.

"I've always been amazed by that," Carl heard Andrea say as the sound faded into the distance.

"It is a truly unique sight, seeing what amounts to an oversized egg rise into the sky on a pillar of fire."

"Oh, stop it. An egg, really?"

"Okay, an *armored* egg," Carl said with a playful smile as he glanced back at Andrea. Too late to react, he took the friendly punch on his arm without flinching. The moment of levity quickly ended, though as Andrea pointed up to a cluster of contrails in the sky.

"Is that our DropShip?"

"No, ours is over there," Carl suggested as he pointed to a single point of light in the sky, about thirty degrees away from the Andrea's cluster. "And that can't be a good sign. I'm not aware of any inbound ships today."

As if on cue, klaxons rang out across the spaceport, announcing a possible raid by hostile forces. Grabbing Andrea's hand, he sprinted for the operations building but stopped suddenly. Carl watched as one of the clusters of lights separated from the rest and was rapidly closing the distance with their outbound DropShip. He stared in abject horror as the newcomer closed within combat range, flashed several times, then began heading back to the main group. The lights heralding the location of the *Silent Sword* briefly brightened, then quickly faded out. The actions of the attacking vessel, with its quick return to formation, told Carl one key piece of information. The *Sword* was dead, and there would likely be no survivors. *And given that no active MechWarriors were aboard, probably no mention in the memorial.*

"We need to get out of here, now. Come, this way," Carl ordered, heading rapidly to ops.

CAPELLAN CURASSIERS HQ
PHACT
CAPELLAN CONFEDERATION
29 OCTOBER 2840, 1302 HOURS

"For the moment, the Curassiers are holding the League raiding forces at bay. The Free Worlders seem content to sally forth from their ships, wear down our forces with constant small scale raids, and then pull back as night falls. While inconvenient for our techies, who have to repair the damage, they aren't doing much to reduce our combat power just yet. It's almost as though they are trying to get the measure of our unit before committing to a wholesale battle. For now, First Battalion will stay in contact with League forces, while Second Battalion protects the factory complexes near the capital. Third Battalion will remain here in reserve. Any questions?" The briefer paused, though clearly not expecting any questions from this disciplined crowd.

"Okay, next, we will be conducting a special rescue and salvage mission at the recently discovered crash site of the *Silent Sword*. The primary objective will be to recover any usable combat equipment before the Marik forces stumble across the wreckage." Expecting the next question, the briefer continued, "Of course, *if* there are any survivors, a secondary objective is to provide first aid to our citizens and stabilize them for transport to nearby medical facilities. This mission will commence at 1425 and be composed of elements from..."

As soon as the briefing ended, Carl gathered the members of his tech team and boarded the transport supporting the salvage mission.

PLAINS OF FURY
PHACT
CAPELLAN CONFEDERATION
29 OCTOBER 2840, 1511 HOURS

As the heavy VTOL touched down near the two-kilometer-long scar left by the disintegrating *Union*-class DropShip, Carl Lipetsk could only hope they would find something useful in the wreckage.

He watched with anticipation as the security element scrambled out the lowering cargo door to secure the landing zone; using a mix of lightly armed and fast multi- and single-passenger vehicles, Carl knew they wouldn't last long in a standup fight against dedicated combat units, but he appreciated having them around nonetheless.

Three minutes after they departed the bay, an all-clear signal rang across his communicator.

"Saddle up, boys and girls, and signal your status as soon as you are ready. Looks like we are clear to begin our mission."

"Ready," came Andrea's voice, followed by that of Richard Liu, the team's primary BattleMech technician, and Antonius McGhee, the resident combat-vehicle tech. Two additional assistant technicians responded, filling out the salvage team for this mission. Having received responses from the whole team, Carl applied gentle pressure to the salvage rig's throttle to coax it out of the VTOL's cargo bay.

Surveying the area around the bulk of the wreckage, Carl felt almost certain that no one could have survived the crash. It was equally unlikely that anything else useful would have survived either. Five hundred meters to the north, Carl found the largest piece of the ship resting in a shallow crater.

"All right team, let's go inside and see what's there. Antonius, take point, and everyone be on your toes."

The team dismounted and carefully climbed down to the battered hulk. Greeted with the stench of burned flesh and plastic, Carl fought, successfully, to keep from vomiting. His victory was short-lived, however, as he saw Andrea and at least one of the other astechs lose the contents of their stomachs.

A few moments later, Carl directed the team to proceed down a darkly lit passageway, expecting it to lead to one of the maintenance bays; he was not disappointed. As he stepped into the crash-ravaged bay, Carl's mouth dropped in utter shock. Most of the room was completely destroyed, with smoldering structural bars hanging from the ceiling in a haphazard fashion, ready to burn anyone not paying attention to their surroundings. Autocannon turrets from armored vehicles littered the bay, along with barely recognizable debris that once formed a Curassiers *Locust*. On the far side of the bay, however, still mounted in its maintenance cubicle, sat the *Grasshopper* destined for Bryant.

"Well, I'll be damned. Andrea, check out the maintenance cube at three o'clock."

"What bay? You mean the one over..." Andrea's words caught in her throat as she spotted the *'Hopper*. "How could it have survived?"

"I don't know, but let's not look a gift horse in the mouth. Team, assemble at the base of that 'Mech. We need to determine how to free it and get it ready for the journey home—before the Leaguers find us out here on the open plains..."

Several hours later, as the setting sun turned the western horizon a brilliant orange, the 'Mech was finally free of its mountings. Since it was too big to ride in any transport available to the salvage team, Carl directed Andrea to begin the journey back to the nearest Curassiers facility, 237 kilometers to the south. With a top speed of only sixty-four kilometers per hour, the 'Mech would have to travel exposed over open terrain for nearly four hours, assuming there weren't any unexpected problems. Carl decided to ride in the 'Mech's jump seat, in case he could provide assistance during the trip.

Barely ninety minutes into the journey, Carl heard a sudden increase in transmissions between the salvage team's transport VTOL and Cuirassier headquarters.

"Tango Six, this is Tango Base. We are tracking possibly hostile airborne and land-based activity in your vicinity. Recommend altering your path to rendezvous at waypoint theta-four until further notice. How copy?"

"Copy, Tango Base," the VTOL pilot nervously responded. "Realigning flight path to theta-four. Can you send anyone to assist us?"

"Stand by, Six." The communicator stayed silent for a brief interval, but moments later, Cuirassiers HQ came back on the line. "Tango Six, be advised hostile aerospace craft and ground units have adjusted to intercept your new trajectory. We are scrambling Rumble One and Two to assist, but their ETA is about seven minutes. Hostile bogies will overtake your position in less than four. Recommend going nap-of-the-earth and attempt to outmaneuver."

"R-Roger Tango." Carl could hear the stress in the pilot's voice as he drove the VTOL down as close to the ground as possible. It became quickly apparent that evasion was not in the cards. "Base, they have locked on to us, please help us, please he–Mayday! Mayday! Mayd–"

Carl listened intently for the pilot's voice, but heard nothing but static. The VTOL that brought them and their teammates out to the crash site was now likely one of its own. He exchanged a worried glance with Andrea, knowing that they might have just lost a lot of their friends and coworkers.

"You better activate the large laser and the two working mediums," Carl ordered Andrea. "Let's just hope we don't have to use them."

"I've never fired a weapon, Carl. I don't know if I can do it."

"It's okay, Andrea. When the time comes, you will do fine. If need be, I'll tell you when to trigger the lasers. Just focus on the task at hand right now."

Andrea guided the 'Mech for another twenty-five minutes before the balky fire-control computer began intermittently painting targets. "Carl, we have a problem. The T-11 is detecting at least four targets, none of them apparently friendly."

"Swing a little further to the west. Remember, fighting in this bucket is our last resort."

Carl kept his eyes glued to the monitor as Andrea shifted the 'Mech's path. If they were lucky, it might be possible to skirt the cluster of units without detection. But luck remained elusive. As they came abeam of the group, two hostiles broke away from their formation and began rapidly moving toward the *'Hopper.*

"Andrea, we are about sixty seconds from contact with hostile forces. Remember what I told you. Take a deep breath, and remember what I said. Aim for a small area, and it will be easier to hit your target. And make sure to control your breathing."

Andrea nodded nervously in response.

Dialing up a different communications frequency, Carl called out to Curassiers HQ. "Tango Base, this is Seven. We are about sixty seconds from hostile contact. What is the status of Rumble One and Two?"

"Both are headed your way. ETA is six minutes. What's your current status?"

"Certainly not combat ready, Base. We are attempting to evade, but two ground units are closing." Carl unclicked the transmitter and turned to Andrea. "About thirty seconds until contact. We should have support in about six minutes."

"Keep us informed, Tango Seven. Good luck. Base out."

And just like that, they were on their own, at least for the moment. In exchange for their exclusive rights and privileges, Confederation MechWarriors were expected to perform great acts of heroism. Carl just hoped they'd arrive in time.

His eyes glued to the cockpit windows, Carl was the first to spot them. Two *Wolverine* BattleMechs, most likely 6M versions, rose on pillars of fire over the tree line. A staple of the Free Worlds League, Carl knew they each carried a large laser and two medium lasers, eliminating the light autocannon from the base 6R model.

"Maximum speed now, Andrea," Carl ordered as he grabbed onto any available handhold. Fired from the edge of its range, the first large laser missed the accelerating *Grasshopper* as the beam carved a scar into the forest floor. The second laser found its mark, liberating half a ton of armor in a shower of orange sparks and sending the 'Mech stumbling to the left. To Carl's surprise, Andrea kept them upright, using the momentum to gain extra ground. *Perhaps she's a better pilot than I give her credit for,* he thought, shaking the stars from his vision.

"Keep up this speed as long as possible. We need to close the distance to HQ."

"What about our friends? Shouldn't we go back to see if they're okay?" Andrea responded while trying to focus on piloting the *Grasshopper*.

"There'll be time. Right now we need to stay alive and report what has happened."

"Oh...okay, I understand." Andrea said, reluctantly returning to her piloting duties.

With a slower speed profile, Andrea's speed run of the *Grasshopper* managed to keep the *Wolverines* at long range for only a few minutes, briefly limiting the shots they could make on the fleeing 'Mech. Eventually, however, the *Wolverines*' speed got the best of the *'Hopper*, bringing the League 'Mechs quickly into closer range.

"We're going to have to fight them. Keep your speed up, but twist right and let them have a shot from the large laser," Carl directed as the *Wolverines* began firing rapidly at them.

Andrea dutifully complied, her shot going wide of one of the *Wolverines*. Carl cringed as the return fire savaged the right side and rear of the *Grasshopper*, drawing a yelp of surprise from his fellow technician as she fought to keep the 'Mech upright.

As the *'Hopper* steadied, he shouted to Andrea, "Nice work! Now fire again! Keep it up!" Heat flooded into the cockpit, quickly soaking Carl in sweat as she complied with his order.

Andrea's second shot showed more success, melting armor from the attacker's right leg but doing no critical damage. The

Wolverine stayed in the fight, returning fire and blasting more armor from the beleaguered *Grasshopper*, knocking it off balance.

As the 'Mech began to topple, Carl barely managed to yell "Brace yourself!" before the *'Hopper* slammed into the hard-packed forest floor and blackness took over.

As the darkness receded from his vision, Carl realized he couldn't hear Andrea. Reaching over to her seat in the dim cockpit lights, a wet, sticky substance seemed to be dripping from the combat couch. Sniffing the liquid on his hand, he smelled the unpleasant coppery scent of fresh blood. Panicking, he tried shaking Andrea, but she remained unresponsive.

Carl looked up as a shadow descended over the cockpit, in time to see one of the *Wolverines* align its medium lasers with the 'Mech's spider-cracked viewport. He could see the bright red laser light building up in the weapon's firing cavity. A crushing sensation of failure overwhelmed him, for the loss of every member of his team—for the failure to successfully recover the 'Mech—for a variety of other things. Resigned to his fate, Carl hung his head and awaited the killing blow—

Blue sparks danced across the shattered viewport as a PPC discharged, but the end did not come. Carl looked up in time to see the *Wolverine* topple outside his field of view, a target of Rumble Two, the unit's lone VND-1R *Vindicator* BattleMech. As the *Wolverine* raised its large laser in answer, Carl saw the arriving *Vindicator* disgorge five long range missiles from its chest-mounted launcher. Leaving swirling smoke trails in their wake, the missiles savaged the *Wolverine*'s cockpit. While not a killing blow, Carl realized the missiles must have hit just the right spot. The medium League 'Mech stumbled a few steps, came to a stop, then unceremoniously collapsed to the ground. *That pilot is either unconscious or dead.*

As the second rescuer, an OTL-4D *Ostsol*, moved into view through the shattered ferroglass, Carl directed his attention back to Andrea. Knowing he was now safe from the other *Wolverine*, he could focus on Andrea's apparently serious injuries.

"Andrea, Andrea! Can you hear me?" No response. Carl fumbled around in the dark for the emergency cockpit lights, desperate to provide aid to the assistant tech-cum-pilot. Once those were activated, he checked her pulse—slow and thready— and sought the source of the sticky blood dripping from the command couch.

Carefully checking his friend over in the reddish hued darkness, Carl found the source. A long gash had opened along the right side of Andrea's face, extending from her ear all the way down to her neck. *My god*, Carl thought, *I've got to stop this bleeding before it's too late.*

Completely focused on Andrea's injuries, Carl did not notice that the battle raging outside of the cockpit had ended. When he finally looked up again, both friendly 'Mechs were towering above the fallen *Grasshopper*, and the *Vindicator*'s pilot was on his way down via a cockpit ladder.

A few minutes later, the cockpit hatch hissed open to reveal Rumble Two's MechJock with an armful of medical supplies. Carl noted the moment of shock as the responding MechWarrior realized that mere technicians were at the controls of the high-tech war machine. In the background, the staccato sound of VTOL blades steadily grew louder as a rescue craft raced to the still searing-hot battle scene.

THREE HOURS LATER

In the seven hours since the salvage team departed, the Curassiers' HQ had undergone a significant transformation from peacetime garrison to wartime nerve center. Where infantry and armor units formerly provided perimeter security, each checkpoint now had a BattleMech in attendance for added firepower. Carl counted no less than six 'Mechs actively patrolling, keeping the League forces away from the facility.

Buoyed by news that his salvage team had survived the crash and escaped into the nearby foliage before the raiders had reached the crash site, Carl nodded in appreciation at the pilots of Rumble One and Two, the 'Mechs that had raced to his rescue. If not for their quick arrival and equally speedy dispatching of the *Wolverines*, he knew Andrea and he wouldn't be alive right now.

While Andrea underwent emergency surgery in the Curassiers' medical facilities, he knew he had to make her near-sacrifice worth it. He quickly drew up a plan to restore the *Grasshopper* to a semblance of fighting trim. The following morning, he put the plan into action.

"Richard, I need you to gather up all of the scrap armor you can find, as well as these other items," Carl explained as he handed a parts list to the team's chief 'Mech tech.

"Roger, sir. I think I can get all of this in about three days."

"You've got two," Carl ordered with a determined grin on his face.

"I'll do my best."

Hours became days, but soon the derelict *Grasshopper* began to look like the combat machine it was. Key components, such as the balky Allet T-11 targeting computer, still needed replacement, but a skilled MechWarrior could now take the machine into combat with at least an even chance of surviving the first few minutes of an engagement.

Ten days after he started, Carl presented the *Grasshopper* to the unit's chief technician for return to combat duty. "This can't be the same *Grasshopper* that flew aboard the *Sword*," he said in disbelief.

With a proud smile, Carl responded to his boss. "Not only is it the same machine, it now has a fully operational weapons package." All of the combat systems onboard have been restored, and its armor complement is back to specification."

"You've done well, Carl," the chief tech replied, pausing to carefully phrase his words before continuing. "I know Andrea would be proud of your team if she wasn't still in a medically induced coma, thanks to the injuries she sustained. I just want to make sure you don't harvest too much of your anger and hate to perform these miracles. That kind of thing will burn you out faster than you can imagine, and won't help the Curassiers in the long run."

"I understand sir, and I'll try to keep my desire for revenge under control."

"You do that, Carl. And good work."

THE LONESOME DOVE
COLUMBA, PHACT
CAPELLAN CONFEDERATION
2 NOVEMBER 2840, 1323 HOURS

Carl sipped his lemonade as he watched the restaurant patrons come and go. Made from genetically engineered Terran lemons transplanted to the planet in the 2600s, he enjoyed both the extreme sour taste and the nearly orange color of the beverage. After coming to this restaurant almost daily for the last six months, Carl had a reserved seat near the bar and never needed to order. All he did was show up, and a few minutes later one of the wait staff brought him a tall glass of his favorite beverage. *At least there's an island of calm in this chaotic world.*

Five minutes later, Carl's mind snapped back to the here and now as his communicator chirped with a message from HQ. Several 'Mechs returning from a raid against the League forces had sustained heavy damage and needed immediate attention.

Well, it was good while it lasted. Draining the last of his lemonade, Carl dropped a few L-Bills on the table to cover his tab, climbed into his personal hovercar, and headed back to base.

"What have they done to you?" Carl asked the 'Mech rhetorically as he pulled up to the maintenance facility and got a look at the *Grasshopper*'s damage.

"Hi, boss," Antonius called out from the ground near the 'Mech's pitted right-foot armor. "We've begun an inventory, and here's what we have so far."

Peeling his eyes away from the 'Mech that had been in near pristine condition just hours ago, Carl quickly read the proffered list. *Damaged armor, most locations; destroyed left arm, up to shoulder; combat computer failure; partial engine shielding damage, gyro instability.*

"Damn. I really hoped we wouldn't have to deal with that T-11 computer while we try to find a replacement, but I guess it's just not to be. Salvage some engine shielding from the *Warhammer* that was scrapped yesterday, and start working on the armor replacement. Have Richard start rebuilding the arm and try to hunt down another replacement Diplan laser."

"What about the gyro? Andrea was the best at fixing those, given her slim build and talented hands."

"Tell me about it." The image of Andrea laid up in the hospital's intensive care unit, with machines keeping her breathing, came unbidden to Carl's mind. With a pang of regret, he said, "Since she won't be back with us any time soon, if ever, we'll have to make do with one of the astechs. Have the smaller of the two get up in the gyro cavity and try to find out what's wrong. I'm going to get started on trying to rig up a bypass on the T-11. Questions?" With none forthcoming, Carl said, "Let's get to work."

As he worked on the Allet targeting computer, Carl found new uses for several curse words in his vocabulary. The board itself already had bypasses around several key components, no doubt the cause of its intermittent function. Damage from this last engagement had shorted most of the remaining functional circuits, as well as about a third of the bypasses. To restore full functionality, Carl had two choices: replace the computer entirely or basically rebuild it from the ground up. As both of those options required time and resources he did not have, Carl chose a third option. He wired the board so that all five lasers would fire simultaneously, bypassing the burned-out weapon-selection circuitry. Carl knew the MechWarrior who currently piloted the 'Mech wouldn't be terribly happy, but he really didn't care. It was either use the 'Mech with all of the lasers firing, or none.

The next morning, the team was working hard on re-armoring the 'Mech when Carl heard the distinctive sound of inbound artillery. As the sound of rippling linen passed by his head, Carl threw himself to the ground and yelled out, "Take cover!" Six shells landed nearby in rapid succession, showering the team with dirt and a few chunks of shrapnel.

Carl was helping to bandage a shrapnel wound when the raid sirens began sounding. "Everybody out of the 'Mech and into the bunkers!" he ordered. As the techs scrambled for the underground shelters, Carl saw the *Grasshopper*'s pilot headed up to the cockpit.

"She's not finished," Carl called out in warning.

"Just tell me what I have! We have hostile 'Mechs converging on the base!"

"All right. The gyro is still shaky, and all your lasers are on a single circuit. Best we could do in twenty-four hours."

Carl thought he heard the MechWarrior mutter something under her breath as she sealed up the cockpit, but quickly forgot about it as he headed toward and inside the bunker. For the next thirty minutes, Carl worked to keep his team calm while the battle raged overhead. Complicating the effort, several near misses seemed to shake the facility to near collapse, complete with flickering emergency lights and chunks of ferrocrete raining down on those inside the bunker. As the senior person in the underground facility, he quickly became the focal point for everyone taking shelter from the combat above. When the all-clear finally sounded, Carl was certain he was more relieved than anyone else to be leaving the death trap they were all crammed into.

"Is everyone okay? Then let's go find our 'Mech." Carl ordered as they exited the battered and pockmarked shelter. Scanning the area where he last spotted the behemoth headed to meet the onrushing assault, Carl was relieved that he did not see it among the destroyed BattleMechs scattered around the base's perimeter. Stepping carefully to minimize the chances of disturbing any unexploded projectiles, Carl quickly surveyed the wreckage. He found seven downed League 'Mechs, four Curassiers 'Mechs, and several combat vehicles from both sides, but no sign of the *Grasshopper*. He watched as two MechWarriors were carefully extracted from their stricken 'Mechs and rushed to a field medical facility, but counted many ground infantry soldiers that would never fight again. The price of this battle was high, but the base had held.

A cacophony of noise soon got the team's attention. Looking back towards the maintenance bay, Carl's brief sense of elation quickly turned to disappointment. The *'Hopper* had indeed survived the battle, but it looked worse than it had before the ill-fated refit flight. Loose armor panels dangled off the 'Mech's savaged frame, and it walked with a pronounced limp. Also missing now was the right arm and its attendant laser. Seeing the same shock and dismay on the face of each technical team member present, Carl knew he needed to act quickly.

"Curassiers, I know how you must feel right now. Each of you has poured your heart and soul into our *Grasshopper* over the last several weeks, taking a virtual wreck and making it combat ready. Now you gaze out and see your hard work dashed yet again. But have heart. If not for your hard work and dedication, that 'Mech would not have been available to defend this base and our comrades. If not for your perseverance, we may well be part of the Free Worlds League now."

Carl let that last statement sink in for a moment, seeing the anger and then pride welling up in his team. "The Chancellor has chosen each of us because we are the best. Let us once again honor his Celestial Wisdom. Each of you knows your position on this team. Let's roll our sleeves up and make her whole once again. For the Chancellor!"

"*For the Chancellor*!" the team responded with one voice, and got back to work.

LANTREN CORPORATION
APOPKA, BRYANT
CAPELLAN CONFEDERATION
18 MARCH 2843, 2044 HOURS

Lightning flashed across the sky as the storm hammered the domes protecting the Lantren factory complex. At one time terraformed and protected by a global weather-control network, the planet was now constantly wracked by intense storms. Most of Bryant's inhabitants lived in the less volatile polar regions, with only a select group of people remaining in the factory complex. Once a major producer of the *Grasshopper* BattleMech, continued damage over the decades had reduced the factory to a shell of its former self. Now only capable of producing a few parts and performing factory refits, the facility nevertheless remained a constant target of raiders.

As Jansen Rivetti looked through the dome's reinforced windows, he swore he kept seeing crimson flashes in addition to the powerful lightning bolts lashing down from the turbulent weather front. *Maybe I'm just seeing things.* As he was about to turn away from the window, the ground-level flashes, now intermixed with emerald bolts, grew more intense. *That can't be a coincidence.* "Rebecca, contact security, I think we may be under attack. And then take cover."

As he kept watch out the dome's viewing portal, his peripheral vision caught Rebecca reaching for the nearest comm and relaying the information to facility security. Splitting his attention, he watched his coworker become pretty animated as she spoke, something Rebecca was not known for. A particularly loud thunderclap drowned out her words as she cut the comm off, but by the agitated look on her face, Jansen got the gist of it.

Moments later, he heard raid sirens sound throughout the complex. Satisfied that he'd done his part, Jansen backed away from the window, quickly walking toward where Rebecca was using a coat closet as protection.

Halfway across the room, he was suddenly knocked off his feet by a powerful blast from where the window he'd just vacated had been. The biodome's pressurization, in place for the comfort and safety of Lantren's workers, now became a liability as the sudden shift in pressure peppered Jansen with shards of sharp ferroglass.

Holding on to the edge of consciousness thanks to the intense pain wracking his body, Jansen looked up as a shadow loomed over the remains of the dome.

"*Well, what do we have here?*" boomed a synthesized voice. A bolt of lightning backlit the shadow, revealing none other than the unmistakable shape of a GHR-5H *Grasshopper*. As Jansen watched, the 'Mech raised its arm and fired at Rebecca's closet, almost certainly ending her life.

Jansen wanted to scream, but the ferroglass shards had done their job. Bleeding from nearly everywhere on his body, Jansen was unable to summon the strength to make even the smallest sound. He knew, however, that destruction of the domes signaled the end of Lantren. Unable to rebuild the Star League-era domes, the storms would certainly destroy what remained of the facility. *How ironic*, he thought, *that a* Grasshopper *would be the 'Mech to finally finish off the factory.* Any further thoughts were cut off as the crimson beam swept across his body, reducing it to ash.

CAPELLAN CURASSIERS HQ
PHACT
CAPELLAN CONFEDERATION
23 APRIL 2843

> *The Curassiers Memorial Halls. Once a tribute only to MechWarriors in the unit, one person's brave sacrifice finally opened the doors to the rest of history. The Curassiers are a team: MechWarriors, cavalry, aerospace, infantry, and yes, support staff. We will never forget that—or you.*
> *Goodbye, Andrea.*

Carl wiped a single tear from his eye as he slowly walked away from the freshly installed tiles commemorating the 2840 defense of Phact. He knew it would be some time before he returned to these halls.

As he headed to his next meeting, Carl reflected on another tribute he'd paid to Andrea, this one more personal and private.

Knowing most MechJocks leave a mark of some sort in their 'Mechs to signify their tenure as its pilot, he felt Andrea should be no different. During one of his many maintenance sessions in the 'Hopper, Carl ensured that her name would remain a part of its history until the day it was destroyed or retired.

Unexpectedly summoned to the chief technician's office, Carl wondered if they would finally get the chance to send the Grasshopper back to Bryant for its refit. Knocking on the heavy wooden door, he could hardly contain his curiosity.

"Come in."

"Technician Carl Lipetsk reporting as ordered, sir."

"Take a seat, please." Carl noticed the edge of tension in his boss's voice, which only made him more curious. "I know you really want to go through with the Grasshopper's refit, but I am afraid that is no longer an option."

"I don't understand," Carl replied, trying to figure out what was holding up the refit plan. Thinking back over all that had happened over the last three years, he felt his anger welling up inside. Andrea had succumbed to the injuries sustained during the aborted attempt to get the 'Mech to Bryant. To not go through with it now would cheapen her sacrifice, making it worth nothing.

With scarcely concealed frustration, he asked through gritted teeth. "May I ask why not?"

"Carl, we all loved Andrea, each in our own way. Given her passing, I know this refit is now even more important to you than ever. The reason, however, is a simple one. The Lantren factory no longer exists. Intel suggests that raiders in Marik livery damaged the facility's biodomes, and the planetary storms did the rest. I felt I at least owed you the notification in person. I am very sorry."

After a moment of disbelief, Carl composed himself and thanked his boss for the explanation. Stepping out of the office and into the crisp morning air, he headed to the only place he found peace since Andrea had passed—the maintenance bay.

Carl selected some tools from his kit and got right back to work on the Grasshopper, as though he'd never known about Lantren's offer. Since a full factory refit was no longer feasible, he'd have to fix it up himself, and that meant nearly disassembling and reassembling the entire 'Mech one component at a time. A nearly insurmountable amount of work, especially for a lone technician.

He told the other techs he was putting so much solo effort into restoring this one 'Mech for the glory of the Chancellor, and maybe there was some truth to the idea. But each component he repaired, each replacement part he machined by hand, each rivet he punched into place—he did it all with meticulous care, for he could think of no better way to honor Andrea's memory and keep her alive just a little while longer.

And as long as this 'Mech persisted, Carl knew a part of her spirit would persist along with it.

THE FORGOTTEN PLACES
ALAN BRUNDAGE

CAMP SCINDIAN
NEAR SHALMIRAT, KESAI IV
DRACONIS MARCH
FEDERATED SUNS
12 APRIL 2973

The darkness enveloped Olivia like a thick and comforting blanket, smothering the fresh pains recently inflicted upon her body. Beside her, rhythmic breathing, heavy and slow. He was still asleep. Opportunities like this were rare, and she had already squandered several.

Slipping out from under the covers, Olivia padded quietly across the room to her pile of clothes. There, she located her tool belt by feel and pulled out the dagger she had concealed there weeks ago. Slipping back to the bed, she looked down at her "master." Cicero Arne had made her life a living hell, all because she was a native of Kesai, which meant that a few hundred years ago her ancestors had been Dracs. In his mind, that gave him free rein to treat her as subhuman.

She let down the internal mental wall she'd erected to shield herself from the abuses constantly heaped upon her. She let the rage and hopelessness from a life of servitude and abuse surge through her, giving her the strength for the next action. She drew back the sheet twined about him and raised the dagger, holding it aloft with both hands. Guided by the moonlight from the window, she plunged the dagger down with all her strength, just as she had dreamed of doing for years. She felt the tip glance off bone before sinking in. Blood gushed out, splashing everywhere.

Cicero's eyes shot open, as did his mouth. She let go of the dagger with her left hand, jamming her arm across his open mouth to smother his cries. His eyes were wild with pain and anger as he struggled to buck her off. Failing that, he bit her, his teeth puncturing her skin, but she hung on tight. She even managed to draw out the dagger and stab him repeatedly in the sides, hoping to pierce some vital organ.

She could feel his cries for help, muffled against her arm, even as she felt his strength waning, his attempts to dislodge her becoming less and less effective. Their eyes locked, his now pain-filled and terrified, hers empty and cold.

Leaning down, she whispered into his ear what he had so often asked her: "How does it feel?"

He never answered, giving one last violent shudder, before sagging limp, lifeless. Olivia looked at his face, the eyes glassy and fixed on nothing. She sat up, wincing as she pulled her mauled and bloody arm out of his mouth. She leaned back, staring at the ceiling, waiting for the relief and feeling of triumph, but there was... nothing. Only emptiness.

She had no idea how long she sat like that, but it was still dark when she came to her senses. She prized herself off the sticky mess of the bed and stumbled to the washroom, leaving the dagger and everything else behind. On autopilot, she filled the small tub and climbed in, the water quickly turning pink with diluted blood. She grabbed a cloth and began trying to scrub herself clean, trying to peel off the past along with layers of her skin. Rinsing herself with the shower head before moving to the sink, where the medicine cabinet was. The functioning part of her brain knew she had to clean the wound on her arm lest it become infected. The antiseptic burned, but that just meant it was working. After wrapping her arm tightly with gauze, she looked into the mirror.

The face looking back at her was the same as always. Thin and sharp-featured, nose crooked from a previous break...Cicero's work. Thin lips on a small mouth, covering a prominent overbite. Shoulder-length black hair slicked straight back. Dark brown eyes. Eyes that were haunted now, surrounded by dark circles and filled with the inescapable knowledge of what she was capable of.

It was the face of a murderer.

A *murderer*.

She began to shake, trembling, short of breath and sick, bile struggling to escape. A single sob escaped her as she took a step back. Her legs collapsed beneath her and she fell to the floor. The edges of the poorly grouted tile dug into her skin, but she didn't care. She curled up into a ball, tears streaming from her eyes, mouth open in a silent scream.

More time passed, she wasn't sure how much, but less than before.

"Get up," she whispered. But she continued quivering on the rapidly cooling floor.

"Get up, you stupid bitch," she growled. Slowly, she uncurled herself and sat up, letting a wave of vertigo wash over her. Standing, she quickly splashed water on her face, washing away the tracks of her tears.

Returning to the bedroom, she ignored the mess on the bed, going over to her clothes instead. She shrugged into her jumpsuit, fumbling as she struggled to lace up her boots. She grabbed her tool belt and turned, facing the bed, and her handiwork.

"I feel like I should say something witty or profound, like they do on the holovids," she addressed the corpse, "but I'm not going to waste any more thought on you."

She headed to the door, exiting into a darkened hallway illuminated only by a few flickering bulbs. She made sure the door was locked, and in a fit of inspiration, filled the keyhole with quick setting resin from her repair kit. Then she turned on her heel and left.

Walking through the camp was surreal: nothing had changed, yet everything was different. She nodded to the guards and other astechs she passed, same as always. They largely ignored her, again same as always. No one sensed the profound change that had come over her. It left her feeling oddly giddy.

Everything was proceeding smoothly until she got to the hangar. All the camp's 'Mechs and vehicles were stored there, but given that it was the middle of the night and the generally pathetic discipline, there usually wasn't anyone on duty.

So of course tonight there was.

"Hey, Liv!" The voice cracked slightly, betraying the youth of the speaker.

Taking a deep breath, she forced herself to act normally. "Hi, Bobby, I don't usually see you here." *Calm, calm. Act normal.*

"Yeah, my leftenant figured I could use the experience of having to stay up all night protecting our stuff from vicious sand dunes."

He rolled his eyes for effect. "Personally, I just think she's pissed I beat her at poker."

She pasted a smile on her face. "Never does to anger the boss."

"Uh—yeah." Bobby winced and looked down. So he'd heard about her and Cicero then. Poor kid's illusions of glory and service were being shattered. She couldn't bring herself to care.

His response was muted. "True. So, uh, what brings you down here at oh-god-I'm-tired hundred hours?"

She weighed her options lightning quick: she could be honest, or press her luck and try to knock out a trained soldier.

"I need a buggy—I need to get out of here." She fumbled desperately for his arm. "Please, you've heard what it's like here for me. I can't take it anymore." She felt a twinge of guilt about not being completely honest.

"I..." He stopped and sighed. Bit his lip. "Okay. I never saw you here."

"Thank you," she said, and this time the smile was genuine.

Wasting no time, she retrieved her small duffle of carefully scrounged supplies and threw it in the buggy. Climbing in, she felt free in a way she hadn't since she was a small child. She gunned the ICE and drove off into the night.

NORTH OF CAMP SCINDIAN
KESAI IV
DRACONIS MARCH, FEDERATED SUNS
14 APRIL 2973

The sun hung hot and harsh in the evening sky. Olivia stood beside the buggy, its engine now depleted. Luckily, she had cleared the canyon before the engine gave out. The rocky terrain had left no tracks to follow, and she hoped that if the militia was looking for her, they would assume she was heading for Shalmirat and Cochi Spaceport.

Instead, she had gone the opposite direction, hoping to reach the oasis northwest of the camp and once there join one of the bands of nomads. She knew life in the desert was harsh, but it would be a harshness of her own choosing. And that was all that mattered.

"Time to start walking, Liv."

Having waited for nightfall, she walked all night. Her meager supplies hardly weighed her down at this point, and the activity kept the night chill at bay. The activity also prevented her from dwelling on what she had done.

By the time the sun began to rise, she was so very tired. It was a struggle to move, but she needed to find shelter before the sun was out in full force. That was why she was fixated on a tantalizingly near hill. With luck there would be a cave, and at the very least there would be shade for part of the day.

Passing several sand-buried mounds, too small to offer shelter, she knew she was close. The hill was in sight now, its lines strangely regular. The closer she got, the odder it looked. Unnatural. But there wasn't any other option, so she pressed on.

Eventually, she arrived at the hill, which looked strange even close up. Tired though she was, she walked all around it, searching for a cave or overhang. She was ready to give up when she came across a slightly triangular hollow and crawled into the space. Collapsing onto the mildly warm ground, her exhaustion a palpable thing, she heard a steady trickle of falling sand behind her.

"I don't care," she muttered, but the sound continued, snagging her attention. What if the hollow were collapsing?

Forcing her weary body to move, she dug in her jumpsuit and pulled out a penlight. A small cone of brilliant light burst forth. She had to blink several times to adjust her eyes to the change in light. When she could make out what the light revealed, she almost cried. Refracted light revealed an obviously manmade interior of some kind, maybe a bunker left over from the days of the Star League.

Sleep now forgotten, she crawled inside. Flashing the light around revealed a cramped hallway, the floor oddly tilted down and to the side. Proceeding farther into the hall, she came to a hatchway. There had been labels of some kind, but the elements had scoured them blank. She spun the wheel on the hatch and pushed. An agonized metallic squeal tortured her ears, but she managed to get the hatch open enough to squeeze through.

Her breath escaped in an echoing gasp. The cavernous space beyond was a 'Mech bay of some kind with what looked like four berths. Heedless of the scattered debris, she ran farther in, panning her light over everything.

The body pulled her up short.

It lay on the floor, brown and desiccated, clad in the cooling vest and shorts of a MechWarrior. Slowly now, she stepped around the body and shone the flashlight ahead. A giant foot emerged from the gloom, followed by a torso and distinctive head arrangement. Lying slouched against the far wall was a BattleMech. Battered and in need of repair to be sure, but still a 'Mech.

The laugh began slowly at first, bubbling up from nowhere, and finally transcending into a hysterical fit that had her doubled over and completely robbed of breath. Once she'd regained her equilibrium, she patted the foot. "I don't know where you came from, sir, but now that I'm here, we can both escape."

DROPSHIP WRECK
NORTH OF CAMP SCINDIAN
KESAI IV
DRACONIS MARCH, FEDERATED SUNS
15 APRIL 2973

Her first order of business was survival. To that end, she had explored the "building" and discovered it was actually a DropShip. How it had arrived here was unimportant. What was important was that some of the onboard supplies were still usable. She'd even managed to get an auxiliary generator running. It didn't provide much more than lights and fans, but that was enough.

The body of the MechWarrior was something else. After stripping it of its cooling vest, she'd wrapped it in a tarp and dragged it to a storeroom she wasn't using, apologizing all the way.

At last, she was ready to tackle the 'Mech. The distinctive head marked it as a *Grasshopper*, a 70-ton 'Mech she had only ever read about. It was an unusual combination of heavy and mobile, with a reputation for being difficult to destroy. Obviously, she'd never worked on one before, but that didn't matter. Inside, all 'Mechs were the same.

She looked up at the *'Hopper*. "Where to start with you, sir?" She peered up at the head. "The basics, I suppose."

Climbing the awkwardly slumped 'Mech up to the cockpit actually proved easier than she thought. The hatch was ajar, allowing a quick entry. Inside, she noticed how cramped it was compared to other machines she'd worked in. Probably due to the head-mounted LRM launcher.

She plunked herself decisively in the command couch. "So," she muttered as she began flicking toggles. "First things first. Power." She pressed the reactor button and held her breath. Displays and lights flickered on, their light more welcome than anything she'd seen in a long time. The wireframe display came up, showing a few minor amber patches, but overall armor integrity was excellent. The weapons board was a different matter. "Wow, your guns are a mess, but hopefully we won't need those, eh?" She patted the console affectionately.

Plugging her own diagnostic board into the console, she ran a more detailed scan. "Hmm, reactor mass low, but acceptable. Myomer control...ouch, fifty percent? Must be dried out in parts. Heat sinks at sixty percent, that will have to do. Actuators? Lower responses than I'd like, but not bad considering you've been languishing here for who knows how long." She looked around the cockpit. "Don't worry, sir, we'll get you fixed up."

Turning around, she pulled the neurohelmet up from the floor. The model was less bulky than she was used to, but less robust as well. A large crack, like a gaping wound, exposed the burned out circuits to the air.

"Dammit, this could be a problem." She bit her knuckle anxiously. "Maybe there's another in ship's stores?" Setting the reactor to idle, she programmed her board to run a detailed scan for any other problems. She exited the head and shimmied down the arm, dropped the last meter to the ground.

"Okay, time to get things done."

Heading to the end of the bay, she opened the doorway heading for the supply locker she'd found previously. The inside was as jumbled as she remembered, and an hour of fruitless searching turned up no sign of a spare neurohelmet.

Slumping to the ground, she could feel despair threatening to engulf her. Giving each side of her face several slaps, she scolded herself. "No, no, no. You don't get to give up now. Not after everything you've been through. On your feet and *think*. There's no time to wallow."

She stood and began to pace the small room. "Think, think, Olivia." Suddenly stopping, she smacked her forehead. "I'm an idiot!"

Racing back to the 'Mech bay, she counted the racks, then faced the *Grasshopper*. "Aha! Four berths! So where are your friends?"

Even with a damp T-shirt wrapped around her head, she could feel the heat from the sun. She should have stopped hours ago, but she knew she was close. The panel she was using wasn't as good as a real shovel, but it did the trick.

Hacking into the DropShip's computer had revealed that it had been shot down years ago. After the crash, a fierce battle had raged around the spacecraft. She didn't know who had won, but the survivors must have died elsewhere, otherwise the ship and 'Mech wouldn't still be out here. More importantly, the record meant that the wreckage of several other 'Mechs were nearby. All she had to do was find them.

Easier said than done.

Which was why now that she'd found one, there was no way she'd give up until she'd gotten inside.

Scooping down, she felt the panel rasp along metal. Flinging the sand aside, she finally uncovered the canopy of what she suspected was a *Locust*. The hatch was closed. Whooping for joy after finding the manual release she gave it a fierce twist, succeeding only in twisting her wrist.

Dashing down the hill, she retrieved the prybar she had brought for just this occasion. Wedging it against the manual release, and heaving with everything she had, she forced the hatch open. Sprawling out on the sand, dripping with sweat, she smiled triumphantly. Still wobbly from over exertion, she dropped into the *Locust*.

Shrapnel to the chest had been the end of this MechWarrior. The mummified remains were still strapped into the harness. Quickly, she examined the neurohelmet. It looked intact, with no obvious sign of damage. Disconnecting the leads, she lifted the heavy helmet off the corpse's head. A brittle cracking, following by a *thud*, and the helmet was in her hands. She looked at the floor and hissed out a breath at the sight of the head. "Sorry."

Climbing out, prize in hand, she felt elated. This might actually work.

Fingers crossed, she plugged in the final connection. Her diagnostics board lit up, doing its thing. "Please, please, please..."

The lights turned green. "Yes!"

Scrambling into the couch, she pulled down the neurohelmet. "Okay, okay, okay, calm down. Deep breaths." Following her own advice, she breathed deeply, calming her nerves. Centering herself, she began the calibration process.

The calibration took hours, but was finally done. "Moment of truth." She connected. A wave of nausea washed over her, fading quickly. In its wake... She grinned.

She could feel the 'Mech around her. Feathering the foot pedals, she watched with glee as the *Grasshopper*'s feet responded in kind.

"Okay, let's get you on your feet, sir."

Moving cautiously, she pulled the legs up, knees to chest. Next she braced the arms on the ground to either side of the torso. Everything worked. So far, so good. With everything aligned, she pushed with all the limbs. The *Grasshopper* moaned, its gyro squealed and several armor plates popped, but she had succeeded. The 'Mech was on its feet at last. The angle of the floor was giving the gyro fits, but that was okay. She backed the *Grasshopper* into one of the berths and idled the engine. She pushed up the neurohelmet, giddy despite the pain in her shoulders.

"Just a couple more things and we're good to go," she said, patting the console.

Her supplies were all loaded in a cubby inside the cockpit. The large laser and one of the mediums were functional, although barely. The LRM ammo had been ditched. It was time to go.

Only one of the bay doors still worked, but that was all she needed. She activated the door, then sprinted for the *Grasshopper*, scrambling up the ladder while across from her sand cascaded into the bay, filling a good third of it. Knowing how ridiculous it looked, she knelt the *Grasshopper* down and crawled out of the ruined DropShip. Emerging into the sun, she grinned fiercely.

"Well then, now that we have our freedom, where to, sir? The spaceport? Why that's an excellent idea!"

NEAR COCHI SPACEPORT
SHALMIRAT, KESAI IV
DRACONIS MARCH
FEDERATED SUNS
25 APRIL 2973

Avoiding Camp Scindian had been easy. Getting into Cochi Spaceport less so. And even if she could, there were no ships on hand. It was a conundrum. So here she sat in a powered down 'Mech. Waiting. If only she knew for what.

After nearly a week of waiting, she had her answer. The militia radio band was panicked, a heavy raid was inbound.

She had the perfect vantage point to witness everything unfold. The DropShip descended on a pillar of flame visible for kilometers. Punching up her magnification showed it to be an *Overlord* with some kind of tree painted on the side of it. It touched down in the center of the spaceport and disgorged just over a company of 'Mechs, far fewer than should have been onboard a DropShip that size.

The Davion militia was slow to respond, and late in arriving. A company of 'Mechs from the far side of Shalmirat finally arrived, all in heavier designs than the raiders. She finally decided to make her move after the raiders lost a full lance to the militia's zero. She took it slow, careful of the bad actuator in the right knee. Once among the warehouses she picked up speed, nervous because she couldn't see the battle.

Emerging into the thick of the fighting, she suffered a stray shot. She was rattled but focused. Light 'Mechs were bounding back to the DropShip, all but one *Stinger* that seemed to have suffered a jump jet failure. Advancing on the *Stinger* was a much heavier *JagerMech*. The inequality of that fight got under her skin, to the boiling sea of rage and shame that she tried so hard to hide from.

And she lost it.

Despite rarely having used them, and then only for maintenance tests, she stomped on the jump jet pedals and flew toward the offender. The jets cut out early, leading to a rough landing and a red warning light on the right knee. She didn't care. The *JagerMech* pummeled the poor *Stinger* with multiple bursts from its autocannon. The *Stinger* struggled to maintain its feet and bravely returned fire with its medium laser, the *JagerMech* shrugging off the damage.

She was finally in range for her jury-rigged large laser. She whooped triumphantly when the shot connected with the *JagerMech*'s upper back. Not bad considering her utter lack of target practice.

The *JagerMech* sidestepped and twisted its torso, bringing its weapons into line on her. The shells spattered damage up and down the entire front of the *'Hopper*. Olivia bounced and rattled around the seat, her teeth chattering, but there was little actual damage.

The large laser was cooling slowly, so she moved forward, hoping to get into range for her medium. In the meantime she acquired a lock for her LRMs. The other pilot had no way of knowing the weapon was nonfunctional.

The feisty *Stinger* closed in and let loose with all its weapons: a medium laser and two machine guns. Not enough to do anything major, but the Davion MechWarrior now faced a two-on-one fight, never good odds.

Olivia finally closed enough for her medium laser. She fired, burning a trough across the *JagerMech*'s torso.

That decided the Davion pilot. The *JagerMech* broke off, retreating back toward its own lines.

She turned and found the *Stinger* motioning towards the DropShip. Perfect. She dropped in beside the smaller 'Mech and, limping, escorted it to the DropShip.

At the DropShip, she found a scene of chaos. 'Mechs and vehicles laden with spoils were hastily boarding the massive ship. Figures of infantry scurried passed her legs, rushing to help.

The *Stinger* halted, and after a moment, a figure emerged and gestured to the ground. Olivia shrugged and powered down. She pulled off the neurohelmet, wincing at how bruised her shoulders felt. She too disembarked and clambered down to meet the *Stinger* pilot.

The other pilot was a rangy woman easily twice Olivia's age. She gave Olivia a thorough visual inspection. "You have my thanks, MechWarrior. What's your name?" Her accent was thick and strange.

"The name's Olivia, and I'm no MechWarrior, I'm an astech." A surge of pride followed that assertion.

"Oh really? And where did you acquire that big boy?" She gestured at the *Grasshopper*.

"I found him in the desert. Took a while, but I got him more or less operational."

The woman nodded, then stuck out her hand. "I'm Ysabel Vassy. This sorry sack of scoundrels are my boys and girls, the Witchwood Warriors."

"Mercenaries?"

Ysabel grinned, exposing a mouth full of missing teeth. "Is there any better way to fight? I don't have much time, what with the Davvies reinforcements on the way, but I could make use of you and your 'Mech. Interested?"

Olivia didn't even have to think about it. "Absolutely. Anything that gets me off this rock."

"Outstanding. Then get yourself aboard."

Moving quickly, Olivia got the *Grasshopper* fired back up and up the ramp. She followed the crew's directions to a berth. Once she was secured, she powered down and let herself slump. She could finally leave this hellhole behind. She could forget about it and the terrible things that had been done to her. By her.

The ramp closed and the DropShip rumbled up and out of gravity's clawing embrace. As the ship ascended, she reflected that starting anew among the stars was the perfect salve for her wounded soul.

She leaned back and, for the first time in ages, slept soundly.

ONE MAN'S TRASH
PHILIP A. LEE

KALI-YAMA FACTORY ANNEX
WESTPORT, KALIDASA
SILVER HAWKS COALITION
FREE WORLDS LEAGUE
27 FEBRUARY 3004

Sergeant Virgil Armstrong couldn't wipe the giddy schoolboy grin off his face—even when his shorts snagged a ragged edge—as he slid into the beat-up BattleMech's cockpit. He'd been trying to suppress the smile since it first appeared while climbing the chain ladder, but seeing the cockpit and semicircular array of instruments in front of the command couch only deepened his euphoria, made the moment that much more real.

Something about the poorly lit interior called to him in a way nothing else could: a beggar that had been inexplicably invited inside a resplendent palace. He imagined Toni from Panther Assault Group's tank company hovering over his shoulder, her hypercritical voice chiming in his ear—*"What a dump!"*—but not even she could've dampened his excitement. After the seemingly permanent purgatory of the Panthers' reserve MechWarrior ranks, sitting inside his own honest-to-goodness BattleMech—not a trainer, a loaner, or a simulator pod—even one as abused as this one, meant the first step in clawing his way up from the hell of reserve pilot duty.

Ignoring the partially melted headrest where a laser beam had punched through the *Grasshopper*'s ferroglass canopy to kill its former pilot, Verge slid into the seat, the cracked and roughed-up leather cool against mostly bare thighs. His body seemed to sink into the command couch as though it was made for him. Too bad the 'Mech's previous pilot had to die in order for him to be sitting here right now.

Always "on the verge" of being promoted to active MechWarrior status, the full members of his company liked to joke. Until today.

Without a 'Mech to pilot, Verge's MechWarrior diploma from Allison MechWarrior Institute wasn't worth the verigraphed paper it was printed on. AMI had churned out far more MechWarriors than the Free Worlds League Military needed, and not enough viable 'Mechs to go around either meant temporary assignment to an armor or infantry regiment or to a pool of reserve pilots until more 'Mechs came available or their original pilots got WIAed or KIAed. Temporary, his ass. One full tour of duty in the Twenty-fifth Marik Militia, and not even a bite. Not a single BattleMech-qualified soldier from his whole armor regiment had ever transferred to a 'Mech regiment, so he'd bowed out and took his chances with the Panther Assault Group mercenary regiment...where he was immediately assigned to the MechWarrior reserves, to wait in line with all the other would-be MechWarriors in the event of casualties or a windfall of salvage.

And then just two days ago, right after the on-planet Silver Hawk Irregulars got recalled to another Silver Hawks planet, some misguided probe from the scattered Seventeenth Arcturan Guards battalion ran afoul of the Panthers' patrols. The quick but decisive clash broke the Lyran Commonwealth troops and sent them fleeing into the hills southeast of Westport, but enough salvage remained for the Panthers to equip a short lance of BattleMechs. All Major Szalinski needed to do was promote some reserve pilots to helm them.

One of the senior techs, Barbara, had followed Verge up the chain ladder, but so rapt was he in absorbing every little detail in the cockpit that he barely paid attention to what she was babbling on about—something about jump jets. Instead he ran his fingers over the instrument panel, relishing the *clickety-clack* of the square buttons as his fingertips grazed their yellowed, transparent plastic tops.

The keys themselves were undoubtedly older than him. Most of the fixtures inside this cockpit, from the multifunction displays to the control sticks to the foot pedals, all of it bore unmistakable signs of age. Cracked housings. Once textured plastic that had been worn to a mirrored sheen. Discolorations on the secondary display. Rust stains on the right-hand bulkhead. A strange musk permeated the whole cockpit, a sick-sweet *mélange* of hot metal, old sweat, lubricant, mold, and something else he couldn't readily name.

To him, it was a perfume. He didn't own this 'Mech—*yet*; he was merely a hired pilot—but maybe in another handful of years or so...

"Hey." Barb reached into the cockpit and swatted his shoulder. "You listening?"

Verge shook his head. His shorts caught on something again when he turned to give the tech his full attention. "Sorry. What?"

"The jump jets," she repeated. "They're all kinds of screwed up. Bent baffles on the right leg, malfed-up 'draulics to boot." She shrugged. "They'll *work*, yeah, but don't expect perfect tens on the landing. Maybe not even sixes. *Capisce*?"

Verge nodded. "*Capisce*."

He didn't have to ask why she hadn't bothered to fix the faulty systems. Parts for GHR-5H *Grasshopper*s were hard to come by even in the best of times, and if he was honest with himself, this 'Mech served as little more than a glorified hangar queen for Major Szalinski's own *Grasshopper*, which his techs kept in far better repair. It was a mercy Szalinski was even letting him drive the damn thing. The most valuable part of the whole 'Mech was its VOX 280 fusion engine. If the major's *Grasshopper* got cored, Barb would cannibalize this 'Mech's heart in a nuclear second—and leave Verge 'Mech-less once again.

"I know she's still got Lyran markings," Barb added, "but we switched over the IFF transponder, so you shouldn't hafta worry about friendly fire. Repainting a junk heap like this just ain't worth the trouble right now, and the camo'll do you just fine in this area anyway." She sighed in frustration. "All right, lemme check a few more things, and then you can take 'er for a spin."

The tech vanished back down the ladder, leaving Verge alone in his new home.

He turned back to the instrument panel, snagged his shorts yet again—dammit, he'd have to file that down, whatever it was—and studied the interior more closely. On the bulkhead above him, just next to the curve where the head-mounted long range missile launcher partially intruded into the right-hand side of the cockpit, a strange texture on the metal caught his eye in the semidarkness. He shined a penlight on it to get a better look.

Someone had carved a series of names, ranks, and dates into the plate, each one etched in a different hand. If he remembered his history lessons, the first date—2779—was somewhere around the fall of the Star League.

Hell. Forget the beginning of the war. This 'Mech was positively *ancient.*

Try as he might, he couldn't quite make out the name. Age and rust and bubbled paint had obscured it beyond legibility. Many of the others in the list had suffered similar fates, but the most recent one he could read well enough: *Leutnant Christiane Kühn, 3001.* The inscription looked like it'd been carved with the tip of a corkscrew, which seemed like an awfully Lyran thing to do.

He made a mental note to add his name to the list, but first things first. This junk pile wouldn't drive itself.

He spent a half-hour going over the controls and running through the prep checklist in his head: waking up the VOX 280's fusion reactor, checking the temperature and coolant systems, verifying weapon systems—the whole nine meters. After each step, he referenced the corresponding multifunction display and monitored the constellation of bright telltales across the instrument panel. When he shifted his knees to reach a distant switch on the comm board, his MechWarrior shorts stuck on whatever ragged metal they'd discovered, and this time a stray thread tore free of the olive-drab fabric.

"Confound it!" Verge yanked the thread until it snapped, then he ran flattened fingertips underneath the instrument panel. "What in all the goddamn—"

His fingers felt a jagged seam that shouldn't have been there. Craning his head to peer under where he'd felt in the small space, he spotted a slapdash weld joint that seemed to have come loose. A sigh escaped his lips. Sure, this *'Hopper* was a mess, but a tech of Barb's caliber knew better than to let the cockpit fall apart around him. In the meantime...

He rammed his knee into the panel in hopes of temporarily jamming it back into place long enough to last through this maiden voyage without cramping his legs. The first bash only worsened matters, jarring the seam even further off true. The second offered greater promise, but wasn't good enough to jam it back into place.

The third popped the whole damn panel open.

And a small object rolled out from inside the panel. It smacked his bare shins and clattered to the cockpit floor, somewhere out of sight within such tight confines.

"Hey, Armstrong, you up there?" Toni asked from below. The chain ladder dangling from the entry hatch's lip rattled and jiggled as she climbed up to see his new assignment.

Sudden panic stole the delight from his discovery. Whatever had fallen out of the hidden panel was bound to be some kind of contraband—which meant he probably shouldn't broadcast what he'd found until he could be sure it wouldn't land him in trouble. For all he knew, Barbara or one of her techs had left a secret stash of some kind of narcotic in here, and that could get the whole tech crew suspended—or worse, *fired*. Not a great idea when Panther Assault Group still had Lyrans to hunt down.

"Verge?" *Chink, chink, chink* went the ladder.

What the devil *had* he found anyway? He strained to reach down between his legs and blindly fumbled beneath the foot pedals until—aha! His fingers curled around a small metal cylinder about a decimeter long and two or three centimeters in diameter. Before he had a chance to examine it fully, the familiar face of Sergeant Antonia Johnson popped into view outside the cockpit hatch. Normally he would've flashed a genuine smile at her dark features and wide, mischievous grin, but not today.

As she ducked her head further into the cockpit lights, Verge palmed the tube and surreptitiously dumped it behind his back, the only place he could think of that wouldn't draw her attention. The cylinder soundlessly rolled down the leather to settle at the small of his back—a hard, uncomfortable lump between the command couch and his lumbar vertebrae, but at least it was out of sight.

Toni's playful grimace didn't quite reach her dark eyes when she gave him a good-natured punch in the shoulder. "You deaf or somethin'?"

"Sorry," he said. "Now's probably not a good time."

"And that's where you're wrong, soldier. 'Now' is *always* the best time for anything." She rested her forearms across the hatch threshold, hands laid atop each other, chin resting on the back of her topmost hand. "So c'mon. Spill the goods. Show me what this beat-up old bitch can do."

Verge squirmed at her suggestion, the tube poking him in the spine as he readjusted. "I...uh, gotta take her out on a test run first," he said, scratching the back of his buzzcut. "If we can figure out where the damn Lyrans are, I don't wanna take her out on a dry run and get killed 'cause I don't know what her quirks are. Lotta stuff to sort out, and I could do without any distractions right now."

Toni's eyebrows quirked. "'Her?' Don't tell me you've gone and left me for this ol' garbage heap?" she said with an accusatory-but-amused smirk.

And then she climbed into the cockpit with him with a mirthful laugh.

Verge had been in 'Mech simulator pods far roomier than the GHR-5H cockpit, and even those had been too small to properly conduct any sort of romantic liaison. This 'Mech had an interior just roomy enough for some overhead storage space, a foldable toilet, and a jump seat, but the LRM launcher took up a large amount of a *Grasshopper*'s cockpit—too much, in fact, meaning Toni couldn't reach the jump seat without crawling over him, so there was nowhere for her to go except to "accidentally" fall on top of him, on top of the entire command couch.

Her whole weight pressing onto him.

Digging the secret metal cylinder into his back. Probably pulverizing a vertebra or two.

Completely ruining the moment.

Her in his lap, with her arms thrown around his neck, their kiss lasted only a few seconds before he had to break away and reposition her to avoid suffering irreparable damage to his spinal column. The pain alone made him want to share his discovery, but a tingling in the back of his mind, like fingernails slowly grazing his brain, made him rethink the idea. Whatever contraband he'd found, she didn't need to know about it until he knew more about it himself. Better he get drummed out of the Panthers for it than her. And Major Szalinski would be more protective of his MechWarriors—reserve or otherwise—than a tanker sergeant.

"Toni..." he wheezed from squashed lungs, "as much as I appreciate the visit..."

She scooted around and sat lotus-style on his lap, barely fitting in the already-cramped space. Her right boot almost mashed the comm board when she swiveled into place; had she activated the external speakers or somehow radioed the whole company, a lot of people would've gotten an earful, and they both would've gotten a stern reprimand—or worse.

"Okay," she said, "I want you show me *everything*. What's this do?"

Verge always appreciated Toni's company—he'd lost track of how many times they'd hooked up in the command seat of her Von Luckner tank during off hours—but this was serious business. He had nothing but respect for her and her tank crew as soldiers, but shenanigans like this might prompt Major Szalinski to find a different reservist to pilot this junkpile.

And the pressure on his lumbar was lancing up into his spine. Any longer, and he'd need to see if Corpsman Ghirardi knew any chiropractic techniques.

"C'mon," he said, trying to rock her up and out of the cockpit. "I really need to get this done. I appreciate the visit, I do, but you're really not helping. And besides, you're not even authorized to be in here. We could get in a lot of trouble."

Toni readjusted to mischievously glare at him, moving just enough to relieve the worst of the spinal pressure from the tube. "It's fine. Barb owes me a favor anyway."

Verge forced a pained smile back at her. "We'll have mess together later, I promise. All right?"

She huffed and caressed her fingers across the throttle lever. "All right. But you *owe* me an official tour of ol' Trash here, got it?"

"Got it," he said, and meant it.

"For the record," she said, pressing her forehead to his own, "I'm glad you finally got your ride. Even if it is a shit pile."

A shared laugh.

A kiss long and deep.

And then the agony of the metal pea digging into his princess back vanished as she headed back down the *Grasshopper*'s chain ladder.

PANTHER ASSAULT GROUP BARRACKS
WESTPORT, KALIDASA
SILVER HAWKS COALITION
FREE WORLDS LEAGUE
27 FEBRUARY 3004

With two unannounced visitors to his cockpit in so short a time, Verge decided he couldn't trust anyone with his new find, so he chose to wait until later, when he could steal a few moments alone in the barracks to investigate.

He spent the entirety of his test run of "Trash," as he'd taken to calling the 'Mech, balancing on that razor's edge between euphoria and anticipation. Even the simplest piloting actions, ones other MechWarriors took for granted—walking, running, juking around broken terrain, low-powered weapons testing, dummy missile launches—drew out a whoop of celebration or a fist pump. Just sitting in Trash's cockpit twelve meters above the ground lent him a heightened sensation of invincibility, regardless that the 'Mech had clearly taken a dive off Ugly Mountain and struck every boulder on its way down. But every now and again, his thoughts wandered back to the tube, to the maddening mystery it represented.

His bunkmate, van Leuwen, was long asleep by the time Verge felt safe enough to sit at his desk and open the mysterious cylinder without interruption. Two end caps were screwed on as though it were a tiny pipe bomb. He steeled himself, bracing for some kind of antitheft countermeasure—an explosive, thermite, acid, or worse—confident in the knowledge that if this *did* kill him, he wouldn't be alive to face the consequences. And he'd never liked van Leuwen all that much anyway...

The end cap popped off easily; no explosion, no surprises. He tipped the tube just enough...and a data crystal tumbled out into his cupped palm. A few more taps deposited some rolled-up papers in his hand as well—

He held the data crystal up to the light, wondering what might be stored in its prismatic depths.

The papers—no, photographs—proved easy enough to decipher. The smiling face of a blond, green-eyed man stared back at him in one of them; another showed faces of similar-looking kids, all of them about ten shades paler than Verge's own complexion. Someone's husband and kids, most like.

Wait—

Something else in the tube. He rattled it again.

A small, white-gold engagement ring plopped into his palm.

Verge swallowed, a sick feeling sneaking into his gut. This was all wrong, like he was rooting through a dead soldier's footlocker in search of valuables. Which meant the data crystal was probably the personal journal of Trash's previous pilot, this Lt. Kühn. And that crossed some kind of inviolable line. Other mercs might take trophies and pull golden teeth out of skulls, but Major Szalinski had a zero-tolerance policy for looting. The Panther Assault Group fought cleanly and acted professionally, both before and after an engagement.

But on the other hand, he reasoned, why would some photos, a ring, and a journal be welded inside a hidden compartment? What if the personal touches were meant to throw off the value of what was on the data crystal?

What if it wasn't a journal at all?

Verge pocketed the ring for now. If he had time, he'd get it appraised when he had liberty, to see if it was even worth anything. He didn't really want to sell it: for all he knew it was probably just cut glass on a cheap metal band. But he had to know.

From his footlocker he pulled out a beat-up old noteputer, a secondhand model with a cracked screen he couldn't afford to replace and a dim, fuzzy screen, and slotted the data crystal.

A bunch of random characters flooded the screen, all the hallmarks of corrupted files. Verge shook his head in dismay. *Garbage from "Trash"–how typical–*

Wait a minute... No no no—this wasn't garbage at all. Were this from an ancient magnetic disk from some low-tech, backwater planet, sure, but data crystals weren't as volatile or susceptible to failure as magnetic storage media. Certain patterns seemed to repeat themselves, which suggested he'd stumbled on encrypted data.

Now why in the world would some poor Lyran sot's personal files be encrypted? Only classified military or intelligence documents would use–

Cold sweat broke out across every centimeter of exposed skin.

He checked over his shoulder to make damn sure van Leuwen was still dead asleep before turning back to the garbage-filled screen.

"I can do this, I can do this," he told himself.

Everyone—well, everyone but Toni—assumed he was just a dumb, meathead 'MechJock, only capable of thumping his chest and doing whatever it is dumb 'MechJocks are supposed to do. But he was smarter than anyone gave him credit for. He always appreciated a good puzzle, and if he could decipher this and turn it over to Major Szalinski, it'd save them some time in figuring out what to do. Plus, if all of this gobbledygook did turn out to just be some paranoid MechWarrior's personal ramblings, then he'd save himself some trouble and embarrassment for wasting the major's time.

Even though he had to report for duty at 0400 the next morning, he stayed up long past the witching hour trying to crack the encryption. Just before he was about to pass out from sheer exhaustion, he figured out the missing piece of the puzzle.

It wasn't a journal.

He tried to get a few hours of rack time before he had to report for morning PT, but the words, those damned words on that fuzzy noteputer screen burned into his retinas and danced through his head while he tried desperately to fight sleep.

But they would not let him fall into the grip of oblivion.

They spelled damnation no matter how he looked at them.

PANTHER ASSAULT GROUP BARRACKS
WESTPORT, KALIDASA
SILVER HAWKS COALITION
FREE WORLDS LEAGUE
28 FEBRUARY 3004

Verge's morning run with the rest of the company and Toni's tank battalion passed in a blur. While a staff sergeant shouted jogging cadence, Verge looked at each person in formation and realized he was staring at the dead. Even Toni.

The sickening churn in his gut made him double over along their route, and he begged off once the rest of the company got too far away for him to catch up. Instead of heading to morning chow, he went straight to Major Szalinski's office, hoping to make some good out of what he had learned.

Szalinski's aide tried to invent excuses, but Verge pressed the urgency of the matter, and eventually gained an audience with the Panthers' CO. Szalinski was a lean whip of a man whom Verge had only ever personally spoken with less than a half-dozen times.

The uniformed major stood up from his desk and cut straight to the chase when Verge stepped into his office. "Sergeant Armstrong—aren't you s'posed to be at PT, soldier?"

"Stomach troubles, sir," Verge half-lied. "I, uh—"

"Spit it out, son. I haven't got all day. I've got Lyrans to hunt."

Lyrans, Lyrans, Lyrans...

Verge suppressed the urge to throw up again. "It's, uh, about my 'Mech, sir."

"You're in the GHR-5H, right? What about it?"

He stared at the floor, away from the major's interrogating eyes. "Yes, sir. I, uh…"

"You got a *problem* with it, Sergeant?"

Dammit, just tell him. "No, sir…" Verge bit his lower lip and sank into an empty chair in front of Szalinski's desk. "It's just that—"

The major loomed over Verge's seated form. "Look, son, I *know* that 'Hopper's a wreck, but we need all hands on deck for this operation. And you should be *thanking* me for it. The only reason—the *only* reason—I assigned you to it is because Sergeant Jemison's giant ass couldn't fit a cockpit that cramped. He's got the better sim scores, and frankly, a much better attitude than yours. *He* wouldn't barge in on me unannounced like this. In fact, I'd bet he's out there at PT right now, busting his ass and hoping the next 'Mech we salvage is big enough to contain him."

Verge's eyes filled with moisture, but he blinked it away before it could betray him. The truth hurt. But if Jemison had been assigned to Trash, if he hadn't found that hidden compartment…

"Sir, with all due respect, it's not about any of that. I, uh…I found something you should know about."

From the pocket of his silkies he withdrew the probably fake photos, the likely worthless ring, and dumped them in the major's hand. The data crystal he kept to himself for now; handing it over wouldn't change anything. "I found these in a hidden compartment in the 'Hopper. Didn't wanna take 'em to Lieutenant Solomon or Captain Pandev because I didn't want all this to disappear and then somehow get me in trouble for looting. It's not that I don't trust them, sir. Just…covering my own ass."

Szalinski stared in response. The ring jiggled about in his palm as though it were some foreign object. "And what do you expect me to do with this?"

Verge shrugged. "We always pride ourselves on fighting clean engagements, sir. If those belong to someone, we should probably try to return them to the family. Keeping them just feels *wrong*. I mean, we signed a contract with the League, but that doesn't mean we have any bad blood with the Lyrans. It's just a job. Just business. But something like this is personal. I mean, if my sister got KIAed, getting her personal effects returned would almost be like resurrecting her from the dead, even for a little while."

"Your concern is noted." Szalinski set the ring and photos on his desk. "And I appreciate your honesty. That goes a long way toward recommendations for officer candidacy."

In the morning light filtering through the window, the major's face softened with something Verge wanted to take for pride. "Jemison may have better sim scores, Sergeant, but from reports, I believe you have more of what it takes to become an officer. Remember that."

Szalinski's face hardened again. "You might be too sick to run, son, but you're well enough to pilot that *'Hopper*. I want to see it and the rest of your lance shipshape by oh-nine-hundred. Now get the hell out of my office."

KALI-YAMA FACTORY ANNEX
WESTPORT, KALIDASA
SILVER HAWKS COALITION
FREE WORLDS LEAGUE
28 FEBRUARY 3004

While climbing back into the *Grasshopper*'s cockpit, Verge ignored the half-melted headrest as best he could. If he didn't do *something*, he'd likely meet the same fate.

Laser straight through the *'Hopper*'s "eye hole," his whole head and shoulders vaporizing from megajoules of energy pumped through the cockpit.

He'd never even feel it. He'd just be living and aware one moment, and be gone the next. No one but Toni would mourn him. The next batch of techs to care for this junk pile would fix up the cockpit, probably bitch about having to clean up the mess his corpse had left behind, and then someone else—a Lyran, probably—would clamber up into this 'Mech and add their name to the list.

He ran fingertips across the faded names on the bulkhead. How many of them had perished in similar fashion? For a dark moment, he wondered whether this 'Mech, having somehow survived since the Star League days, was a curse rather than a treasure.

In a deathly silence, he stared at the controls without truly seeing them and strapped himself in; each belt of the five-point safety harness clicked home one at a time, each dull *clack* as loud as an autocannon discharge in the small space. Yesterday he'd done all of this deliberately and with rapture, but today, he knew the grim truth behind their situation.

In the closed, cramped interior of his steel coffin, he went through the rest of the startup sequence textbook style, lifeless, joyless. Not even the weight of the neurohelmet pads on his shoulders could comfort him. And then the security protocols prompted for voiceprint authorization and passphrase.

He swallowed and enunciated the phrase he had encoded the day before:

"One man's trash is another man's treasure."

The suite of controls came to life, and Trash was now at his command. Exercising more caution than yesterday, he walked the 'Mech out of the hangar one step at a time and went out on scheduled patrol alongside the rest of his lance. No one else, not even Lt. Solomon knew what he wrestled with in the lonely confines of his cockpit. But out here, in the relatively safe environs of Westport, he finally had time to think.

On the data crystal was an official Lyran Commonwealth Armed Forces dispatch from the local ComStar station. This very 'Mech he was sitting in had been entrusted with delivering it to the on-planet Lyran forces in hiding, until the former pilot had the bad luck to run into the Panthers' pickets. The decoded orders, from a Colonel McCrae, were in German, but translation software on his noteputer made short work of that. And once he'd read them, they turned his world completely upside down:

Hold position at Crater Hollow. Reinforcements en route to L1 Lagrangian point: 10th Skye RGT, ETA in system 1 Mar '04.

The Panthers had spent the past month hunting down a few fractured companies, all that remained of the Seventeenth Arcturan Guards' Second Battalion, but these encrypted orders were a complete game changer. The Panther Assault Group could boast an on-paper complement of three battalions, one each of 'Mechs, armor, and infantry—more than enough to scour the planet of Lyran forces. But the Lyran Commonwealth was determined to wrench Kalidasa and her 'Mech production capabilities from Marik hands. Now a whole regiment of reinforcements were incoming, and the Panthers owned no DropShips of their own. Unless they wanted to break their contract and steal a civilian DropShip, they were trapped on this rock, with nowhere to go but charge straight into Lyran guns.

Unless something happened before these reinforcements could arrive, the whole Panther Assault Group would be dead within a week. Kalidasa natives probably knew of some useful boltholes they could hide in, but that would only delay the inevitable. Everyone, from Major Szalinski all the way on down to the infantry privates, wouldn't survive the fight. There was no way an understrength combined-arms regiment of mercs and a handful of Kali-Yama's corporate security forces could best a fresh BattleMech regiment. The major could get on the horn and request off-planet reinforcements, but those would arrive far too late to do the Panthers any good—assuming Parliament and the FWLM could even agree on something as simple as national defense.

Might as well just stand at attention in the middle of Westport Square and let the Lyrans open fire.

Verge followed behind Lt. Solomon's *Crusader* on the scrublined path, not truly seeing the terrain around him anymore. He navigated solely by feel, letting the 'Mech's gyro bear the brunt of the piloting work. He would've set Trash on autopilot so he could think better, but the *'Hopper* lived up to its moniker once again. Its autonav circuits were completely fused, and not even Barbara herself could remove them without replacing the whole navigation and radar system, which—surprise, surprise—was almost as hard to come by these days as a VOX 280 fusion engine.

He sighed. How different his life would've been had he stuck with a Free Worlds League Military unit. Regular FWLM troops didn't get stranded against unbeatable odds like this. But he couldn't hack it, not even in a Marik Militia regiment. He wasn't cut out for regular military service, regardless of how much he wanted to serve. FWLM regs didn't care about provincial or even national patriotism. Regs were regs, and those regs had gotten him drummed out of service. And getting drummed out of service—and eventually landing into the Panthers—would ultimately get himself and those he cared about killed.

There had to be a way out of this.

He idly settled Trash's crosshairs on a distant shrub while ideas tumbled through his head like broken minerals in a rock polisher.

Did the ragtag remnants of the Seventeenth even know reinforcements were en route? And if not, might they be willing to trade for that information? Intelligence for a chance to step out of the way?

Or what if the orders were falsified? The Seventeenth could've easily planted the document, knowing that if it fell into enemy hands, it would incite enough fear and panic to give them ample time to regroup and strike back. Was he playing right into their trap? The electronic ComStar watermark on the file seemed legitimate, but was it? Only a ComStar acolyte would know for sure, and attempting to leave the barracks to travel all the way to the HPG station at Sakuntalem before the reinforcements arrive would waste precious time that could be better spent preparing for inevitable destruction.

If he shared his find with Major Szalinski, then they would all stand and fight. The major never broke a contract, regardless of the odds. *"We get paid to fight, not to win,"* Verge had heard him say countless times. That was why he hadn't handed over the data crystal when he'd had the perfect opportunity.

However, if he tried to negotiate with the Lyrans, things could go just as horribly awry. They might grant him and Toni safe passage off planet...or they might just shoot him down on the spot.

Damned if you do...

Verge ground his teeth. There seemed to be no way out of this one. A quick glance at the ever-advancing numbers of his HUD chrono reminded him that in two days, Panther command would get notification of several JumpShips arriving at one of the system's pirate points.

There had to be *something* be could do to keep from running headlong into the jaws of certain death.

CRATER HOLLOW
WESTPORT, KALIDASA
SILVER HAWKS COALITION
FREE WORLDS LEAGUE
29 FEBRUARY 3004

Verge slowed Trash to a stop at the crest of a hill overlooking a sprawling, forested basin and drew in a deep lungful of that heady, old-cockpit scent he'd quickly come to appreciate.

According to the natives, a meteorite had struck the area millions of years ago, and this concavity, overgrown with grass, trees, and other vegetation, was all that remained. Its shape made a perfect hiding spot for enemy troops by providing a natural defiladed position from which to attack incoming forces, but the gentle, furrowed slopes leading up to the crater's lip proved empty.

Good. All the better for making contact.

He checked his short-range scopes one last time, paying special attention to the hills he'd spent hours crossing, and they came up empty. Also good.

This whole undertaking, just the notion of walking alone into the Seventeenth's clutches, was dangerous, incredibly dangerous, and maybe even a little bit stupid, but he had convinced himself this was the only way he could see this through.

At a slow and unthreatening pace, he walked the *Grasshopper* down the grassy crater slope.

Verge caught a flash of forest camo rustle through the forested basin. A brace of light 'Mechs, a *Commando* and *Firestarter*, dashed out from the tree line, their meager weaponry pointed his direction with obvious hostile intent.

A 70-ton 'Mech, even one as beaten up as Trash, had little to fear from 25- and 30-ton 'Mechs, but Verge's pulse sped up regardless. He had only ever participated in simulations and field training, not actual BattleMech combat.

This was such a bad, bad idea. But the Lyran 'Mechs hesitated.

Barbara had been so consumed with trying to get Trash from "salvage" to "functional"—let alone combat ready—that her crew hadn't a chance to repaint the old bitch yet. Aside from the handful of primer-gray armor panels the techs had replaced, the *'Hopper* still bore its Seventeenth Arcturan Guards markings, albeit chipped and sun-faded all to hell.

Verge lifted Trash's arms in the universal gesture for surrender, just high enough that the Lyran MechWarriors would see the arm-mounted medium lasers weren't aiming at them, and continued his approach. Throat dry, he swallowed and keyed up the general frequency.

Thank goodness he'd written his speech down.

"I am Sergeant Virgil Armstrong, Charlie Company, Panther Assault Group, BattleMech Battalion, and I come bearing a proposal. You will see I have come alone, and my weapons are powered down."

The 25-ton *Commando* stood right in Verge's path and aimed its right-arm short range missile launcher toward Trash's head, the pilot apparently uncaring about the size disparity between them. "State your business," barked a fierce female voice in thickly accented English.

Verge pulled back on his sticks to wave Trash's arms and overemphasize his nonthreatening posture. "I wish to speak with your commander."

The little *Commando* shook with palpable rage. "We do not listen to mercenaries, swine! We will not tolerate your theft of one of our—"

"That will be enough, Leutnant," a stern male voice interrupted. From its labored edge, the voice sounded old and battle-worn. A battered *Zeus* stepped out from the trees alongside a handful of other 'Mechs. The 80-ton assault 'Mech had certainly seen some action within recent weeks. Laser-melted gouges crisscrossed weathered armor panels, as though the BattleMech had wrestled with a bear its own size. The left-knee poleyn was mostly torn off, the knee actuator's myomer fiber bundles exposed to the elements. And everywhere else across the armored surface was pitted and scarred by autocannon fire, missile blast craters, and shrapnel.

The *Commando* settled; its arm lowered.

"I am Kommandant Nielsen," the *Zeus* pilot radioed. "How did you find us? How is it you come to pilot one of my BattleMechs?"

Verge gestured his hand in a circle, hoping to speed things up. The longer this exchange took, the worse off things would be. "Battlefield salvage."

"And Leutnant Kühn?"

He checked his scopes. Good. Still empty, aside from the nearby Lyrans. "Don't know, honestly. Techs just fixed up this 'Mech, and I got assigned to her."

The *Zeus* shifted uncomfortably, lurching on its damaged knee actuator. "A shame. She was one of my best."

"With all due respect, Kommandant, she's not what I'm here to talk about."

Trees swayed, and two more Lyran 'Mechs, a *Rifleman* missing its left arm and a beat-to-hell *Warhammer*, emerged to flank the *Zeus*.

Verge swallowed, his throat so dry it pained him. "I...I found something hidden in this 'Mech," he continued, reading off the script he'd written. "A communiqué from LCAF High Command that sheds some interesting light on your rather precarious situation here on Kalidasa."

"We've received several dispatches from High Command, *mein freund*," said the kommandant. "You will have to do better than that."

The *Commando* and *Firestarter* both circled around Trash's flanks. "Tell me why I shouldn't order my troops to open fire on you."

Shaking his control sticks, Verge repeated the *Grasshopper's* yielding gesture. "All right, all right. You have reinforcements coming. They'll be in system at any moment. So—" he consulted his written speech, "—if you can grant me and my closest friends amnesty and safe passage off this planet, I will..."

Toni's face, that heart-melting smile, intruded in his thoughts, and he almost couldn't bring himself to utter the words.

"...I will provide you with intelligence on the Westport defenses. Panther patrol schedules. Logistics reports. Anything I know that might give you an advantage."

The *Zeus's* left arm lifted, its autocannon barrel trained at Trash's torso. "And why should I believe you? Why would you give up this information, betray your own people?"

Hot tears welled in the pits of Verge's eyes. "Because what's coming is a fight we cannot win. Your people will slaughter us wholesale just because we signed a contract to feed our families, and I have since lost my desire to sacrifice myself or my friends on someone else's war." He paused to let the words sink in. "I just...I just want to go *home*."

The autocannon arm relaxed. "I have one condition. You must surrender Leutnant Kühn's *Grasshopper*."

A spider of revulsion writhed in Verge's gut. Trash was *his*.

He checked his scopes one last time, noting the *Commando* and *Firestarter* nearly facing his rear armor. His fingers danced across his comm board and keyed in a preset command.

"All right, Kommandant. I will comply. Starting my powerdown sequence in three...two...one..."

Even through the cockpit's sound dampening, Verge witnessed the sky fill with the roaring churn of hundreds of long range missiles sprouting from above and beyond the crater's lip. A sheer avalanche of warheads, a smoky tidal wave of contrails rained down from the heavens, arcing in toward the forest edge.

Verge smirked. *Right on time.*

Before the wave of devastation could hit, before the confused Lyrans even realized what had happened, he stomped down on both of Trash's foot pedals to escape the 'Mechs encircling him—

His stomach remained somewhere on the ground behind him as the jump jets catapulted all of Trash's 70 tons skyward. But then everything turned sideways.

Literally.

One of the right-leg jump jets cut out mid-flight, slewing his whole view to the right.

Dammit.

Dammit!

DAMMIT!

He hadn't initially planned to fall back this way, but the lack of options forced his hand.

In mid-air, Verge fought the controls and used his own sense of balance to try throwing the 'Mech's mass in the opposite direction. Partial thrust from the right leg's remaining jump jet helped somewhat, but he braced for a rough landing.

While chaos reigned in the skies above, Verge went down toward the grassy crater hard, all 70 tons of mass. In horror he watched the altimeter count down from thirty-nine-odd meters to zero...

A curtain of black flashed across his vision. Jaw clamped hard enough to crack a molar. Safety harness wrenched his collarbone. Absorbing the worst of the landing, the whole chassis reverberated with the awful groan of crunching, twisting metal. Verge felt the *'Hopper*'s right leg crumple beneath the 'Mech's weight as lasers from the *Firestarter* and missiles from the *Commando* whipped centimeters above his cockpit, right where he'd been an instant before. Armor panels burst free as the interior bracing joists collapsed. The faulty leg hydraulics couldn't take this kind of stress, Barbara had said. And of course, she was right.

His helmet filled with migraine-inducing alarms, but the 'Mech didn't go down all the way, not yet. Damage readout showed the leg armor was largely shredded, but its steel endoskeleton remained mostly intact—not pretty, but intact. Trash might've looked like a polished turd, but Barbara and her team had made damn sure it would hold up under fire.

Verge regained his bearings, freed the safety on Trash's array of weapons, and turned to face the pair of light 'Mechs attempting to get the better of him.

Two breaths later, the avalanche of missiles from the hillside struck. Both enemy 'Mechs vanished in a wall of smoke punctuated with the crack and flash of indeterminate explosions farther within the cloud, like a string of firecrackers detonating at random. Thermal and mag sensors carved through the murk to reveal both the *Commando* and *Firestarter* lying in ruinous craters.

Lasers and autocannon tracer rounds answered, stabbing from the smoke in Verge's direction. Others aimed far higher, beyond him.

In his rearview, he saw numerous silhouettes emerging at the crater's lip behind him. The humanoid shapes of various BattleMechs and the squat, boxy outlines of Von Luckner tanks all lined up side by side in perfect formation, using the surrounding hills for cover. Another mass salvo of LRMs shot off like firehoses, and units lacking missiles charged down the hillside toward the waiting Lyrans.

"Armstrong!" Major Szalinski himself was on the horn. "Get out of there! Fall back now!"

Verge didn't need to be told twice. Still facing the enraged Lyran remnants, he jerked the throttle lever in hard reverse while taking shots of opportunity on the nearest target, a *Stinger* at ninety meters that had burst from the tree line. Verge's LRM salvo overshot the target, but his large laser cleaved the *Stinger*'s left arm clean off at the elbow, robbing the light 'Mech of a machine gun. Then more incoming LRMs from the hillside caught the 20-tonner and blasted it into scrap.

Kommandant Nielsen's *Zeus* stepped back from the fray, withdrawing to the forest's minimal protection, but its *Rifleman* and *Warhammer* cohorts demonstrated no such illusions of cowardice. The 60- and 70-ton 'Mechs could match an undamaged *Grasshopper* in a footrace, but with Verge having a crippled leg and the good sense to not turn and expose his vulnerable rear armor just for some extra speed, they would inevitably catch him. He could stand and fight, but not even Major Szalinski wanted to risk the replacement for his precious VOX 280 engine

Verge retreated in an awkward zigzag pattern, doing everything he could to keep the mangled leg out of the direct line of fire. Together the *Rifleman* and *Warhammer* advanced in his direction with a disturbing synchronicity. Not slowing. Keeping perfectly abreast of each other. Autocannon chattering from the *Rifleman*'s sole functioning arm. The *Warhammer*'s PPCs charging to fire...

Verge dry-swallowed, loosed an ineffective LRM salvo at the heavier *Warhammer*, and waited for his large laser to recharge.

Another combined LRM salvo from atop the ridge arced down on his pursuers, wreathing them in vibrant explosions and smoke until they vanished from visual sensors entirely. Large-bore autocannon shells followed the missiles. But like avenging demons, the Lyran BattleMechs emerged from the wispy billows and rain of tracer rounds, leaving smoke eddying in their wake.

The already scarred *Warhammer* had suffered even more wounds than before, but it retained full combat effectiveness, despite torrents of green coolant leaking from the rents along its right side.

Still the Lyran giants pressed, one implacable step at a time.

A series of thunderclaps—the battering rams of explosive autocannon shells—pummeled Trash's torso, so close to Verge's cockpit he could see sparks shower just outside the ferroglass canopy. Close enough to reach out and touch, had the cockpit glass not separated him from the elements.

The back of his neck grazed the partially melted headrest. The next shot—any shot—aimed just a few decimeters higher... A stream of charged particles from the *Warhammer* missed, plowing a smoking furrow in the ground right where he'd just been a step before.

The second PPC shot caught him full in the chest.

Kinetic force threw Verge against his harness hard enough to knock the wind out of him. Felt like he'd been mule-kicked right in the sternum. He gasped for air, but it was too late.

Autocannon fire hit him in the leg, and blackened fragments of structural supports in the right leg blew outward like a bloom of fireworks. Damage warnings *gronk*ed in his headset.

Trash lurched and stumbled.

Verge felt the 'Mech—*his* 'Mech—teeter backward...

But the leg wasn't quite done. Not yet. What internal struts remained somehow managed to support the 'Mech's weight, but a pillar of greasy smoke trailed behind his line of retreat.

One more hit, and he'd be down for the count.

The smoke obscured visuals, so he switched to thermal and aimed his weapons solely on instinct.

One wobbly step back at a time... Had to time this just right...

He led the *Warhammer* just enough to get tone, then fired laser and missiles in unison.

He wasn't be sure which weapon tagged the 70-ton 'Mech, but it no longer mattered. Heat from the *Warhammer* spiked, flooding the thermal channel with a bright white flash as something ruptured deep inside. In mid-run, it keeled forward limply into the grass, the pilot seemingly knocked unconscious from the internal explosion.

The loss of the *Rifleman*'s partner did not deter its advance. The amputee continued its headlong charge, and Verge could do little more than limp backward while trying not to fall flat on Trash's jangly metal ass.

His radio blasted to life with a familiar female voice. "Armstrong! Clear my lane of fire!"

Toni.

The Panthers' tank battalion was finally in place on their way down the crater slope.

They were right behind him. Right in his line of retreat. Right in their line of fire.

He had no choice but to stomp his jump pedals once more. This time at least, he was ready for the faulty jet and compensated for it.

"Platoon, weapons free!" Toni shouted while he was almost to the jump's apex. "Fire at will! Fire at will!"

From the air, the sound of an entire platoon of Von Luckners unloading their medium-bore autocannon and cutting the *Rifleman* in half warmed the cockles of Verge's heart.

The hard landing that greeted him at the end of his jump did not. His fractured arm, even less so.

KALI-YAMA FACTORY ANNEX
WESTPORT, KALIDASA
SILVER HAWKS COALITION
FREE WORLDS LEAGUE
1 MARCH 3004

Left forearm in a sling and a breathable composite cast, Verge waited silently at the foot of the work gantry and craned his neck up to take in the full image of the broken, 70-ton BattleMech. Trash's right leg had crumpled completely, but Barbara and her techs swarmed over it like carpenter ants, rebuilding the internal supports as quickly as humanly possible.

Toni leaned in next to him, and recoiled when he subtly winced in pain from the touch. "Glad to see you're all right. That was a pretty nasty spill back there."

"Yeah, well, I have you to thank for pulling my bacon out of the fire."

A smirk curled her lips. "One of these days, I expect *you* to be the one saving *me*, all right? I mean, it's kinda embarrassing if a 'MechJock has to have his lowly tanker girlfriend come save his sorry ass all the time."

"Thanks." He drew her in and kissed the top of her head when she nestled into his arms.

"Hell, I'm just glad you're *okay*."

He swallowed. Couldn't bear to tell her about the reinforcements, that pretty soon they'd all have to fight for their very lives a second time.

Over his shoulder he spotted the major headed his direction with intent. Toni saw too and pulled away. "Looks like you've got a visitor," she said. "I'll see you later." With a quick kiss on the lips, she was gone.

Verge turned back to the torn-up *Grasshopper*, listened for Major Szalinski's boots clopping on the ferrocrete behind him.

"Sergeant." The major stood alongside him, shoulder to shoulder as they both surveyed the 'Mech undergoing repairs. "Thought you'd like to know we caught a lucky break, son—no pun intended. The Arcturan Guards battalion has been taken care of, Kommandant Nielsen is in custody until the Leaguers decide to repatriate him, and we just got confirmation of a Lyran JumpShip arriving at the nadir jump point."

Verge wrinkled his nose in response, unsure how a JumpShip arrival constituted a lucky break. "Sir?"

"*One* JumpShip," Szalinski clarified. "Preliminary reports are saying she's loaded with no more than a full battalion. And a *battalion*...now that we can handle. Especially since they didn't jump in at the pirate point mentioned in the communiqué."

So much fuss over nothing. Verge shook his head. "I don't understand, sir."

"My guess is the Tenth Skye Rangers had some kind of jump trouble. Could be mechanical trouble, could be a mis-jump, any number of things. Could be sabotage by SAFE agents, for all we know. Either way, I'm glad you eventually decided to bring that message to my attention. If you hadn't, we'd be trying to fight nearly two battalions instead of one. And I commend you for volunteering as bait while we moved into position."

"Yes, sir. It was..." Verge hung his head. "It was just the right thing to do."

Szalinski nodded. "I take back what I said earlier. You've got a lot more going for you than Jemison ever did." He gestured at the sling. "You up for a fight, son?"

Verge lifted the arm just enough to show its mobility. It ached like a sonovabitch, but the cast was good, and Corpsman Ghirardi had cleared him for duty. "As ready as I'll ever be. But...I'll need something to pilot."

The major scratched his stubbly chin. "Well, that *Warhammer* you took down didn't have a full mag of missiles left when it blew, so it's pretty clean, apart from the arm and torso damage. And it's got a functioning VOX 280, so that means we'd have a potential replacement from this *Grasshopper* here. You're welcome to the *Warhammer* once we get 'er fixed up."

Verge swallowed but said nothing.

"Or..." Szalinski said. "Fancy piloting a *Zeus*? Only slightly used. It's yours if you want it."

Verge had to admit that inheriting an assault 'Mech once piloted by a Lyran officer of a rank equivalent to Szalinski's, that had some prestige to it.

But then he looked up at Trash, this 'Mech full of secrets that had somehow saved his life during their first engagement. He thought of the partially melted headrest, the hastily welded panel, the photos, the ring. The rush of terror when those two heavies nearly killed him back on the crater slope.

"With all due respect, sir, thanks, but no thanks. Think I'll stick with this one."

Szalinski crossed his arms and frowned at the 'Mech. "Why would you want to stick with a kludged-together piece of garbage like this?"

"Me and her," Verge said, beaming with pride, "we've got history."

LIGHTNING STRIKE
GEOFF "DOC" SWIFT

THIRD LYRAN GUARDS HQ
BURGUNDY, BAXTER
RYDE THEATER
LYRAN COMMONWEALTH
12 DECEMBER 3038

Hauptmann Miles Shelley stared up at his new 'Mech. Well, *new* was certainly inaccurate—it looked older than the Lyran Commonwealth. The *Grasshopper*'s upper body had yet to be painted, clearly showing that the arms were not original to it. A stylized horse's head on the left leg identified it as a Lyran Guards 'Mech, while the crossed swords over a purple shield on the right leg showed it was part of the Third RCT. He could practically hear the poor thing groaning like an old man who just missed the last of his favorite food at a buffet.

"Who did I piss off?" he mumbled.

Laughter from behind surprised him. Recognizing it as coming from Kommandant Rickard Feldstein, Shelley restrained the urge to turn around. Feldstein commanded the battalion Shelley's new command was attached to.

"One would think you'd be happy to have something faster than your old *Stalker*." A huge hand slapped his back. Shelley'd been expecting that. His CO was hardly a model of formality.

"I suppose it's faster, sir, but not by much. How am I supposed to keep up with the rest of the company?"

"Tell them to walk while you run ahead?"

Shelley couldn't resist looking to his right. Seeing the huge smile on Feldstein's face brought a matching one to his. "I'll take that under advisement, sir."

"Given her a name yet?"

"Not yet, sir." Shelley couldn't keep the sourness from his voice.

"Mmm. Bad luck to take a salvaged 'Mech out without a name. Might be she's still loyal to her last pilot... Try to find one in the next few weeks. Word is we'll be moving out soon, so get trained up. We'll be waiting on Vega. But cheer up! This thing's survived more wars than you'll likely fight in! And it's been fully upgraded."

"Fully. Upgraded?" Shelley's doubt was clear from his sarcastic tone.

"Well, maybe not *fully*. But it's got all new weapons. Fancy kit from your new pals on New Avalon..." Feldstein trailed off intentionally.

Shelley looked back at his new 'Mech, uncomfortable under the scrutiny. He had spent the last two years learning mobile combat from the Cadet Cadre of the New Avalon Institute of Science. There were few in the Lyran Commonwealth Armed Forces who liked the thought of adopting Davion tactics now that the two nations were linked by marriage between their ruling families. Shelley had been given command of the Third's new Lightning Company. How he was supposed to reconcile his new role while piloting a slow *Grasshopper* was far more than a challenge. He turned and looked at the rest of the company's 'Mechs, all standing in their own cradles in the 'Mech bay. His was the slowest of the lot.

His resigned sigh brought another burst of laughter from Feldstein.

THIRD LYRAN GUARDS HQ
CLARION, VEGA
VEGA PREFECTURE
DRACONIS COMBINE
10 MAY 3039

Hauptmann Miles Shelley stood outside the briefing room door, listening to the raised voices within. He felt no shame about eavesdropping. It was the members of his company arguing. When he caught his first CO, just before the Fourth Succession War, doing the exact same thing, Hauptmann Meraldine Wulfstein had winked and whispered that it never hurt to hear what your subordinates really think about you and your plans. It was Shelley's first real command instruction. None of his instructors at the Coventry Academy had taught him that.

"*Gott im Himmel,* he's a *believer*!" Shelley recognized the voice of First Leutnant Mut Hobson, commander of Krypta Lance. He piloted one of two *Charger*s reassigned from an assault lance in the Third, and considered being assigned to the Lightning Company a demotion. Hobson had graduated from the Blackjack School of Conflict. Like most Blackjack grads Shelley'd met, Hobson was always trying to find a way to take credit for others' work without doing any of his own. He was also always the first to retreat from even the slightest hint of circumstances turning against him in the last two months of training.

"He's got a job to do, same as us. You don't like it, you should have requested a transfer." Shelley smiled at the calm tones of First Leutnant Alexis Gantikul, Box Lance's commander and pilot of one of the lance's two *Wolverine*s. Gantikul was an exceptional officer who had the misfortune of being assigned to a recon company. The *Wolverine* was a big upgrade from the *Commando* she'd been piloting the last three years.

"I did! *He* denied it!"

"Well, what do you expect? You've got one of the fastest 'Mechs in the regiment that has actual armor to speak of. And it's not like there was a lot of time to find another lance commander before the invasion!"

Shelley'd heard enough. He took a few steps back and began walking boldly and loudly down the hall and into the room. He restrained a smile at the embarrassed silence in the room as those within came to attention.

He stepped to the front of the room and turned to face his eleven MechWarriors with a glare, letting them stand at attention for a few moments longer than necessary. A few years ago, Shelley would never have commanded this company. Instead, a member of some wealthy or powerful family would have gotten the high-profile assignment. He had no family fortune to fall back on. He couldn't afford to fail.

"We've got a mission. It's not exactly our preferred mission profile. But few soldiers get to choose their missions. Let's start planning."

Shelley spread a map on the table at the front of the room. As the company gathered around to examine the terrain they would be covering, Hobson was, predictably, the first to complain. "A city? Oh come on."

Shelley stayed silent. He actually agreed with the obnoxious leutnant. The Lightning Company was best suited to open-field combat. The tight confines of a city were far from ideal. But he'd never agree with Hobson in disapproving of a mission assigned by regimental HQ. Not in front of the company, anyway.

"A recon company just went silent. They reported some sort of jamming or other sensor interference. We have to find the scouts and get them out, but with the Fourteenth Legion of Vega dug in like they are, expect heavy resistance."

"Do we know what they've got in that area? Heavies, lights, or what?" Gantikul was all business, a true professional. Shelley really appreciated her focus on the mission.

"No clue." Shelley was going to force a confident smile, but a genuine one appeared on its own.

Hobson groaned, though he leaned in to study the map. "We're going into Delta Quadrant. First, let's set up rally points in case we have to regroup."

The planning took less than ten minutes. Every minute wasted was another nail in the recon unit's coffin. Shelley watched them file off to change out of their fatigues. He looked at the map one last time. He couldn't shake the feeling that his company was being set up to fail. The diehards hated change. Would they sacrifice a company just to say "I told you so"?

BRODE STREET AND NINTH AVENUE
NEUCASON, VEGA
VEGA PREFECTURE
DRACONIS COMBINE
10 MAY 3039

Shelley was one of many MechWarriors in the Third who'd fought on Vega in the Fourth Succession War. That invasion had ended poorly. This one would succeed thanks to changes in the Third's tactical doctrine. A new commander was a big improvement, but mostly it was the intensive training with the Commonwealth's Davion allies. There were many old guard Lyrans in the Third who refused to embrace change. They preferred the old "stumble and bumble" mindset, sending the Commonwealth's massive assault 'Mechs straight into the enemy, and trusting mass and momentum to win the day. Shelley had been one of those adherents, holding tight as defeat rushed them with superior mobility, tactics, and planning.

He didn't put much stock in superstition or fate or the positions of the stars. He put his faith in metal and myomer and coherent light and fusion power. He was not entirely sure about this *Grasshopper*, though. She was slower and much heavier than the medium 'Mechs he'd driven during his NAIS training. He'd barely gotten acquainted with the salvaged old girl in the few weeks of training on Baxter.

Shelley was among the vanguard of change in the LCAF. Two years of constant training against the First NAIS Cadre's light 'Mechs drove home how fundamentally different the Armed Forces of the Federated Suns approached warfare. The LCAF could only benefit by embracing a new mindset. Shelley would prove the skeptics wrong. Anything other than overwhelming success might stymie that effort.

Shelley commanded the new Lightning Company attached to the Third Lyran Regulars. Lightning Companies, composed of faster, lighter 'Mechs than those commonly associated with the Commonwealth, were still comparatively new in the LCAF. The Third had resisted incorporating the formation, despite many Lyran regiments making good use of them in the Fourth Succession War a decade ago.

Shelley intended to show the Third what lighter 'Mechs could accomplish—not that a *Grasshopper* was very fast or very light. Still, it was the fastest 'Mech available after he returned to the Commonwealth. It wasn't all bad. Its upgrades included a new large laser with a longer effective range, and the so-called pulse lasers were much more accurate than the standard mediums they had replaced, even if they were heavier and had a shorter range. The techs had removed the missile system and some armor to accommodate a fourth pulse laser, giving him more space in the cockpit and eliminating ammunition dependency. His armor was some new type that was lighter but much bulkier. The techs complained of the difficulty working on internal components now, but the new armor's greater coverage made up a bit for the reduced mass.

Shelley's *Grasshopper* was possibly the most expensive 'Mech in the Third due to all the prototype components. Apparently, the upgrades were part of putting the former Free Worlds League *Grasshopper* back into service after moldering for most of a decade in a salvage yard on Hesperus II.

Now it was his. He eased it to a stop on the debris-littered pavement still smoking from a recent battle. The missing recon unit had fought here. And they had died here. BattleMech carcasses littered this stretch of Brode Street for at least seven blocks. Three buildings had been reduced to rubble. Shelley could imagine Legion 'Mechs bursting through them and surprising the *Commando*s and *Locust*s on their scouting run. With the jamming that was also fouling Shelley's sensors, the scouts didn't stand a chance.

His instruments had been giving false returns since he led his company into the suburbs of Vega's capital. Steel frames and electrical wires could be to blame, but command believed the Dracs had some sort of Jammers hidden in the buildings. Looking at the debris that was all that remained of his comrades, Shelley feared two things. First, that his sudden desire for vengeance was shared by his company and, second, that his company had just stepped into the same trap as the scouts.

Without trustworthy sensors, visual scanning was the order of the day. He imagined he looked comical, pausing at a building on the corner of the nearest intersection and peeking around the edge.

The response was less than encouraging.

A fusillade of missiles and armor-piercing shells shredded the edge of the building. Shelley pulled back before his armor disappeared along with the rest of the structure. A *Dragon*, two *Archer*s, and a *Marauder* had been lying in wait.

"Contact! One lance of heavy movers! Two hundred meters east! Box Lance, pen 'em in! Krypta Lance, hit 'em hard! Airborne, on me!"

Shelley didn't wait for acknowledgments before stomping the pedals for his jump jets. Pillars of flame erupted from the *Grasshopper*'s legs. His stomach plummeted as the 'Mech rose into the air.

He cleared Ninth Avenue in an instant, landing in the shadow of the building on the north side of the thoroughfare with a heavy jolt. Pavement cracked under the impact of 70 tons of BattleMech returning to earth on flexing legs. A punishing wave of heat washed through the cockpit and the status board flashed yellow. He hoped the actuator wasn't acting up again. The yellow turned back to green as he throttled forward. Shelley breathed a sigh of relief and darted back into the street as the rest of his lance landed on his side of the street, lasers blazing into the enemy 'Mechs.

The Fourteenth Legion of Vega knew their capital. They were arrayed in staggered formation between the buildings. Shelley needed to keep their attention. A Legion *Marauder* ignored the pinpoint precision of Shelley's ER laser and riposted with twin blue beams of PPC fire. Shelley rocked under the assault, delivering a second laser shot before ducking back into cover. The building shuddered under the barrage from the non-humanoid 'Mech.

Shelley pressed up against the building as First Leutnant Lorenzo Torrio's *Quickdraw* stepped past and fired his long range missiles. Before the *Quickdraw* stepped back, though, a wall of missiles slammed into it. Shelley watched in horror as Torrio's 'Mech rocked and juddered, disappearing in a cloud of rocket exhaust, warhead explosions, and destroyed armor. Shelley felt a tremor as his XO hit the ground. "Torrio!"

The lack of response was a bad sign.

"Airborne, displace and close!" Shelley's voice was getting raw from shouting over the titanic sounds of BattleMech combat. He braced himself for the shock of heat as he engaged his jump jets again. The right knee didn't protest this time. He hoped it wouldn't trouble him again before he could put it back into the 'Mech bay. He crossed the street again, moving one block closer to the enemy.

The Dracs were prepared this time. Missiles arced into the sky toward him. His teeth rattled as impacts and explosions buffeted him. The *Grasshopper* landed hard, slamming into the building he'd wanted to use as cover. Pain lanced through his shoulders and waist as he hit the restraints. He tasted blood and smiled. It was the taste of combat.

He yanked the left control stick back and pushed the right one forward, pivoting against the building's crumbling façade. He skittered left, spotted the *Marauder*, and fired his large laser. An angry red welt scored the crablike 'Mech from left shoulder to hip. A pleasing tone informed Shelley his pulse lasers were in range too. He indulged in an evil grin and triggered his secondary target interlock circuit. A quartet of stuttering beams formed a dashed line between the two 'Mechs. Shelley adjusted his aim and walked the pulsing light across the *Marauder*'s face.

Shelley imagined the MechWarrior shaking in his seat. But the enemy didn't take cover. The close range made Shelley too tempting a target. The Drac fired everything he had. A pair of red laser beams lanced into his *Grasshopper*, the left one tearing into his right leg and the right one vaporizing armor from his left arm. Fortunately for Shelley, the close range inhibited the Drac's PPC effectiveness. The left one missed entirely, blasting a building down the street to rubble, while the right one danced across Shelley's torso. Armor sheeted off in a cataract of destruction, scarring the road to match Shelley's ruined paint job. The *Marauder's* cannon thundered away, sending explosive shells into the *Grasshopper*. Individually, they were mere annoyances, but a continuous fusillade was a genuine concern. Shelley dodged back into cover, barely able to keep his 'Mech upright after absorbing such punishment.

His seismic sensors, unreliable at the best of times, recorded a sudden spike. Shelley smiled and slid back into the street. The *Marauder* had fallen to the pavement. *Guess I gave better than I got.* The enemy was trying to stand back up. *None of that, now.* He dropped his targeting reticule over the bucking 'Mech and braced himself for the blast of heat as he fired all his lasers again. Missiles and PPC bolts from the *Griffins* of Danielle Jackson and Jackamar Matteus, the "Jumping Jacks," kept the *Archers* and *Dragon* honest while Shelley focused on the *Marauder*.

A gout of greasy smoke erupted from the Drac 'Mech's back. Shelley knew the telltale sign of a gyro's destruction. The *Marauder* was out of the fight. He turned to find a new target and smiled again.

Box Lance slewed into view down the street, running flat out toward the enemy rear and blasting away. Box's two *Phoenix Hawks* concentrated on the *Dragon*, lasing its rear with perfect accuracy. It collapsed to the ferrocrete with a loud crash.

Box's two *Wolverines* focused on the *Archer* on the north side of the street. It returned fire with its rear lasers, scoring the torso armor on Milton's 'Mech before it also crashed to the ground.

The remaining *Archer* turned to flee south, only to meet Krypta Lance. A pair of *Chargers* lived up to their name, plowing into the *Archer* and smashing it to the ground. They quickly stepped aside, allowing Krypta's two *Ostsols* a clear field of fire. Megajoules of laser energy speared into the *Archer*, joined by PPC fire from the two *Griffins* of Shelley's lance. The *Archer* soon exploded as its ammunition stores were touched off by the sustained barrage.

Shelley's grin was sobered when he remembered Torrio. He spun about and ran back down the street toward his fallen comrade. The *Quickdraw* had certainly seen better days.

He thumbed the external speakers on. "Torrio! You alive in there?" He punctuated his query by nudging the downed 'Mech with his left foot. "On your feet, XO!"

As an answer, the *Quickdraw* twitched and rolled onto its face and pressed itself up like a recruit doing pushups. The ragged 'Mech shakily regained its feet, leaning against the nearest building like a drunken reveler.

"You okay, Torrio?"

"Been better, Hauptmann, been better. But I think I can—"

Shelley would never know what Torrio's last words would have been. A furious torrent of lasers and PPCs blasted into the two of them. Shelley tried to dodge the fire as it poured down the street from the north. He spun west and collapsed to the buckling ferrocrete.

Shelley gaped at the oncoming enemies just before his vision washed out from white-hot fury as Torrio's LRM ammunition succumbed to the attack. The *Quickdraw* exploded, battering the buildings and Shelley's *Grasshopper* with debris.

He screamed into his comm. "Drac company incoming! Disperse and regroup! Rally point—" he searched his memory for the closest safe zone,"—Delta-seven! Move, move, move!"

Blinking away the afterimages of Torrio's death, Shelley muscled his 'Mech back to its feet. He immediately stomped his jump jets, hurtling into the air to the south. He came down behind the building he'd first peered around at the start of this engagement. He chanced another peek around that same corner once more, relieved to see the other lances withdrawing in good order. Enemy fire was lancing into them, but they were returning fire to slow the oncoming Dracs. Box dashed east and turned south several blocks away. Krypta did the same, the *Charger*s leading the retreat since their popgun lasers weren't much use against the closing enemies. Shelley saw the dissipating smoke trails from the Jumping Jacks' *Griffin*s. He sighed with relief. One casualty was more than enough.

He narrowed his focus on the intersection one block east, fingers ready on his triggers, prepared to spin and jump as soon as he fired on the enemy. A Legion *Thunderbolt* surged into view. It spun and raised the huge laser on its right arm. Shelley smiled in triumph, knowing he had the advantage of surprise. He mashed the triggers.

An alarm klaxon sounded in his ears, sundering expected joy in a terrifying instant. None of his weapons had fired. His gaze flicked from one status board to the next, seeing red indicators everywhere. Before he could try to diagnose the problem, a huge laser beam stabbed into his left shoulder and another two into his torso. More red lights lit up his status display, indicating critical damage to his shoulder. Shelley lurched behind the building, falling to the ground again, this time in shock at the sudden attack. He slammed into the seat restraints with a heavy grunt as his forehead smashed into his neurohelmet.

His fancy new weapons had failed him. He was defenseless. And an enemy company was closing in. He blinked against a shower of sparks from his control panel as he fought to stand his 'Mech up, wondering if he would survive the next few minutes.

Shelley forced himself to breathe slowly and deliberately. Panic beckoned from a deep pit in his gut, and he couldn't allow himself to fall in.

He could radio for assistance from his company. They would surely come to his aid if he called. Well, maybe not Hobson. But his company wasn't suited for standup fights. Isolating heavy lances was doable. Engaging even numbers of heavier units? No chance. Shelley reached a decision. He opened his comm and said, "*Rinnsal!* Repeat, *rinnsal!* Confirm!"

"*Rinnsal* confirmed," First Leutnant Gantikul's voice was grim. The rest of the company's acknowledgments followed quickly. *Rinnsal* was the code word for falling back in successive step. If Delta-seven were compromised, or if some of the company didn't arrive fifteen minutes after you did, you fell back to the next rally point.

They were all faster than he was, so they were sure to arrive before him. But if he led the enemy there... He couldn't lose his company. He had to lead the enemy away.

Shelley trudged along an alley separating two long rows of abandoned apartment buildings. His sensors were no more use in this setting than his nonfunctional weapons. Seismic readings were the best gauge he had of the enemy right now, mainly because the Fourteenth apparently had heavy and assault 'Mechs defending the area.

He debated pausing at the intersection. Instead he stomped the pedals and jumped across instead. A trio of PPC bursts flashed underneath his feet. An *Awesome* was positioned half a klick down the thoroughfare. If the range had been a little less, Shelley'd be picking himself up off the ferrocrete again.

He was sprinting as soon as he touched down. Delta-seven was still two klicks south. Or at least that's what Shelley thought. He wasn't entirely sure where he was at the moment.

A large parkland appeared before him. Now he knew he was lost. But the wooded area might allow him to lose his pursuers. The *Grasshopper* dashed into the thick cover.

Shelley ran straight for sixty seconds, then took a hard left and plunged ahead for another thirty. He stopped at the edge of a pond and allowed himself to breathe for a moment. The lessons from NAIS came back to him. The Davions were experts at mobile warfare, relying greatly on lighter units than the Steiners favored. They were used to being outmassed by their enemies. They didn't let that deter them from engaging those enemies, though. They had to rely on trickery. It was not first-nature for Shelley, or even second-nature, but he liked to think he was among the best in the LCAF at the concept. He was hurting, but at least some of the enemy had pursued him. Did the concealing foliage even the odds? Shelley checked his sensors and was pleased to find them functioning now that he was away from the buildings. A few red lights glowed at the edge of the park. Some of them withdrew into the sensor-fuzzing haze of the city proper, disappearing from his panel. But two moved into the woods.

Shelley smiled. *Time to try some trickery.*

He could just make out the enemy *Crusader* through the forest canopy. It was moving along a narrow walking path, widening it considerably and damaging its esthetic value. Shelley was about to enhance that destruction.

The Drac was moving slowly. The MechWarrior within was likely watching his sensor board closely for any sign of Shelley. He wouldn't see one until Shelley made his move.

The urge to act was painful. Shelley restrained himself as the enemy approached the chosen spot. Waiting. Waiting. Waiting. Now! He activated his reactor from standby, knowing the Drac would detect him now. Hesitation would mean death.

Shelley throttled as fast as the water would allow. As soon as his panel showed green for his jump jets, he knew he was clear of the water and stomped his pedals. He rose on flames, wreathed in steam from the pond he'd been partially submerged in. He had waded in, finding the pond surprisingly deep, leaving only his head above the surface, masking the telltale heat from his engine.

He had measured the distance to his chosen site very carefully. It was at his maximum jump range. And the Legion of Vega *Crusader* had just crept into that position. It was facing the opposite direction from the pond. Even so, the MechWarrior reacted incredibly fast. *Getting out of the water took too long, dammit!*

A fusillade of lasers sliced into the *Grasshopper*'s left side, lighting up the status panel. Shelley's stomach swam as his 'Mech shook from the beams searing armor off his side.

Desperate, he feathered his left pedal and soared over his enemy, turning a complete 180 degrees from his original orientation. Shelley landed directly behind the *Crusader* and threw a pair of massive punches. The *Grasshopper*'s fists drove through the thin rear armor once, twice, a third time.

The *Crusader* spun before it dropped like a puppet with its strings cut. Shelley had destroyed its gyro in the most brutal, personal manner imaginable. The 'Mech flailed its arms, chopping into the *Grasshopper*'s shoulder and grabbing onto the arm as though for support. Shelley lurched backward, trying to pull free. A tremendous *screech* of tearing metal and myomer presaged horror as his left arm, already damaged by the Drac's lasers, wrenched free at the shoulder and hit the ground with the crippled *Crusader*. Shelley stomped the arm, wincing as he crushed the pulse laser in it. *Can't leave that for the enemy.*

Unable to enjoy his victory, he immediately jumped again, deeper into the forest. *Never rely on the same trick twice*, he recalled. He might have crippled the *Crusader*, but the MechWarrior could relay what had happened to him. The pond was now off-limits.

Shelley had to keep moving and figure out what to do about the other Drac. Especially since he now had only one arm to do it with. Plus, his 'Mech was limping; the right knee was acting up again. *Nothing I can do about it now.* His gait smoothed as he ran, but the balky joint concerned him almost as much as the enemy.

The *Dragon* advanced cautiously. Shelley admired the skill of the Legion MechWarrior. The thick cover opened out into a clearing. It was some sort of memorial garden, by the looks of it, but Shelley had no time to try reading the plaques around the perimeter.

The trail took a long straight run into the clearing before a dogleg right. He watched the *Dragon* pause at the edge of the clearing, just as Shelley would have done.

He should have focused his attention on the beginning of the straightaway.

Shelley restarted his 'Mech from standby mode and ran through the trees to the path. He pivoted on his left foot and swung towards the *Dragon*. Shelley accelerated to maximum speed and closed in seconds. But this MechWarrior was even faster to react than his comrade near the pond.

Shelley absorbed a fusillade of cannon rounds and a medium laser hit before he reached the enemy. He lowered his shoulder to charge. The *Dragon* reacted as Shelley had hoped. It braced itself to receive his charge, leaning forward to meet the expected impact rather than trying to avoid it. Instead, Shelley kicked his own feet forward and slammed to the ground. He slid into the *Dragon*'s right foot, throwing the right leg up in the air. The unbalanced 'Mech flopped to the ground face-first.

Shelley rolled to his right, got his remaining hand on the ground, and shoved. He thrust back off the ground with the remaining momentum from his charge. Two quick steps had him standing over the downed *Dragon*. He threw a series of kicks and stomps into the right leg he'd already damaged. A blast from the *Dragon*'s rear laser nearly caught Shelley in the face. He allowed himself one more stomp, confident the leg would not support the 'Mech anymore, before jumping off to the south.

Shelley hoped his company was still alive.

Shelley's heart sank as he approached Delta-seven. The rally point was a scene of carnage. The narrow alleyway no longer existed, the buildings that once formed it now rubble. There were no 'Mech carcasses, though. He ran with abandon through the city to the next rally point. It was the same story there and at the next two rally points, each one closer to the edge of the city. Shelley was three blocks from Delta-three when he caught the first hints of disaster over the comm.

He came into view of the city circle he had designated Delta-three. A classical clock tower glared down from the north end of the circle, while a statue commemorating some Drac hero or other occupied the southern part. Fine cobblestones formed walking paths leading into and through the circle, which was ringed with aesthetically pleasing brick barriers to prevent vehicle traffic. These were no impediment to BattleMech strides, making the circle a scenic redoubt to assemble a small force like the Lightning Company.

At least that's how Shelley remembered it. The scene that greeted him was far from beauteous. The cobbled walks had great rents torn in them from BattleMech feet moving and turning at high speed. The elegant brick barrier walls were sundered from weapons fire, dripping mortar and molten brick the evidence of laser fire, shattered cinders and flinders the proof of autocannon rounds and errant missiles.

The western rim had been burst by the fallen torso of Chad Milton's *Wolverine*, which had lost both arms before succumbing to enemy fire. The shattered canopy sang the song of Milton's fate more bitterly than any after-action report would do, assuming Shelley survived to write one.

The Jumping Jacks were in constant motion, leaping from building to building and engaging target after target with their PPCs. Their missiles were probably exhausted, given the level of visible damage to both 'Mechs. One of them landed on a building that had been weakened by weapons fire. As the *Griffin* touched down, its arms flew up as it plunged through the roof and the floors below. Only a cloud of dust emerged.

The other *Griffin* now leaped over the shielding row of buildings to the south and out of Shelley's view. Alexis Gantikul's *Wolverine* fought from the lee of a pair of heavily damaged buildings. Gantikul was only firing her lasers, likely having run dry on ammo. Behind the *Wolverine* were Douglas and Bauer's *Phoenix Hawks*, blazing away with their large pistol-like lasers. There was no sign of First Leutnant Hobson's Krypta Lance. Shelley cursed.

The *Griffin* reappeared over the building row, landed while firing, and immediately jumped away again. Shelley nodded in appreciation that one of his comrades was utilizing the tactics they'd spent weeks drilling. The enemy couldn't hit such frenetically moving targets.

The enemy was what remained of the company that had drove them off earlier. Seven of them were still standing. Four were on the far side of the circle from him, moving closer to the three 'Mechs taking cover between the buildings. The other three were firing on Gantikul's *Wolverine* as cover for the other lance, and had their backs to him.

He diverted left and ran up a block, slewed around a right as he ran another block, then skidded through another right turn. He throttled up to maximum and hoped luck would be with him. He couldn't risk the comm for fear of alerting the enemy. Since they hadn't fired on him yet, they might not know he had arrived.

He thought idly about how he was falling back on classic Lyran tactics rather than relying on the Davion techniques. But what's a MechWarrior to do without weapons? He wore a grim smile as he remembered another lesson from NAIS. *You're never out of the fight. Improvise and adapt and overcome. A direct assault can often bluff a superior enemy into believing he's outmatched.* In truth, he realized that, sometimes, classic Lyran tactics had their place.

Shelley braced himself as much as he could as the left shoulder of the Legion *Warhammer* rushed at him.

RALLY POINT DELTA-THREE
NEUCASON, VEGA
VEGA PREFECTURE
DRACONIS COMBINE
10 MAY 3039

First Leutnant Alexis "Kull" Gantikul was shouting in fury. She never truly believed Hobson would desert his comrades. *Rinnsal* required they stay unless forced out. He'd left before the enemy had even arrived. Now she was desperately holding off two Drac lances with the scraps of the company. They were pulling out when Danielle Jackson's *Griffin* went through a nearby roof. Gantikul couldn't leave a comrade behind. Not like that bastard Hobson.

The *Warhammer* on the west landed a devastating hit with both PPCs. Gantikul's status board was entirely red. It was now or never.

She stabbed the comm. "Delta-two! Go! Go! Go!"

Before she could switch off the comm, she saw the unbelievable. Many MechWarriors were superstitious. She had always prided herself on her rational mindset. But she could only classify what she saw as an apparition. Unless she was hallucinating.

A one-armed *Grasshopper* covered in dirt and leaves, rent in at least a dozen places from weapons fire, charged from the north and plowed into the *Warhammer* that had just blasted her.

The *Warhammer* crashed into the *Dragon* next to it, which crashed into the *Crusader* next to it. The four 'Mechs slid down the street in a single pile of metal and myomer until they passed from view. The *Grasshopper* was on top of the heap.

Her comm crackled with Leutnant Sven Bauer's voice. "Hey, Kull. Did that just happen?"

She was too stunned to respond.

Apparently, the enemy MechWarriors were just as shocked. She could imagine their mouths gaping open. Whatever kept them from taking advantage of her momentary lapse of concentration by reducing her to ash was good enough for her. "Targets right! Fire!"

Shelley floated on a sea of unconsciousness. He tasted blood and didn't know where he was. Dimly, he realized he was rocking back and forth in his restraints. His face was mashed against his neurohelmet. He shook his head and realized immediately what a horrid mistake that was. White pain lanced through his skull. He groaned and pushed against his armrests. Fresh pain ignited his left arm.

"How long was I out?" he muttered through broken teeth. The view through his canopy was filled with the insignia of the Fourteenth Legion of Vega painted across buckled armor panels. *Right. The* Warhammer.

Something underneath the *Warhammer* was jostling the scrap pile of 'Mechs. *Guess my idea worked.* It took considerable effort to get his 'Mech's legs operating from the top of the heap. His attempt to stand failed miserably, and he returned to the bruising embrace of his restraints. Growling, he forced the *Grasshopper* back to its feet with a banshee shriek of shredding metal. Data from his right arm disappeared from his status board as the limb was left underneath the *Warhammer* trapping it. Shelley groaned as new alarms shrilled. He acknowledged the alert, sparing his ears the *Grasshopper*'s wails of pain.

The stub of a *Dragon*'s autocannon stuck out from the pile, wiggling in an impotent effort to extricate itself. The *Warhammer* was otherwise motionless. The arms of another 'Mech protruded—motionless—from beneath the *Dragon*. A distant sound intruded upon him.

He turned, so slowly, and realized a battle was still being fought. Cold hate banished the fog of pain. Armless, he limped toward the battle, the right knee refusing at first to bend at all.

Shelley was awed by his comrades' constant motion. None of the four operational 'Mechs stood still for an instant. Instead they continually hopped, firing from the air, not letting the enemy draw a bead.

Even so, their firepower was limited by expended ammunition. Their enemies were not so afflicted. Missiles and explosive shells shattered building façades and ruined the hand-laid cobblestone walkways beyond hope of repair.

Shelley couldn't believe that the Dracs would do this to their own homeworld. They didn't deserve to keep what mattered so little to them.

He had no weapons save mass and momentum. He didn't expect to survive another impact like he'd just experienced. Ending the threat was all that mattered. Damn the rest.

He pushed his throttle to maximum. Damage to his right leg put a hitch in his step, slowing him slightly, but the knee smoothed out a bit with higher speed. The loss of two limbs reduced his mass by a couple tons, perhaps reducing the stress on the joint. He lurched across the formerly beautiful pavilion toward a familiar *Thunderbolt*.

The distance closed quickly. Then the *Thunderbolt* was gone. Shelley blinked and throttled back. He stared at a most unexpected vista.

A *Charger* braced itself against a building while two *Ostsol*s sped across the gap between buildings on the edge of the square. At the *Charger*'s feet lay the *Thunderbolt* Shelley was about to ram. The *Charger* laid about with kicks, battering the Legion 'Mech into inoperability. The rest of the Legion lance was in flight, pursued by the *Ostsol*s and *Phoenix Hawk*s.

"Glad you decided to join us, sir." Leutnant Gantikul's voice over the comm was a welcome relief to the silence Shelley'd forced himself to operate under.

"Report, Leutnant." Shelley realized how thick his voice sounded. He coughed and hawked up a wad of something unspeakable, leaning down to clear his neurohelmet and spitting it onto the floor of his cockpit.

She related the details of the downed MechWarriors sharing cockpits of the operational 'Mechs. Shelley was happily stunned to learn that Milton had survived and was with Breanna Douglas in her *Phoenix Hawk*.

They surrounded the pile of Legion 'Mechs Shelley had created. The trapped MechWarriors had abandoned their downed 'Mechs and fled into the warren of buildings. Shelley had Leutnant Bauer extricate his right arm from the wreckage.

"Area secured." Gantikul sounded surprised. "Apparently, Krypta decided to fight after all."

"Roger that, sir."

Shelley recognized MechWarrior Marlowe Winter's as the *Charger* joined them. "Report, Winter."

"Well, sir, when Box Lance didn't follow we wanted to come back. Leutnant Hobson ordered us to continue to Delta-two. When we refused, he said we'd be arrested, but we'd rather be in the stockade than leave you guys behind."

"I guess not all Blackjack grads are bad, eh, sir?" He could hear the smirk in Gantikul's voice.

"There are rare exceptions, sir." Winter laughed.

"Okay, Winter. Krypta Lance is yours now. You've got rear guard." *I'll deal with Hobson when we get back to base*, he thought.

Box Lance formed up echelon left behind Shelley, while Krypta formed echelon right a hundred meters back. Shelley led the Lightning Company at a snail's pace back to base as his damaged 'Mech began to falter more and more as they progressed.

Less than a kilometer from the city's edge, they found Leutnant Hobson. He hadn't made it out of the city after all. Some Dracs must have caught him from behind. The rear torso on the *Charger* was a gigantic open wound showing the cratered street underneath the metallic corpse. Whoever did the deed made sure he wouldn't be getting back up. The 'Mech's head had been stove in so that it resembled a crushed raisin.

No one in the company said a word about Hobson as they paraded by.

By the time they reached their base, Shelley's left leg was frozen at the knee and ankle, while his right hip was locked tight. He hobbled it into the makeshift repair bay in the suburb of Clarion.

He gratefully pushed the neurohelmet off his shoulders and shrugged out of his restraints. His left arm was swollen around a new joint between elbow and wrist. He didn't even remember breaking it.

He popped the canopy and gingerly climbed out with one arm, letting his left hang loose. The broken arm, thankfully numb, was the only part of him that didn't hurt. Lacerations covered him from the restraints, and he was sure he looked a fright from making out with his neurohelmet.

Kommandant Feldstein was waiting for him at ground level. Shelley was wobbly on his legs and couldn't stand at attention. Feldstein was still looking up at the *Grasshopper* when he spoke. "Shelley, you give her a name yet?"

Oddly, Shelly realized that he had. "Yessir. 'Survivor.'"

Feldstein gave Shelley the once-over as the rest of the company gathered around. "Sounds about right." Feldstein looked over the rest of the company and nodded. "Report?"

"The recon unit's a total loss from what we could find. Torrio and Hobson're gone. Four 'Mechs lost. Took out a Drac company."

Feldstein nodded again. "I know this was a tough mission for you guys. Don't worry, Hauptmann, I'd say your company proved their worth. Now get to the medics. Full briefing once you're fixed up."

"Yessir." The survivors of the Lightning Company's first mission escorted Shelley to the medbay. He was on the verge of collapse when they finally arrived. He looked at the concerned faces of his company. "Don't worry about me. I'm a survivor, too."

CHOICES AND CHANCES
CHRIS HUSSEY

NEW HOUSTON, BLACK EARTH
BLACKJACK OPERATIONS AREA
FEDERATED COMMONWEALTH
8 JULY 3049

The dying screams of her lancemates cut into Lieutenant Sigland Idelson's heart as she switched off her comm.

She yanked off her neurohelmet and threw it, as if it might make the sounds leave her head. The tight confines of the cockpit of Chances, her *Grasshopper* BattleMech, only caused the helmet to bounce off a panel and land back in her lap. The helmet's viewscreen stared up vacantly at her, mirroring how her soul felt. The familiar rumble of a DropShip launch caused her emotional walls to break and the tears to flow. The roar of the launch drowned out her sobbing as she mourned the fate of those left behind because of her betrayal.

It was supposed to be an easy smash-and-grab mission. A facility owned by Shatterdog Shipping on the outskirts of the planet's capital. Her mercenary lance, the Idle Hands, was perfect for the job. Small and agile. *And desperate,* she reminded herself.

It had started easy enough; they'd broken through the site security, found their target, and got moving.

That's when it went south. Shatterdog had brought in reinforcements and caught Sigland and her unit flat-footed. She wanted to tell herself that her unit fought well and she had no choice, but it was a lie.

I panicked and fled.

The truth stung bitterly, and she dropped her head in her hands as the g-forces from the escaping DropShip weighed down on her.

Sigland wished they would simply crush her.

It wasn't long after the craft cleared Black Earth's atmosphere that her comm began blinking. She knew who it was but didn't want to talk. She didn't want to do anything.

She keyed the comm. "Yes."

"I'm very sorry about your unit, Lieutenant."

Sigland grunted.

"I'm sure you're a bit upset, but I must ask. Did you retrieve the core?"

Sigland found herself hating her employer, Kelly Hunt, more by the second. She sighed. "Affirmative."

"Good." Hunt sounded relieved, then quickly turned business. "Of course, you realize you won't be receiving their portion of the contract. There is a 'survivors only' clause."

Sigland's red-rimmed eyes narrowed. "You're doing this right now?"

"I'm sorry, Lieutenant. But often with merc units—" Hunt paused "—in your situation, many MechWarriors betray their comrades for more pay. It's an occupational hazard I've seen before."

Hunt's words hit her like the blade of a *Hatchetman*. "Understood." She killed the comm. *You want to be an asshole about payment? How about I be an asshole about the mission?*

Reaching into a cargo pouch, Sigland fished out a data cable and connected to her 'Mech's system the storage drive that had cost so much. In a few keystrokes, half the files were transferred to the *Grasshopper*'s internal memory. *You cut my pay, I cut your product.*

Time dragged after leaving Black Earth, and Sigland's guilt grew heavier and heavier as she sat in her cabin. This new failure only called up the long string of bad decisions, losing battles, and cowardice that dotted her career. Her promising start as a lance commander with the Third Lyran Regulars had ended when she got into a brawl with members of her own company. A dishonorable discharge led her to a command position in a defunct mercenary unit called Cash & Combat. When they hit hard times, piracy was an easy choice. Sigland knew where that path led, so she got out and formed her own unit, the Idle Hands, thinking she could turn things around.

She was wrong. Sigland knew she wasn't cut out to be in command. She was a MechWarrior, but not a leader. That truth was painfully obvious now. She wanted to run from it all: 'Mech combat, questionable contracts, life itself. The faces of those she had abandoned and betrayed haunted her.

The comm on her door dinged. A canned voice followed. "Lieutenant Idelson?"

"Enter," Sigland called out.

The cabin door slid open and Kelly Hunt stepped in. Well-groomed, with graying hair and a lean build, the merchant had a face that made you double-check your wallet or keep your valuables just a bit closer. Normally well-dressed, Hunt was casual within the confines of his ship.

"A commander without her unit. I'm very sorry."

Sigland stared blankly at the man. "If that's sympathy, you're pretty lousy at it. What do you want?"

"The database is rather...small." Hunt sounded annoyed.

Sigland shrugged. "So? That's not my problem. The mission was to recover it. We recovered it. Didn't have time to look at it."

Hunt persisted. "But it's not all there."

Sigland mocked his tone. "But that's not my problem. You never put a clause in the contract for a portion of the data. Maybe you received bad intel."

Hunt's eyes narrowed. "Maybe I should check your 'Mech's databanks."

Sigland moved a hand toward her holstered pistol nearby. "Maybe we should end these negotiations right now."

Hunt held both hands up. "No need to escalate." He sighed. "You'll be paid your portion, and just to show I'm not completely heartless, I'll give you a percentage—in supplies and munitions— for those in your unit that didn't make it, so you can repair your *Grasshopper*."

Blood pay for blood parts. Sigland swallowed hard as she felt tears well up again.

Hunt turned toward the door, then looked back. "We never discussed where you'd like to go, now that the mission is complete. Do you have a destination in mind?"

Sigland turned away and pressed the button to close the door to her cabin.

"Anywhere I can forget any of this ever happened."

TORNED'S HIGHLANDS
EREWHON
GREATER VALKYRATE
3 AUGUST 3049

The sheep bleated angrily as Sigland Idelson prodded it forward with the end of her staff. Despite the protest, the animal lumbered into the pen where four others waited and wandered.

Her sheep secured, Idelson leaned the staff against the attached shed, grabbed the powered shears, whistled one of the flock over, and wrangled the animal into position. Within minutes, the thick coat of wool was a distant memory. Idelson whistled for another while her dog, Cadbury, barked his approval.

Idelson was about to start shearing again when a voice made her look up.

"Need any help?"

She looked at the man standing in the doorway. His sweat-soaked shirt clung to a chest powerfully built from years of farm work. One hand held a long rake, while the other removed his hat to wipe moisture from his face.

Idelson smiled as she let the sheep go. "Yeah. Where's my lunch?"

The man set the rake next to the other tools in the shed and moved toward her. "That's why I'm here. It's all ready."

Idelson rose and walked to the man, pulling at his shirt. "You worked up this much of a sweat making lunch? August Lauer, what the hell did you make?"

August smiled at her playfulness. "Cutting bread is not easy, even with one of your fancy combat knives. Still squished the loaf."

"Dumb farmer." Idelson smiled as she pulled August close.

"What does that make *you*, then? You're learning how to farm from me."

Idelson nodded. "Good point." She gave him a quick kiss, broke the embrace, and went back to the remaining sheep. "Let me finish, and I'll be right in."

August waved her off. "Nah. It's nice out. I'll bring it out. We'll eat under the canopy."

She bit into her sandwich and watched the quintet of freshly shorn sheep dart about the field, chased by Cadbury, her border collie.

August pointed toward the group. "You're a pretty quick study." He broadened his gesture to the entire small farm. "In fact, you've done pretty good for yourself overall."

"Well, you get a lot of credit. If I hadn't met you after getting here, I'd probably still be trying to lick the last bits out of my MREs."

August laughed and placed a hand on Idelson's thigh. "Happy to help. Besides, there's benefits for me too."

She looked at him and raised an eyebrow. "Oh, is that all you're in this for? The sex?"

August opened his mouth to respond, but she cut him off. "Well, you'd probably get that regardless. I get bored and lonely, and you're the only one who comes around." She smirked.

His open-mouthed expression changed to a smile. "I love you too," he offered sarcastically.

She smiled back. "And I love you."

"You coming here is the best thing that's ever happened to me."

She grabbed his hand and pulled it close for a kiss. After a moment, she returned her gaze to the sheep. "You think I'll have enough for the festival? All I've got is the wool, some lamb jerky, and a few jars of preserves. It's not much."

August chuckled. "Are you kidding? Don't forget, you offered free use of that." He jerked a thumb behind him at the twelve-meter-tall *Grasshopper* standing at attention. From a distance, it was impossible to tell that a 'Mech even existed on the small farm. Tarps fanned out from all sides of the oblong-shaped head. Secured with taut lines, the structure looked like a small circus tent. Indeed, Idelson had used the makeshift structure as her initial home while renovating the farm gifted to her by the citizens of the small town of Torned. It was one act in a string of kindnesses given to her by people she barely knew.

Now, almost a year later, she was more than happy to return the favor, offering her *Grasshopper* as a mobile power plant during the town's festival. "Of course I offered it. It's the least I can do after all they've done for me." She kissed August's hand again.

"And all you've done." August nodded. "A lot of the people here aren't natives.

They've come for different reasons. And those that are native, well they've seen plenty of people come here seeking peace, so they understand. To them, you're a kindred spirit." August paused. "And you follow the rules. You help out and pay taxes to Maria."

Idelson exhaled, recalling the tense encounter with members of Maria Morgraine's Valkyrate when they arrived on the world to collect tax. They wanted Sigland and her *Grasshopper* at first, something she wasn't ready to give yet. After running from fighting, she thought she might have to take up arms again.

That's when August intervened. He'd argued to keep Sigland and her 'Mech on-planet, using them for recon and gathering intel on Erewhon's long-abandoned cities. The pirate's commander, Senda the Shiv, agreed—but only after Sigland pledged fealty to Maria and Valkyrate.

Idelson was convinced that the welcome she'd received on Erewhon saved her life. With a satchel filled with supplies, 5,000 kroner, and her *Grasshopper*, Sigland thought she'd come here to die. Even the last words spoken to her by Kelly Hunt had been a disingenuous "Good luck."

The first week had been rough. Sigland spent far too much time in the cockpit of the *Grasshopper*, staring at the bulkhead just above her. Scratched into the steel were the names of all the previous owners of Chances. Some with dates of ownership. Some with planet names. Some listed kills. The most recent owner, *Hauptmann Miles Shelley*—who was he? What battles and glories had he and the rest of these former MechWarriors faced in this 'Mech? Her mind endlessly contrasted them against the failure after failure she'd endured, until finally winding up on a dead-end world few people knew of, and even less cared about.

It wasn't until she had run out of liquor, and August had scooped her up out of an alley, that things turned around. Now, instead of ending lives, Chances would be used to enhance them.

Idelson rose and pulled August to his feet. "Well, break's over, Mister Lauer. We only have two days left, and there's still plenty to do."

TORNED
EREWHON
GREATER VALKRATE
5 AUGUST 3049

Idelson sat patiently in the cockpit of Chances. She was beginning to think Mayor Richards would never finish her speech. She'd been blathering on for the past ten minutes; something about hard work, togetherness, praise for the Greater Valkyrate, and the wonderful freedom from the conflicts of the Inner Sphere.

Despite her impatience, she had to concede that those last lines did resonate with her. She looked around the cockpit—the controls, monitors, her cooling vest. It almost seemed foreign to her. She nodded knowingly to herself. *I'm really ready to let this all go. Heh. Looks like the real chance you gave me, Chances, was to start over.*

She scanned the crowd gathered in the park below. Her gaze drifted over many friendly faces before finally landing on August, who smiled lovingly at her, then rolled his eyes in frustration toward the mayor. *I've never felt more sure about anything before.*

The 'Mech's external mics picked up the end of the mayor's speech. "...And as we always do, we mark another year of prosperity. With one hand, we embrace old friends, and with the other, we reach out to new ones, welcoming them and the new lives they seek. And with that, I declare the Forty-Fifth Annual Torned Freedom Festival underway!"

Sigland exhaled. *Finally.* Calling up her targeting reticule, she did a double check confirming all four Diplan M3 medium lasers were locked on their targets, as they'd been prone to drift ever since being replaced years ago. She let fly with each beam on four-second intervals.

Mayor Richards had wanted something extra special to kick things off. After mulling over several ideas, the mayor, August, and Idelson settled on using the medium lasers to target four nearly empty fuel pods on the edge of town. The resulting fireballs were sure to make a statement and be a big hit.

Each laser struck its target, causing a massive ball of flame to burst skyward. With each subsequent blast, the roar from the crowd grew. With the final explosion triggered, Idelson turned to her next trick.

Set to "paint" mode and programmed to strobe, the Diplan HD large laser, also having been swapped out at some point (making

Idelson wonder what had been in there previously) flashed only meters above the heads of the crowd as it made a 180-degree arc. The light show was augmented, by loud, classical music through the *Grasshopper*'s external speakers.

The crowd hollered and applauded the finale, with some adding to the cacophony by drawing their sidearms and firing into the air.

As Chances finished its turn, Idelson faded the music out, then shifted power from the 'Mech's fusion reactor to the external cables that would draw power for the park's lights and festival's machines. Smiling, she crawled out from the cockpit to join the fun.

Idelson kept her arm tight around August's waist, a thumb hooked in one of his belt loops. Her other hand held a drink, positioned deftly in front of her mouth, shielding the growing smile and occasional giggle.

A drunk Mayor Richards swayed as she spoke to the pair. "I'msohappyyoudidthishforus." The words fell over each other as she spoke.

Idelson watched as August reached out a hand to steady the mayor. "It's really no problem, Mayor, after everything you've done." She pulled August closer. "Everyone has been so welcoming. It's saved me."

"Yesh. Shaved you." The mayor steadied herself against August briefly, then gave the pair a loopy-eyed stare. "I thinkIneedtosit... down."

"Good idea." August broke free of Idelson and helped the mayor to a bench. Once she was secured, the pair moved away, allowing Idelson to release the laughter she'd barely able been able to contain. August joined her.

"That's why I don't drink anymore." Idelson coughed out a few more chuckles. "Well, one of the reasons anyway."

The first night of the festival had been a success, with the music, food, dancing, and revelry enjoyed by all. Idelson enjoyed herself as well, and was further pleased when August informed her this had been the best festival he'd seen in years.

The pair strolled lazily back to Chances. The first night's fireworks began as they approached the 'Mech.

"C'mon. Let's get a better view. We climb up top and it'll be perfect." Idelson scaled the small chain ladder hanging in front of the 'Mech, with August following. As they reached the top, she scrambled onto the *Grasshopper*'s shoulder and curled up, wrapping her arms around her knees. August settled in next to her as they watched the bright, colorful explosions of the fireworks show.

"This really is pretty amazing," Idelson remarked after a minute.

"The festival means quite a bit to everyone here. Out in the Periphery, especially on worlds like this, you feel very much like it's you against the universe."

Idelson nodded. She knew the feeling all too well.

"What really amazes me," August began, "is that you sold all your preserves. I didn't want to say anything, but...that stuff was awful." A huge grin spread across his face.

"The other folks here simply have better taste than you!" She elbowed him playfully, then shared a deep kiss with him. "I'm so happy here."

"I'm happy *you're* here," August answered her. They kissed again, but it was cut short by an exceptionally loud boom from a firework. They both smiled under the pink glow of the fading blast, then a steady pin of light high among the evening stars caught Idelson's eye. She immediately knew what it was.

"There's a DropShip up there."

"What?" August looked to where she was pointing. "Now I see it. Probably a merchant. Perfect timing."

Sigland felt herself tense. "I don't think so. Unless it's headed to another settlement, it should be getting brighter and closer." She looked down into the cockpit of her 'Mech. An amber light on the comm panel blinked in a steady rhythm. Sigland knew something was wrong. Sliding away from August, she keyed in her access passcode. The hatch hissed open, and she climbed inside.

As Sigland reached for the comm panel, August poked his head inside. "What's going on?"

Sigland shushed him as she opened the comm channel indicated by the blinking light. Static crackled briefly, before being replaced by a deep female voice.

"—Repeat. This is Star Captain Sophia Thastus of Delta Trinary, Fourth Talon Cluster, Clan Jade Falcon's Peregrine Galaxy. I am issuing a batchall for a Trial of Possession of this world. What forces defend it?"

Sigland looked back toward August, who seemed confused. "Clan Jade Falcon? What the hell is that?"

She shook her head. "I have no idea." "Well, what do they want?"

The message repeated itself again.

Sigland scratched her head. "Sounds like they want to attack."

The message ran its course again. Sigland grabbed the small headset that rested on the panel and put it on. She opened the comm channel.

"This is Sigland Idelson. Who is this?"

"This is Star Captain Sophia Thastus. I ask again, what forces defend this world?"

Sigland paused, looked up at August once more, then turned to the comm panel. "Just me, I guess." Mercs had scoured the planet for Maria Morgraine's forces just last week, but Kirkpatrick's Bandit Killers—a name Sigland couldn't help chuckling over—had left once they came up empty. Where the mercs had gone, she didn't know, or care.

Even so, Sigland wished she had their help—or anyone's help—right now.

SHAKENSWAY FOREST
EREWHON
GREATER VALKYRATE
6 AUGUST 3049

Sigland willed herself to stop sweating as she ran another diagnostic check on the weapons and internal system of her *Grasshopper* as it lumbered through the massive timbers of the forest. Her body responded by excreting another layer of salty moisture over her skin.

She had every right to be nervous. The last several hours had been a whirlwind of confusion, chaos, conversation, panic, and planning.

For all of her arrogant bravado, Star Captain Thastus proved to be somewhat reasonable. Once it was revealed that Erewhon did have other defending forces, all of which were tanks and infantry in the capital city of Rangitata, the Star Captain told Sigland that something called an Elemental Binary would be heading there. Her 'Mech, however, would be engaged in single combat by the Star Captain herself.

Thastus then let Sigland pick the site of the battle. August pushed hard for the abandoned portions of Torned. He argued there were plenty of places for the *Grasshopper* to hide, and he could rally enough troops and weapons to use as a sniping infantry force. Sigland shot that idea down immediately. Soldiers stood little chance against an angry MechWarrior in a 'Mech. Sigland also feared the battle spilling into the city's inhabited regions. She loved the people in Torned. The last thing she wanted was to put their lives at risk.

The Shakensway Forest seemed the best option. Located on a high, hilly expanse north of the city, the forest was exposed to near year-round wind. This would provide cover and possible interference with visual sensors of the Star Captain's 'Mech. Sigland prayed the region would also have some of its signature seismic activity, but so far, nothing.

What worried her most was the tone in the Star Captain's voice. *And that title.* Normally she'd write off someone with a rank of "Star Captain" to be nothing more than a pirate drunk on too many episodes of *The Immortal Warrior*, with an overinflated ego and little skill. This woman's speech hinted at strict military training. Sigland knew there were no such ranks in any Inner Sphere military. *This "Jade Falcon" clan must be from outside the Valkyrate. Maybe King Grimm has changed things up?*

The final worry gnawing at Sigland was her lack own of practice. She'd been out of her 'Mech for months as far as combat was concerned. Not even one training drill to keep her skills up. *Let's just hope this is like riding a bike.*

Sigland stole a glance at the bulkhead above her. The names, places, and dates. The history. She finally settled on her own name, added not long after she'd taken possession of Chances. An odd sense of finality crept over her. *I hope my service in your 'Mech makes you proud. If there's any help you can give me, I'd sure as hell would appreciate it.*

Then she thought of August. Doubts about never seeing him again crept into her mind. She failed to push them away. *C'mon, Sig–focus!*

A voice crackled over her comm. "You have chosen an interesting location for our engagement. I look forward to finding you and showing you the might of the Jade Falcon."

She's here. "I've fought pirates before," Sigland answered. "Your words mean nothing."

Thastus chuckled. "Pirates? You think us pirates? You are sorely mistaken, MechWarrior Sigland."

She liked Thastus's tone less and less. "Yeah, that's what they all say before their 'Mechs end up as trash heaps."

She slammed her feet down hard on the foot pedals, activating the 'Mech's jump jets. The *Grasshopper* hurtled into the pre-dawn sky, high above the trees in search of its enemy. *Where are you hiding?*

She was answered as a score of missiles arced up toward her position, followed immediately by laser fire which came in a rapid, almost burst pattern. Several missiles found the 'Mech, blasting armor off its *v*-shaped chest. The volley of laser fire passed harmlessly to Sigland's left. *What the hell was that?*

On instinct, Sigland returned fire with her Conan/S missile launcher. Aiming on the fly, she sent the quintet of rockets toward where she guessed the enemy 'Mech was hiding. Steadying Chances against the wind, she brought it down with a massive thud in a thick patch of trees. She caught the glow of the fires from the explosions in the distance. *Maybe the heat will mess with your sensors. Time to go hunting.*

Turning to the nearest tree, Sigland placed the *Grasshopper*'s hands around the top, then slid them down quickly, stripping the timber of its limbs. Then she gripped the tree trunk farther down, braced Chances against it, and heaved. Rocking back and forth, the tree ripped free of the earth within seconds, unable to resist the strength of her 'Mech.

The makeshift club in her hands, Sigland began walking carefully through the overgrowth. "Looks like you have a problem with one of your lasers. You can retreat at any time," she taunted.

A pause, then a reply. "I will admit I was not prepared for your *Grasshopper* to jump. I could not bring my pulse laser to bear in time, but fear not, it will find you soon."

Sigland couldn't stop the words from leaving her mouth. "Pulse laser?"

Thastus chuckled. "Oh, perhaps it is not true what we had heard, that your technology has regressed since the fall of the Star League. Regardless, I shall make this quick and merciful for you, though you do not deserve it."

Doubt trickled into Sigland's thoughts. *Maybe this isn't a pirate force.* Her radar pinged a target at two o'clock, and she whirled Chances toward the position.

Zooming in, she could see the 'Mech lumbering toward her. Her tactical computer struggled to identify the design, switching between an *Archer*, a *Rifleman*, and a *Catapult*. The approaching 'Mech bore similarities to all three. The reverse-kneed legs of the latter, the missile bays down each side of the chest of the former, and the twin-barreled arms of a *Rifleman*. From a distance, the enemy 'Mech appeared to be a coherent design, but Sigland's confidence rose that this had to be a mash-up built by a desperate tech. An easy target. *It must be the Oberon Confederation.*

Sigland pushed the *Grasshopper* faster through the woods, closing the distance. *If I can get inside those missile racks, I can go toe to toe with my lasers*—she glanced out the cockpit windows at the club in her 'Mech's hands—*and this.*

Thastus's 'Mech stopped and opened fire, cutting down trees in a 180-degree arc in front of her. The pulse lasers made short work of the trunks and limbs, mowing them clean like so much grass. "I am clearing a space for your demise, MechWarrior Sigland. Please, come forward and meet your death with some tiny shred of honor."

Sigland smiled at the verbal jab. "I'll be right there. Just hold still." She pushed the *Grasshopper* up to top speed, closing sixty meters in a dozen steps.

Thastus finished her assault on the trees, but not soon enough. Sigland reached the edge of the makeshift clearing, and skidded to a stop as she brought her targeting reticule dead center on the mash-up 'Mech and opened fire.

A trio of bright beams erupted from the chest of the *Grasshopper*. The Diplan HD large laser bore a straight line, gouging a deep scar across the chest of Thastus's 'Mech. The paired Diplan M3 medium lasers hit lower, raking the left leg from hip to knee. Sigland grinned in satisfaction.

Thastus returned fire. Two score missiles blasted from the chest of her 'Mech. Sigland's eyes widened. *That's too close inside range! What the hell is she doing?*

Only ninety meters away, Sigland expected the speeding missiles to either overshoot the *Grasshopper* or fall short. Less than half did that. The remainder blanketed the *Grasshopper* head to toe in explosions and fire, sending her stumbling to recover. Keeping Chances upright, Sigland glared at the strange 'Mech. *Not going to let that happen again. There's no way she can do that face-to-face.*

The wind raged, taking the gray smoke from the missiles, mixing it with the blasted remnants of the trees, creating a debris-filled dust devil that swirled between the two foes.

Pressing her feet to the floor once more, Sigland sent Chances into the air on jets of plasma flame. The gusts pressed against the 'Mech, but she was ready for them. Staying low and soaring fast, she tried to angled Chances to come down behind Thastus's 'Mech, but the invader reacted quickly. The bird-legged 'Mech held fast, only adjusting its position to face Sigland as she landed. The *Grasshopper* touched down only meters from the strange 'Mech, and Sigland once again triggered her chest-mounted lasers. The large laser cut a straight scar across the enemy 'Mech's chest, but the paired medium lasers shot wide, only bracketing her enemy. Sigland saw the twin-barreled arms of Thastus's machine glow with deadly intent. She raised her makeshift club quickly and swung.

The massive trunk shattered as it slammed home. Splinters flew in all directions, but the damage was done. The housing of the left-side missile launcher groaned in protest as the punishment caved several launch tubes, but not before Thastus could use them.

Both launchers coughed out another forty missiles, assaulting her *Grasshopper* up and down. Armor plating blasted free, and one round struck the cockpit armor. Sigland pitched hard against the safety straps in her cockpit, yelping in pain as the straps cut through her tank top and into her skin.

The assault from the Jade Falcon pilot wasn't over. Sigland caught multiple staccato flashes of emerald as strobes of pulse laser fire jabbed at Chances. Warning tones sounded as most of the armor indicators on her 'Mech turned from green to amber, with her right arm and leg threatening to go red.

As Sigland recovered from the cockpit hit, she felt her 'Mech teeter sideways. Fighting the controls, she struggled to keep Chances upright, but the momentum was too great. The *Grasshopper* stumbled and fell clumsily on the ground.

The impact was harsh. Sigland once again was driven hard against the safety straps, and felt new cuts in her shoulder. She bit her lip hard and tasted blood. The crimson dripping from her lips matched the armor warning lights on her right arm. As the 'Mech skidded to a stop, Sigland heard the distinct grinding of a damaged actuator. *Great.*

Rolling Chances quickly to the side so she could move to stand up, she froze as Thastus's 'Mech towered over her.

The Star Captain spoke over the comm. "Though you are an insufferable *surat* for engaging in melee combat with me, proving your barbarism by using a tree no less, I will allow you to rise so that I may end this and give you the chance to be honorably beaten while standing on your feet."

Sigland's mind raced, desperately seeking some way out, some way to still win, but there was nothing. Thastus was better than she was, her 'Mech in better shape. Her thoughts drifted to August. She couldn't bear to lose him, and after so many years of running and abandoning those close to her, she wasn't about to do it again.

Then an idea hit her.

"What if I surrender and give you my 'Mech? I'll be Dispossessed, but you'll have the best prize on this planet."

Thastus laughed. "You offer me nothing I will not soon have. Your 'Mech is no prize to me. It is a small miracle it still functions after all these centuries. You are clearly undisciplined and an obvious failure, and only continue to embarrass yourself. Now. Get. Up."

Sigland sighed and brought Chances to its feet. The two 'Mechs stared at each other briefly before Thastus spoke. "Go to the edge of the clearing, and we shall begin again."

Sigland marched the *Grasshopper* forward as a fiendish idea wormed its way into her head. *All I need is one lucky shot—*

She whirled Chances on its heels and brought all her weapons to bear.

Thastus was waiting for her. *"As I suspected."*

The invader opened fire with a quartet of pulse lasers and a salvo from her remaining missile launcher. Sigland briefly felt the impacts before her world went black.

CAMP DETERMINATION
PERSISTENCE
JADE FALCON OCCUPATION ZONE
19 APRIL 3050

The simulated damage readings on Sigland's *Grasshopper* went from amber to red. The tactical computer registered the 'Mech's left arm as gone, and the fusion reactor that powered the machine showed damage, venting excess heat.

Not again, she thought as she moved Chances toward a nearby pillar for cover.

Her opponent, another bondsman named Datu, a Lyran ex-pat from Icar, was piloting a *Thunderbolt*. She could tell he was feeling confident after that last exchange. He moved from his cover position, coming in for the kill. Sigland did not want to lose another test match.

I'm not done yet. She charged forward, then cut left. Three steps in, she activated her jump jets, lifting the *Grasshopper* high into the air.

Spinning in mid-flight, she angled the 'Mech's chest toward Datu's 'Mech. The reticule centered over the *Thunderbolt*, and Sigland let fly with the large laser, followed up by her missile launcher. The computer registered a solid hit from the laser, as well as all five missiles.

Undeterred, Datu returned fire. A near mirror of Sigland's attack, his large laser stabbed out while his Delta Dart launcher arced simulated missiles at her.

Warning klaxons sounded as the hit registered massive damage on the left side of the 'Mech's chest, not only from the *Thunderbolt*'s laser, but from several missile impacts. The remainder struck Chances's other arm, breaching the armor. Sigland grimaced when the computer told her the shoulder actuator and the arm-mounted medium laser were out.

A wave of heat blasted through the cockpit as she shakily landed the 'Mech. With her arm-mounted weapons out, her options were very limited. She started backing the *Grasshopper* toward cover when Thastus's voice broke in on her comm.

"That is enough. This test is over. Power down your 'Mechs, and get out. MechWarrior Datu, you may return to your bondholder. Sigland, wait for me."

The neurohelmet she wore suddenly felt even heavier. *Failed again.* She punched the wall of the cockpit, took a deep breath, and exited.

The last six months had been a harsh education, and Sigland knew she hadn't been the best student.

After the defeat on Erewhon, Star Captain Thastus had claimed her as a bondsman and took her offworld, away from all she knew and loved, especially August. She'd never even gotten a chance to say goodbye. For all she knew, August thought her dead.

At times, Sigland wished she was.

Thastus was a good teacher, but harsh. Sigland's skills as a MechWarrior had improved, but her heart was no longer in it. Her time on Erewhon had taken that fight out of her, giving her a new path in life. Thastus had tried to force her back into the warrior mold, but it wasn't happening. This latest test proved it.

Thastus approached. Her face was grim. "You can take heart, Bondsman Sigland, in that you are not the worst to fail me, even in these dilapidated machines. Were we on the Clan homeworlds, you would be training in second-line Clan 'Mechs, not Inner Sphere detritus like this. But here in the occupation zone, we must make do."

"Is that supposed to make me feel better?"

"I do not care *how* it makes you feel," Thastus answered.

Sigland lifted her hands in surrender. "Thanks." A pause. "Am I to be a tech then?"

"*Aff.* And you will be leaving now. I am freeing you of your bond. This way."

The haste of it all surprised Sigland, but she complied. Still learning Clan ways, and their sometimes rash decisions, she accepted her fate. Time had not healed the sting of having her happiness ripped away. Rather than live out her days with August, she would repair the machines she once piloted somewhere deep behind enemy lines.

Sigland wanted to know more about her new role, but it was pointless to ask. Now free of any remaining obligation to her, Sigland knew Thastus would offer no information.

They exited the testing field, marching to the 'Mech bay in silence.

Entering a small office, Sigland found herself in the presence of Thastus's CO, Star Colonel Yasukai Shambag. Out of reflex, Sigland saluted in time with Thastus as the Star Colonel stood. It was then that she saw the man standing next to Shambag.

While still fit, Sigland could tell he was not a warrior. His midsection pressed too hard against his olive jumpsuit, and he wore no rank. Draped behind his shoulders was a mid-length emerald cloak. Sigland noticed the rings the man wore, at least six over both hands. Her eyes focused in. Each one bore a symbol from either a Great House or Inner Sphere military unit. *He clearly did not earn those.*

"Thank you for bringing her, Star Captain. Is she the last one?"

"*Aff,* Star Colonel."

Thastus fixed Sigland with her usual harsh stare. "Enjoy your new life," she whispered. "You were never fit for a warrior. Perhaps this will suit you better." With a quick motion, Thastus drew a combat knife, slipped the blade under the bond cord on her wrist, then cut it free with a quick turn and flick.

Sigland gasped at the action and frowned. "How is this possible? I know I have not earned for any of these virtues to be removed."

Thastus remained stone-faced as she produced a second cord. "You are correct. I was prepared to have you serve as a tech under my supervision." She paused, her voice angrier. "But the Star Colonel has seen fit to relieve me of your burden." Thastus fashioned the new cord around her wrist. "You will now have to prove your worth to him." Her head jerked toward the other man.

Turning on her heel, Thastus marched off. Sigland looked after her for a moment, then turned back toward the pair. The Star Colonel stood stone-faced, her jet-black hair adding emphasis to her grim expression.

The man with the many rings smiled. "And remember, their 'Mechs as well. That is the only way I am going to get everything you need, Star Colonel."

A curt nod and unhappy grunt was her only response.

The man pulled his cape around and strode toward Sigland. "This way, please."

Sigland followed him out of the office and across the 'Mech bay. "May I ask where we are going?"

Without turning to face her, the man pointed out of the 'Mech bay toward a DropShip in the distance. "Technician Sigland, I am taking you to your new home."

NADIR POINT BETA VII
JADE FALCON OCCUPATION ZONE
5 JULY 3050

"You present a unique opportunity, Technician Sigland, but I am no fool. Your suggestion has deception written all over it. Indeed, I could even have you killed for speaking to me of such things."

Sigland knew he wouldn't. Mattox, the Jade Falcon merchant captain she'd been turned over to three months ago, was an opportunistic man, and the wealth offered by deals within the occupation zone (including the one that had brought her into his service), as well the illegal temptations beyond the border, was something she knew he wouldn't ignore.

"*Aff.* But you will not." Sigland smiled. "At least, I hope you will not."

Mattox was skeptical. Sigland realized he needed more convincing.

After learning what Mattox was truly like, a plan slowly came together. The data files she had stolen from Kelly Hunt what seemed like a lifetime ago were locations and inventories of a variety of caches hidden throughout the coreward portion of the Federated Commonwealth. Apparently, Shatterdog Shipping had numerous illegal operations, and were using the caches to store much of their ill-gotten loot.

Sigland realized she finally had some leverage to get back what she had lost. She knew the cash and other economic assets would hold little interest for the merchant, but the artwork, raw materials, spare parts, and other goods would.

Sigland had started small, dropping suggestions to Mattox of places where certain items of interest could be found while on certain worlds in the occupation zone. Once she felt she had earned his trust, she presented him her plan.

Now he only needed to accept it.

"So you will grant me access to the remainder of your information if I authorize a transfer for you?"

Sigland nodded.

"You obtained this intel from someplace." Mattox paused to think. "Perhaps, it is stored somewhere. You once owned that *Grasshopper.* Perhaps I order another technician to scan its files?"

Sigland smiled and tapped her temple. "Unless you can crack this open, you'll find nothing."

Mattox sighed. "You would make an excellent merchant. Where is it you want to go?"

Sigland took a deep breath. "Erewhon."

Mattox winced. "Ugh. Why?"

Sigland was earnest. "I want to go home."

Mattox sat silently behind his desk.

She pressed on. "My life before the Clans was unpleasant. I did much I am not proud of. I went to Erewhon to die, but instead I found a new life. Found happiness. I left my shameful warrior life. Then the Clans came, and I was forced to become a warrior once again, and I failed once again. You have been good to me, and I have proven my worth as a tech, and I swear I will not leave the

Falcons, but I want to spend the rest of my life with that family I found on Erewhon."

Mattox nodded. "Ah. So it is for love, then?"

Sigland let a brief smile cross her lips, then lowered her head.

"We are not aliens, Technician. The warriors may not know love, but the lower castes certainly do." A gleam showed in his eye. "I agree to your proposal. Give me the rest, and you will be sent home."

INBOUND, EREWHON
JADE FALCON OCCUPATION ZONE
13 SEPTEMBER 3050

Sigland ran her hand along the cockpit bulkhead inside Chances. This would be the last time she would ever see these names scrawled there. She smiled as she looked at her own which she had just added to the bottom of the list.

In just a few hours, she would be on the surface of Erewhon, but Chances was bound for somewhere else. She told Mattox that trading a 'Mech in the Inner Sphere would easily get him what he sought when he crossed the border to make a deal. Mattox told her such actions might be treason. She responded by saying it would only be treason if he was caught.

Sigland read each name above hers on the bulkhead, and wondered one last time about each MechWarrior. Their battles. Their enemies. Who they saved, who they lost and the sacrifices they made. *I bet none of you fought any enemy like the Clans.*

Her hands left the bulkhead and ran along the cockpit's interior. Each switch, button and control stick. After one last look out of the ferroglass viewport, she crawled out of the 'Mech and stood on its shoulder. A wave of joy washed briefly over her as she realized where she was headed and whom she would soon see.

Thank you, Chances. You've lived up to your name. You've given me many over the years. I promise I will not waste this last chance.

THE THIRD PILLAR
JASON HANSA

OUTSIDE DALIAN, TSINGTAO
CAPELLA COMMONALITY
CAPELLAN CONFEDERATION
21 DECEMBER 3057

"Well, Sergeant Major, I suppose that's it for this location," Kommandant Philip Giacomo said as he lowered his binoculars. Taking care to ensure they didn't reflect the evening sunlight, the cocoa-skinned man passed them to his older companion.

Sergeant Major Ken Franks carefully raised the binoculars to his eyes to study the new garrison. He looked for a moment and whistled. "Looks like the mercs rotated in a full company. If they're maintaining their normal ratios..."

"That means the entire battalion is now on-planet," Giacomo finished for him. "Say what you will about the Redfield Renegades, but they're not stupid. You're the engineer. See anything they did wrong that we can use?"

The sergeant major, the senior enlisted man of the Giacomo's guerilla force, studied their enemy's deployment for several moments, and then shook his head. "No sir, I don't," he admitted. "Like you said, they're not stupid." He lowered the binoculars and passed them back to Giacomo. "If the lance is now outnumbered nine to one, maybe sitting tight until pickup is our best option."

"They didn't leave us behind to be safe, Sergeant Major," Giacomo said, some humor in his tone.

"They didn't leave us here to die, either," the sergeant major said, laughing slightly. But his face cleared, and his tone dropped. "I know our mission is to continue to attack, but these are long odds, and we still have a month to go until pickup." With that, the two slinked back into the woods, careful to not draw attention from any enemy lookouts.

Thirty minutes later, they had picked their way through increasingly thick forest back to their temporary headquarters. A small bowl valley with near impenetrable tree coverage, it was just big enough for the force that had volunteered to remain behind when the Thirty-sixth Lyran Guards had obeyed Katherine Steiner-Davion's come-home order.

As they entered the perimeter, Giacomo sent word for the unit leadership to meet him around the map table. As a pair of infantrymen ran off to carry the message personally— eschewing the use of radios that the enemy could detect—Giacomo and Franks took a moment to grab cold-cut sandwiches from the mess tent. From there, they headed deeper into camp, past the perimeter where the four BattleMechs were laagered in a rough circle, facing outward.

When they arrived, the sergeant major waved the two MechWarriors near their 'Mechs—Hauptmann Adam Braun in a camp chair behind his *Scarabus* and Marcos leaning against a tree— over to the table.

"Romero, is Jones in her *Axman*?" asked the sergeant major. Before Marcos could answer, the heavy BattleMech in question rotated at the waist to look at Franks. Jones opened her 'Mech's hand and patted the air, progressively lower. Giacomo smiled at her adherence to noise discipline; not only was she not using her radio, she wasn't even using her external loudspeakers. It was unnecessary—the Renegades were close, but not *that* close—but still good to see.

"No, stay up there, I'll brief you personally after," the sergeant major called up.

"Debrief her, you mean," Marcos said with a laugh, and Giacomo shook his head for the response he knew was coming.

"Romero, one more outta you, and I'll put you back in the hole I signed you out of," warned the sergeant major.

"I know, so I can 'wither away in starvation before the Capellans execute me,'" replied Marcos good-naturedly, and Giacomo suppressed a sigh. Marcos was huge, seemingly as thick as the ankle of his *Whitworth,* and had "volunteered" to join Giacomo's stay-behind force to get out of the stockade. Apparently running a little side action at a couple of pubs in town, he had run afoul of the local cartels, but instead of backing off, he'd marched his *Whitworth* to the house of a local affiliate and destroyed a van full of merchandise. The sergeant major had signed for his release from the military police, promising to supervise Marcos at all times. Though he wouldn't have been Giacomo's first pick as a lancemate, the large man had created no problems since, grateful to remain out of prison and keep his BattleMech.

His relationship with the sergeant major, however, was constant bickering. They seemed to know instinctively how to get under each other's skin; after two months, however, it had transformed from meanness to a routine sparring match. Like an old married couple comforted by repetition, Giacomo suspected they probably both enjoyed having someone to match wits with.

The other MechWarrior joining them stood off to the side a bit, a carry-over from his noble upbringing. Hauptmann Braun was Lyran-born and proud of it. Confident almost to the point of arrogance, he would have taken up Katherine Steiner-Davion on her come-home request in a heartbeat if it hadn't been for one person—and from the way Braun's stance shifted and his head spun, Giacomo knew she was approaching from behind him.

He turned around and nodded to welcome his remaining officers—Leftenant Roberts, in charge of Karnov Platoon that had been doing yeoman's duty moving the infantry and artillery around the continent to ambush the Renegades. Next to the rail-thin pilot was a tall hauptmann in full infantry kit. Taking off her combat helmet, she took a moment to shake out the long dark braid that draped halfway down her back, and then moved over to hug Braun, eliciting a smile on his normally stern face. Hauptmann Alicia Stillwater was the commander of Giacomo's infantry detachment, and was one of the first to volunteer to remain behind. As Braun's longtime girlfriend, she'd caught him between his love for her and to his home: to his credit, it'd only taken him a moment to pick.

Despite his ongoing condescension from his upbringing—which Alicia was slowly beating out of him—Giacomo was happy to have him. Piloting a light, fast BattleMech with a two-ton hardened-steel hatchet in place of a right fist, Braun was one of the best pilots Giacomo had ever worked with. Using his ECM suite, he could sneak up and ambush enemy BattleMechs or vehicles before they knew he was there, then disappear without a trace.

Giacomo coughed, getting everyone's attention, and they assembled around the map table. Within a few minutes, Giacomo and the sergeant major brought everyone up to speed on the Renegades' increased deployment size. There was silence for a moment.

"Kommandant," Marcos asked, "what were our orders, exactly? Were we ordered to destroy all the enemy 'Mechs?"

Giacomo shook his head. "No, we were ordered to slow down the occupation force by denying them some combination of resources or area, with a secondary task of forcing them to commit as much material, time, or money to Tsingtao as possible."

Marcos nodded. "What if we attacked the processing center?"

"We'd never get close enough," said the sergeant major. "You trying to get us all killed?"

The Montebahn Processing center in Fairmont was Tsingtao's main node for agricultural and lumber exports. The Renegades kept at least a third of their force there at all times, plus the majority of the conventional defenders the Capellans had sent in. They'd kept one of Alicia's infantry platoons in the city to occasionally conduct a mortar attack or do some sniping, but it was far too tough a nut to crack for one BattleMech lance.

"Not everyone, just you," Marcos replied, humor in his voice, and even the sergeant major smiled as they all chuckled. They lapsed back into silence as they studied the map again.

"We could blow up the refinery in Cairo," said Braun finally.

Giacomo shook his head. "No, that drives a large part of Tsingtao's economic base. We destroy that, it'll have ripple effects."

"Maybe...that's not a bad thing," the sergeant major said slowly. The group turned toward him. "Kommandant, you said the goal was to deny them resources and cause them to sink money into this world. Among everything else, that refinery generates diesel for armor units. With the Cappies standing up a Home Guard regiment here, the refinery's a legitimate military target. More than that—there's three pillars that hold up a world government: the military, the government, and the economy. We can't destroy that 'Mech battalion, and the governor has gone over to the Cappies, but maybe we could wreck the economy and force the Cappies to rebuild it. If they don't, and then the mercs leave..."

"Then the government could easily get toppled, and the world becomes ours again," Giacomo finished, nodding as he caught up to the sergeant major's train of thought. "We take out the refinery, we essentially tie the battalion to the world until it's rebuilt. The Renegades aren't destroyed..."

"But they're off the table for a bit. 'Bout the best a lance can do, I figure."

"Not bad, but your plan is still too small, gentlemen," a voice called out from behind Giacomo, and he turned toward it.

Approaching the table was one of the most beautiful woman Giacomo had ever met, wearing fashionable jeans, a near-sheer top, and a skin-tight leather jacket; beautiful, that is, except for her eyes. Steel gray, they were the cool eyes of a professional: no matter how laughing and carefree she could act, she was relentless and ruthless when the situation called for it. Philip had personally watched her knife a double handful of wayward militia during their time on-world, and there was a pool going in the unit estimating how many Capellans she'd actually put down in the past ninety days.

"Hello again, Alysheba," he said to the woman everyone referred to—when she wasn't around, of course—as "the spy." She nodded to the group as she approached. "Have any problems slipping past the Renegades?"

She grunted and rolled her eyes as her answer, then put a noteputer and a new rolled-up map on the table; as she unrolled it, Giacomo thought about asking where she'd gotten them before changing his mind.

"Kommandant, events are happening as the Capellans consolidate their grip on Tsingtao," she said in a flat accent that could be from anywhere. "The good news is, this should blend into your little idea perfectly. You want to wreck the economy, well..." She trailed off before pointing to a spot on the map. "To do it right, you should rob a bank."

TSING CITY, TSINGAO
CAPELLA COMMONALITY
CAPELLAN CONFEDERATION
28 DECEMBER 3057

A week after the initial conference in the forest, Hauptmann Alicia Stillwater felt incredibly uncomfortable as she followed Marcos and Alysheba through a seedy bar. The room was dark, with only the reverse coloring from black lights and dark purple neon signs lighting most of the area. To her right, two naked women danced on opposite ends of a catwalk, with drunken viewers vying for their attentions with handfuls of cash; along the walls, darkened booths hid any number of sins, punctuated by an occasional laugh or splash of flesh. The threesome weaved between tables, following a bruiser even larger than Marcos.

As she turned to slip past a table, Stillwater brushed her hand across the well-hidden hold-out pistol concealed in the waistband of her leggings, finding comfort in its presence. They were all dressed in conservative civilian clothes, maintaining a low profile from the Capellan secret police they were sure had landed alongside the mercenaries.

For the first three days after Alysheba had proposed her plan, the unit had planned as they moved. The Renegades were too close, so Giacomo had ordered them deeper into the woods, using the sergeant major's infantry company to blaze a trail and Leftenant Roberts's Karnovs to haul out supplies in one direction, and some of her infantry platoons to act as distractions in another. Once they were situated in a series of rocky hills deep in the forest, they began the serious work of planning a bank robbery. But not just any bank robbery: the planetary reserve would receive approximately 3.8 billion bills of various denominations from the Capellan Confederation. They would store two billion of it on-site and distribute the rest, sending all six central city banks 300 million bills each. The city banks would then distribute the cash to smaller local and rural branches.

It was one of the six main convoys that they wanted to rob, but 300 million bills—at 1,110 bills per kilo—came out to just over 135 tons. The armored trucks transporting the bills could carry twenty tons each, but a Karnov's six-ton cargo bay was too small for carrying even a single truck.

So the plan now included the "acquisition" of larger aircraft from the capital. They'd found two likely candidates the first day, crashed in a seedy hotel that night, and found the third the next day. All three were Capellan-built variants of the King Karnov VSTOL, locally known as "Walruses." They were essentially unguarded, and would be easily stolen once Alicia summoned Roberts and his pilots to Tsing City.

After that, they had come here to meet one of Marcos's contacts, apparently the man he owed some money to. Alysheba hadn't explained why—Marcos seemed somewhat worried, and Alicia was unsettled by that and being so far out of her element. Her parents were both infantry officers serving in the Third Federated Commonwealth Regiment, a proud defender of the Sarna March. She'd been born in a Third FedCom field hospital, and gained her love of the local worlds from them and their regiment. Even loving Braun as she did, she'd be *damned* if she'd scoot off-world without even attempting to slow the Capellan invasion down.

But I didn't realize fighting the Cappies meant strutting around in civvies in a strip bar, she thought. *Why can't I just be doing something easy—like a combat insertion under fire—instead of this sneaking-around spy stuff?*

The bouncer gave all three a cursory pat-down, then led them past a red velvet curtain, down a tight hallway, and to an unmarked door in the back. He knocked twice and someone on the inside opened it. She blinked at bright white light that flooded the corridor, and they walked through

The room was all white, with a Greco-Roman theme down to the busts adorning various pedestals around the room. A pair of near-naked ladies sprawled on a pile of plush pillows in the corner, their unfocused stares indicative of mood-altering substances. More threatening, however, were the burly guards—one at the door, and two standing behind a desk of polished black wood. Sitting at the desk was a greasy man with a comb-over and a sneer.

"Marcos, my boy, you must be an idiot to come here. I admire your courage, at least." He looked at all of them quickly, gauging and dismissing Roberts before undressing Alicia and Alysheba with his eyes. Alicia felt disgust at his open leer at Alysheba, but sensed the malice behind it when he turned it on her. Resisting the urge to draw her hold-out, she exhaled and just hoped she'd live through the night.

Moretti's eyes finally fell back on Marcos. "I have no idea why you brought your friends to watch you die." His eyes flicked over to Alysheba again. "Perhaps we can get better acquainted after I kill you."

"Actually, I want to strike a deal with you, Mr. Moretti," Alysheba said.

His slitted gaze swiveled toward her again. "Marcos owes me a lot of money, young lady, and I'm not inclined to even talk to any of his friends right now."

Alysheba made a show of pulling a paper notepad from her pocket—a motion that made the guards twitch and a drop of sweat roll down Alicia's face—and flipped through it. "According to my notes, Marcos owes you ninety-five K in FC-Bills, plus a moving van and various...sundries. Does a quarter-million L-Bills sound fair?

The room was quiet for a moment, silent enough that Alicia could hear the faint pounding of the music from the bar behind her. *This room is almost soundproof,* she realized even as she noticed the floor was a waterproof marble veneer, and there was a dark-stained drain almost directly in front of her. *The strippers will never hear us die back here.* A drop of cold sweat ran down her back. Again, she resisted the growing urge to shoot first.

"Who are you?" Moretti demanded.

"My name's not important," Alysheba replied. "Marcos told me you control the garment factories in this city. I need a... *specialized* order filled, quickly and discreetly. I'm also willing to pay a reasonable amount for your time and discretion."

"Where's the money?"

"Also not important."

He leaned back. "What do I get out of this, besides a lot of money?"

"Besides a *reasonable* amount of money," she corrected, "you get my friendship. That's worth more than you might think."

He laughed, shaking his head. "Your friendship?" He laughed again, then his face turned dark. "If I thought you were kidding, I'd let you live. I'm still killing him, of course," he said, pointing to Marcos, "but I'd let you go for the fun of it. But I'm going to kill him, and then do horribly painful things to you and your friend here until you tell me where your money is. Boys?"

At that, his two goons stepped forward to grab Alysheba. Alicia swore and went for her hold-out pistol. She felt the trigger guard catch for a split second and the thought *I'm going to die here* raced through her mind as she pulled the gun free.

Marcos simply stepped back and to the left. Alicia had a moment of confusion at his actions, then heard two small pops: the right-hand guard's head exploded into a bloody red mess, duplicated a split-second later by the head on the left hand guard.

He was clearing her line of fire, Alicia thought as she swung her pistol up. She saw Alysheba spinning on her right heel to bring her own concealed pistol to bear on the guard at the rear entrance, so Alicia pointed her pistol toward the two drugged women. They hadn't reacted at all to the first two deaths, and didn't flinch as Alysheba fired twice more.

Alicia heard the guard to the rear collapse, then saw Alysheba swing her pistol toward Moretti.

In a perfectly calm voice, the spy said, "I can be a powerful friend or a powerful enemy, Mr. Moretti. I *came* here to make a deal: I'll kill you if I have to, and you'll die knowing that one of your competitors will agree and will rise up in your place. *Or...*" she said, drawing the word out, "we can all put this minor disagreement behind us and move forward."

He licked his lips, looked at the men on the floor, the gun in her unwavering hand, and then her face. "Uh...perhaps I was a bit... *hasty,* not letting you fully explain your offer," said Moretti. "You said something about a, ah, special order?"

Alysheba holstered her pistol and pulled out a data chip. At her nod, Alicia slowly put hers away as well. Alysheba gave her a slight smile, and then, focusing back on Moretti, put the data chip on the desk and slid it toward him with one finger.

"Uniforms. Our special order is several different varieties of uniforms."

CAIRO, TSINGTAO
CAPELLA COMMONALITY
CAPELLAN CONFEDERATION
22 JANUARY 3058, 1425 HOURS

Hauptmann Philip Giacomo, commander of Tsingtao's remaining Federated Commonwealth defenders and soon-to-be bank robbers, stretched in the cockpit of his *Grasshopper.*

Loaned Grasshopper, he corrected, looking around. For hundreds of years, each pilot had signed on the upper bulkhead their name and the dates they'd piloted this particular 'Mech. Some end-dates were written in a different handwriting, testimony to a life violently led, and probably violently ended. Some had written notes to their children; some had written notes about long-since repaired quirks.

He was surprised when he got it: he'd been piloting a unit-owned *Griffin* when he received word his aunt had passed on the Falcon front. He'd been surprised for a number of reasons when the *Grasshopper* arrived on a DropShip, along with his aunt's will.

He knew that side of the family came from money, but he never knew she'd had enough socked away to buy a BattleMech from "a discreet merchant," as she'd described it. He was also surprised that she hadn't put it into storage, waiting for his niece to graduate from the Nagelring. She'd said she trusted him to maintain it and care for it more than she trusted a storage facility—but he doubted she'd anticipated a war with the Capellan Confederation. When he wrote his name on the cockpit bulkhead, he'd solemnly listed his aunt's date of death under her name. Since then, he'd nearly lost his niece's inheritance a number of times during his long guerrilla operation.

Months ago, the Captain-General Thomas Marik of the Free Worlds League had revealed to the rest of the Inner Sphere that Archon-Prince Victor Steiner-Davion—Giacomo's liege lord—had substituted a duplicate for his son undergoing medical treatment in the Federated Commonwealth. The Captain-General declared war to avenge his son, joined by his tenuous ally, the Capellan Confederation.

Immediately following the declaration of war, Victor's sister, Archon-Princess Katherine Steiner-Davion, separated her half of the Federated Commonwealth in protest of her brother's actions. She then issued a come-home order to any unit with historical ties to her rechristened Lyran Alliance.

Giacomo's unit, the Thirty-sixth Lyran Guards, had been split almost fifty-fifty between MechWarriors that wanted to remain in Federated Commonwealth space and those wanting to return to its traditional home in the Lyran Alliance. However, of the fifty-plus pilots that had elected to remain, only thirteen owned their BattleMechs: a baker's dozen out of a full regiment, a near unfathomable ratio just a decade before.

BattleMechs like the *Grasshopper* had been passed down in families for centuries, the physical act of ownership conveying a near-noble privilege. But everything had changed when the descendants of the original Star League Army returned to the Inner Sphere: known as "the Clans," they had continued advancing their technology while the Inner Sphere's had stagnated. Intent on recapturing Terra, they had been stopped at great cost in men and materiel.

Regiments once consisting almost entirely of owner-operators— with just a leavening of "federal" BattleMechs—now found their ratios reversed, the Great Houses providing new BattleMechs to their pilots in exchange for continued service against the Clans. This had never before created any issues until the come-home order; MechWarriors piloting new BattleMechs for almost a half-dozen years were suddenly reminded which nation actually possessed the title.

The Thirty-sixth Lyran Guards had lifted off for Alliance space, leaving behind thousands of militia troops, dependents, a hundred or so troops from the Thirty-sixth, and only thirteen BattleMechs to protect them.

Unwilling to simply cede the planet, Marshal Harold Andrews had asked Giacomo to remain behind with just a lance and two mixed battalions of conventional militia to delay and harass the occupiers. For four months they'd obeyed their orders, did their best, and the bank robbery was their final mission: their headquarters and armor elements were already on their hidden DropShip. By nightfall, win or lose, the DropShip would depart for the pirate point and the anticipated Commonwealth JumpShip, because there was no second pickup scheduled.

There was a flash on a secondary monitor as a data transmission was received. Giacomo nodded as he read a report from one of Stillwater's scout teams, confirming that the convoy had just passed their location, and on time. It had departed the central reserve in Tsing City, capital of Tsingtao, to Burlington's central bank two hours prior, and should reach the kill zone in thirty minutes. There was still time to abort, but barring any last second problems, the operation was a go.

According to information Alysheba received from Moretti, if the armored cars were past the halfway point and an emergency sounded elsewhere on world, they would accelerate forward toward the destination. His goal in attacking the refinery first— besides the economic damage—was to spook the convoy *without* them realizing they were the intended target.

His team would start. The city of Cairo was on the west coast of the continent, bordering a bay. His *Grasshopper* and Marcos in his *Whitworth* were on its south side, and a battery of sniper artillery pieces had been airlifted to the north side the week prior. Once scouts reported the convoy entering Burlington, about twenty minutes from the kill zone, the BattleMechs would break cover and drive toward the refinery, attempting to destroy as much equipment or buildings as possible. Simultaneously, the artillery would target the million-liter fuel tanks on the north side; the 'Mechs—theoretically—far enough away from the tanks to ride out the shockwave when they went up.

If it went well, the mercenaries would focus the Capellans' attention on the refinery, pulling them away from the armored cars until the sergeant major and Braun sprang their trap. For weeks, while Alysheba and Alicia were coordinating with Moretti and helping Roberts steal the Walruses, the sergeant major and his engineers had been working in disguise in Burlington. Infiltrating under the guise of a civilian construction company, they had turned the convoy's route into a veritable maze of tank traps: no easy route for reinforcements coming in, and only one preselected route for the armored cars going out.

Giacomo frowned, waiting for the signal that would launch his attack. There was one more piece of the puzzle out there, one he wasn't even briefed on. Alysheba had asked for Alicia and one platoon of infantry to work with her during the robbery, with no explanation given. She wanted Alicia for a mission she wouldn't divulge, saying only, "Your missions are a distraction for mine," and asking them to trust her.

The sergeant major was in Burlington at the time, so Giacomo conferred with Alicia, hoping her time with Alysheba would give her better insight into the spy's methods. The young infantry hauptmann was beginning to understand the other woman better and, wanting to continue striking at the invaders, was more comfortable accepting a mission sight-unseen than he was. Trusting her judgment, he'd agreed: right now, Alicia and her hand-picked platoon were with Alysheba doing God-knew-what, and he just prayed the spy remembered that his DropShip was Alicia's only ride home.

His secondary monitor finally blinked again, stating the convoy had entered Burlington. Immediately after that came a simple word from the battery to his north: "*Firing.*" He was too far to see or hear them, but he knew the snipers were now laying down a mix of high-explosive and white phosphorus shells that would ignite anything they stuck.

Time to make an inferno, he thought, bringing his *Grasshopper* up from standby to full power. "Get ready, Marcos—those rounds might not take long to set off a tank, so be prepared to—"

He didn't finish as a flash of light lit the daytime sky, and a thunderous explosion shook the earth, rattling his BattleMech three kilometers away from the explosion.

As they charged north toward the burning refinery, Giacomo typed "*Attacking*" into his keyboard and sent it out, letting everyone know the operation was proceeding as planned. Aiming the lasers in his right arm toward a structure he thought looked important, he squeezed his main interlock trigger, and the *Grasshopper*'s lasers blasted it into kindling as he ran by.

"Follow me," he told Marcos, heading toward the twenty-story control and administrative center in the center of the refinery. Another tank exploded to the north, shaking the ground and sending another fifty-story fireball into the sky. "Stay close, the artillery will do their best not to fire near us, but things are going to get hot pretty quick."

BURLINGTON, TSINGTAO
CAPELLA COMMONALITY
CAPELLAN CONFEDERATION
22 JANUARY 3058, 1455 HOURS

"Bravo team, the convoy has accelerated. XO, they're five minutes from the kill zone, and we're still a go. Stand by," said the sergeant major over a low-powered transmission the convoy wouldn't be able to pick up.

Braun smiled tightly. Franks and a platoon of his engineers were still in construction-company disguise and set in place in their heavy equipment, waiting for their part in the heist. The other two platoons of engineers were set in position alongside two platoons of infantry, each engineer armed with an extra pair of LAWs and ready to initiate the attack.

Half-assault, half-masquerade; the attack on the convoy had been scripted and rehearsed by the infantry, engineers, and the pilots as much as possible. Braun's team—himself, Jones in her *Axman*, and a company of infantry in APCs—were the free-floating reserves. They weren't sure what direction enemy reinforcements would come from once the convoy cried for help, so they would have to handle variables as they arose.

They were hiding in empty warehouses in north Burlington, the most likely direction any assistance sent to the convoy would arrive from. They had a good picture of the local police response and Capellan troops, but they had no clue how the mercenaries would respond, or in how much force—even just a fast lance would outnumber him and Jones two-to-one, and they had nine lances.

For the hundredth time since Alicia had disappeared with Alysheba two days ago, he wondered where she was, and hoped it was safer than his upcoming afternoon.

He looked at the edge of his BattleMech's hatchet. *She gets Alicia killed, I'll slice that spy in half with my blade,* he thought, *and there's not a person in this unit that would stop me.*

1459 HOURS

"Contact, contact," reported the spotters on the far side of the kill zone. "One minute out, we have twelve vehicles, I say again, twelve vehicles moving at forty klicks. Seven targets, a police car, and I count five escorts. I identify as two Brinks, two Enforcers, and—shit!—a Hetzer! I say again, a Hetzer is in the convoy!"

"Where's the Hetzer in the convoy?" asked the sergeant major. The Brinks were armored cars used to haul secure goods on hundreds of worlds; they probably held jewels, coins, or important papers. The Enforcers were common Capellan police tactical vehicles, with moderate civilian armor and a response team in each. Both types of vehicles had been expected alongside the target tractor-trailers.

But the Hetzer was a 40-ton military vehicle with the largest available autocannon mounted in the nose. The good news was it could only fire forward—a liability in a city fight—but that was the *only* good news. Two hits could rip apart the XO's *Scarabus* or put the *Axman* into a world of hurt; left unchecked, the Hetzer could easily level the surrounding buildings containing the infantry and his engineers.

"Up front, just behind the cop car, Sergeant Major," the scout replied.

"Team, they're coming in dumb," Franks transmitted while looking at Corporal Wyle in the bulldozer next to him. Hiding inside a heavy building with a good line of sight, the dozer was lined up to burst through the sheet-metal door when the time was right. She gave him a tentative thumbs-up, not understanding.

"Fine by me, Seven," replied Hauptmann Braun, all business. "Can you take it out without killing the cops?"

"I can try," said the sergeant major, "but they'll probably get rattled quite a bit. Best I can offer. Okay, Bravo team," he continued, "the Hetzer is the drop target. Ignore the cop car if possible, and every escort gets a platoon of LAWs. If the Hetzer somehow lives, it gets the entire second volley of LAWs. Everyone stand by."

He glanced up at the corporal, who still looked confused. "What?" he asked her.

"What did you mean, 'coming in dumb'?" she asked. Wearing little more than a pair of work jeans and a reflective vest, she'd used her good looks to distract more than a couple inquires during the weeks while they'd worked.

Using their engineering equipment, repainted a garish safety yellow, they'd spent weeks pretending to be a civilian road repair and repaving company. Apologizing for the inconvenience and noise while they mostly worked at night "so we don't disrupt morning commutes," they'd dug trenches across a number of strategically planned intersections wide enough to accept a drainage pipe. Doing that without getting noticed was the easy part.

Carefully mixing thousands of liters of homemade plastic explosive in a cement mixer without killing himself and his whole unit had been the nerve-wracking part of the operation. He'd heard it discussed as a theoretical concept, but Alysheba promised him she'd seen it done safely at a class she'd attended once; despite his sweating bullets every time they began a new batch, it had worked. They'd laid a half-meter-wide drainage pipe filled with plastique into every trench and then repaved the entire street to hide their work. Besides the initiating bomb, there were additional ones keyed to the same circuit, one behind the convoy and on each side street. He almost felt bad for the calamity to come—from what some civilians had said, the street had never looked better.

"Coming in dumb means they're not going by the book," Franks explained. "Standard convoy-protection doctrine says they should have put the Hetzer in the middle, where it could react to attacks from either end. Instead, they're rushing, trying to get to the bank and safety with their best asset up front."

She nodded, and he saw the convoy turn the distant corner. "Hearing protection in, everyone," he said, and then put in his earplugs. No one would be able to hear until after he initiated the ambush, but the earplugs would ensure he could hear after it.

Up first with lights flashing was a Burlington police car in its standard white-and-amber livery. Directly behind it was the forty-ton wheeled Hetzer, the monstrous autocannon barrel mounted off-center on the vehicle's right-hand side. Behind that was an Enforcer and the two Brinks armored cars, both in Capellan Central Bank paint schemes. Behind the armored cars were the seven target long-haulers.

They're military variants! Franks realized with a smile—the scouts hadn't reported that the trucks were military "ten-twenties," not their civilian "twenty-twenty" counterparts. Civilian tractors had lighter armor and weighed twice as much as their military counterparts, but were faster and could haul more weight. The military tractors were lighter, slower, but had better armor. In this case, heavier armor was a nonfactor—they weren't planning on attacking the trucks—but every gram counted during an airborne escape.

A final Enforcer brought up the rear, but Franks was focused on the front of the convoy. They were in a long straightaway with only one cross street; once they hit his intersection, he'd blow all the charges around the kill zone and seal the convoy into a linear ambush.

Franks let the police car pass his trigger point unmolested, then triggered the explosives as the Hetzer arrived.

The wheeled vehicle was ripped in half as a thousand kilos of homemade plastique detonated under it, just behind its front wheels. The autocannon ammunition went off in an immediate secondary explosion; the double-tap explosion shattered every window in a two-block radius, and knocked the sheet-metal door off its hinges. Franks was knocked backward, and had to take a knee to keep from falling over. Glancing over at Wyle, he could see her cheering, but Franks couldn't hear over the ringing in his ears, despite his earplugs.

Each drainage bomb had ripped a three-meter-wide, two-meter-deep trench when it detonated: the convoy was stuck behind the burning Hetzer and unable to cross the trenches down the side streets. From his now-windowless vantage point, Franks could see—but still not hear—the infantry and engineer platoons lash into the escorts, firing dozens of the light, disposable rockets into each Enforcer. He didn't trust himself to speak, so he sent *"Bravo team attacking"* as a data burst. Within seconds he received *"Charlie team en route"* in response.

The convoy is headless, he thought, *and Roberts is on his way. Once the escorts are dead, we give the trucks the way out.*

CAIRO
1501 HOURS

Giacomo nodded as he saw the sergeant major's transmissions. *Perfect. If they keep to the schedule, me and Marcos will be out of here in a few more minutes.*

The snipers had stopped firing once they'd pushed deep into the refinery, the sprawling installation covering nearly nine square kilometers, about half of which was now on fire. A corporate security infantry platoon was taking intermittent shots at them as they continued melting anything that looked important with their lasers. Fires from the burning fuel were everywhere, with smaller buildings and vehicles randomly detonating from secondary explosions, and they were careful to fire at anything that might explode at maximum range. He saw Marcos aim at a square sided maintenance truck with his lasers and slag it in one volley.

Excellent, he thought, *that'll slow down repairs, costing them time and money.* On his monitors, he saw the platoon forming up for another attack around a three-story, fifty-meter-wide fuel drum just out of range of his lasers. Slamming his foot pedals to the floor, he activated his *Grasshopper's* jump jets and launched forward over a maze of pipes and walkways that had been slowing him down. The 'Mech swayed slightly in the crosscurrents created by so many burning fires, but he easily corrected and landed safely.

Now in range, he aimed—seeing the platoon begin to scatter, he held his fire for a few seconds. *You guys should have backed off a while ago. No job is worth this.* He squeezed the trigger, and a massive fireball immediately leaped into the air. *Hopefully a few of you lived to perform first aid.*

"One, this is Three," said Marcos. "I'm getting some weird contacts—I think the Renegades may have finally arrived."

"Magscan?"

"Seismic."

Giacomo frowned and flipped the secondary display, showing the local map, through its settings. A BattleMech had an array of sensors that could see across the spectrum, but the burning refinery had eliminated the usefulness of most of them: the fires made infrared worthless, and the mad mix of machinery and steel played havoc on the relatively short-ranged magnetic resonance scan.

Seismic was also relatively short-ranged, and the explosions were sending tremors through the ground that overrode his ability to detect even Marcos. But, standing still for a few seconds, he finally saw what Marcos had seen—a series of uneven thumps that weren't aligning with falling buildings or explosions.

"Agreed, looks like we have company. Three, form up, let's start drifting north."

Heading down a paved side road between a pair of burning maintenance sheds, they stood before a 300-by-200-meter rectangle of low pipes and erratic crosswalks. Slowly picking their way into the mess, they were about halfway across when red triangles began to appear on three sides.

"One, this is Three," said Marcos. He was slightly ahead and to the northeast of Giacomo. "I've got a lance to the east."

"I've got a lance each to the south and west. This is well past our worst-case estimates," Giacomo said.

"I'm sorry, Philip," Alysheba cut in. "I warned the Renegades you were going to be there, to pull attention away from me and the sergeant major. If we live through this, I promise I'll make it up to you."

"That's a damn big 'if,'" he replied. "Three, follow me." He jumped his *Grasshopper* north, to the safety of the sprawling refinery. Marcos followed in his *Whitworth*.

As the two 'Mechs climbed into the sky, lasers, PPCs, and missiles crisscrossed the field, some impacting both. Giacomo grunted as the hits knocked him slightly off course, and landed hard. He flexed his 'Mech's knees to take the impact and stood, searching for targets.

"Still here?" he called to Marcos.

"Barely," Marco replied, and he could see it was true—the *Whitworth* had caught most of the fire, its armor now paper-thin in some locations.

"Head north, find a spot, then cover me with your LRMs," Giacomo said. "I'll cover you."

Marcos acknowledged and ran north into the zone the artillery had ignited, which contained the worst of the fires.

"XO, Ken, we're in trouble. We'll hold them as long as we can, but if we fall off the net, don't wait for us. Take off on time—that's an order."

BURLINGTON
1505 HOURS

Hauptmann Braun was tracking the ambush of the convoy on a secondary monitor when four red squares appeared on his display. He looked at the range—kilometers away, coming fast across the rolling fields toward Tsing City.

"Three, Two," he said to Jones. "Looks like a lance of reinforcements are approaching from the capital." While she acknowledged, he studied the enemies: they were too far out for the computer to identify them, but their rate of approach at least narrowed down what they weren't.

"From their speed, I'm guessing lights, maybe with a fast medium or two. Probably the battalion quick-response force. They must not know we're here, or they would have sent something heavier to be your dance partner."

Ensuring his ECM was on, he moved his *Scarabus* toward the warehouse door. "Find a good ambush spot, I'll lure them to you. If we're lucky, we can kill this whole lance and buy the sergeant major some time."

1508 HOURS

"Seven, this is Five, two minutes out." Franks heard over the radio. He slapped the side of Wyle's cab and motioned her forward. The Hetzer had been blown up on the west side of the intersection, severing the east-west road; the exits to the north and south had been detonated at the same time. The trucks had pushed forward, trying to find a way out while bullets from the infantry rifles ricocheted off their military-grade armor. But the trenches were just too deep—which was part of the masquerade.

Franks and his team approached from the south, one squad wearing their construction company coveralls and three squads dressed in imitation Renegades uniforms they'd received from Alysheba the week prior. They weren't perfect copies, but they didn't expect the truck drivers from the Capellan bank to notice the slight inconsistencies in the middle of battle.

He directed Wyle to push a car into the south-side trench, and then jumped onto the car, then across to the main road. Crouching down to avoid ricochets—even though his men wouldn't aim near him, bullets went where they wanted after they bounced off armor— he jumped onto the running board of the closest truck and banged on the window.

"Follow me! We're gonna get you out of here!" He saw a pair of stressed faces nod at him through the bulletproof glass, the older woman behind the wheel clenching it with whitened knuckles.

Franks made a show of placing his "infantry" into firing positions while two dump trucks dumped loads of gravel into the trench. Wyle cleared the road, pushing cars and debris out of the way, rifle shots occasionally glancing off her dozer blade for show. His "Renegades" troops fired back, the truck drivers not noticing they were all armed with carefully powered-down laser rifles: Franks had personally checked them all to ensure they were on minimal strength, so even an accidental strike on a friendly wouldn't create a casualty.

"Seven, this is Five, wheels down."

Franks nodded. *Finally.* He thumped the window again and motioned the driver to head down the freshly opened south side street. He held on as they carefully went over the now-filled trench, and then accelerated down the narrow lane. It was a tight fit for the trucks, running straight for three blocks until it opened up into an empty stadium parking lot.

In a loose triangle at one end sat the trio of 200-ton stolen Walrus VSTOLs, cargo ramps down, rotors idling, and freshly painted in Renegades colors. Armor crewmen—their tanks already loaded on the hidden DropShip—were set up in a perimeter around the Walruses. Also wearing false Renegades uniforms and carrying laser rifles, some waved the trucks toward the loadmasters frantically signaling the trucks to board.

Franks banged on the window to get the driver's attention. "Keep going! That's your ticket out of here!"

The terrified driver nodded and headed towards the left-hand Walrus, slowing and following the directions of the loadmaster. Franks jumped off as it hit the ramp and ran toward the center of the perimeter to guide in the next truck. *It's working. If Braun can keep those Renegades off us long enough, we might actually pull this off.*

CAIRO
1513 HOURS

Giacomo gasped in the overheated air of his *Grasshopper*'s cockpit. Between the fusion engine that powered a 'Mech and the waste heat its weapons generated, a MechWarrior always left a cockpit drained and dehydrated. It was worse fighting in a raging fire, though, as the inferno itself contributed to the 'Mech's heat woes.

At least the upgraded mercs are suffering worse than we are, he thought, aiming at a *Shadow Hawk* 5M that had been pestering him. Apparently receiving an upgrade package when the Renegades served the Free World's league, it had been pestering him at ranges he was disadvantaged at. Though his *Grasshopper* outmassed the pesky medium, it sported only five long range missiles to throw at the *'Hawk*'s brand-new twenty-rack, and his lasers were outranged by the *'Hawk*'s new Ultra-class autocannon. But thankfully the new weapons were crippling the *Shadow Hawk* in the inferno, forcing it to move sluggishly lest it overheat further and shut down.

A full score of long range missiles streaked in from Giacomo's left; hiding behind a stone building, Marcos finally had a clear shot, and all but two he'd launched spattered across the *Shadow Hawk*. The missiles exploded across the 'Mech's torso: a handful went deep into the left-hand side, making it shudder. It took one more step before falling on its left side into a smoldering garage.

"Nice shooting, Three. That got him."

"That also cleaned out my bins, One," Marcos replied. "We got a plan to get out of here yet?"

Giacomo grunted—but before he could reply, a new voice cut in. "One, this is Nine, my spotters have eyes on you. If you keep pulling back toward us, we can give you some cover fire."

Nine? It took Giacomo a second to work through his confusion and put the call sign with a name: Sergeant Brooke Zide, the sniper battery commander. "Nine? What the *hell* are you still doing here? You should have left a while back!"

"You didn't tell us to evac, One. Can you head north? We'll cover you." That, he knew, was at least a partial lie. The plan never required him or Marcos to release the battery: once the fuel tanks had been destroyed, the crews should have limbered and departed to get some distance from any potential Capellan counter-fire assets. He had no doubt Zide and her team had decided to stay "just in case" unexpectedly large numbers of Renegades arrived.

Bless the artillery and their "why haul ammo when you can fire it?" tradition, he thought. "Roger that, Nine. We'll cut through the tanks and see if we can give you something to shoot at. Marcos, same plan as before. You lead, I'll follow."

As the *Whitworth* broke into a run, weaving between tanks, some burning, some still intact, Giacomo took a moment to check his tactical display. Of the twelve enemy BattleMechs that had attacked them at the field, Giacomo was pretty sure they'd destroyed four and put a hurt on the rest. He'd taken out a *Cicada* and an *Anvil*, Marcos had taken out the *Shadow Hawk*, and he was pretty sure he'd seen another 'Mech swallowed in an explosion when a *Griffin* had fired at him, missed, and hit a fuel tank next to a second *Griffin* that was trying to flank them.

Of the remaining eight Renegades, Zide's spotters had eyes on six, which was pretty decent odds. He picked the largest of them and clicked open his microphone. "Nine, One, put a barrage down on that *Thunder* that's bringing up the rear. If it ever catches up to us, that's game. Hit him, and then fire at your discretion."

"Understood."

Giacomo broke from cover and ran down an asphalt street that was starting to buckle from the heat. To his left and right were burning fuel tanks, but with lower flames. They were starting to enter the area the artillery had initially fired at, so the fires were now in burning structures or open pools of burning oil. Still hot, but still jumpable if necessary.

He saw Marcos behind a one-story building, the *Whitworth* leveling its lasers down the road. "I have you covered, One. There's... crap," he said, starting to turn toward Giacomo's left. Whatever he was going to say next was lost as a silver streak screamed in from the flank, struck the *Whitworth* in the side, and burrowed deep into its center torso. The 'Mech immediately fell backward.

Giacomo spun the *Grasshopper*'s torso to the left, ready to fire. *Dammit*, he thought, watching two 'Mechs leaping over a burning building. Both were new; one was a Capellan *Snake*, an anti–battle armor specialist that was a little undergunned for a 'Mech fight. The other was a *Tempest*, a heavy 'Mech that traded speed for firepower. *That was a helluva shot from the* Tempest–*this ain't gonna be easy.* "Marcos, you okay?" he asked while firing his large laser into the *Tempest.*

The heavy 'Mech landed and spun toward him as the *Snake* cut north, trying to block their avenue of escape.

"One, this is Nine, the rest are falling back. If you guys can break contact, I think you're home free."

"Boss, just run. I'm not going to make it out of here," Marcos replied. Giacomo saw the *Whitworth* rising to its feet, slowly and unsteadily. "Gyro's damaged. I'll cover you."

Giacomo lined up his reticule on the *Tempest* and pulled his main interlock trigger. His large laser sliced up the heavy 'Mech's left side, melting a half-ton of armor in seconds. Two of his medium lasers went wide, but the other two hit top and bottom on the mercenary's right leg, one above the knee, one below. His five LRMs seemed to be heading straight for the *Tempest*'s cockpit before the 'Mech's anti-missile system swept them from the sky. His cockpit swam with heat, and he slammed the override button to make sure the *Grasshopper* didn't conduct an automatic shutdown. He saw the *Tempest* taking careful aim, and braced for impact.

The *Tempest* fired its Gauss rifle, magnetic coils accelerating a watermelon-sized slug of nickel straight from the mercenary's right arm into the *Grasshopper*'s left arm. It slammed through what little armor was left and crashed deep, destroying the medium laser there and locking up everything south of the elbow. Judging by the schematic, it was hanging on by myomer or two, and a small laser could sever it. The bright green bolts from the *Tempest*'s large pulse laser sliced into his right torso, luckily hitting only internal structure. The *Grasshopper* shook when it also absorbed the hit from one of the mercenary's three medium lasers, but luckily the other two went wide.

The *Snake* and Marcos both fired at almost the same time; the *Snake* fired a shotgun-style round with its LB-X autocannon, and a half-dozen small explosions rocked the *Whitworth*. Marcos's cockpit window starred as it took a direct hit, and then four of the *Snake*'s six SRMs spun in. The *Whitworth* staggered—firing back with its three medium lasers, the big ex-con managing to hit the *Snake*'s knee with two. Both 'Mechs crashed to the ground about a hundred meters apart, with the hazmat building halfway between them.

"Nine, this is Three...full barrage...my position," gasped Marcos.

"Nine, ignore that order!" yelled Giacomo, running his 'Mech toward the *Whitworth*. "Eject, Marcos! I'll get us out of here!"

"Can't eject. Hit me, Nine. I don't want to burn to death down here. Do it."

Giacomo hesitated for a split second. Burning to death was the fear of every MechWarrior. They were trained to ride the heat curve, managing their heat as they fought hard and died hard, death usually coming in an instant on a battlefield where every moment could be their last. No one wanted to go out by fire, slowly and painfully consumed by heat and flames.

"Get clear, One," came Nine's calm voice, and the *Grasshopper* rocked as it was struck again. The *Tempest* had hit him with the lasers first, stitching the pulse laser across his left torso before hitting each leg with a medium laser. Giacomo rode out the impacts and screamed in pain as the *Tempest*'s third laser hit his cockpit, the strike hitting hard enough to knock his neurohelmet into his display. The *Grasshopper* staggered as he struggled to keep it upright, the *Tempest*'s Gauss slug slicing through the air it had just vacated.

Thanks, God, that probably would have finished me, he thought.

"Rounds en route. One, get clear now!" came Zide's shout, much more forcefully this time.

"Go, boss...Spend my share on booze. Really...really good booze," came a pained whisper from Marcos.

Giacomo slammed his foot pedals down, leaping his *Grasshopper* to the north.

The artillery barrage landed just as he jumped, a pair of rounds bracketing the *Snake* trying to get to its feet and sending it right back to the ground. Another pair landed in the space between, and one struck the immobile *Whitworth*, burying itself deep into the shoulder superstructure before exploding, sending the hapless 'Mech's right arm flying into the air.

The last round crashed through the roof of the hazmat building and exploded—Giacomo saw a series of secondary explosions as various canisters leaped into the sky, and then a large explosion sent a green flowing cloud of gas across the area, completely covering the *Whitworth* and *Snake*. The *Tempest* leaped away to the south.

Giacomo landed and turned around. He heard Marcos cough wetly once, and then silence, and the *Snake* was no longer struggling, either. He looked down the long asphalt road at the motionless *Tempest*, staring him down across the gas and through a path of burning buildings.

Another barrage landed, the artillery laying a mix of white smoke and high explosives to cover his retreat. Giacomo stared at the *Tempest*, neither moving nor firing, until it was hidden behind the white smoke and finally, slowly, turned and headed north.

BURLINGTON
1515 HOURS

Leaving Jones in her *Axman* and a platoon hidden at a crossroads, Braun hid two blocks east and one north from her. He kept one platoon in APCs as a reserve, with the last platoon broken up into teams of spotters. Spread out at key intersections, he would have real-time tracking of the Renegades lance, a key advantage in a city fight.

All he could see were buildings around him, so he was watching his secondary display as the four Renegades 'Mechs continued their sprint to the city.

"Two, this is Ten," called the infantry company commander with the forward-most of the spotters. "We've got eyeballs on the Renegades—still too far for our equipment to tag them, so this is best guess."

"Understood. What do you have?"

"Pretty much bad news all the way around. Looking at one light and three mediums."

Braun swore. "Of course we are." He sighed. "Go on."

"A *Raven* out front. A pair of *Assassins*—my human warbook of an assistant tells me one's an upgraded version, one isn't. I can't tell the difference at this range, but he's never been wrong."

"Okay, I'll assume he's right until the computer says otherwise."

"And a third fast medium bringing up the rear. I've never seen one in person, but superfan here says it's a *Wraith*."

Braun frowned, and typed "*Wraith*" into his battle computer. It instantly brought up the specifications, and he swore again.

"Sarge, if he's right, that's bad news," Braun said. "Jones, you tracking?"

"I am, and the kid's almost never wrong," his lancemate added.

"I was afraid one of you would say that," Braun said. *Raven*s were light BattleMechs filled with ECM and advanced probes—it could certainly discover Jones in her hide if it got close enough, and would certainly notice the distortion his ECM would inflict on it. The *Assassin*s were very light mediums, trading armor and weapons for maneuverability. But the *Wraith* was almost double his *Scarabus* in weight and armed exclusively with pulse lasers, which would negate a lot of his speed advantage.

"Jones, I'm going after the *Raven* first and will then try to lure the *Wraith* to you. The *Assassin*s we'll just have to handle as best we can."

"Agreed."

When the Renegades 'Mechs finally hit the city perimeter, they slowed down, but continued on a steady pace toward their convoy. Heading down two parallel multi-lane roads, Braun focused on the *Raven*, working his way closer until he was only an intersection away.

"Two, Ten, they've stopped," reported Jones.

"Yeah, I see it." The four enemy 'Mechs were about 100 meters away from Jones, the building her *Axman* was hiding in directly between the two roads.

Braun thought quickly. "Jones, come out of your building toward the *Raven*. I'll cut east, then up. If I'm right, you'll flush him straight at me."

She didn't acknowledge verbally; he just saw her icon moving on a secondary monitor and began running. The *Raven* and an *Assassin* were on an intersection, and Braun figured instead of running south, toward the angry heavy 'Mech with an ax, they'd cut east a block and then south again on the side road he was on. He smiled as his secondary monitor updated with data from an infantry spotter: he'd called it right. Which meant the *Raven* should turn the corner into him right about...

Now.

The *Raven* spun around the corner, and Braun already had his hatchet up high. He could tell Jones had gotten a volley into the *Raven* with her twin LRM 15s: the right torso and arm were covered in damage from her missiles, and he estimated about half the armor was gone in each location. The *Raven* skidded slightly as the MechWarrior struggled to stop and hold it upright simultaneously, and Braun almost laughed.

He's already bracing for the hit, he thought. *Everyone always forgets I have two arms.*

He squeezed his main interlock trigger. The designers of the *Scarabus* had placed all four energy weapons into one solid block in the 'Mech's left hand, something a lot of enemies forgot when they saw the hardened-steel hatchet in front of their cockpit.

One of the small lasers barely missed, skimming just behind *Raven*, but the other three connected. His second small laser sliced into the 'Mech's beak-like center torso, just behind the cockpit, but the two medium lasers dug deep into the *Raven*'s already-damaged right torso. One cut into the SRM launcher, and he saw the distinctive sputter of the system going offline. The mercenary fought to stay upright and returned fire, the twin medium lasers in its right arm blasting into the building right behind Braun.

He pushed his *Scarabus* forward slightly and swung the hatchet in his Mech's right arm. He had to work the swing, crossing his body as he was—the *Raven* had turned slightly to his right, so his hatchet swung just under the *Raven*'s cockpit before arcing upwards and cutting into the right torso from below. He felt the recognizable *crunch* of internal structure yielding to his hatchet's momentum, and suddenly it cut free. He stood motionless for a split second, watching the *Raven*'s right arm and torso fall one way while the rest of the BattleMech staggered the other. From his vantage point, he could see into the *Raven*'s interior, where huge chunks of engine shielding had fallen away with the torso. The 'Mech collapsed into a heap on the street in front of him just as the *Assassin* turned the corner.

Braun flicked his microphone to an open, unencrypted frequency. "You're next."

The *Assassin*'s only reply was to raise its arm and fire.

1518 HOURS

Franks checked his chrono as the first Walrus departed. *Six minutes to load, not bad with a well-rehearsed team and drivers scared for their lives.* The infantry had moved up, continuing to lay down occasional rifle shots to maintain the illusion for the drivers, while farther away, the XO kept up a running battle against Capellan reinforcements.

They always knew it would be tight fitting two tractor-trailers in side by side, but luckily, they'd calculated for civilian vehicles. The military variants were smaller, giving them a little more room to work with: as soon as the truck backed into a Walrus and stopped moving, crewmen swarmed it, using two-centimeter chains to lash it to the deck.

Once the second Walrus had two trucks loaded, his "civilian" squad swarmed onboard. Wyle jumped from her dozer, gave it a sad pat goodbye, and ran up the ramp. Turning, she gave him a thumbs-up and a huge grin as the ramp started to close. The huge VSTOL began rolling across the parking lot before slowly lumbering into the sky.

Franks jogged over to Wyle's dozer and quickly attached a pair of thermite grenades. *Just because it's too heavy for us to take doesn't mean we should leave it for the Capellans,* he thought. Yanking the pins, he sprinted towards the last Walrus.

He slowed to a walk as he approached, and keyed his comm. "Six, this is Seven. How far out are you?"

"Seven, we're circling a minute away," replied the lead Karnov pilot. "The moment the last Walrus is in the air, we'll touch down and grab your engineers."

Franks acknowledged and walked toward the seventh and final truck backing into the third Walrus. Once the Karnovs grabbed his company, the infantry would leave via APCs with Braun and his team.

With two trucks already loaded, the final truck had to drop its trailer on the Walrus's ramp and then park outside, left behind like Wyle's dozer. The driver clambered out of his cab about fifty meters away and started sprinting back to the Walrus, the crewmen already on board cheering him on.

He hit the ramp hard and kept jogging, the final dismounted tankers pretending to be guards following him in. The ramp began to close, and he started walking toward Franks with his hand outstretched when he paused and slowly turned around. He bent to the side to study the outside of the Walrus just as the ramp snapped shut.

He slowly turned back toward Franks, his face pale and shocked.

"Hey, are you okay?" the sergeant major asked. "If you get airsick, we have bags for that."

"No," he quietly replied. "This is painted Renegades red, but whoever painted this missed a spot. This Walrus was reported stolen. I saw the police reports." His eyes focused on Franks. "I also saw classified intelligence that said Davion agents might have been behind the theft."

Franks bowed. "And so we were." He waved some crewmen forward. "Find the detective a seat, if you don't mind," he instructed, mirth in his voice.

As they led off the now-irate driver, Franks keyed his microphone. "All stations, this is Seven, en route to Oz," he said, using the code word for the DropShip. The stolen Walrus did a rolling start and finally shook itself into the air, and the interior rang with cheers from the tankers and crewmen.

Franks keyed his comm again. "All teams, Shakespeare," he gleefully said, using the code word for successful completion of the ambush and robbery. "I say again, *Shakespeare*! *We did it*!"

CAIRO
1522 HOURS

Giacomo stood in the forest, his *Grasshopper* standing guard over the artillery battery as they finally pulled out of their firing position, their cargo trucks and towed artillery bouncing down an old logging road. His 'Mech was scorched and burned, nearly all of his armor gone—he had more armor remaining on his back than any other section, including his cockpit. He got a thumbs-up from Zide as she passed, the entire battery on the move.

"Good work, Seven. One, Nine, and Alpha team will meet you at Oz."

BURLINGTON
1526 HOURS

Braun gasped for air as he sprinted his *Scarabus* towards a Renegades *Assassin*. The *Wraith* and *Axman* were having a private little war, while the two *Assassins* had teamed up to worry Braun's *Scarabus* to death with numerous little attacks.

One-on-one, his *Scarabus* was an even match for an *Assassin*— but the two-on one advantage had left him receiving the lion's share of damage. Despite the fact he was faster, their ability to jump meant that every time he tried to close with one, the second would jump behind him. He was slowly trying to work his way back toward

Jones, but they were keeping him separated. His *Scarabus* was badly damaged, and while he'd managed to hurt both mediums, he knew it was only a matter of time before one of them got lucky and took him down.

He saw the messages reporting that the commander and his team—minus Three—and Franks and his team had evacuated. Only his team was left—and Alicia, wherever the spy had dragged her off to.

The standard tech *Assassin* came soaring over a building, firing as it approached, and Braun realized it was going to land closer than its MechWarrior had probably expected.

He smiled a vicious, tight grin. *Finally*. He raised his hatchet and charged, quickly closing the distance.

"Ten, this is Four, the *Wraith* is down. Mount up and help Two so we can get out of here."

Braun heard Jones's report over the radio, but didn't have time to reply. He fired and struck the *Assassin*'s right leg with a medium and small laser. Too close for LRMs, the *Assassin* returned fire with its SRMs and his laser. One missile missed, but the other hit his heavily damaged left torso. The laser went in right behind it, and Braun knew from the sudden rush of heat that his engine had been hit.

Engine's not dead yet, he thought, *and neither am I*. He raised his 'Mech's right arm, the polished-steel hatchet gleaming in the Tsingtao sunlight. The *Assassin* shifted, protecting its cockpit, but Braun bypassed the difficult target and struck the Capellan 'Mech dead center. Already damaged from a previous hit from a medium laser, the hatchet struck the wound just below the *Assassin*'s bulbous cockpit and sliced deep. Anticipating that the hatchet wouldn't penetrate, Braun pulled his right arm back and slammed the *Scarabus*'s left arm right against the fresh hole, squeezing his main interlock trigger when he felt the jar of impact.

Placed directly against the chest of the *Assassin*, all four lasers burned deep into the mercenary 'Mech. The *Assassin* shuddered as it was cored, the upper half of its body seeming to collapse two meters downwards onto its own engine, and then the Renegades BattleMech fell directly backward. Braun gasped in the heat; before he could find the second *Assassin* again on his monitors, the *Scarabus* reeled as a series of missile explosions hit him in the back. Braun fought for control as his control board lit up with red.

No armor there; that's it for the engine, he thought. His monitors flickered as the Scarabus began to die; he grabbed his overhead handles and ejected, feeling his spine momentarily compress as the seat immediately launched him up and out.

The chute on his chair opened and he drifted to a landing about 300 meters up the street from where his destroyed *Scarabus* had fallen. He could see the upgraded *Assassin* in the distance closing quickly when he heard a loud roar from behind him. Turning, it was one of the infantry's tracked APCs, already dropping its ramp to let him in. In the gunner's hatch was an infantryman with an SRM launcher—he fired, as did the first trooper down the ramp. Both missiles landed far short, but set the street on fire when they detonated.

Infernos, Braun realized. *Warning shots.* Inferno missiles were short range missiles containing a gel that ignited on impact instead of exploding. Capable of setting a 'Mech alight, they were one of the few equalizers infantry had for fighting a 'Mech: any exposed internal areas would get destroyed by the burning gel, and a lucky inferno hit against a cockpit could burn the MechWarrior alive.

The mercenary apparently got the hint and backed off, content to let Braun escape at the cost of his 'Mech. Braun quickly unhooked himself from his command chair and sprinted for the APC, crouching as he entered. The APC was already lurching into motion before the ramp was fully up.

The interior was dark, lit only by a few overhead lights, and smelled of fuel and sweat. Braun crinkled his nose but said nothing, thankful to be alive. He moved forward to get next to the company commander.

"You okay?" he asked. At Braun's nod, the commander keyed his radio. "Four, this is Ten, I've got Two, we'll follow you to Oz."

Braun leaned in. "Has anyone heard from Eleven or Twelve?"

The infantryman shook his head. "Not yet. But trust me, Alysheba's a stone cold killer. Wherever Hauptmann Stillwater is, if she's working with the spy, then she's safer than we are."

TSING CITY
1429 HOURS

Hauptmann Alicia Stillwater fidgeted in an unfamiliar uniform, watching the buildings and skyscrapers of Tsingtao's capital blur by the windows. Riding in the front of a train engine in a separate compartment she'd heard was normally reserved for brakemen, it was only her and Alysheba, the engineer separated from them in his own compartment by a sheet of glass. The brake compartment had dirty, greasy benches; both women had eyed them and elected to stand. Alicia didn't want anything to get on the pure white Com Guard uniform she was wearing, half-cape and all, and she assumed the beautiful spy felt the same way about the fashionable—and presumably *expensive*—business suit she wore.

"The convoy just entered Burlington," Alicia said.

"I heard," Alysheba replied politely.

"The commander should begin his attack in about ten minutes," Alicia continued.

Alysheba just shrugged.

Alicia felt her weight shift and said, "We're decelerating."

"Are you going to state the obvious *all* day?" Alysheba asked with a slight smile.

"No," Alicia quickly replied, sensing the edge behind her innocuous question. "But of all the teams, we were the only ones that didn't get a mission briefing. You told us at the last second to put these uniforms on and defend this train," she said, waving her hand around to encompass where they were. "We don't have an escape plan, we don't know the opposition, we don't know *anything* but to guard this train and any cargo."

The spy nodded. "Hauptmann, I told your team only what they *must* know—their job and nothing more—so they can maintain their covers. If they truly believe their only mission is to guard this train, anyone questioning them about it will believe it too."

"Our mission *isn't* to guard the train?" Alicia asked, confused.

"We're here," Alysheba replied. She waved at the engineer up front in the separate compartment, and then turned back to Alicia. "I shouldn't have even told you that." She paused, biting her lip for a second. "Look, I like you. You're good people, and under different circumstances, I think we could even be friends." Her voice dropped, and her eyes became as cold as an airless moon. "But—and I mean this with all of my heart right now, Alicia—I need you to shut up and pay attention, because, I swear to *God*, if you ruin this, I'll kill you myself."

Alicia's eyes widened and she swallowed at the very real threat. Then she nodded once to show her understanding and followed Alysheba out of the engine.

They were in an underground loading bay, a thick ferrocrete loading dock next to the short, ten-car train. Every car, including the fore and aft engines, was heavily armored; directly behind each engine were passenger cars from which her troops spilled out, quickly taking up a perimeter around the six empty boxcars in the center.

For the next thirty minutes, her troops, in their Com Guard uniforms, escorted and assisted the Capellan Central Bank officials and guards as they swept the train from front to back. Finding nothing of concern, a thick armored door swung open on rails, and a large forklift appeared, holding a twenty-meter-long armored container. It slid the container into the empty first car, and as Alysheba and other bank officials sealed the car and confirmed paperwork, the forklift returned with another container. The next five cars were loaded in the same manner, the entire process taking just over thirty minutes.

Finally, only a little over an hour since they'd first arrived, Alysheba and the bank manager shook hands. She nodded once to Alicia, and the infantry officer signaled for everyone to quickly board the train.

Alicia had her squad leaders quickly count noses as the engine slowly began to move. She sighed in relief as they confirmed everyone was on board. *I won't leave anyone behind, but I've been around Alysheba enough now to read her body language and know she wants us the hell out of here.*

The engine cleared the underground facility, and Alicia blinked in the daylight. As the engine continued to accelerate, she turned around and strained to see where they had just left.

"We were under the Global Reserve!" At the other woman's nod, she asked, "Can you tell me what the mission was? What are we guarding?"

Alysheba chuckled. "Remember when I said the Capellans brought approximately three-point-eight billion bills to Tsingtao? They left two billion here, and sent the other one-point-eight to the six secondary reserves."

"Right. That was half of today's missions—steal one of the shipments, hurt the economy."

She shook her head. "It was one-*third* of today's missions." Moving her hands to imitate a schoolteacher, she asked, "Now, Hauptmann, once the Capellans dropped off their L-Bills to the reserve, what do they do with the FC-Bills? They're not going to want people to use money from outside the Confederation, so they're going to collect it up and do...what?"

"Destroy it?"

Alysheba shook her head. "Some, but not all. Remember, the Succession Wars ran for centuries, so there's a standardized process to this. No, what they do is trade it to ComStar. C-Bills are a universally accepted form of currency. The Capellans exchange the physical FC-Bills to ComStar for electronically deposited C-Bills. ComStar then sells the FC-Bills back to the Federated Commonwealth—it's pricey, but ComStar keeps it more affordable than the Commonwealth reminting them all. Eventually the Commonwealth Exchequer will send a DropShip to ComStar's holding site, retrieve the currency, and return it to the Commonwealth's financial system.

"Some border worlds do it more often than others, of course, but it's routine," she continued. "An established routine leads to complacency, and complacency leads to people like us—" she waved a hand towards Alicia's snow-white Com Guard uniform "—sliding in unnoticed."

Stillwater's head swam as she worked through the process. "So, we're dressed as Com Guards, but ComStar never physically handles the invader's money, just the physical bills of the original Great House." Realization started to come. "We don't have L-Bills on board, we have FC-Bills! The Capellans think we're taking the FC-Bills back to the compound, and then they'll electronically receive C-Bills in return. But in reality, we're stealing them?"

"Well, technically we're *liberating* the FC-Bills, because we serve the Federated Commonwealth. But, yes, the Capellans won't get paid, so we're stealing from them, too."

She laughed. "Two billion in FC-Bills! Oh my God, we just stole two-billion-with-a-*b*!"

Alysheba smiled slyly as she grabbed her radio, holding up a finger to make Alicia wait. "Oz, this is Twelve," said Alysheba to the DropShip. "Relay to all stations that Eleven and Twelve have left the target without contact or casualties. Will offload in half hour, ETA to Oz is two hours." After receiving confirmation, Alysheba turned back to Alicia.

Smiling widely, Alysheba *tsk*ed her theatrically. "*Nyet*, Hauptmann, you missed part of what I said. Not two billion *in* FCBills, but two billion *bills*. The average bill is a ten."

"The average is a ten?" Alicia started to giggle.

Alysheba smiled and grabbed the cord to the train's horn. "Yes. T—" she pulled the cord, and the train blared a flat *blahh* sound "—E—" *blahh* "—N—" *blaaaahh*, she finished with relish, holding the last note a little long. "What I wouldn't give to see the look on their faces when ComStar tells them the money never arrived."

Alicia thought about the portly bank manager looking at an empty account and began laughing. "You're killing me, Aly," she gasped, her sides starting to hurt from laughing.

The spy chuckled. "And you wondered why I didn't tell you the mission ahead of time. Lordy, Alicia, never play poker, 'kay?"

The two women laughed together as the train raced toward freedom.

LYRAN SECTOR
HARLECH, OUTREACH
5 APRIL 3058

Sitting in the *Grasshopper*'s cockpit, Giacomo put the date under his name on the bulkhead above him, happy both starting and finishing dates were in his handwriting. Looking around the cockpit one last time, he then gave a thumbs-up to the customs official watching him.

"Looks good," said the thin, bored man. In a monotone, he added, "Please climb out so I can do a final check, and then I'll release the 'Mech for shipment."

Giacomo climbed out and let the crew do their job. Once the customs inspector had sealed the cockpit, a crew boxed up the prone *Grasshopper* and prepped it for travel.

"Almost done, One?" said a familiar voice. "I only have an hour or so before I have to report to customs myself."

Giacomo turned to see Braun and his now-fiancée Alicia Stillwater approaching. During the transit to Outreach, Braun had formalized their relationship in the crew galley. Giacomo wasn't sure that it had been the most romantic spot, but Alicia hadn't complained, so he'd kept his mouth shut and simply congratulated them both.

"A few more minutes, Adam. They have to seal it while I watch. I thumbprint the documents, and it's done."

"I'm surprised they got it repaired so quickly," Braun said with what Giacomo thought was a hint of jealousy. He completely understood—no MechWarrior wanted to be without a 'Mech for long. He did feel uncomfortable packing the *Grasshopper* for shipment before getting his new ride, but the timetable couldn't be helped.

"The Dragoon techs can work miracles when you throw enough money at them. Of course, they kept it in the standard 5H configuration: the Lyran embassy was willing to pay for speed, but there was a limit to their generosity."

Braun laughed. "I can't believe you managed to convince them to both repair it and ship it under the come-home order."

Giacomo laughed too. "Paying for shipping was always included in the order. I just had to convince them that if you were going to pay to ship a 'Mech, it might as well be fully functional at the end." He got serious and said, "I appreciate you escorting this to my cousin. Do you have a line on your next ride yet?"

"My pleasure," Braun said, then shrugged. "My dad thinks he's got a lock on something out of Coventry. I'm hoping for another *Scarabus*, but beggars can't be choosers." He was about to say more, but they saw the customs official approaching. "I'll let you go."

"You're a helluva light 'Mech driver, Adam," Giacomo said, shaking his hand. "I hope we work together again."

"Thank you, and I'd like that too. Once I get my 'Mech, I'm on my way back." Braun tilted his head toward Alicia. "Wherever she is, you'll find me." With a final nod, they turned and walked away.

Giacomo finished up the shipping documents, and as the customs official left, he gave a final pat on the side of the shipping crate. "Keep her alive, 'kay, big guy?" he said, before heading back toward the crowded terminal.

As he walked through the frantic cargo shipping and receiving wing, he saw someone familiar leaning against a support beam. Changing direction, he cut through the crowd and headed towards the short, fashionably dressed woman.

"Alysheba," he said. "You're looking well."

She smiled. "I did some shopping. I appreciate the officer share," she said.

He shrugged. "It *was* your idea," he replied, glad they were back on better terms.

Deep in the bowels of the DropShip en route to Outreach, they'd had a long, private argument about the ambush at the refinery. "The

Renegades were beginning to suspect something, and of all the teams, you were the farthest away and had nothing to do with the heist," she'd explained. "You were, bluntly, expendable." Once he'd cooled off, Giacomo had eventually understood her reasoning, though her phrasing still bothered him some.

"Off to your niece?" she asked, tilting her heads toward the shipping area he'd just left.

"Yes," he replied, his mind back in the present. "She's in the Northwind Highlanders, and it's technically always been hers. My late aunt let me pilot it until she came of age and qualified as a MechWarrior. Since I get my new 'Mech tomorrow and this is her final year at the academy, it's time to let it go."

Alysheba frowned in confusion. "Shipping to Northwind's not free."

"She's an exchange student at the Nagelring. Ships for free under Katrina's come-home order, and Braun even volunteered to escort it that far."

Alysheba gave him a playful punch in the shoulder. "You cheapskate! You've got millions in the bank and you charged it?"

Giacomo smiled despite himself. They'd divided up the L-Bills based on rank: everyone received at least a quarter million, with the officers—including Alysheba and those among the DropShip and JumpShip crews—clearing just over two million L-Bills each.

Their original mission directives had left their jump away from Tsingtao at "the commander's discretion," as no one knew at the time where the front might be. Alysheba had suggested to Giacomo that they head for Outreach. While it was numerous jumps away, as an independent world with embassies for all five Great Houses and ComStar, it would be the perfect place to exchange the stolen L-Bills into C-Bills.

They'd turned over the FC-Bills to the Davion embassy on Outreach upon planetfall. Though they hadn't expected a reward, the Davion ambassador authorized everyone a blanket million FC-Bills each, in gratitude for the morale boost it would provide. With the League and Confederation pushing deep into the Sarna March, good news was scarce across the front; the embassy made holos of the triumphant reception and inventory of the almost twenty-two billion FC-Bills for distribution across the Federated Commonwealth.

"Well, I *was* trying to save money. I originally thought I'd have to buy a 'Mech, but the AFFC bought me a replacement, free and clear," Giacomo replied. "I go to the factory tomorrow to receive a brand new *Gallowglas*."

"Do you, now?" she asked slyly.

He quirked his head. "You knew?"

"I suggested it. Where're you heading?"

"Back to the hotel, I guess. I don't pick up the *'Glas* till tomorrow."

She nodded. "Well, let me buy you dinner." Before he could say anything, she went on, "Word on the street is your unit hasn't been reassigned yet. The whispers also say the honchos at High Command haven't decided whether to break you up or use you to rebuild one of the units that's retreating from the front."

He looked at her strangely, before looking around to see if anyone was listening, then turned back toward her. "No, we haven't been reassigned yet. How do you know the rest of that?"

She gave him a half smile. "Because my boss told me. He also suggested another option. What if you could stay together—off the books—working for a Federated Commonwealth organization long on ideas but short on firepower?"

"Work for you?" he asked.

She nodded, giving him another half-smile while she fingered what appeared to be a *very* expensive bracelet. He glanced at it, looked over her outfit again, and then thought about his pleasantly plump bank account.

He gave her a half-bow, and a wave toward the spaceport exit. "It's a little early for dinner, but I know a quiet place where we can talk."

EARTHBOUND

AARON CAHALL

PAHN CITY FACTORY COMPLEX
HUNTRESS
KERENSKY CLUSTER
CLAN SPACE
12 MARCH 3060

The barracks alarm klaxon blared through the early morning gloom, but Ean was not asleep. Sleep came rarely now. His mind raced far too much, his well-toned muscles twitched too often, and his senses crawled too far into every darkened corner of the large, bunk-lined room. When the alarm's shrill tone roused his fellow warriors, Ean was already awake.

It had not always been this way. Once, Ean had known how to sleep. He was one of Turkina's chosen, an aerospace pilot soaring with the mightiest of Great Kerensky's children. He spent his days among the clouds and stars, unfettered and free. When he returned to his roost, he would fall into deep, nourishing slumber, secure in the knowledge that one day, very soon, he would be among those to swoop from the sky and fall upon the barbarians of the Inner Sphere.

Now, somehow, the barbarians had struck at the very homeworlds of the Clans themselves.

Ean bounded lightly from his bunk, landing on the balls of his feet, a small twitch in a quad muscle causing him to stumble slightly. He crouched and retrieved his special bodysuit from where it lay, carefully folded, beneath his bed. He stood and tugged the lower half on, beginning to move toward the exit as he shrugged the top portion over his shoulders.

His time as a Jade Falcon felt very distant. Years of training had culminated in the glorious invasion Ean hoped for, but nearly too late for his career to achieve its full measure of glory. Then came Apollo. His injuries were slow to heal, and when the year of peace descended, he was sent back to the homeworlds and consigned to the fate of *solahma*. Worse, his wings were clipped—rather than be assigned to even a second-line aerofighter, he was cast down among the general garrison troops of the Falcon's Eyrie, an enclave his own Clan seemed barely interested in maintaining.

The Trial of Possession six years ago changed all that. Why the Smoke Jaguars would target aging aerospace pilots was a mystery to the entire garrison, and Ean's rapid adoption as a warrior by his new Clan was stranger still. When the Smoke Jaguar scientists finally revealed their intentions and made their offer, the new Point Commander felt the skies open to him once more, just for a moment.

Ean shook away the memories as he crossed the short distance to the hangar where techs had already prepared his true skin. The five-meter tall, 7-ton *Roc* was assigned to him as a concession to his origins as a Jade Falcon, but Ean felt an immense kinship that went far beyond man and machine. When he wore his true skin, he *was* a roc, transformed into the great bird, Garuda—

—my people have a legend, that of a great bird named Garuda, who stole immortality from the gods themselves—

He halted a few meters from the machine, closed his eyes, inhaled, and repeated the mantra the medtechs had taught him. *Self, place, duty.* He was Point Commander Ean of Clan Smoke Jaguar. This was Huntress. His duty now was to cast down the invaders and remove their taint from his home. Vikram was back on Apollo, and his legend was just a meaningless Spheroid story shared years ago.

Ean exhaled. The medtechs' mantra helped root him in a reality which seemed to drift farther away every month. It was a temporary measure, they said, and eventually it would have no effect against the deterioration of his implants. A cost, to be sure, but Great Kerensky, the *freedom* it purchased...

"Point Commander! Your ProtoMech is ready. Please embark." The tech's voice carried above the din of hundreds of tons of moving metal, the clamor of the remainder of the garrison completing their startup sequences and taking the field. Ean skirted up the gantry stairs and clambered into the small hatch in the machine's breastbone, folding himself into a tight fetal position. A moment later, the hatch slid home, cutting off the thin light offered by the pre-dawn murk.

This dark and claustrophobic moment, Ean knew, was when many of his would-be comrades washed out of the unique training program required to pilot such a weapon. Still balled into the tiny cavity, he had to find the direct neural interface cord, insert it into his implant port, and power up the ProtoMech. Many were unable to do so without panicking. Ean accomplished the task with practiced ease.

The moment he inserted the cord, his physical confines melted away. Suddenly, he was in his true form—towering above the now infantile-looking technicians, on par with the other titans of the battlefield. He quickly ran through the full range of the *Roc*'s motions. Gone were the damnable twitches in his limbs, the phantoms lurking just out of sight, the wandering sense of place and time.

As the gantry swung away, he strode forward with a mighty swing in his step, no longer aware of the tiny scrap of human flesh powering his metal form. He called to his Point, his silent vocalizations automatically triggering the ProtoMech's radio.

"Ocelot Alpha, check in."

A pause, as the two other *Roc*s and two *Centaur*s confirmed their status. Motioning the four forward, Ean bounded across the cement pad, falling in behind the BattleMechs striding toward the invaders. A few minutes later, advance scouts reported contact—his blood began pumping even harder—with the Northwind Highlanders *lucre*-warriors, bearing the sacred Cameron Star.

"Attention, all commands." The voice of Star Colonel Cara rang clear in Ean's ears. "Engage and destroy the invaders. I do not want even one of the *surats* to survive. Command Star, on me."

Cutting in a different circuit, she added, "All Ocelot Points— weapons free. Dynamic assault."

Without even acknowledging the order, Ean and his two fellow *Roc*s fired their jump jets, bounding in a great arc above the battlefield. Not true flight, as Ean had once known, but he could still feel the momentary skybound jump in every fiber of his metal body. Lacking the shock absorption of his larger BattleMech cousins, Ean tucked and rolled as he fell back to earth, taking two quick steps over pockmarks in the field and hitting his jets again, exulting in the feeling of his imminent test in true combat.

Ahead, a thin line of 'Mechs in garish tartan stretched across the immediate horizon. Moving rapidly under the first long range volleys, Ean's sensors scanned the interlopers and locked in on a *Komodo*, identifying the dangerous anti-Elemental hunter as the most immediate threat. In the depths of his ProtoMech's heart, Ean squinted with one eye to lock on the ungainly 45-ton machine and mark its position to the remainder of his Point.

Sprinting to the top of a nearby rise, Ean again leaped into the air, timing the discharge of his laser to the apex of his jump. His attack pulled the *Komodo* pilot's attention skyward, exposing his 'Mech to the lasers of the other *Roc*s darting across his feet. All three beams converged on the hapless giant just as SRMs from the two *Centaur*s slammed into its torso. Ean landed and bounced out of the way of the falling shreds of melted armor plates, rolling under the *Komodo*'s legs and bounding upward once more.

Another swirling volley struck home, and the 'Mech grew suddenly sluggish. *Engine hit*, Ean thought, then jumped atop the *Komodo*'s broad back and triggered his laser down through the suffering machine's barrel-shaped torso. As pieces of the 'Mech's gyro shot up through the gaping wound, a hatch flung open a meter in front of Ean, and a command couch rocketed into the lightening sky.

Ean rode the slumping BattleMech to the ground, rolling across the roof of the now-vacant cockpit and onto the soft grass. His Point's first kill had not gone unnoticed, however—his sensors warned him of a targeting lock. He traced it to a tartan-wrapped *Grasshopper* bearing some sort of large star-snake insignia moving smoothly across the field in their direction.

Ean began running, building speed for another leap as the 'Mech threw all its lasers at one of Ean's *Centaur*s. Two connected, coring through the ProtoMech's torso. Pilot Olena died without a sound.

Ean snarled, perhaps loud enough to send a harsh rasp through his machine's external speakers. Squinting again to mark the 'Mech on his Point's tactical display, he double-blinked to summon the attention of the nearby Jaguar BattleMechs to the formidable opponent. Surging forward, he alternated jumps with his Pointmates, triggering his laser in concert with the other converging ProtoMechs.

If the *Grasshopper* pilot was intimidated by the swarming Clan machines, he did not show it. Slowly backpedaling, the 'Mech unleashed its large laser at a *Roc* from Ocelot Beta. The hellish lightning burst through the ProtoMech's legs, and Ean's local tactical channel filled with the screams of the pilot experiencing the equivalent sensation of having both his own legs ripped off.

A flight of LRMs exploded across the *Grasshopper*'s chest, signaling the approach of BattleMechs better suited to engaging the heavy machine. Ean beamed a prearranged set of instructions to his Point, ordering them into a series of flanking maneuvers to distract the Highlander. Spotting a Jaguar *Warhammer IIC* closing on his position, Ean fired his jump jets and briefly touched down on his larger cousin's arm-mounted PPC.

Drawing a bead on the invader's cockpit, Ean instantly jumped once more to avoid overbalancing the *Warhammer*. He was barely a meter into the air when the *Grasshopper*'s laser discharge struck the arm on which he'd stood a second earlier.

Razor-sharp electrical fire filled Ean's world. Capacitors blew and synapses fried, the difference between the two meaningless as Ean's body—or was it the metal form of his *Roc* itself?—writhed in unspeakable agony and sprawled face-up onto the ground. As the smell of ozone and cooked skin filled his nostrils, his vision dimmed to a single sight: a large star-snake symbol painted on the *Grasshopper*'s torso.

It was a serpent, coiled around the holy Cameron Star.

A new wave of white-hot pain lanced through Ean's brain.

The serpent.

The *naga*—!

TERRA PRIME GENERAL HOSPITAL
APOLLO
JADE FALCON OCCUPATION ZONE
28 MAY 3050

"The naga." A voice cut through the semiconscious fog filling Ean's senses. "Natural enemies of Garuda."

His temples throbbing from both pain and painkillers, Pilot Ean opened his eyes and regarded the newcomer, a portly, aging man with thick black hair and dark skin. "Leave me."

"That would violate my oaths as a doctor, and this IV bag won't change itself." The man's cheerfulness inflamed Ean's already titanic headache.

"You are a lowly Spheroid medtech," the pilot said, gesturing at the simple tunic and lab coat the other man wore, "and I am a warrior of Clan Jade Falcon, an heir of Turkina chosen to soar the skies and stars. Heed my command. Leave me."

"Well, two weeks ago, you were apparently chosen to be shot down and soar your fighter into our fine countryside," he beamed. The doctor moved to the other side of the hospital gurney, and began checking a datalog on a nearby machine. "And a month ago, I was Dr. Vikram Khatri, chief resident of this hospital. Pleased to meet you, Pilot...?"

"Ean."

"Ah! Well, as I was saying, Ean, my people have a legend, that of a great bird named Garuda, who stole immortality from the gods themselves, to free his mother from his sworn enemies, the serpentine nagas." Vikram chatted as he made a few notes on a tablet. "It's a story I've been thinking about quite a bit lately."

Ean pressed his head farther back into the bed's thin pillow and screwed his eyes shut. "Stop. Speaking."

"I suppose if I don't, I'll be subject to one of the beatings that passes for your people's delightful chain of command." A smile which actually felt genuine to Ean crossed Vikram's broad face. "But you have multiple spiral fractures of both tibia, and I have thoughts regarding our present circumstances and how they relate to a four thousand-year-old Hindu epic. So, as I was saying—"

Ean groaned. "Spare me your barbarian fairy tales."

Vikram continued, unabated. "In our Mahabharata, the eagle-king Garuda is opposed by the naga, a race of poisonous cobras." As he spoke, the doctor puttered around Ean's bed, adjusting his leg braces and medical sensors. "The nagas and Garuda were actually cousins, or even half-siblings depending on what version you read. It's a rather long work, so I'm summarizing here, of course.

"You Jade Falcons clearly fancy yourselves as Garuda, the king of birds." Vikram leaned in. His smile faded slightly, and his voice took on a hard edge. "If that's true, then I wonder...who will be your nagas?"

The doctor paused, staring silently at Ean. After a moment, his beaming smile returned. "Well, I do have other patients to attend to, and you're not going anywhere. Perhaps tomorrow we'll start at the beginning. After all, if you fancy yourself an heir to a bird, then this is your story too."

Days passed, and by degrees, Ean found himself less inclined to do harm to the rotund, talkative doctor. Each afternoon, Vikram made his rounds through the critical care ward, and each afternoon he would stop for a few minutes and—without invitation—continue the story of Garuda.

Perhaps it was the monotony of bed-bound life, or perhaps it was the high-grade painkillers, but Ean began to anticipate Vikram's visits. And, even more surprisingly, he began to lose himself in the tale of the conqueror bird. Vikram did not exaggerate—the epic poem was one of the longest in human history, approaching nearly two million words. With liberal summary and paraphrasing, Ean eventually learned the outlines of the story.

Garuda's mother, Vinata, lost a bet and became enslaved to her sister, Kadru, who was mother of the naga. Seeking his mother's freedom, Garuda asked the naga what they wanted in exchange for her release. The naga gave Garuda a significant challenge, demanding that he steal the elixir of immortality from the gods themselves. The elixir was carefully protected; it was ringed by an enormous fire, blocked by a device of razor-sharp rotating blades, and guarded by two gigantic snakes.

Resolving to free his mother at any cost, Garuda flew to the home of the gods. He smashed through the pantheon, dispersing their mighty host. He took water from the world's rivers into his mouth, dousing their ring of fire. The great bird cannily shrank himself to a small size and clambered past the blades of their hideous machine. Finally, he confronted the serpent guards and destroyed them. Taking the elixir, Garuda's honor and love for his mother would not allow him to claim the gift of immortality for himself. Instead, he would uphold his side of the deal, and flew back to the naga, intending to deliver the elixir to them in exchange for Vinata.

Ean saw parallels between Garuda's portion of the Mahabharata and his Clan's own glorious quest. Like Garuda and the naga, the Clans shared a common origin in the Inner Sphere. Garuda's mother was held hostage, and so too was his Clan's "mother"—the Inner Sphere—held hostage by the barbarian snakes of the House Lords.

As Garuda overcame the will of the gods themselves, so would the Jade Falcons liberate their mother in a glorious campaign.

Eager to hear how Garuda's exchange with the naga played out, Ean was disappointed when, one afternoon several weeks after they first met, Vikram did not visit. Nor did he appear the next day, or the next. Having regained a measure of mobility in a wheelchair, Ean finally cornered a passing Star Captain in the hospital's administrative wing.

"Star Captain, there was a doctor, Vikram, who treated me when I first arrived. He has...additional intelligence I wish to acquire. Have you seen him?"

The Star Captain scowled and produced a noteputer from his pocket. "Many personnel were transferred three days ago to an understaffed hospital elsewhere on the continent to meet the needs of our Clan. The man seems to have been among them. You say he has important information? I will pass along your request for additional questioning, and others will see that it is acquired."

Before Ean could object, the Star Captain paused, then tapped a new series of commands to access the aerospace pilot's codex. "Pilot Ean. You were among the few pilots defeated in the battle for this planet." The man glanced down at the wheelchair-bound warrior and scowled again. "I suggest you focus on your recovery, and the training needed to reclaim your place in the *touman*." He repocketed the noteputer and continued down the hallway.

Ean knew the senior officer was right; his sole concern should be finding his way back to the skies, not whiling away hours with ancient stories. But even without Vikram, he had to learn the conclusion to Garuda's quest. Perhaps it would help motivate his recovery and future performance as a Jade Falcon warrior—if so, the tale could have some value to the Clan, *quiaff*?

Long minutes passed as Ean remained in the hallway, wrestling with the question. Finally, taking one of the wheelchair's grips in hand, he spun around to consult a nearby directory, then wheeled himself toward the hospital's library terminals.

SMOKE JAGUAR BIVOUAC
SHIKARI JUNGLE, HUNTRESS
KERENSKY CLUSTER
CLAN SPACE
12 MARCH 3060

Ean jerked awake, his head and neck straining high off the crude gurney on which he lay. A moment later, it occurred to him that the rest of his body did not seem to heed his commands. He strained again to sit up, with no better results. He could barely see, the world smearing into a series of light and dark shades.

"Point Commander, please." The voice of a medtech cut through Ean's momentary, unClanlike panic. Ean took a deep breath—disconcertingly, he could only tell he took the breath by the raspy sound of his mouth, not the rise and fall of his chest. He heard the man tapping on a noteputer. The air around him felt hot and sticky. A jungle, most likely. Why not Pahn City?

"Where...where...?"

"We are in the Shikari Jungle, east of Pahn City, Point Commander. Our remaining force repositioned here under Galaxy Commander Howell's orders after the Pahn City factory complex fell."

Ean's mind spun. They had lost the factory to the Spheroid mercenary scum. Selfishly, his thoughts turned back to his own condition.

"Why...cannot..." He attempted to sit up once more, and once more failed.

"You were gravely injured in the battle four days ago, Point Commander. An Inner Sphere 'Mech engaged a *Warhammer* near you and destroyed its PPC a moment after you leaped from it. The damaged capacitors of the weapon discharged directly onto your ProtoMech.

"MechWarrior Rohan marked the position where you fell. We recovered you and your machine in our withdrawal, but the rest of Ocelot Star was killed or captured. I am sorry to say it, but you are the last ProtoMech pilot among the forces here with us."

The medtech paused briefly, the eternal sign of preparation to deliver difficult news. *It is bad*, thought Ean. "We have kept you sedated because you suffered severe electrical burns across much of your body, exacerbated by your EI implants—they carried the current farther than it might have otherwise gone, and sections of your implants fused and melted. Bringing you fully out of sedation would kill you. Your eyesight was severely damaged, likely permanently, and, with the damage to your nervous system... you will not walk again."

Ean shut his eyes. Like any warrior, he often wondered how he would meet his end. Begging for a mercy killing while strapped to a medical gurney was not among his preferences.

After a moment, the medtech spoke again.

"I am telling you this because your...unusual...abilities provide an opportunity," he said. "Galaxy Commander Howell has given standing orders that any remaining warriors should be returned to duty regardless of their condition. A new raid on the Pahn City factory is being organized. With several hours' work, our technicians believe we can reroute around your damaged implants and create a stable interface with your *Roc*.

"It will only last for a short time, and you will not exit your ProtoMech alive. However, the unique neural interface should block out most of the pain, and the machine's sensors already replace most of your impaired senses. You will have the chance for a warrior's death, if you want it."

New hope for a less bitter end bloomed in Ean's chest. "*Aff.*"

"As you wish. You should know that while you will be combat-effective, the interface process will almost certainly wreak significant psychological effects. You may not be fully...you...when you awake."

Ean turned toward the sound of the medtech's voice and nodded. It did not matter. He would take the field one last time. He would have a chance to steal immortality from the clutches of a meaningless death.

He would face the naga once again.

PAHN CITY FACTORY COMPLEX
HUNTRESS
KERENSKY CLUSTER
CLAN SPACE
15 MARCH 3060

Garuda exulted in his rebirth, rearing back to stretch his new metallic limbs before racing forward and, in a great bound, leaping skyward. Some of the other mottled-gray creatures around him were larger, but none were mightier. He was Garuda, the great roc, reborn now in new form. The small seed of flesh he bore inside his chest no longer mattered—it was a pale husk, the shattered egg left behind in the nest. Garuda soared.

Nothing mattered now but claiming the gift of immortality, and freeing his mother from the serpents. Flashes of a strange icon superimposed themselves over the battlefield, a snake coiled around a many-edged star. The symbol of the naga. Were the naga guarding immortality? Or was he retrieving the power of the gods for them? The side effects of his rebirth muddled things, but it did not truly matter. The large, crescent-headed naga bearing the snake-star blocked his holy path.

He was Garuda. This was the battlefield of the heavens. His duty now was to seize immortality.

There! Clambering through the entryway to a series of massive buildings and warehouses was the naga, standing with two of its kind in a vain attempt to defend the large building. Garuda knew his lesser comrades had intended to draw off the others, and their plan appeared to have succeeded.

Finishing his previous leap, he rolled, took a few steps, and launched forward again in a line toward the larger, clumsier machine. As he closed in, a few ruby-red beams issued from his foe—clearly, he was not the only one who had been reborn in a metal body.

Finding in his hands a weapon of his own, Garuda triggered it twice in succession, melting hot slashes across the naga's breast and ankle. Not the same as rending a foe with beak and talon, but effective. The naga turned to him and again sent bright lances of energy toward him, but Garuda flew far too fast for them to connect.

Sidestepping lightly off his left foot, Garuda paused and drew a bead on the naga's injured ankle, boring deeper into the weakened joint. The naga now appeared hobbled, stumbling significantly as it turned toward him. Standing his ground against the behemoth, Garuda paused, took careful aim, and sent a lash of energy against the naga's crowned head. The giant recoiled as if struck, and droplets of superheated metal cascaded from its face, but it did not fall. Instead, it lurched forward toward Garuda. He was clearly the sole focus of its attention now.

Just as he had planned.

Racing under the serpent's feet, the mighty bird darted down a passageway between two of the enormous factory complexes. Not daring to turn around, he felt the thumping of the monster's feet keeping pace behind him, and grinned slyly. In these close confines, he could choose his attacks and keep the naga off balance. In here, he had a chance.

As if in answer, a rush of heat flared too close behind him, reminding the reborn warrior that his opponent was still lethal. He turned a corner but heard a rush of thrust from the alley he had just departed. A moment later, the ground rumbled directly behind him. The naga had somehow leaped into the sky itself and vaulted the far corner of the intersection to land in line with Garuda. Only an instinctual jump aloft saved his life—a bright laser beam attempted to track his flight, but instead carved into a nearby building. As he descended, the beam cut off, leaving a red-hot trail up the side of the structure. After a moment of silence, a soft *ker-whump* emanated from inside the building, followed by a terrific explosion. Two enormous jets of magma sprayed from the structural wound, perfectly bracketing Garuda.

—a ring of fire, filling the sky!

The tiny, fading voice in Garuda's breast called out in recognition. But the great bird had no time for such imaginings. As sheets of red-hot slag poured down on either side of him, the king of birds found salvation.

Mounted halfway up wall of the building in front of him was a large, ovular containment cistern used for collecting rainwater driven to the facility by the jungle's weather patterns. Garuda sprang into the air and latched onto a service rung near the tank's valve ring. One hand fused to his weapon and the other needed to hold onto the rung, only one option remained. Garuda wedged his mighty beak around the ring, gaining leverage and viciously thrashing against the metal. With a groaning creak, the metal slowly parted. Garuda jammed his beak farther into the breach, rending and tearing. Far below him, the two waves of bubbling slag had met and turned the ground beneath his dangling feet into a superheated cauldron.

A final *crack* sounded, and then the rush of water nearly swept him from his perch. When the tank gave way, the weight of the water rapidly widened the crack until the tank's entire contents became a waterfall pouring directly into the magma pool. Plumes of boiling vapor screamed upward as the water rapidly cooled and hardened the slag. After a moment, Garuda released his grip and glided back to the ground.

From the other side of the intersection, the naga paused, as if considering what it had just witnessed. The momentary respite was shattered by a fusillade of lasers from the serpent. Garuda bounded away once more—but not quite quickly enough. A smaller column of light caught his foot, sending a lance of white-hot agony up the great bird's leg. Landing in a heap, Garuda barely managed to regain his feet and hobble down the street toward another flat-roofed facility. Bursting through a door meant for a much smaller figure, next to a gigantic retractable entryway, Garuda tried to catch his breath.

A *whoosh* from down the street signaled another leap by the titanic serpent. It landed just outside and, without a moment's hesitation, crashed through the large metal door.

Garuda scrabbled forward, trying to gain traction on the smooth floor. Taking stock of his surroundings, he saw the building was stuffed to overflowing with long, wide belts, piles of raw materials, tools and machines of every height, and multi-limbed columns on which were poised razor-sharp cutting implements.

—the many bladed device! The tiny flesh voice again cried out its half-remembered dream.

In such an environment, Garuda knew his smaller stature would offer a significant advantage. He darted into the thickest knot of machines, weaving his way deeper into the metallic wilds of the strange room.

Behind him, the naga blundered through the machinery, unleashing an occasional blast as if to announce his frustration with the fruitless hunt for his quarry. The bird-king dared not leap again and risk surrendering his location. The great snake continued tearing randomly across the floor, while Garuda reached a broad, yellow-line lane between the bank of machines he occupied near the building's side wall and another section a short distance away. His position was secure for the moment, but the time to mount an attack approached.

As always, the sky provided the answer.

Above Garuda, hasty repairs had reinforced a partially collapsed portion of the ceiling, but daylight shone through in several places, and the makeshift patches shifted and groaned thanks to the damage wrought by the naga's entry. A bold plan formed.

Garuda fired his laser randomly into the air. The crashing footfalls of the naga ceased instantly, then picked up in intensity as the titan sprinted toward him. As the dark pool of the snake's shadow fell on him, Garuda launched into the air on an arc across the wide lane toward the new bank of machines. He fired his weapon with devastating effect on the patched portions of roof, and boulder-sized chunks of metal and stone rained down on the naga, partially obscuring it in a cloud of dust.

Garuda's leap carried halfway across the broad passage when the stricken naga, half-blind, lashed out with a foot. The kick might have staved in his chest, but instead only clipped his torso, flicking him through the air. The world inverted, righted, then inverted again. An instant of solid resistance crashed a wave of pain across his back, until it gave way, and Garuda completed his trip through the nearby wall by landing in a crumpled heap back outside.

Struggling to his knees, the warrior saw he was in a broad park plaza at the heart of the facility. He backed away from the shattered wall and farther into the park. A heartbeat later, and the naga's lasers cored through the same wall. The beast followed, tearing apart the thin sheeting with a giant metallic hand. The horrible weight of the roof section had mauled the head and shoulders of the serpent, and a large beam stuck through its left shoulder. But the metal snake strode onward.

The plaza was wide open. No cover, no hope for escape. The last moments of his quest had finally arrived, and Garuda's chest heaved with pain and expectation in equal measure. Face to face with the great serpent, he knew immortality waited beyond.

He leaped in a one more mighty arc, clawing up through the sky toward the star-snake's head. Straining against gravity, he flew, truly flew again, if only for a brief moment.

As he screamed toward the serpent, it leveled its large-bore laser to meet him, the point glowing with an imminent release of energy.

Earthbound no longer, Ean soared.

UNDERFOOT
ROBERT JESCHONEK

ARD RI MOUNTAINS
NEWTOWN SQUARE
FEDERATED COMMONWEALTH
23 APRIL 3063

The battlefield was calm and dead. The wreckage of lifeless and devastated 'Mechs lay inert in the mud. The skirmish that had happened there could have just as easily happened days earlier instead of a half-hour ago.

Anaya Okeke, war correspondent, stood on the far fringe of the field, straightening her black pantsuit. Looking around, she saw a scavenger picking through debris some meters away, and a doctor working on a wounded survivor. It was just another day on the Federated Commonwealth world of Newtown Square in the heat of the FedCom Civil War.

Anaya pressed a green stud on the remote control gauntlet strapped to her dark brown forearm, and one of her two airborne drones snapped a burst of photos of the scene with its onboard camera.

Same old, same old. More wreckage, more bodies, more mud. Time to deliver another recap of another battle over another plot of so-called strategic territory. She'd been doing it for so long, she could hardly stop herself from rolling her eyes on camera...but that's what it took to get the story sometimes.

Though there wasn't much of a story here yet. The two sides had been pounding each other for days, Victor Steiner-Davion's Thirty-ninth Avalon Hussars of the Federated Commonwealth fighting to take Newtown Square from the Fourteenth Donegal Guards holding the planet for his sister Katrina's Lyran Alliance. In all that time, neither side had held a decisive edge for long. The fighting just kept going for what was starting to feel like forever.

Meaning Anaya's coverage had long ago passed the point of turning stale. In fact, the wire service she worked for hadn't picked up a post from her in twelve days. If she went one more day without making the feed, she would have to admit defeat and go elsewhere...in this case, home.

Because, against her will, Newtown Square had become the last assignment of her career. After twenty years in the field, the wire service had decided not to renew her contract. A younger face was needed, and that was the one thing Anaya, forty-two, couldn't provide, as much as she wanted to. As much as she couldn't bear the thought of never again doing what she loved most—reporting for the top news organization in the Inner Sphere.

But the one thing she *could* still provide was a powerful story, a high note to go out on...*if* the raw material for one would present itself.

Just as that thought crossed her mind, she felt the ground tremble underfoot. Eyes wide, she froze, instantly understanding what the trembling foretold. Something big was coming her way.

'Mechs were approaching.

When the ground started to shake, Barr Benfico was working over a slab of cherry-red armor. There was gold in that armor, so to speak—or *on it,* rather. Collectors of 'Mech memorabilia would pay good money for pieces of plating adorned with squad insignia. This one—a firebreathing 'Mech head with black, bat-like wings on either side—was one he'd been hunting for since the start of the action on Newtown Square. It was worth a lot...and there were more than enough people around to make the risk he was taking to get it worthwhile.

That was how Barr made most of his money these days. Scavenging parts and selling them on the black market was one thing, but the market for 'Mech memorabilia, hot off the battleground, was ridiculously good.

Barr grinned from his dirt-and grease-smudged face as his laser cutter sliced free one side of the hunk of painted metal. Armor was tougher these days, but he still knew just how and where to cut it loose. He understood the properties of 'Mechs as well as he had ten years ago, when he'd gotten to know them inside-out.

Back when he'd kept 'Mechs running as a top-flight field engineer instead of scavenging memorabilia on a battlefield.

Before Barr could finish cutting away the insignia, however, the ground trembled. Immediately, he stopped working and got to his feet. He knew what that rumbling meant, and it wasn't anything good.

Cursing, he shoved the cutter into his backpack. As the rumbling intensified, he heard loud clanking and crashing noises in the distance—but not for long. Those noises, and the 'Mechs that made them, were quickly coming closer.

He'd been in this situation before, and he knew how ugly it could get. Though the initial battle was over, a secondary action had pushed back in this direction. The 'Mechs and pilots who'd survived the first skirmish were bringing the fight back to the same battered ground.

And Barr was caught in their path.

The best Anaya could do was take cover behind a fallen blue 'Mech on the far edge of the field. Just as she threw herself down behind its huge body, the approaching 'Mechs lumbered up from the south, appearing from between two dusty brown hills.

A gray-skinned *JagerMech III*—one of Victor's war machines—was first to enter the field, charging through the wreckage from the first fight on the run. Suddenly, it stopped and spun around, blasting away with its Gauss rifle.

A heavy slug from the rifle slammed into the *Hauptmann* pursuing it. The *Hauptmann*, fighting for Katrina, fired back with its own Gauss rifle, which tore a hole through the *JagerMech*'s steely hide.

As the shock of renewed battle wore off, Anaya started thinking like a newswoman again. Playing the buttons on her control gauntlet, she took her drones off standby mode and pulled them back into action, having them sweep around the perimeter at a respectable distance...far enough away, she hoped, that they wouldn't be mistaken for enemy weapons and shot down.

Anaya brought up two views on the tinted visor in her flak helmet—one from each of the drones. As the little 'copters swooped around the battlefield, flying on autopilot, they beamed back continuous video of the struggle in progress.

The *Hauptmann* lashed out with two of its extended-range medium lasers, slashing the *JagerMech*'s left side, Anaya felt the ground tremble from another direction—east. Peering around the downed blue 'Mech, she saw a silver *Barghest* burst out of a towering treeline with an *Enforcer III* hot on its heels.

Anaya dropped back down and frowned. Her best routes off the battlefield were blocked. She'd wanted something interesting to happen; now she was stuck in the heart of it.

The ground shook from the footfalls of the Davion *Enforcer* as it hounded the Steiner *Barghest* with its Blazefire extended-range laser blazing. The *Barghest* spun and got off a volley from its LB 20-X autocannon, though no direct hits impacted the *Enforcer.*

Breathing in the acrid, smoke-filled air, Anaya watched the video feeds from her drones with heart pounding. If the action continued to heat up, losing her job might soon be the least of her worries.

Just then, a surprising new player dropped into the frame, and things suddenly got infinitely more interesting.

A green-skinned 'Mech came in so fast, propelled by the flaming jump jets in its feet, that Anaya caught her breath.

"*Now* we're talking." Anaya's fingers danced over her gauntlet. "Maybe I can finally get some viral *vid* out of this bore-fest." The gauntlet signals sent both drones to capture whatever the newly arrived *Grasshopper* 'Mech did next.

After all, it wasn't every day that a *celebrity* landed in the picture.

Barr was darting from one heap of wreckage to another when the new 'Mech leaped into the fight from above. It was the mere *sight* of that 'Mech, a *Grasshopper*, that made him stop in his tracks. He knew the demand was higher for its insignia—the flaming locusts on either side of its chest—than for any 'Mech on Newtown Square.

Because if the rumors were true, it had gone rogue. It was picking its battles without regard for command or faction, interceding wherever it chose and switching sides without apparent rhyme or reason.

Not that any of that was the most interesting thing about the *Grasshopper* to Barr. What fascinated him the most was the 'Mech's *history*.

The one he shared with it and would never forget.

Huddled by some boulders at the perimeter of the battlefield, Dr. Dmitri Popov tended a dying female pilot whom he'd found on the ground next to an ejected command couch after the first action at the site.

"H-hey...look at that." The dying woman's shaky hand fluttered in the general direction of the *Grasshopper*. "Big bug s-saved my life once...at the b-battle of Kathil."

Dmitri smiled as he injected more painkiller into the woman's arm. She didn't have a chance of surviving; most of her lower body was gone. All he could do was make her comfortable until the end.

"It's the same 'Mech, huh?" Dmitri withdrew the syringe from the woman's arm. "You're sure of that?"

The woman didn't answer. Her eyes flickered shut, and her head rolled sideways in the mud.

Dmitri felt for a pulse and barely found one. It was only then that he tipped back his helmet's visor and cast his eyes up for a glimpse of the *Grasshopper* midway across the suddenly reactivated battlefield.

Just as he did, the smoke parted, and a red sunbeam stroked the *Grasshopper*'s bright green skin. This, then, was the god of Dmitri's new life. Without it and its brethren, he might never have come to this little factory world of Newtown Square. The group he belonged to—Doctors Under Fire—might never have sent him there to do the good work of saving lives and relieving suffering in the war zone.

And he might not have had to bear witness to such atrocities that he was rethinking not only his mission, but his calling as a physician.

"D-doctor...?" Just as the *Grasshopper* opened fire on the *Enforcer* that had been harrying the *Barghest,* the dying woman opened her eyes and looked up from the mud. "Do you think I'll ever...p-pilot again?" The telltale electrodes of a 'Mech neurohelmet were stuck to her forehead.

Dmitri smiled, even as his heart broke for her. "Is that what you want?"

She nodded. "It's all I've *ever* wanted."

"Why?" Dmitri met her gaze.

The woman beamed. "The r-rush...is indescribable. And f-fighting for something you b-believe in..." Her eyes closed as her heart beat its last. "There's nothing like it," she said, and then she died.

Determined to make the most of the dangerous situation, Anaya stared resolutely into the mini-camera resting in the palm of her hand. "The rogue *Grasshopper* has arrived," she said for the benefit of the microphone mounted in the camera. "Reports from other battles indicate that this 'Mech has taken up arms against both sides in the conflict. Those reports, I can now see, are accurate."

Pausing the recording, she watched the drone feeds in her helmet. Sure enough, the *Grasshopper* was fighting both the Davion and Steiner forces.

As she watched, the great green 'Mech blasted away with its torso-mounted large laser at the *Hauptmann*, scorching its legs and sending it staggering backward. Seconds later, the *Grasshopper* leaped up and came back down behind the *Enforcer*, pounding it with the medium lasers in each arm, knocking it down.

It was a sight to behold, and a real mystery. No one knew why the pilot of the *Grasshopper* had gone to war against both sides. Was he or she trying to stop the war, prove a point...or was madness at the root of the rogue action?

No one was even really sure of how the *Grasshopper* had gotten involved in the fight on Newtown Square in the first place. Searching its registration revealed that it had disappeared months ago, dropping off the radar after serving with Victor's forces. According to rumor, the 'Mech had served Task Force Serpent alongside Victor Steiner-Davion himself, which meant they'd fought the Clans in their own backyard. Sensational as that story sounded, not even Anaya could believe it without substantial proof.

Everyone wanted to know the rogue's story. If Anaya could somehow deliver it, she might be able to save her job.

Swallowing hard, she got to her feet and moved in closer from the edge of the battlefield.

As Barr watched, the four medium lasers in the *Grasshopper*'s arms and on either side of its torso hacked into the *Barghest*'s chest and blew its power plant, causing a blast that shook the battlefield like an earthquake.

As the debris from the shattered *Barghest* streaked across the field, the *JagerMech* surged up from the *Grasshopper*'s right flank, cutting loose with its two PPCs. The *Grasshopper* answered that fire by leaping over it. Landing twenty meters away, the *Grasshopper* unleashed a missile salvo from its LRM 5 launcher, toppling the *JagerMech* with a precise hit to its left knee. The *Grasshopper* followed that with a series of hits from its medium lasers that separated the *JagerMech*'s left leg from its body, leaving it crippled.

The *Grasshopper* was now the last 'Mech standing, though only the *Barghest* and *JagerMech* were permanently out of action.

The sight struck a chord in Barr, as he remembered past battles on other worlds. He remembered working as the chief mechanic on that very *Grasshopper*, which he recognized from various markings and customizations that had been the work of his own hands. In the old days, he'd watched as it conquered one enemy after another—at least until the accident that had laid it low. The accident that Barr himself had been blamed for...and rightly so.

After all, he was the one who'd missed the faulty seal in the *Grasshopper*'s left-leg hydraulics, the one that had failed and crippled it in the middle of a blistering firefight. The *Grasshopper* had gone down hard, leaving a gaping hole in the front line and turning the tide in the enemy's favor. Good men and women in other 'Mechs had died that day as a result...and all of it had been laid at his feet when the after-action investigation had turned up the failed seal.

It was the reason Barr had been cashiered out of the service, the moment that had led him to his lowly life of scavenging. Now, suddenly, past met present, as the unexpected happened. As another accident took its toll on the *Grasshopper*, right before Barr's unbelieving eyes.

Anaya was in the middle of shooting a stand-up (though maybe "crouch-down" would have been more fitting, as she kept her head low in the heat of battle) when the *Grasshopper*'s luck ran out.

"So you see," she was saying for the benefit of the camera in her hand. "This rogue BattleMech has again proved to be the wild card in the conflict on Newtown Square. Seemingly without loyalty or sympathy to any side or cause, the *Grasshopper* has defeated all comers, regardless of affiliation or—"

It was then, with a resonating *crack*, that the ground under the *Grasshopper*'s feet gave way. The big green 'Mech dropped through the surface up to its ankles.

Anaya continued the stand-up. "I may have spoken too soon. It appears the ground under the rogue 'Mech has been subsumed. Is some tunneling 'Mech at work, attacking from below? Or is this another of the sinkholes that are all too common on Newtown Square, the result of the many hydraulic fracturing wells used to mine fuel for this planet's factories?

"Whatever the cause, how deep will the rogue go?"

Anaya punched buttons on her gauntlet, zooming in the view from the drones on her helmet visor. She couldn't see any sign of pilot-controlled movement from the *Grasshopper.*

Then, suddenly, the *Grasshopper* shifted. Its left side lurched downward.

The drones scattered and regrouped, beaming back a less hopeful image. The *Grasshopper* was canted left, sunk up to its left knee and then some. At least the fighting was done for the moment, as the trapped 'Mech and its pilot were sitting ducks.

Heart hammering, Anaya ran toward the sinkhole. She didn't know if she could do anything to help anyone, but she knew she had to get over there. Others—the scavenger and the doctor—were running in the same direction.

Barr scowled as he raced toward the *Grasshopper.* From what he could see, the 'Mech's situation was quickly going from worse to *much* worse.

Not only was the *Grasshopper* caught in a sinkhole, but its pilot wasn't doing anything to free it. Either the 'Mech had gone offline, or the *pilot* had.

And it looked like the one person in the best position to do something about it was a washed-up 'Mech scavenger who'd been stupid enough to get caught in the middle of a firefight.

Stopping thirty meters from the trapped *Grasshopper,* he gazed up at it, considering options. As he stood there, the crimson-uniformed doctor he'd seen on the field earlier ran up and stood beside him.

"You think the pilot's dead?" asked the doctor. Barr glanced sideways at him and didn't answer.

"I'm a *doctor*. Dmitri Popov." The man's face and hands were streaked with blood. "I'm with Doctors Under Fire. My only concern is the pilot in that machine over there. Do you think he is dead?"

"Or unconscious." Barr snorted and returned his gaze to the 'Mech. "Don't know why the damn thing wouldn't blow outta there on its jump jets otherwise."

Dmitri took a step toward the *Grasshopper*. "Someone needs to go up there and find out. Render assistance if needed."

"Be my guest," said Barr.

Dmitri looked back at him. "I don't have the gear or the expertise."

Barr shook his head as the *Grasshopper* kept sinking. He knew where this was headed.

"That's what I call a dead man's detail," said Barr. "Just as likely to fall or get shot off that thing when the other 'Mechs recover as make it to the cockpit."

Just then, a woman wearing a reporter's feed helmet ran over and interrupted. "Anaya Okeke for the Interstellar Wire Service! I'll get you on *all* the feeds for rescuing the pilot of that rogue 'Mech!"

"Not interested." Barr saw what looked from a distance like flickers of flame around the *Grasshopper*'s head, where the cockpit was located.

So now the question was, would the 'Mech burn and blow, or fall deeper underground first?

"What's your name?" asked Anaya. "Doesn't matter," said Barr.

"At least tell me your name!" said Anaya.

"Barr," he said simply, his mind elsewhere—up in that cockpit. What if the pilot *wasn't* dead already?

"What do you say?" Anaya touched controls on her gauntlet, and two drones zipped overhead. "You're on camera, see?"

Barr ignored her...even as he made a decision about what to do next. He couldn't stand by and let the pilot perish. Or the *Grasshopper*, for that matter.

"Stay outta my way." Barr reached into his backpack for his grappling gun. "There's something I've gotta do."

Marching toward the *Grasshopper*, Barr gripped his grappling gun with a coil of line attached. He'd used it plenty of times to climb downed 'Mechs in search of treasures—just never when they were still live.

Ten meters out, Barr aimed the grappler up at the base of the *Grasshopper*'s neck. He fit his finger against the trigger, steadied himself, then squeezed the trigger.

He was ready for the recoil as the gun kicked hard against his right shoulder. There was a blast of compressed air, and the metal grappler leaped upward, right on course. It reached the neck of the *Grasshopper* and struck metal with a clang. Two of its four prongs caught the upraised edge of an armor plate.

Barr tugged hard on the line with his gloved hands, further securing the prongs of the grappling hook. Then, he walked forward to the edge of the sinkhole.

We meet again. Gazing up at the *Grasshopper* from so close, he was struck by how beautiful a machine it was. Flashes of memories and dreams flickered through his mind, reminding him of the attachment he'd always felt for it.

Then the 'Mech shifted again, snapping him back to the present. He tested the line once more, then put all his weight on it and jumped off the sinkhole's edge.

Hoping the 'Mech didn't shift much more, he swung over the gap and landed with his boots against the plating above the left knee. Determined not to waste time, he immediately started climbing, pulling himself glove over glove as he walked up the familiar green armor.

He breathed evenly, trying not to think about how much more precarious his position became the higher he ascended. If the 'Mech shifted suddenly, it might shake him loose. If it made a sudden drop, it might drag him underground along with it.

Then there were the other three 'Mechs on the field below. If any of them recovered enough to get off a shot, it might incinerate him or blow him clean off the *Grasshopper*'s skin.

Blinking sweat out of his eyes, he kept climbing...then stopped when the *Grasshopper* trembled. He held his breath and heard his heart pounding in his ears. Was the 'Mech about to plunge underground?

The trembling didn't stop, but the *Grasshopper* didn't make another violent lurch. Barr decided he should keep moving in case it did, to beat the next one.

The thought of it made him climb a little faster.

When Barr got to the top of the chest, the *Grasshopper* shuddered again, more roughly than before. Again, he froze and held on tight... and the 'Mech eventually stilled.

Waiting for aftershocks, he looked up toward the *Grasshopper*'s head. Low flames danced around the base of the head, and wispy black smoke swirled from vents in the neck.

When Barr was relatively sure no aftershocks were coming, he resumed climbing, hand over hand, toward the head and the cockpit inside. When he got there, hoisting himself up onto a ledge on the *Grasshopper*'s shoulder, Anaya sent the drones up to hover nearby.

"Don't mind me," she said through the drone's onboard speaker. "Just recording this for posterity."

Barr ignored her. Taking a deep breath, he inched toward the cockpit hatch on the side of the 'Mech's head.

Perched on the *Grasshopper*'s shoulder, he studied the keypad mounted on the frame of the hatch. Had they changed the cockpit passcode in the years since he'd last entered it?

Maybe, but he doubted the override code he'd set up had been altered. Taking care to stand to one side in case fire blasted out when the hatch popped, he typed in the numerical sequence. He knew it by heart, without a doubt; after all, that 'Mech had been his baby back in the day.

He recited the numbers as he typed them. "Seven, seven, three, four, one, zero, niner."

The hatch hissed open on the first try. Luckily, no flames burst out when it did.

There was smoke, though...but not a lot of it. It swirled out and cleared quickly, revealing the inside of the cockpit for Barr and the drones' cameras to see.

The occupant—a young woman with bright red hair and a faceful of freckles—was unconscious, head tipped back under the neurohelmet, mouth hanging open.

Just then, Dmitri's voice spoke up from one of the drones. He must have been watching the video feed with Anaya. "Is there a pulse?"

Barr stepped through the hatchway. Reaching out, he pressed his fingers against the side of the pilot's throat. "Not much of one."

"You need to restart her heart," said Dmitri. "Is there a first-aid kit? White box with a red cross on the lid?"

"I know what a first-aid kit looks like, and I know where it is." Reaching into his backpack, Barr pulled out a silver fire-suppression wand, eight centimeters long. It had come in handy many times before in the field, when his salvage or something near it had caught fire unexpectedly.

He pointed the wand at the back wall behind the pilot's couch. Flames were visible, licking from a control panel set into the wall at waist level.

Barr activated the wand, and pink chemical foam shot from its tip, smothering the flames. As soon as they were all the way out, he pushed closer and grabbed a charred, white first-aid kit that had fallen on the floor.

"Look for a red syringe labeled 'Hot Shot,'" said Dmitri.

"I *know* what a Hot Shot is." Barr opened the kit and reached in. "Got it."

"Remove the plastic cap from the needle," said Dmitri. "Then drive the needle into her heart and squeeze the plunger. And do it quickly! The compound in that syringe can restart her heart, but not if it's been stopped too long."

Barr snorted. "Like I haven't done this before."

"Hurry!" shouted Dmitri. "You might be too late already!"

Just as Barr was about to administer the Hot Shot, the *Grasshopper* lurched under him. How much longer until the whole 'Mech sank all the way underground?

"What are you waiting for?" howled Dmitri. "Do it!"

Barr hoped the 'Mech would stay still as he raised the syringe over the pilot's heart. Jaws clenched, he steadied his grip—then plunged the needle down into her chest and pushed the plunger. The Hot Shot's contents pumped into the pilot...yet she remained silent and still. Barr pulled out the needle and threw it aside, waiting.

"She's not reviving!" said Dmitri. "I need to get up there!"

"Hold your horses!" snapped Barr. "Give it a minute to kick in."

"She doesn't have a minute!" yelled Dmitri.

Then, suddenly, the pilot gasped. She was alive after all.

Her hand lashed out and seized Barr's arm, tightening like a vise. "Who—?" Her voice a hoarse croak, she locked eyes with him. "What—?"

"Hi." Barr managed a tight smile. "I'm here to help. Nothing to worry about." Just then, the *Grasshopper* shifted violently. "Except for the giant sinkhole, that is."

The pilot's free hand flew over a nearby keyboard, and her eyes focused on the heads-up display of her neurohelmet. A moment later, she cursed and punched the side of her couch. "It's 'giant' all right! And it's about to give way completely!" Releasing Barr's arm, she worked the keys some more, then flipped a switch on one of the joysticks. "I need to fire the jump jets *now*."

"No, wait!" Barr shook his head. "I can't stay."

"Forget it!" The pilot pushed buttons on a panel, and the jump jet engines whined to life, ready for launch. "No time!"

It was tempting to ride off in his beloved *Grasshopper,* but Barr felt like he needed to leave. Though he'd done what he'd come to do, though maybe he'd made up for his mistakes of the past, he still felt like he didn't deserve to be there.

"Gotta go." Leaning out, he saw the grappling line still firmly secured to the armor plating near the neck. He realized he needed to get down that line much faster than he'd come up it...but even his heavy gloves wouldn't protect his hands during a slide.

Ducking back inside, he quickly looked around the cockpit for something to hold on to while sliding down the line. Spotting a length of thick, plastic-clad cable hanging from above, he wrenched it free, drawing sparks, and wrapped one end around his gloved left fist.

"Good luck!" Barr told the pilot, shouting to be heard over the whine of the jump jets. "Whatever reason you have for doing all this, I hope it's worth it!"

"I just want the war off this planet!" The pilot scowled. "They don't *get* to wreck *my* homeworld!"

"You ever need an engineer, look me up!" Barr grinned back at her, then lunged out of the cockpit and slammed the hatch shut.

As the *Grasshopper* shuddered before takeoff, he hurried to the grappling line and dropped down to wedge himself under it. Then he wrapped the length of cable around the line and twisted the ends around his gloved fists. Taking a deep breath, he pushed off into a fast slide, letting the

He heard the jump jets roar to life as he plummeted toward the ground ten meters below.

Barr landed just as the *Grasshopper* bolted from the pit. Dmitri grabbed him the second his feet stumbled into the mud and wrenched him away from the line just in time. It whipped away from them violently as the 'Mech burst skyward.

Everyone watched as the *Grasshopper* leaped free. Just as it escaped, the rim of the pit caved in completely, dumping thousands of tons of dirt and rock into the depths of the hydraulic fracturing well below.

Dmitri grinned and waved as the big 'Mech hurtled into the crimson sunset. Meanwhile, Anaya stood off to the side and did a stand-up for the camera with the *Grasshopper* in flight in the background.

As for Barr, he stood and watched silently, tears rolling down his dirty cheeks. Finally, after all those years, he felt like he had redeemed himself for his mistake. He felt as if he'd made it up to the *Grasshopper* and was ready to move on.

Without a word, he saluted.

Anaya called him and Dmitri over for an interview, but only Dmitri went. Barr was too busy staring at the contrail the *Grasshopper*'s jump jets had left in the sky. His thoughts were elsewhere, remembering years gone by and all the adventures he'd shared with that 'Mech.

"You go give 'em hell, kid," he said softly. "You get the war off this planet of yours."

Barr was so caught up in the moment that he didn't hear the *Enforcer* stir across the battlefield. He didn't hear its extended-range laser powering up or its targeting system blowing out, ruining the shot its pilot had intended for the *Grasshopper*, sending it low and wild instead of high and on-target.

Since Barr didn't hear any of this, he didn't even try to get to cover. The crimson beam from the *Enforcer*'s laser sliced through him, cutting his body in two.

As he fell, he smiled.

Because there it was a moment later, the *Grasshopper,* leaping down onto the battlefield after making a distant landing and leaping back the way it had come, the jump jets in its feet blazing like shooting stars. Lasers flashing, missiles launching, it descended, blowing the hell out of the *Enforcer* to stop it from harming those who'd saved the *Grasshopper* earlier—all but one, who was already beyond saving.

All but Barr himself, the man with the smile, who in the fading light of his mind's eye was climbing the *Grasshopper* all over again, all the way to the top and beyond, long after his heart stopped beating.

HOMECOMING
ALEX FAUTH

BREIN, BRYANT
WORD OF BLAKE PROTECTORATE
2 MARCH 3078

"Uncle Lewis, is it always going to be this windy?"

Lewis Carter looked down at his five-year-old niece and smiled warmly. This wasn't her first Storm season, but certainly the first she would be aware of and remember. Even protected by the combination of geography and the city storm walls, life in inner Brein was still subject to the whims of Bryant's constant storms.

"For a little bit, Anna," he replied. "But then it will be a lot nicer in time for your birthday."

That seemed to bring out a small smile on her otherwise concerned face. "I don't like it when it's windy. Why is it always windy?"

He took a deep breath before continuing, glancing sideways at Sarah as she walked past him in the apartment's small living room. She just shrugged, sending a subtle hint that it was his turn. "Well, Anna, a long time ago—"

"Before Grandpa Charlie was born?" she interrupted.

"Before even then," he replied with a laugh, "there were magic mirrors in the sky that made the winds go away." Right now his niece was probably not ready for the intricacies of terraforming techniques and an in-depth explanation of how storm inhibitors had controlled Bryant's atmosphere, so that would suffice.

"Thanks to them, it was always sunny and always bright and never ever windy."

"What happened to the magic mirrors?" she needled. "I like it when it's sunny."

He could understand how she felt. Even here, in the heart of what was left of human civilization on the world, the effects of the planetary windstorms were still appreciable at best, and devastating at worst. "Well, one day there was a very bad man who—"

A loud beep from the communicator on his hip interrupted Lewis, directing his train of thought away from any talk of bad men and magic mirrors. The look of concern on his sister's face was quickly matched by his as he picked up the device, looking at the simple message on the screen.

Blake's blood. It's happening.

"I need to go," was the best he could manage. He was not trying to be cold or distant, or to give his sister and niece the brushoff. Rather, Lewis was trying to remain calm, given the enormity of what the message had suggested. His face was stoic and impassive, a mirror of the look that his sister quickly shot him.

"How bad?" Sarah whispered as her eyes went back to her confused daughter. "If it's the Capellans..." She let her eyes once more dart to him, if only for a moment, sparing him a clearly fearful glance.

He didn't even want to think about that. Life on Bryant was fragile enough as it was, a tiny population who stayed on a world that had turned so very hostile long ago. And two of those lives seemed suddenly especially vulnerable all of a sudden. "We don't know yet." Lewis quietly replied. "I'll tell you as soon as I can."

He took a deep breath. "This won't be like before, I promise," he offered, trying his best to be reassuring. "The Word have made sure you'll be protected this time." Lewis knew more about the steps the Word had taken to protect Bryant from further harm, but at the moment, much of that was still classified. On the other hand, the presence of a Protectorate Militia Division on world was meant to be a reassurance in and of itself.

It was a far cry from the ad-hoc unit both he and Nicholas had served with following Bryant's independence in the fifties. Professional, regimented, and well-equipped, a visible sign of the Word's commitment to protecting its world and their people. More than the Capellans or the Commonwealth had ever done for them.

That last thought mixed with another nervous glance from Sarah, bringing his eyes back to her daughter. His niece. *Blake's blood, why did it come to this?* The Word of Blake Protectorate was meant to be about protecting those worlds of the former Terran Hegemony that had been ravaged by the Successor States and their greed; plundered, despoiled and left for dead.

In Bryant's case, at least, the world was still clinging to life, but everything about that existence was so precarious. The idea of war returning to the world made him shudder.

But he suppressed it, maintaining an air of outward confidence for her sake.

UNION-CLASS DROPSHIP DCS *BENJAMIN SUNRISE*
INBOUND BRYANT
WORD OF BLAKE PROTECTORATE
12 MARCH 3078

"There is no greater honor than to serve the Dragon."

A series of beeps served as a confirmation to *Tai-i* Shintaro Gustavson that his *Grasshopper* had accepted the security code. Even in what should have been an unquestionably secure locale, the heart of a DropShip in the service of the DCMS, the procedure was still required to activate a BattleMech. As soon as the systems started powering on, through the pre-drop checklist for his *Grasshopper,* sending a quiet prayer of thanks to the Dragon when everything—almost miraculously—turned up green. That was a quiet blessing in and of itself with the ancient machine, one that he often saw as both a gift and a curse.

After the humiliating loss of his near-new *Ninja-To,* Shintaro had been lucky enough to be assigned a new BattleMech from salvage acquired by the Seventeenth. When that 'Mech had turned out to be an elderly *Grasshopper,* one that, despite being reconditioned, was also more akin to a stumbling wreck than a gleaming engine of war, he had been quietly aghast. The whole thing seemed to be barely running, functioning as it was under centuries of rebuilds, jury-rigged repairs, bypasses, and sheer wishful thinking.

And as awkward as it had been, he had quietly accepted the *Grasshopper,* knowing full well that it was still a sign of the Dragon's generosity, a reward for his humble service. Through this gracious gift, he was fortunate enough to continue to carry out the Dragon's will and strike down its enemies.

"Ikazuchi *Ichi,* all systems green," he finally reported over the company's tactical network after the last of the systems had cleared. The rest of Ikazuchi Company replied in kind, confirming that they were ready to do the Dragon's bidding. "*Benjamin Sunrise* control, we are green for drop."

Shintaro gave the briefest of acknowledgements to control, his mind instead settling on what was ahead, and the opportunity that it presented. *Bryant, once a jewel of the Hegemony, now little more than a wasteland,* he told himself, paraphrasing the mission brief. *And yet, the Word is so determined to fight for it.* That thought made him clench his fists, a tremor of anticipation running through him as he was awaiting the confirmation. *I have waited so long for this.*

Six years ago, the Word of Blake had bought their damnable Jihad to his home, attacking Benjamin with unrestrained fury. Their armies had not cared what they had destroyed in order to wrest the planet from the Dragon's secure clutches. Not the so-called artificial suns that helped warm the world and made life viable, which they had wantonly and knowingly destroyed. Not the cities, bustling with the Dragon's dutiful citizens, which had been relentlessly bombarded and burned in the name of their conquest.

Not one woman and her dutiful son, who had the misfortune to be caught in the crossfire, their lives ended by the fanatics' cruel reach.

The light outside the *Grasshopper*'s cockpit turned green, accompanied by the heavy, mechanical grind of the hull doors opening, reverberating throughout the ship. "Ikazuchi *Ichi,* launching," he spoke to command, his voice clear despite the whistling of the outside air, which was steadily turning into a deafening roar. A low-altitude drop like this was risky, but far less so then dealing with the murderous Space Defense Systems that had already wreaked bloody havoc on the Coalition fleet. With a heavy clang of metal feet on the ramp, the huge war machine began to advance towards the door.

And yet, the pilot's mind was elsewhere. For Shintaro, the fall of Benjamin had been a shocking blow. Not for the loss of one of the Dragon's military-district capitals, an act that seemed unthinkable. Not for the stain on the Dragon's honor that came with it, knowing that its arm had failed such a key world. And not for the way the

Word had ravaged and despoiled the world in their savage, brutal conquest. But for those two simple lives, ones taken for no reason.

When the Seventeenth Benjamin had been selected to be a part of Operation SCOUR, the reclaiming of the Protectorate from the Word of Blake, he had been elated. But unlike many of his fellows, this feeling had not come from the honor of the assignment, nor the opportunity to show the Dragon's strength against its greatest foe. Nor was it the chance to avenge the stain on the Dragon's honor that it had suffered at Benjamin and so many other worlds.

But in spite of that, Shintaro had been driven by one thought. His wife and son, taken from him, and the opportunity to seek restitution for their loss. *That starts today. I fight for the honor of the Dragon, yes, but for them as well.*

The *Grasshopper* stepped out of the ship and plummeted into the clouds below.

LUMSDEN, BRYANT
WORD OF BLAKE PROTECTORATE
14 MARCH 3078

"Contact!" Tremayne's voice rang out loud over the tactical network, cutting through the sounds of both the howling winds outside, as well as the thrum of the *Shadow Hawk*'s reactor. "Estimate one dozen BattleMechs, more vees behind them—" The end of the report degenerated into crackling static as enemy jamming tried to shut it down.

"Roger that," Lewis replied as he keyed commands to the rest of his force. "Move out, and try to keep them away from the city walls. There are plenty of people counting on us to keep them safe." His Bryant Protectorate Militia unit had been forward-deployed to the town of Lumsden, which was the nearest community to the invader's landing zone, in the hopes of stopping them dead and driving them from Bryant.

He had quietly prayed that the extensive SDS the Word had set up around Bryant would be enough to deter the invaders. It was a horrible series of ways to die: flash-frozen, sudden explosive decompression, seared and torn apart by weapons fire, and so many other options, ones that normally he wouldn't wish on anyone else. Any yet, at the same time, as horrible as they were, they also seemed infinitely better than the other option.

Despite all their planning, those weapons had ultimately failed. The so-called Coalition's forces had made landfall on Bryant, their troops spreading out to try driving the Word from the planet. In some ways, to Lewis it seemed so unfair. Bryant had already suffered so much: both the traumatic, world-shattering blows laid on it by Amaris and the slow, withering death bought on by the Succession Wars. Only a comparative handful of people still remained on the world, living marginal and fragile lives at the mercy of an environment turned so very hostile.

His *Shadow Hawk* moved forward at a slow, regular pace, keeping formation with the other units around it as it picked its way through the outer city. Like the planetary capital of Brien and so many other of the remaining communities on Bryant, Lumsden was but a tiny shadow of its former self, its small population concentrated in the center of the city. The outer city had been long since abandoned, given over to agriculture and to serve as a buffer against the constant windstorms.

Data from the scouts began to filter back to his unit, new symbols appearing on both the tactical and heads-up display. "Looks like the Seventeenth Benjamin Regulars," Tremayne continued. "Their units—"

His report was cut off by the *whoosh* of missiles and an explosion. *"*Missile fire!" Tremayne called out. "Enemy has opened fire on us!"

"Fall back to our position. Do not engage," Lewis replied, his tone as calm as possible. *Poor kid probably has never faced a live enemy in his life,* he quietly admitted. *I wish he never had to either.* "Don't let them drag you into a fight."

A shaky affirmative suggested that the kid had at least gotten the basic picture.

"Good. Everyone else, get ready. Try to keep them as far from the city walls as possible."

Crunching concrete accompanied the *Shadow Hawk* as it advanced, slowly picking up speed as the rest of the company formed up around it. The tactical display lit up with more and more symbols, angry red points illustrating the approaching Combine force, and the blue of his retreating scouts. To their credit, the members of his company were doing their best to maintain their discipline, resisting the urge to break formation early.

Just as long as we keep it away from the city proper.

Warning alarms began to ring out in the cockpit as more missiles took to the air, sailing towards his position.

You do this for them, for your home. Always remember that.

"Ikazuchi Company, advance!" Shintaro Gustavson shouted over the command channel, his *Grasshopper* pushing forward with the rest of his company. Behind them, tanks rumbled through the long grass; supporting his force, but no less vital to their success. His scouts were already feeding him telemetry data, reporting on the positions of the Word forces around the city and their estimated strength

Despite its nature and history, the *Grasshopper* had served him flawlessly so far. A part of him had been convinced that the ancient BattleMech would contrive to kill him during the drop or quickly succumb to Bryant's hostile environment. Instead, the 'Mech had done neither, continuing instead to function despite its decrepitude.

Behind him, Ikazuchi Company opened fire, streams of long range missiles arcing up and over the *Grasshopper* as they flew towards the Blakist line. Almost immediately, he could see there was something wrong as tight clusters of warheads dispersed and scattered, smoky contrails corkscrewing across the gray skies. While some warheads did make their marks, others scattered across the landscape or disappeared behind this city walls.

"The wind is too high," he reported, only to be cut off by a screeching warning from the *Grasshopper*'s systems. Seconds later, a flight of missiles hammered into the BattleMech's chest, rocking the titanic war machine on its feet, but failing to shift it. "Somebody get me a more accurate reading." The *Grasshopper* stomped forward, powering between the ruins of several long-abandoned and collapsed buildings.

An affirmative from one of the scouts came back to his order, only to be nearly drowned out as the *Grasshopper*'s lasers opened up. Bolts of searing ruby-red energy leaped from the BattleMech's weapons, stabbing at a Protectorate *Lineholder*. Rather than make their mark, however, the beams instead slammed into a nearby section of city wall, cutting through concrete and steel to very little effect.

"We got the course correction," *Chu-i* Yoo-Sool cut into his command channel. "With your permission, *Tai-i*?"

"*Hai*," he confirmed. "Fire at will."

Behind their main advance, the quartet of Schiltron artillery tanks assigned to support the company opened up, their launchers sending deadly payloads skyward. Half of the warheads rained down across the Word force or scattered into the city itself, brilliant blossoms of fire erupting where they fell. The others broke open as they neared their destination, dispersing bomblets across a broad front.

"Continue fire!" Shintaro ordered.

Another flight of missiles erupted from his company as his own *Grasshopper* pushed forward. This time they were tighter and more closely packed, more of the warheads finding their marks on the enemy force. Shintaro followed through with his own assault, lasers again lashing out to savage the flank of the *Lineholder* that had evaded him before.

His BattleMech surged ahead now, breaking into a run before its jump jets fired, lifting the massive machine into the air. As he rose, Shintaro got a better idea of what was going on, seeing the Protectorate Militia forces splayed out in a line before the city's inner wall. Their early attacks had done little damage to their 'Mechs and vehicles thus far, but he could already see where their missiles and artillery had made their marks, both on the combatants and the city around them.

The *Grasshopper* landed to the sound of cracking pavement, already in a run as soon as it was down. He opened fire again, this time letting a quartet of lasers fly. Savage red energies ripped into the *Lineholder*'s body, carving through the armor before greedily devouring chunks of its structure. Wounded, the Word BattleMech staggered, black smoke erupting from the gaping hole in its flank.

"Push forward!" he commanded, his voice dripping with excitement. "We are the might of the Dragon! Our strength is unmatched, our cause is just!"

This was what he had wanted, what he had yearned since that one fateful day. *All you have taken from us, all the suffering you have inflicted upon us. This is where it ends.* Images flashed in his mind again, those two faces that were so dear to him, now lost forever. This was not Terra, nor was he facing those same forces that had defiled his home, but to Shintaro it didn't matter. This was his chance to redeem his honor, and that of the Dragon, and he was not going to let it slip through his clutches.

The intelligence brief on the Seventeenth Benjamin Regulars had mentioned their love of artillery and LRM attacks. From the cockpit of his *Shadow Hawk*, Lewis witnessed the horrible truth of that statement. The first rounds of missile fire had been scattered by the winds, falling lightly across his force, and more worryingly, the city behind him. Subsequent attacks had been more tightly grouped but no less indiscriminate.

"Close ranks!" he ordered over the command channel as his *Shadow Hawk* ran forward, its Ultra-class autocannon belching shells and adding to the noise of its metal footfalls. "Get in close under their LRMs, and try to keep them back from the city walls!"

Shells slammed into a Combine *Wolverine*, stitching a pattern of fire along its shoulder. The BattleMech stepped back, whirling around to spit fire from its large pulse laser. Ruby-red darts splayed across the *Shadow Hawk*'s thigh, doing little more than melt armor. Tremayne's *Nexus* darted forward, the scarecrow-like 'Mech weaving between ruins as it attempted to draw a bead on the *Wolverine*. For a moment, it seemed to have an opening—before the ground around it erupted in a ball of fire and mud that obscured the light 'Mech. Moments later it cleared to reveal the *Nexus* lying on its back, its right leg simply gone below the knee.

"They're using FASCAM mines," Lewis warned as he tried to close on the *Wolverine*, each step much more carefully measured. "Watch where those missiles are coming down." He knew it was a difficult request; in the midst of a heated battle, the last thing his men needed was another thing to watch for. He opened up on the *Wolverine* again, missiles and cannon fire peppering the Combine 'Mech's flank as it tried to find some cover.

Its response was not what he expected. Wheeling around, the *Wolverine* opened fire on the *Nexus* as the slender BattleMech tried to prop itself up. Hungry red-energy darts ate into the crippled 'Mech, erasing its head in an instant, along with the MechWarrior within.

Tremayne.

"Bastards," Lewis spat. He pushed forward to further hound the *Wolverine*, a quiet rage simmering within him over its merciless attack. He pushed forward, advancing on the ragged 'Mech, only to be interrupted by a screeching warning from the *Shadow Hawk*'s sensors. A new icon entered his display, its identity made clear a moment later as a *Grasshopper* stepped forward, laser fire leaping from its weapons.

One of the beams slammed into the *Hawk*'s side, a crackle of static filling Lewis's ears for a moment as the tremendous energies of the assault ate into the BattleMech's systems. In an instant, the anger over Tremayne's death evaporated, replaced with the very real concern for his own life. Not wasting any time, he fired the *Hawk*'s jump jets, eager to get out of the line of fire of the heavier 'Mech. The *Grasshopper* disappeared behind a section of ruined building, obscured from view for the moment.

Sparing a second, he glanced at the tactical display to try and get a better idea of what was going on. The vision was grim, a swarm of angry red icons closing in on his own blue ones, the symbology doing little to hide the clear eagerness the Combine forces were displaying. More missiles and artillery arced overhead, scattering wildly across their lines and the city itself. *We can hold out, but how long can they?* That was his chief concern, the fragile lives of a population that had already suffered enough. *The Snakes aren't going to give them a chance.*

He had no idea how many of their missiles had already fallen on the city. One was too many, especially given how many of them were scattering minefields as they went. *I can't let this go on.* He keyed his mic, speaking over the channel. "This is Captain Carter to all units. Pull away from the city and head due west. Draw as many Snakes with you as you can."

Lewis took the lead, his *Shadow Hawk* breaking into a run as he pushed away from the city, the metal feet pounding into the ancient pavement beneath it. As he ran, he swung around the 'Mech's torso, bringing his weapons to bear on the *Grasshopper* that had hounded him earlier. The roar of the autocannon accompanied the flash of its muzzle as it sent forth a stream of shells, stitching a line across the *Grasshopper*'s chest.

A Blizzard hovercraft dashed past him, adding its own LRMs to the assault on the lead Combine 'Mech. The missiles went wide, its crew more focused on maneuvering than accuracy. Other vehicles followed behind it, their crews doing their best to harry the invading force, keeping them off-balance and provide an opening for slower-moving elements.

"Keep going!" Lewis called out as laser fire leaped back from the *Grasshopper,* one beam digging into the *Shadow Hawk*'s left arm, setting off red warning lights inside the cockpit. "Don't give them a chance to pin you down."

Behind him, a *Bandersnatch* tried to join the retreat, only to be lashed by fire from several Combine 'Mechs. The heavy BattleMech stumbled, putting out one of its arms to stabilize it as it fell. Instead the limb was torn apart as it landed on another mine, sending the *Bandersnatch* crashing down onto its back. A pair of Protectorate 'Mechs immediately behind it stopped their advance, their MechWarriors clearly wary of the mines and enemy fire.

Wounded and with one arm now little more than a twisted stump, the *Bandersnatch* turned to stand. A pair of PPC bolts slammed into it as it did, burrowing into the BattleMech's rear. The wounded war machine staggered again, only to be further pummeled by more fire from the Combine force. Laser and missile fire greedily ripped into it, driving the *Bandersnatch* to the ground. A glance told Lewis it wasn't going to rise again.

Those Protectorate 'Mechs that had been behind it stopped in their tracks, MechWarriors clearly shocked at the sudden destruction of the powerful machine. Lewis could sense it too, and knew the effect such an act could have on their morale. "Keep moving!" he shouted, only to have another flight of scattered missiles punctuate his statement. Some of them slammed down around a *Crab,* scoring hits against its curved shell while others plowed into the ground.

It was those latter ones that probably frightened them more, the fear of being caught among the mines doing more than the actual damage. The *Crab* turned back, breaking into a run, but not toward Lewis and the rest of his force. Rather, it ran toward the city walls, the MechWarrior inside seeking solid and more tangible cover.

"Come back here!" Lewis ordered as he opened fire on the Combine forces again, his indicators telling him he was halfway through his supply of missiles. Half of his force was with him, sending scattered long range fire back to the Combine lines to harry their ranks. The rest still lagged behind, their morale shaken. "Stay together, and do not—"

Another battery of missiles cut him off, the command channel erupted into a flurry of cries as more 'Mechs and tanks broke formation, following the one *Crab*'s lead. Some of them were making a fighting retreat, turning to fire their weapons as they backpedalled. Others were simply breaking and running, desperate to get away from the Combine advance. Regardless of their method, they still headed in the same direction, to the city, seeking refuge behind its walls.

Endangering the very lives Lewis was trying to protect. All of a sudden he wanted to be back at Brein, just to know how Sarah and Anna were. Under his breath, he prayed things were going better there than they were here, before focusing again on the matters at hand.

"Do not head into the city," he commanded, trying his best to sound authoritative over the crackle of weapons fire and the roar of explosions. "Continue heading due west, and try to draw as many Combine 'Mechs as you can with you." His *Shadow Hawk* was in a flat run now, turning to try flanking the enemy advance. There were others following his lead, but far less than he would have liked.

We take this to the city, and we may as well just burn it to the ground ourselves, he told himself, ruefully glancing at the storm of chaos his tactical display had become. Hopefully, the enemy force would take the bait, and if nothing else, spare some of their number to pursue his force instead. He fired another burst from his autocannon at a Combine *Warhammer*, the shells tearing into its leg, causing the heavy 'Mech to momentarily stumble. *Better we die here then let our people suffer any more.*

Shintaro couldn't help but feel satisfied as the Blakist formation began to shatter under Ikazuchi Company's assault. Intelligence had suggested that the PM troops were largely inexperienced reservists, and they had very much proven it by how their force had scattered. *What a pack of cowardly dogs. I wouldn't even expect Lyrans to fight this badly,* he told himself as his battered *Grasshopper* continued to advance.

The minefields had done their trick, sowing discord and confusion among the enemy ranks. Each move they made had become wary, fearful that they would find their 'Mechs' legs torn off or their vehicles gutted. All the while his company had simply maintained their advance, pouring on fire to those targets who had been isolated or damaged by the mines.

He sent the *Grasshopper* leaping forward, the towering machine landing atop one of the outer walls of the city. Below he could see several Protectorate 'Mechs trying to run, using the densely packed streets of low-lying, hardy buildings for cover. Another round of laser fire reached out to a fleeing *Crab,* with one of the two beams searing armor off its side. The other slammed into a building, tearing through the ferrocrete structure with ease.

"Ikazuchi Company, with me!" he called out. "We have them on the run!" As the *Grasshopper* took to the air again, he spared another glance at his display, seeing the small portion of the enemy force that were still on the move. "*Chu-i* Ishigro, take your lance and follow those still outside. I do not want them to escape." He only barely acknowledged the recon lance commander's reply, focusing instead on hunting down the Blakist forces as they sought refuge. Even if they ran, it didn't matter. His victory was close, and with it, another step towards redemption.

He glanced again at the picture taped to the side of the cockpit, and couldn't help smiling. *My son, my love. Soon.*

APOPKA, BRYANT
WORD OF BLAKE PROTECTORATE
19 APRIL 3078

Each mechanical step the *Grasshopper* took was accompanied by a soft, wet squelch as it pushed on through the marshland. Ahead lay a seemingly endless expanse of dull green stretched out to a stormy gray sky, punctuated by the ruins of long-fallen and clearly forgotten structures that themselves were being slowly subsumed. According to the maps the Seventeenth had acquired, this had once been a major industrial district, home to industries that had fed the armies of the Star League.

Shintaro Gustavson didn't see it himself as he pushed the titanic war machine onward. All he knew was that this ruin was apparently sheltering elements of the Bryant Protectorate Militia after they had scattered. A chance break in the cloud cover had revealed their location, offering an opportunity to end the farce this campaign had become.

After a few initial engagements, the Protectorate Militia force had broken and run, but their acts had not been in desperation or defeat. Many of them had gone to ground, hiding out in the vast, largely abandoned wilderness that accounted for most of the planet. What should have been a quick, decisive victory for the

Coalition forces had turned into a long, drawn-out game of cat and mouse as the Blakist forces continued to elude them.

They should have been consolidating their hold over the planet and then moving on to other, more valuable targets than this deserted graveyard of a world. Instead, they had spent weeks tromping across the wilderness, investigating every farm, every outpost, and every ruin for some sign of their enemy. Even the planet's weather worked against them, its constant storms providing thick cover that shielded their movements and allowed them to strike out and disappear.

About the only upside was the perverse satisfaction that Shintaro felt from knowing that all the units in the Coalition force were suffering just as equally as the Seventeenth Benjamin were. They were only here in this particular swampy hellhole because of a stroke of luck. There had been a break in the cloud cover just as a recon flight had been passing overhead. They'd spotted a group of BattleMechs and hovercraft in among the ruins, and quickly relayed the information. Ikazuchi Company had been the closest force, and the responsibility had fallen on them to investigate and, if the enemy were found there, eliminate them. Any thoughts of an honorable victory had long ago left Shintaro's mind. Now all he wanted was to be as far away from this world as possible.

About the only thing that had gone right was that his aged wreck of a *Grasshopper* had behaved itself. For a patchwork mess, it had performed better than many of the newer 'Mechs in his command. He should have taken that as a sign of the Dragon smiling on him, but instead all he felt was that the BattleMech was somehow mocking him.

"Anything?" he snapped over the company's tactical network, his mood slowly worsening as his force trudged forward. They had already marched for several hours to get here, their DropShips unable to find any closer safe landing spaces due to the treacherous combination of soft ground and hidden ruins. As they had advanced, his company had seen a lot of rubble and plenty of rain, but precious little else to suggest that the Blakists were actually here. A round of negative responses only served to underscore that point, making him feel like this was just another massive waste of time.

Damn them. This should have been easy. A dying world with a tiny population shouldn't be this much of a problem.

A new icon appeared on his heads-up display, the navigation computer indicating that they were approaching the Lantren

Corporation factory. Or, rather, where it had stood centuries ago before it, like the rest of the district, had been destroyed or abandoned or whatever else had befallen it.

Thank you for that useless information. All I see is another empty ruin, he told himself. *That's all this damnable planet has to offer us.* As if the world itself was openly mocking him, drops of rain began to spatter against the *Grasshopper*'s canopy.

The few drops quickly turned into a wall of rain, which amazingly managed to make the already dreary scene before them seem even more miserable. The BattleMechs of his force were quickly turned into little more than silhouettes, looming gray shapes hidden behind a curtain of rain. But it also did nothing to relieve the oppressive heat; if anything, it only seemed to make things even warmer. And all the meantime, his sensors remained almost mockingly quiet, as if to tell him that this whole exercise had been a waste of time.

Focus. He eyed the photo of his wife and son one more, reminding himself why he was here and what this was about. *You do this for them. Every discomfort, every indignity you suffer is for their sake.*

And then the *Warhammer* in front of him simply disappeared, a splash marking its passing as it dropped out of sight.

"Report!" he barked as he glanced down at his sensors, trying to find out what devastating weapon could be responsible.

"I fell in a sinkhole or something," came the almost sheepish reply. "Ruins are probably riddled with them."

"*Baka.* Watch your step, all of you," he snapped over the command channel. "Slow and careful movements. If something feels even slightly out of place, then do not advance. Back up, find a way around it or whatever else." It would make the going painfully slow, but it was still better than losing a BattleMech to carelessness.

He turned back from the *Warhammer*'s watery grave, leaving its idiot pilot to get himself out of his own mess. Looking ahead, all he could see was more of the same, irregular chunks of rubble that jutted out from the morass, their shapes lost to centuries of growth and the rain.

It was only then that he noticed one of them move.

A millisecond later, the *Grasshopper*'s computer blared a warning as a flight of missiles streaked toward the 'Mech. Shots hammered into its chest and arms, shaking the huge 'Mech, its feet fighting for traction in the soft mud. More alarms went off, the tactical display lighting up with new markers as huge, muck-covered shapes emerged from the swamp—primal behemoths rising from the depths.

Muck streamed off the *Shadow Hawk*'s canopy as the BattleMech pushed out of the swamp, Lewis urging it toward the Combine force. Around it, the other surviving 'Mechs of his company did the same, emerging from their aquatic refuges to engage the enemy. Already fire filled the rain-soaked air, cutting through it to seek out their opponents.

A *Grasshopper* loomed large in the center of his sights, Lewis hammered it with missile and autocannon fire as he advanced on the heavier 'Mech. He had no idea if this was the same one that he'd faced outside Lumsden, nor did he care. Right now, his goal was to do as much damage as he could to the enemy force, to slow or even turn back their conquest of the world by any means possible.

The swampy ruins had offered his men a number of advantages. The Combine force wouldn't be able to call on their artillery support, for starters, with the ground being inaccessible to their heavy vehicles. Conversely, his men could use the terrain to their advantage, digging in and setting up an effective ambush.

But to him, the most important advantage that the swamp offered was its location. The ruins had been abandoned for centuries, left behind when war and the planet's reverting ecosystem had destroyed anything of any worth. Out here, there were no innocents that could be caught in the crossfire, no property or lives that could become collateral damage to the battle.

A handful of hovercraft, the few survivors from his original force, sped toward the enemy, kicking up massive clouds of spray in their wake. Infantry took potshots from concealed positions, using the rubble as cover as they opened fire with whatever weapons they had left.

And for a moment, it seemed to have worked.

The Combine forces were caught off balance by the attack, left flat-footed as the surviving Protectorate forces emerged. Their 'Mechs weathered fire as they struggled to get their bearings and figure out what was going on and just what they were facing. Instead, more shots came as them as fast-moving hovercraft and light BattleMechs wheeled around, making the most of the situation to nip at their flanks. The gray skies filled with brilliant flashes of energy and bursts of fire as the two forces opened up, unleashing terrible energies on each other in a desperate battle for survival.

Lewis was at the head of the charge, his *Shadow Hawk*'s autocannon vomiting shells at the nearest target as it pushed forward through the muck. The Combine *Grasshopper* ahead of him stood transfixed for a moment, shuddering as the first shots hammered into it. Wounded, the war machine stood its ground, several poorly aimed shots spitting back through the rain.

As much of an advantage as the initial surprise had given him, he also knew his force would need a lot more than that to win the day. As soon as he could, he yanked the controls hard to one side, the *'Hawk* twisting as it ran, seeking out more cover. Weapons cycled around and Lewis opened up again as soon as he could. The rain and clutter was making it hard to tell how much effect he was having against the heavier Combine 'Mech, but with all the disadvantages he was fighting against, every shot mattered.

The *Grasshopper* seemed to regain its composure, the big 'Mech whirling around to pursue him. Searing red beams flashed out, briefly illuminating the dismal, gray world around them before slamming into the *Shadow Hawk,* searing through its patched-up armor with ferocious intensity. Bursts of static filled Lewis's ears as his BattleMech reeled under the assault, before his stomach lurched as it struggled to keep its footing in the treacherous terrain.

With an almost Herculean force of will, he was able to resist the call of gravity, keeping the BattleMech on its feet and in the fight. Around him, he could see that the initial shock of the ambush had already dissipated, the rest of the Combine force pushing back against his own. Their cluster of 'Mechs pushed outward, and while still surrounded, they began concentrating their fire to punch holes in his line.

To his left, Kranowski's *Buccaneer* reeled back under the force of a missile barrage, the long-legged 'Mech stumbling to one knee. A *Komodo* advanced out of the gloom, its lasers slicing armor from the wounded BattleMech, further driving it back. Other Kuritan 'Mechs, seeing a weakness they could exploit, followed behind it.

"Take that *Komodo*!" he called, the order half about holding the Combine force back, but his focus more on protecting his men. The *Shadow Hawk* pivoted at the waist, Lewis triggering the weapons as soon as his sights dropped onto the squat BattleMech's form. Missiles drilled at the armor over its forearm before the lasers bored through the gaps they tore. Something erupted within the limb, and the small 'Mech took a quick step back as it sought to get away from the barrage.

It was a small moment of triumph. It didn't last.

A pair of shots slammed into the *Shadow Hawk* from behind. Alarms went off as the 'Mech stumbled under the assault. Angry red lights lit up across the board as systems were devoured by the angry energies of the attack, critically wounding the war machine. Both the force of the attack and the damage were enough to send the war machine toppling forward, Lewis able to do little to fight the seemingly inevitable, other than brace himself for the impact.

The *Shadow Hawk* hit the ground with a hard, sharp impact, its 55 tons barely cushioned by the mud. Gravity yanked Lewis against his harness before violently snapping him back, accompanied by sharp shocks as his neurohelmet clattered against the seat. Immediately he reached out with the *Hawk*'s hands, trying to find some purchase in the soft muck.

Around him, he could see the situation unfolding, his men doing their best to fight back against the Kuritan resurgence. A Blizzard reeled under laser fire, the hovercraft spinning out across the water as black smoke belched from its side. An *Archer* pummeled a *Lancelot* with missiles, the slender Bryant BattleMech losing one of its arms in the firestorm. Several 'Mechs poured fire onto the wounded *Buccaneer,* while a *Jackal* desperately tried to escape their attention.

It's falling apart so fast. He pushed the *Shadow Hawk* back to its feet and triggered a burst of autocannon fire to ease the pressure off the *Buccaneer.* "All units, pull back," he ordered, doing his best to stay calm, trying to keep his force together under pressure. It wasn't easy. "I repeat, pull back. We're not going to—"

More shots rocked the *Shadow Hawk* as the *Grasshopper* found its opponent again. The tall, humanoid BattleMech advanced through the mud and rain, seemingly focused on its opponent. Lewis knew he could outrun it still, but that was now his only option, given how badly wounded his *Shadow Hawk* was. Its LRM launcher had been destroyed in that last barrage, and the autocannon was near dry. Even if the BattleMech did manage to stay together for just a little longer, it would be all but unarmed anyway.

But that didn't stop him from trying. "All units, pull back!" He ordered even as his own 'Mech made a stumbling but determined advance toward the Kuritan line. He swung his sights onto the same *Grasshopper* that had he tangled with before, hoping to—if nothing else—slow it down. There was a roar as the autocannnon spat shells at its target, short bursts of fire cutting through the rain to strike their target. Ruby-red laser beams followed, cutting across the enemy BattleMech's heart.

It wasn't enough.

The *Grasshopper* charged, its attention fully focused on the *Shadow Hawk* as it unleashed a hellish assault. Lasers stripped armor from the *Hawk*'s already ravaged frame, drilling into its structure with murderous intent. More sirens rang out inside the cockpit, accompanied by a sudden spike in the temperature. It was all Lewis could do to keep the *Shadow Hawk* upright.

He tried to keep the 'Mech moving, but its wounded systems refused to cooperate. A single step turned into a stumble, driving it down to one knee. More warnings went off as he tried to get it upright again, only to find it struggling even further.

And ahead of him, the *Grasshopper* stepped out of the rain, looming over him. Its armor was pitted and scorched from his attacks, with deep gashes crossing its body. But even from here, he could see that the BattleMech was very much still in the fight, its weapons leveled at his own doomed machine.

"Wait!" Lewis called out. He was trying his best to sound resolute rather than desperate, not letting either the pain or the concern for his men and their lives show. It wasn't easy, given that his 'Mech was literally on its knees before a more powerful enemy. "We surrender. Let my men stand down, and nobody else needs to get hurt. We can end this here."

He looked up, fearful of what would come next.

Shintaro could end this here. This battle would not conclude the campaign for Bryant, but it would bring it another step closer. It would be one less group to chase down through every fetid hole, swamp, and blasted ruin on this damnable rock.

But they could fight. Their victory was close, almost assured. And they could win, but he could still lose some of his men and machines. And some of the Protectorate forces could still escape, to continue their campaign of harassment, striking before fading back into the winds and the rain.

The former would be the pragmatic choice. The latter would let him have his moment, to sate that need for vengeance that had driven him for so long.

Ninjo against *giri*. Himself against the Dragon. Avenging two lives at the cost of so many more.

He wanted to pull the trigger there, to destroy this one *Shadow Hawk* and then every other Blakist he could find. His finger was there, hovering for either a second or an eternity, ready to unleash the terrible energies that would obliterate his fallen opponent.

Instead, he spoke. "Tell your men to stand down," his voice boomed from the *Grasshopper*'s speakers. "I swear on my honor that they will not be harmed."

He glanced at the battered photo in the corner of the cockpit again. *I am sorry.* As much has he knew that he was doing the right thing for the Dragon, it still hurt on a deeply personal level. *Please forgive me.*

The Blakist commander had been true to his word, with the surviving members of his force standing down. There had been a lot apprehension among them, given the reputation of the Dragon for never showing mercy, but Shintaro had personally pledged that they would be under his protection. Even then, as the survivors were being carefully marshaled, it was hard not to see the apprehension in their faces, measured by the very real fear of what might happen to them.

Now technicians and recovery crews were crawling across the battlefield, doing their best to haul damaged and disabled 'Mechs out of the muck and make what they could usable again. He had given the technicians the clearance to do what they wanted, his thoughts distracted by other matters, and questions that needed to be answered.

As pragmatic as his decision had been, there was still something that he needed to know. And, to the best of his knowledge, there was only one man who could answer his questions. It was that train of thought that led him to the temporary holding ground for the Blakist prisoners, itself little more than a crudely fenced off area of ancient concrete with guards and a tarpaulin for cover.

A few quick words singled out their commander. Shintaro took him aside, but kept him in view of both his own soldiers and the Combine guards. The move was to put both of them at ease in what was an unquestionably tense situation.

"*Tai-i* Shintaro Gustavson, Seventeenth Benjamin Regulars," he introduced himself. "There is something that I would like to know."

The man nodded. "Captain Lewis Carter, Bryant Protectorate Militia," he replied. "Well, formally, I suppose. You understand I'm not really at liberty or required to answer any questions about our forces or the like."

Shintaro shook his head. "It was just a simple question," he explained. "At Lumsden. there was a *Shadow Hawk* in among the Word's BattleMechs. Was that you?"

Lewis nodded. "It was. There's no real harm in answering at this point."

"Why did you run? At Lumsden, half your force stood their ground in the city, while you and the others fled. Why?" Shintaro's question seemed earnest, but his thoughts were elsewhere. *Did I surrender my honor to preserve cowards? Or did they have a reason for their actions?*

"Actually, it was the other way around," Lewis admitted. "I tried to lead my men away from the city, and yours with them. I never wanted to fight inside it."

"I do not follow you."

Lewis gave a small sigh before continuing. "Life on this planet is fragile. During the heyday of the Star League, it had a population in the hundreds of millions. Today there's a few score thousand. I wanted to protect this world, yes, but I did not want to put those innocent lives at risk in doing so." There was a hint of anger in his voice, one that rose and then dropped as he continued.

"My brother died fighting for the Word. His wife and a daughter he never even saw live in Brein. It may sound selfish, but it was them I was thinking of when I ordered my men away from the city."

Shintaro winced at the thought. *And I would have done the same in his place.* He thought of those two lives in particular, two faces he would never see again. *They could have just as easily been in Lumsden. What the Word did on Benjamin, we were doing here.*

I wanted vengeance for two lives lost. And I doing such, I didn't care how many more I took with me.

He looked away, out into the rain. His eyes fell on his *Grasshopper,* the battered BattleMech still standing defiantly over its fallen, mud-caked foe. "You did the honorable thing," he finally admitted. *And I know I did as well.*

"You know, there's a certain irony in all this," Lewis suddenly spoke up, a small chuckle in his voice.

"What do you mean?" Shintaro asked, clearly confused.

"Here, this place and your 'Mech." Lewis indicated the Combine machine. "Your *Grasshopper* was built here centuries ago. Of course, it wasn't a swamp at the time, but you get the picture."

"Is that so?" Shintaro finished, a contemplative tone in his voice. "Then I guess this was a sort of a homecoming for both of us."

END OF THE ROAD
CRAIG A. REED, JR.

CAMP LIBERATION
LITTLE ROCK, NORTH AMERICA,
TERRA
WORD OF BLAKE PROTECTORATE
1 SEPTEMBER 3078

Nathaniel Trivedi looked up at the *Grasshopper*. "You're kidding, right?"

"Do I look like I'm kidding?" the woman next to him replied, her annoyed tone carrying her opinion loud and clear. Like Nathan, she wore a set of faded overalls.

The pair were opposite in appearance. Nathan was tall and gaunt, with pale skin and a long face. Goldie McQuistan was short, broadly built, with skin the color of strong coffee.

"My *Victor*—"

"—Is scattered across half of Hilton Head." McQuistan turned her head and spat on the floor. "This is the heaviest unassigned unit we have at the moment."

"Where'd it come from?" Nathan asked. "If the Wob—"

"It came out with a shipment of parts and supplies from Combine forces on Bryant. Why are you bitching? It's just as fast as your *Victor*, can jump just as far, and has more armor. We've replaced the large laser with a Clan model, scrounged up a pair of the extended-range mediums, and found another heat sink."

"But I—"

"Look, Professor," McQuistan snapped. "Hammer said get you into the heaviest 'Mech we have ASAP. You want to bitch at someone, bitch at him!" She grinned. "Besides, I think this one might appeal to you more than some of the others."

Nathan looked around the 'Mech hangar. The 'Mechs of Stone's Lament's Third Battalion were undergoing repairs, the white bones on black making it look as if the place was filled with giant skeletons. Most were assault-class, with a scattering of heavies and medium-class designs. The constant noise echoed through the structure, giving Nathan a headache.

"Well?" McQuistan prompted. "You want the 'Mech, or do you want to face the Hammer's wrath?"

"I don't have a choice, do I?"

"Nope. Come on. Let's get you into the cockpit and get it calibrated."

The *Grasshopper*'s cockpit was dark when McQuistan opened the hatch. She reached inside and flicked on the interior light. "There you go."

Nathan slid inside. Out of the corner of his eye, he saw something on the bulkhead just above the command couch, something written on the steel. He frowned as he read aloud what looked like a list of names and notes. "Sam Tanaka...Klaus Peterson...Randy Peterson... Sigland Idelson... Who are these people?"

McQuistan grinned. "Best bet? The 'Mech's previous pilots."

"There must be thirty names here!"

"Along with units and dates and other stuff."

Nathan followed the dates. "This 'Mech must be three hundred years old!"

"Looks like you got a genuine relic. Let's get you hooked up."

"But...this must be one of the earliest *Grasshopper*s ever built!"

"Probably. But first things first. You can explore your new ride after I get it calibrated to you."

CAMP LIBERATION
LITTLE ROCK, NORTH AMERICA
TERRA
WORD OF BLAKE PROTECTORATE
3 SEPTEMBER 3078

"Yo, Professor, where are you?"

Nathan looked up from the screen and glanced around the cockpit. Only then did he realize the voice had come from his comm headset. "I'm in my 'Mech, Paula."

"The major wants us in our bunks ASAP."

"I'm busy."

"With what? The major said bunk time now, and he sent us to get you. Get out of that 'Mech, or we'll come up there and drag you out."

Nathan looked out and saw the short, slim form of Paula Kranski standing at the *Grasshopper*'s feet. Close behind her loomed the much taller Lou Grace. He sighed. "All right. Give me a minute to shut down."

Reluctantly, he began shutting down the few active systems. Somehow, an auxiliary hard drive had survived everything the *Grasshopper* had gone through, and it contained a number of files, including combat footage. He had already matched several of the names on the panel with files, heard their voices, read their reports. Realizing his find, he had scrounged up some data crystals and copied the data. Another crystal contained his notes and thoughts about what he had learned.

As the last system died, he stood and stretched, feeling tension in his neck and shoulders. He started heading toward the hatch, but stopped and looked at the names panel again. *I know some of you now*, he thought. He stepped out into the night air, closed and locked the hatch, then descended the gantry's stairs.

Kranski and her partner were still waiting at the gantry's base. Despite her last name, Kranski was Asian, an exotic waif of a woman who was also loud and profane, always in motion, and never far from the man behind her. "Took you long enough," she said as the trio began walking toward the hangar doors. "You look over Lear's data?"

Nathan sighed. "Yes. It's hard to sort out, but the Word's pulling out all the stops. There are reports of mobile fortresses, a superheavy BattleM—"

"Is that why you spend all your time in the cockpit?" Grace asked. He was a decade older than Nathan, rangy from light meals and heavy work. He was the opposite of his lover, quiet and still most of the time, Yin to Kranski's Yang. "Lear's data?"

"Nope." Nathan pointed a thumb over his shoulder at the *Grasshopper*. "That."

Kranski looked back at the 'Mech then at Nathan. "Look, I know you're a history professor, but—"

"I'm just a doctoral candidate," Nathan interrupted.

"For all practical purposes, you're a professor. So, what's up? Was Kerensky the first pilot or something?"

"No, but I'm certain it was one of the first *Grasshopper*s ever built."

"So?"

"Do you realize what that means?" Kranski shrugged. "Nope."

"So it's what, two hundred years old?" Grace asked.

"Three hundred."

Kranski shook her head, then pointed at her *Gunslinger*. "I've had that 'Mech for six years. Do you know how old it is?"

"No, but—"

"Neither do I. Don't care either. Lou here doesn't worry about his *Stalker*'s history, and all the major cares about is how fast he can kill the enemy in his *Highlander*. These are weapons of war, Professor, not dusty artifacts stored on a museum's basement shelf."

"But there's a cockpit panel with a list of previous pilots' names, one that goes back centuries!"

Kranski shrugged again. "So?"

Nathan shook his head. "You have no sense of history."

"I don't have time."

Grace nodded. "None of us do."

Nathan scowled. "Someone should."

"Not right now, Nate," Kranski replied. "The major says Stone thinks the Wobbies are up to something."

"Intuition?"

"Either that, or Lear's people uncovered something. Either way, this may be our last chance for sleep for the foreseeable future."

LITTLE ROCK, NORTH AMERICA
TERRA
WORD OF BLAKE PROTECTORATE
8 SEPTEMBER 3078

The Blakist *Trebuchet* stepped into view and fired both LRM racks at Nathan before vanishing behind a building. Nathan sidestepped his *Grasshopper* to the left, and most of the missiles flew past and exploded on the road behind him. Several struck his new ride's right arm, shattering a few armor plates. He cursed under his breath.

The area was open, and what has once been a park was now shattered trees and torn-up turf. The Word's attack on Camp Liberation had occurred on the heels of a nuclear strike on the assembly and supply base at Dallas-Fort Worth. As news about the strike reached the base, the camp's alarms went off, sending the Coalition members scrambling for their machines. The Word forced their way across the Arkansas River, stormed through the city, and slammed into the defenders just outside the camp. After an intense battle, the Coalition forces pushed the Blakists back to the river.

While the Lament's First and Second Battalions pushed forward, Third Battalion followed behind, ready to reinforce the advance and eliminate any Word units trapped behind the lines. The *Trebuchet* was such a unit, now harassing Nathan and the rest of the Third's command lance.

"What are you waiting for?" Kranski sarcastically said over the radio. "Bag and tag him!"

Nathan worked his jaw and started forward again. "If you can do any better, you try."

Kranski laughed. "You're in the way, kid."

Nathan felt a flash of anger, but tamped it down. He was only two years younger than Kranski, but she and Grace had been with Devlin Stone for several years, while Nathan had only been in the Lament for three, the last two in Third Battalion's command lance. There was a perverse sort of seniority in the Lament, based on how long a person had been with Stone. It didn't crop up on the battlefield, but the longer you'd been with him, the more weight your words carried.

The *Trebuchet* stepped out again as something moving at hypersonic speed shot past the *Grasshopper*'s shoulder and slammed into it. The 50-ton 'Mech spun and staggered as armor fragments flew off in all directions. By comparison, the flight of missiles that struck the Word 'Mech several heartbeats later was almost in slow motion, but they followed up on the Gauss rifle's damage. The resulting explosions tore apart the *Trebuchet*'s left arm and torso, and sent it crashing into the building behind it.

Nathan glanced at the portion of the view strip covering his rear arc and saw Major Wozniak's *Highlander* striding forward. The 90-ton 'Mech was painted in the Lament's color scheme of black with white bones, reinforcing the air of menace about it.

"What are you waiting for?" the major asked coldly. "Kranski, left flank, Grace, take the right. Trivedi, you're on point."

Nathan glanced at the downed *Trebuchet*. The enemy 'Mech was buried inside of a twelve-story building, several tons of debris covering it from the waist up. It wasn't moving, so Nathan tagged it with his 'Mech's on-board GPS system and continued.

A few minutes later, he saw the river ahead through the smoke, demolished buildings, and wrecked vehicles. As he reached the riverbank, he saw a black *Atlas* standing at the riverbank with several other 'Mechs.

The *Atlas* turned just as Wozniak's *Highlander* strode into view. "Gideon," Devlin Stone said over the command channel. "How goes it?"

"The Hammers are scattered across this half of the city," Wozniak replied in the same flat tone he'd used earlier. "The Blakists left enough units behind to cause havoc if they ever get organized."

"How long to clear them out?"

"I don't know."

Stone was quiet for a moment. "Take whatever you need. Hunt them down."

"I'll use Johnston's company, a couple of lances each from the Guards and Regulars, along with some of the infantry assets. That should be enough."

"They have twelve hours."

"I'm on it."

"I know, Gideon." The *Atlas* turned toward the *Grasshopper*. "Nathan."

"Sir." Nathan wasn't surprised that Devlin Stone knew his name—Stone knew everyone in the Lament on a first name basis, and knew enough about each person to could carry on a comfortable conversation with any one of them. His charisma, combined with strong political and military acumen, had taken him from the unknown leader of the Kittery resistance to the head of the largest military force seen in the Inner Sphere in centuries.

"How's the new 'Mech?"

"More like an old 'Mech, sir. I think it's one of the first *Grasshopper*s ever built."

"That says something about how well it was built. Very few things survive three hundred years of war."

"Yes, sir."

The *Atlas* turned away. "Sorry to break this up. Bella's reporting the last organized Blakists are back across the river. We're pursuing."

"Right," Wozniak said. "Shouldn't take more than an hour or two to get Johnston and the others hunting."

"Good." The *Atlas* turned and strode toward, the bridge, followed by the rest of the Lament's command lance.

KANSAS CITY, NORTH AMERICA
TERRA
WORD OF BLAKE PROTECTORATE
16 SEPTEMBER 3078

The air was cool on Nathan's skin when he climbed down the *Grasshopper*'s ladder. Around him, the rest of Third Battalion were also getting out of their 'Mechs.

There wasn't much left of the Kansas City Spaceport. Most of the buildings were ruins, the result of the intense battle that had occurred earlier in the day. A heavy aroma and smoke hung in the air, giving Nathan more incentive to descend quickly.

McQuistan, carrying a noteputer, was waiting for him when he reached the tarmac. "Repairs needed?"

"Just a few armor panels. Nothing serious."

She nodded and touched the noteputer's screen. "There's a kitchen set up near the hangar over there." She half-motioned to Nathan's left. "There are field showers next to that, and a resupply station next to that. The major wants you all fed, showered, resupplied, and rested. We move out at dawn."

"Any word on the Wobbies?"

"Still moving away. We've got scouts watching them."

Nathan nodded. He was bone tired, as the last eight days had been hard. The Word had split into several groups and scattered in different directions. Stone was chasing the largest of the Word formations, because the Precentor Martial Cameron St. Jamais's *Awesome* was with them. The last eight days were pursuits punctuated with brief firefights with Protectorate Militia rearguards. Stone had pushed the Lament on, not giving his force or the enemy time to rest.

Only after the Word had destroyed all the bridges across the Missouri River for a hundred kilometers in both directions did Stone call a halt. For Nathan, the idea of something other than Combine ration bars to eat, a shower, and sleep that lasted more than thirty minutes sounded like heaven.

"Trivedi!"

Nathan turned toward the major. Gideon Wozniak was one of "Stone's Immortals"—men and women who had been with Devlin Stone from the start on Kittery, and had fought alongside him ever since. He'd earned the nickname "Stone's Hammer" because Stone called on him and the Third Battalion whenever he wanted an enemy broken or an objective taken.

Nathan nodded. "Sir."

Wozniak walked past him. "We'll talk on the way to the mess tent."

Nathan hurried to catch up. He had just matched strides when Wozniak asked, "Did you look over the technical intelligence Lear's people collected?"

Nathan thought he heard the major's tone become even colder when he said David Lear's name—Stone's most trusted confidant. "Yes, sir."

"Your opinion?"

Nathan inhaled. "The technology...If it's true, it's incredible. The Rattler mobile fortresses were all reported destroyed during the Star League's fall. The idea that—"

"Skip the history lesson. How hard are they to beat?"

"Hard? They're mobile fortresses. It'll be like going up against a walking weapons bunker."

"How do we stop them?"

"Their track systems are the best bet. Immobilize them first, then call in artillery strikes. *Lots* of artillery strikes."

Wozniak nodded. "And these *Omegas*?"

"The idea of a superheavy 'Mech has been discussed for centuries, but if these *Omegas* are something more than hype, they're going to be monsters to fight. They pack one hell of a punch with those Gauss rifles and autocannons, and they must have heavy armor."

"Agreed."

"But they're slow. We hit one from several directions at once and get behind it, we can take it down, but it won't be easy."

The major nodded. "What's wrong?"

Nathan frowned. "Wrong?"

"You've been hesitant on the battlefield lately, and you're spending most of your down time inside your 'Mech's cockpit. What's wrong?"

"Sir—"

"You haven't been the same since you lost your *Victor* at Hilton Head. Something wrong with the *Grasshopper*?"

"No, sir."

Wozniak stopped and looked at him. In the near darkness, Nathan could only see the left side of his face. "I hear the 'but' in your words."

"It's not easy to explain."

"I talked to Kranski. She said you think the *Grasshopper* is some sort of ancient prototype."

"That's not what I said."

"Kranski's not the most focused lens in the laser array, especially around Grace. Tell me."

Nathan inhaled slowly. He thought about telling him everything, about how the research into the *Grasshopper* was his sole island of sanity in this sea of death, destruction, and madness. It cost him sleep and missed meals, but he needed to do something beyond fighting. Or else he'd end up like Major Wozniak—a man whose sole purpose in life was killing Blakists.

Instead, he took a different tack. "Do you know what I was before I joined the Lament?"

"A student of technology. That's why I keep giving you the technical intelligence from Lear."

"I was a doctoral candidate, preparing my dissertation on the military technology curve between the end of the Amaris Civil War and Kerensky's Exodus."

Wozniak grunted and turned toward the mess tent. "Sounds boring."

"I believe that had Kerensky remained, the Hegemony's technology drop-off—"

"Cut to the chase."

"From the evidence, the *Grasshopper* is one of the first ones ever built."

"So?"

They began walking again. Nathan inhaled again. "There's a panel inside the cockpit that lists the MechWarriors that have piloted it over the years, going all the way back to the Star League and Kerensky. There's evidence that it was on Kentares IV during the Massacre. It's a walking history lesson!"

Wozniak stopped again and exhaled. "You're an idiot."

Nathan frowned. "Why?"

"My grandfather had an axe. A large, two-handed axe he used to cut firewood during the Antietam winters. He told me it had been in the family for six generations and was a family heirloom. In the next breath, he told me the axe head been replaced twice and the axe handle three times. The axe wasn't much older than I was at the time. But it was still a family heirloom."

Wozniak pointed back at the *Grasshopper*. "That's a machine," he said. "It's been broken apart and put back together so many times over the years, I doubt anything except that panel is original to the 'Mech. So stop treating it like a museum piece and use it for what it was designed and built as—a weapon."

"But—"

"The Word wouldn't care if you were piloting the first *Mackie*. Thus is war—things are destroyed, people die, and no one cares how old or valuable items are." Wozniak gestured around them. "Some of these 'Mechs are older than you are, while others are less than twenty years old. It doesn't matter—they are all subject to fate and the whims of battle. So treat that *Grasshopper* for what it is, and worry about documenting its history after the war is over, if you're still alive. Understood?"

"Yes, sir."

"Good. Get something to eat, take a quick shower, then get some sleep. Devlin thinks St. Jamais is heading west and intends on losing us in the Rockies. We'll be in pursuit as soon as we finish rebuilding the bridges. This will be the last chance we'll have for a hot meal and full night's sleep for a while. Take advantage of it."

"Yes, sir."

SUNDANCE, NORTH AMERICA
TERRA
WORD OF BLAKE PROTECTORATE
17 SEPTEMBER 3078

The mushroom clouds that rose into the air were the most horrific and beautiful sight Nathan had ever seen.

The attack had come before dawn, with only two minutes' warning. Camped several kilometers southeast of Sundance, Nathan and the others had just enough time to climb into their machines, dog the hatches tight, and hope the NBC seals still worked. The missiles struck in and around the town, creating the awful beauty he'd witnessed.

"All Hammers!" Wozniak growled over the radio. "Check with your company commanders. Company commanders, report to me. Hammer Command, check in."

"Hammer Two here," Kranski said.

"Hammer Three here," Grace replied softly.

"Hammer Four here," Nathan said. "What the hell's happening?"

"Boss," Kranski said. "Perimeter radiation sensors are going nuts!"

"Confirm," Grace said. "Levels are a dozen times lethal levels in and around the town."

Nathan's sensors began screaming an alert. As he stared at the screen, his sensors began picking out individual targets through the nuclear haze. "Enemy contact!"

"All Hammer elements, this Hammer Six actual." Wozniak's tone was hard as diamond. "Form up. First Company on the right, Third on the left. I want—"

"All Coalition forces, this is Stone." The voice was only a little warmer than Wozniak's, but more commanding. "I want a defensive line along the edge of the woods from Adams Canyon to Fish Canyon. Hammer Battalion in the center, Slasher Battalion on the left, Chopper on the right. Regulars on the right, Guards on the left. Gideon, it looks like the Blakists are throwing a couple of heavy and assault Level Threes with support elements right through your position."

Nathan glanced at his sensors and saw that the identified targets matched Stone's information. He gripped the cockpit's control sticks harder.

"They can try," Wozniak said. "Gideon?"

"Yes?"

"If you see an *Awesome*, he's mine."

"Understood. You want him gift-wrapped?"

"Don't bother. I'm pulling together a reserve and making sure our support is clear of the fallout. Give me all the time you can."

"Of course. Hammer Six to all Hammer elements. You heard the man. Move! Hammer Command, we're with the reserve."

In a couple of minutes, Third Battalion's 'Mechs were moving down the slope, with the command lance and the reserves 500 meters behind them. Nathan watched a dozen tanks, mostly Ontoses, Demolishers, and Brutuses, move into positions between the 'Mech companies.

Nathan felt uneasy. Despite the major's warnings, he'd continued researching, using the data on the crystals to document the history of the *Grasshopper* and pilots who came before him. For three centuries, it had served each Successor State in turn, been built, rebuilt, and modified into several different configurations. It had been part of planetary invasions, as both invader and defender, survived hundreds of battles, skirmishes, ambushes, and raids, in all sorts of conditions and terrain. It had stood on over a hundred worlds and survived three centuries of war.

To Nathan, it had become more than a 'Mech—it had become a symbol of the last three centuries of war.

But sooner or later, time and fate would catch up with the *Grasshopper*, and one day it would die, destroyed in the fires of war that had claimed untold numbers of 'Mechs before it. Nathan just hoped it wasn't today.

"Major, what if they hit us with more nukes?" Kranski asked.

"Then you'll be your own personal nightlight," Wozniak replied in a scathing tone. "Heads up, incoming artillery."

Nathan picked up the artillery fire on his sensors as it cleared the smoke from the nuclear strikes. A dozen rounds fell from the sky, some short, others long.

"Hammer to Skull," Wozniak said, his tone steady. "We've got incoming artillery."

"Already on it," Stone replied. "Hold the line."

From his location, Nathan could see only flashes of fire and some movement of vehicles and 'Mechs. The shouts and yells from the soldiers crackled across the radio, mixing with the sounds of weapons fire and impacts.

"—Mad Cat on the left! Jakes!—"

"—Take that, you Wobbie bastard!—"

"—Coles and Ramirez are down! Target the *Masakari*!—"

Thirty-five minutes passed, then: "Hammer Three to Hammer Six. We're retreating! Down four 'Mechs and facing a full-strength assault Level Two!"

"Hammer Command, First Armored Reserve, with me," Wozniak said, sending the *Highlander* into a run toward Third Company's location. Kranski, Grace, Nathan, and a company of medium armor followed.

The slope below, covered with tall, thick-trunked trees, was silent. Half of Third Company, supported by several tanks, were backing up it, laying down heavy fire at the advancing Blakists. One of the Lament's 'Mechs, a *War Dog*, was hit in quick succession by several cobalt beams. It toppled over and smashed face-first into a tree.

Nathan saw a Word *Thor* step into view and fire at him. Two emerald beams sliced into the *Grasshopper*'s right leg, vaporizing most of the armor. The abrupt loss made Nathan stumble into a tree. As the tree cracked and fell, he regained his balance and returned fire, leaving a ragged scar on the *Thor*'s right leg.

To his left, Kranski's *Gunslinger* fired both its Gauss rifles. The *Thor* staggered as the slugs slammed into it, shattering large sections of torso and left leg armor. Despite the double impact and the sudden armor loss, the Blakist stayed on its feet.

"That's how you do it, kid!" Kranski yelled over the radio. Nathan gritted his teeth and moved to his right, targeting the *Thor*. The enemy 'Mech fired again, one large laser beam punching though a tree trunk to Nathan's right, the second carving a long scar across the *Grasshopper*'s right arm. The tree exploded, showering Nathan's 'Mech with splinters.

Nathan fired all his weapons on the run. The sudden spike of heat in the cockpit was instantaneous and intense. The laser barrage struck the *Thor*, liquefying armor across its torso and right arm, exposing the right side to the air.

Before Nathan could follow up, something shot past his cockpit and slammed into a tree behind him, demolishing it.

"*Daishi* on the right," Grace said, his dispassionate tone at odds with the battle around them.

"I'm picking up more enemy units heading toward us!" Kranski shouted. "Heavies and assaults, mostly Clan designs!"

"Hammer One, Hammer Two," the major said. "Can you spare anyone to reinforce Hammer Three?"

"Negative, Hammer Six. The Wobbies are pushing all along the line. We can't spare anyone. Slasher and Cutter are equally engaged."

Nathan stepped back, putting a few more trees between him and the *Thor*. To his right, he could see a *Daishi* leading a *Vulture* and *Guillotine* up the slope.

"Enemy aerospace coming in!" someone shouted. "Three marks, three fifty, angels three thousand!"

Wozniak snorted and said, "Hammer Six to Hammer Command, Hammer Three, and supporting elements. Fall back one hundred meters and consolidate the line. Hammer to Skull. Need some help here."

"We're a bit busy here ourselves," Stone replied. "The Blakists are forcing the issue."

"They've dropped in a second level Deuce against us, and Hammer Three is paper-thin."

"Hold for three more minutes."

"Not any longer. The Wobbies are Clan-heavy and assault."

"Three minutes."

Nathan continued moving up the slope. He saw Grace's *Stalker,* battered and scarred, upslope. Wozniak's *Highlander* was on the *Stalker's* left, with Kranski's *Gunslinger* on the far side of the major. The four Third Company's survivors were also moving uphill, along with half a dozen tanks. He glanced at the view strip and saw the Blakist force charging toward them.

Nathan recognized the battered and scarred *Warhammer IIC* struggling up the hill as Captain Johnston's, Third Company's CO. The Clan 'Mech spun and unloaded both Clan-built PPCs at the advancing enemy. An artillery shell landed near him, showering him with dirt and debris.

Then the enemy fighters, a trio of *Hellcat II*s, came swooping in, light PPC blasts smashing through the trees and into anything else in its way. Johnston staggered as two particle beams found his armor. An extra explosion ripped through the *Warhammer's* right knee joint, and the captain snarled a curse. Nearby, an Ontos opened fire at the *Hellcat*s, raking one with several lasers and short range missiles. The 50-ton aircraft wobbled, then flipped over onto its back and dove steeply before hitting the ground somewhere behind Nathan.

Sliding behind a tree to protect his right leg, Nathan raised his right arm and fired his extended-range medium laser at the Word *Thor*. The emerald beam struck the former Clan 'Mech in its left leg, dissolving large sections of armor.

Fire from numerous war machines flew through the trees at the Lament line. The *Grasshopper* lost more armor on its torso and left arm, but the tree took the brunt of fire directed at it.

"Lou!"

Nathan glanced at Grace's *Stalker* just as the 85-ton 'Mech exploded, scattering remnants in every direction. As he blinked to clear his vision, Nathan saw the *Stalker*'s remains fall over, the left side and cockpit burning fiercely.

A primeval howl of rage and pain ripped across the radio. The *Gunslinger* stepped forward, arms up and pointed at the advancing Word force. "You bastards!" Kranski screamed. "You goddamned bastards!" She fired both Gauss rifles and started forward.

"Kranski!" Nathan felt the snap of command in Wozniak's voice. "They killed Lou!"

The *Highlander* fired, sending a one-two punch of Gauss rifle and long range missiles down the slope. "You can die after the enemy is dead, Paula. Hold the line."

"But—"

"We will hold the line and kill the Blakists before they kill us."

The *Gunslinger* took a step back. "I'll kill them all!" Kranski screamed. "Every single one of them!"

"Good."

The next several minutes were a blur to Nathan, becoming nothing more than a few flashes of images:

—Kranski standing next to Grace's downed *Stalker*, firing her Gauss rifles and lasers as fast as possible—

—The major's *Highlander* slamming a fist into the *Thor*'s cockpit—

—Johnston's *Warhammer IIC* falling after getting savaged by the Word *Masakari*, with the *Masakari* being ripped apart by the rest of the Lament's 'Mechs concentrating fire right after—

—A pair of Lament Ontoses dueling with a Word Puma that left the Puma and one of the Ontoses flaming wrecks—

There were only five Lament 'Mechs standing now, all heavily damaged. A half-dozen Lament tanks, similarly damaged, were interspaced between the 'Mechs. Nathan's armor screen was all red, indicating little or no armor remaining. He felt the *Grasshopper* groan as his moved through the trees. "Hold on," he muttered.

A tree exploded behind and to Nathan's right. He twisted left and fired his large laser. The beam found the Word *Daishi*'s right leg, leaving a long scar along the thigh. The massive 'Mech showed no reaction but swung toward Nathan, intent on bringing its full firepower to bear on the Lament 'Mech.

Nathan's sensors all of a sudden lit up with friendly icons. The *Daishi* staggered as several lasers and autocannon rounds slammed into it, several missiles exploiting the damage Nathan's laser had caused to its leg.

A Lament *Black Watch* lumbered past Nathan, flanked by a *Viking*, both firing at the enemy downslope. Nathan stopped, suddenly finding himself in the middle of a charge. Several more 'Mechs in Lament colors moved through the defenders and tore into the Word force. The *Daishi* went down under the *Viking*'s missile swarm, multiple warheads ripping through its armor. Large swaths of trees vaporized under the reinforcements' fire, and the surviving Word forces fell back.

"Nice timing," Wozniak said. "Thanks."

"I aim to please," Stone replied softly. His *Atlas* stood near the major's *Highlander*. "We can't stay long. The Word is hammering us all along the line. I can only spare a couple of 'Mechs and a platoon of tanks to help you hold here."

"We'll hold."

"Bad?"

"Yeah. Third Company right now is more theory than fact, and Lou's dead."

"I see." The *Atlas* shifted to face the *Gunslinger*. "I'm sorry, Paula."

"I want to kill them all, sir." Kranski's tone was flat and detached. "I want to send every single Robe to hell."

"You aren't alone in that. We'll take care of them." Stone turned toward Nathan. "I see the old dog survived another fight."

"Yes, sir."

"Gideon says you're a historian."

"Well, I... Yes, sir."

"When you write this down, don't forget the people who made the sacrifice today."

Nathan swallowed. "Yes, sir."

"Good. Need to get moving. Hold the line, Gideon."

"We will."

The *Atlas* turned and lumbered up the slope. Most of the reinforcements followed. A silence settled around the few defenders, but the sounds of battle were all around them.

"Kranski, with me," Wozniak said after a couple of minutes. "Trivedi, I'm leaving you in command of this part of the line."

"But—"

"No arguments. This is still my battalion, and I have to know what's going on with the rest of it. Stay and hold the line if they attack again. If you get into trouble, sing out. Otherwise, keep me informed every fifteen minutes."

Nathan sighed. "Yes sir."

It was well after dark when the *Grasshopper* was declared free of radiation and Nathan was cleared to open the hatch and step out into the cool night air. The winds had shifted, blowing most of the radioactive fallout away from the battlefield. Both sides had pulled back, the Word north of what remained of Sundance, with the Lament and their allies rendezvousing at a small village southeast of the battlefield, twenty kilometers away.

Nathan climbed down the ladder slowly. He was tired and sore, his brain in a fog. The Word had broken off the attack an hour after Wozniak had left him in charge of Third Company. Both sides had taken heavy casualties, and neither had the energy or resources to continue.

When he reached the ground, the major was waiting for him. "Walk with me to the mess tent."

Nathan bit back a groan. "Yes, sir." They walked. "Sir, I—" Nathan began.

"We got hit hard today," Wozniak said. "I'm reorganizing the battalion into two companies. I'm commanding one company. I'm promoting you to lieutenant and putting you in command of my second lance."

The announcement was like a shock of cold water. "Me? But Kranski—"

"—Is currently sedated. The only thing on her mind is killing as many Blakists as fast as she can." Wozniak exhaled slowly. "Normally, she'd be pulled off the line and strapped to a hospital bed, but we can't afford to lose anyone else right now. She's an unstable warhead—the best I can do is point her in the right direction and stay out of her way."

"But she needs help!"

"We all need help. Some of us have been fighting nonstop for almost a decade, and all of us have lost somebody..." He scowled as he recalled something, and Nathan saw him tense up. "Or many someones."

"But...I have no command experience!"

"I don't have much of a choice. You're the only one I can give this to."

Nathan sighed. "I don't know if I—"

"We're both going to find out. Get something to eat, then some sleep. Officers' meeting at the *Highlander* at oh five hundred."

"Yes, sir."

DEVILS TOWER MONUMENT
NORTH AMERICA
TERRA
WORD OF BLAKE PROTECTORATE
19 DECEMBER 3078

Nathan stared at the view strip, not believing what he was seeing.

Three kilometers away, Devils Tower, a large rock sitting on a hill overlooking the Belle Fourche River, dominated the surroundings. It was also the centerpiece of a Word fortress—an extensive network of bunkers, weapon emplacements, and minefields built into the hill around the Tower. Stone had been probing the defenses with light 'Mechs, hovercraft, and battle armor for most of the past day, but all they had to show for their efforts were a couple of knocked-out emplacements and a handful of casualties.

The Hammers were in reserve, on a wooded hill. Between Nathan and the Word fortress was mostly flat, open ground with a few trees closer to the enemy.

"Gideon, I need you to break them when the time is right," Stone had said to Wozniak at the officers' meeting that morning. "I need you fresh and ready to go at a moment's notice."

That moment hadn't arrived yet, and the Hammers were getting impatient. Nathan's new command—consisting of First and Third Company's survivors—was muttering over the lance frequency. They wanted revenge for the loss of their friends, and they wanted it now. Nathan didn't blame them, but their orders were to hold until called.

Nathan looked to the left. The major's *Highlander* was a hundred meters away, still and silent as Devils Tower itself. In contrast, Kranski's *Gunslinger* kept shifting its weight, moving its arms, straining at a nonexistent leash. Nathan didn't know how the major kept her under control.

A Coalition artillery volley flew overhead, targeting the Word's emplacements around the monument. No Word field forces had been seen since the assault started, but Nathan knew they would come when the time was right. For now, it was a battle of feint and maneuver, locating and painting weapons emplacements for air and artillery strikes.

"Trivedi," Wozniak said over their private channel. "I want your lance to stand down for now. Sleep, eat, whatever you want, but be ready to move immediately as the order is given."

"Yes, sir. Is Kranski—"

"She's my concern, not yours. Pass along the orders."

"Yes, sir."

Nathan switched to the lance channel and gave the orders. He slumped in his chair, and closed his eyes. He couldn't sleep, not here and now.

He reached into a compartment built into the side of his chair and took out a ration bar and a water bottle. He wasn't hungry, but he'd learned to eat whenever possible. Placing both items on his lap, he leaned over the other side of the chair and took the noteputer out of another built-in compartment. His research would help him relax.

"Enemy contact!"

Nathan snapped out of the half-doze he'd been in and looked around. It was late afternoon now, the long shadows pointed toward him. He hurriedly put the noteputer and the trash into their compartments and wiped the grit from his eyes.

"Location?" Stone asked.

"They're sallying from Devils Tower," the scout reported. "Looks like they're splitting up to hit us on both flanks."

"Type and description?"

"A mix of 'Mechs and vehicles and—My god!"

"What?"

"It's massive! It's... Hold on, we're sending you video feed, because I've never seen anything like it before! Channel four!"

Nathan switched on a small monitor to the left of his chair. The picture was fuzzy for a moment, but then the image stabilized. Nathan felt his blood run cold.

A column of Word 'Mechs and vehicles moved along a road flanked on both sides by trees, but Nathan's eyes immediately went to the armored titan near the center of the column. It was a 'Mech, but it towered over the other ones by several meters. It was hunched forward, had three long barrels on its back, and the two arms ended in muzzles. When it took a step forward, the movement was slow, ponderous, and with authority and power.

"What the hell is that?" someone said.

"It's an *Omega*," Nathan whispered.

There was a babble of voices over the radio, until Wozniak's hard voice cut through the chatter. "Clear the channel!"

"So, St. Jamais is all in," Stone said softly. "Scout Seven, have you spotted the precentor martial's Awesome yet?"

"He's not with the northern force."

"Scout Nine here!" another voice cut in. "The *Awesome*'s with the southern force! There's also...they look like large mobile structures of some sort, bristling with guns!"

"Rattler Mobile Fortresses," Nathan muttered.

"All right!" Stone's tone changed. "Slasher, Cutter, form up on me. We're going after St. Jamais. We've made the snake show his head. Let's crush it before it can retreat into its hole. Hammer, I need you and the rest of the allies to hold off that northern force. I don't care what you have to do, but stop them. I'm leaving you half the artillery tubes and a third of the aerospace cover."

"You can count on us, Devlin."

"I always have, Gideon. Skull Six out."

Wozniak growled, "All right Hammers, move out!"

Once they were on the move, the major said, "Trivedi, you told me we have to hit that *Omega* from several directions, correct?"

"Yes, sir. Have to get in close and in numbers. Fighting it one-on-one or at range is suicide. It doesn't have any short range weapons, so—" He stopped when he saw a second *Omega* appear behind the first on his screen.

"There's more of them," someone whispered. "How the hell are we going to stop them?"

"We're the Hammers," Wozniak replied, his tone hard. "We get the impossible tasks, but we always complete them."

Nathan's lance consisted of Zach Richey's *Cerberus*, Mary Kidwell's *BattleMaster*, and Hans Altschuler's *Zeus*. They, along with a platoon of armor—pairs of Manticores and Zhukovs—were moving along a swale, hidden from the battle by the trees and hills.

Most of the blocker force was to Nathan's left, deployed to stop the Word force from entering the plains. The major had called for and received an intense artillery bombardment that eliminated the fortress defenses closest to the site. Nathan's task was to find the Word flank and either pin it in place or smash it.

Richey led the way in the diamond formation, with Kidwell and Altschuler on the flanks and Nathan at the rear. The tanks were at the center of the diamond, the Manticores leading, the Zhukovs on their flanks.

"Contact!" Richey shouted.

A Word *Mongoose,* flanked by a *Hermes* and a *Jackal,* charged out of a break in the trees in front of the allied force, opened fired, and backpedaled. Richey fired, ignoring the *Mongoose*'s laser hits that melted away armor. The *Cerberus*'s one-two Gauss rifle punch tore into the *Jackal*'s torso, ripping away the armor and leaving a gaping hole on the right side. The light 'Mech wobbled but stayed on its feet. Nathan fired at the *Mongoose,* but the pilot nimbly avoided the laser.

The *Hermes* wasn't so lucky, its armor no match for the tanks' heavy weapons. As the Blakist 'Mech fell, three more charged into view.

Nathan immediately marked the *Black Hawk* as the more dangerous, but before he could say anything, the *BattleMaster* and *Zeus* opened fire. The *Black Hawk* staggered under the bombardment but still managed to fire its lasers at the *Cerberus.* The 95-ton Lament 'Mech shrugged off the few laser hits and again fired both Gauss rifles, the slugs ripping through the Clan 'Mech's right arm and torso. The *Black Hawk* fell over, armor fragments spinning across the grass.

"Keep going!" Nathan shouted and he ran forward.

The next exchange of fire finished the *Jackal* and damaged a Word *Dragonfly.* The *Mongoose* and an *Ostscout* turned and ran back the way they'd come, followed by the *Dragonfly.*

"Keep going!" Nathan shouted. "Don't let them rally!"

The clearing narrowed, then disappeared among the trees. As the Lament force reached the trees, Nathan's sensors indicated a large target was approaching. "Contact!" he shouted. "Large contact!"

"Second contact!" Kidwell shouted. "Also large!"

"Multiple contacts!" Altschuler shouted. "Smaller and faster!"

Nathan's eyes narrowed. "Zach, Mary, go left. Hans with me right. Lacy, take your tanks up the middle. Wait for my word to attack. If these are the *Omega*s, aim for the legs, and for god's sake don't take these monsters head on!"

The lance split up. Through the trees, Nathan saw something large coming into view. A pair of trees behind him exploded when fast-moving Gauss rounds struck them. A cold shot of fear went through Nathan when he imagined what those rounds could do to the *Grasshopper*—and him.

The trees thinned out, and Nathan could see the ground slope up. Word armor, at least two Level IIs' worth, were grouped around a few 'Mechs, including the ones that had just engaged. Just then, two *Omega*s crested the ridge and started down the slope toward them.

"*Mein Gott,*" Altschuler whispered. "They can't be real. They're *Dämonen* given form."

"My sensors say they're real and coming at us!" Kidwell shouted.

"They're real, Hans," Nathan said. "Stay in the woods and pick your targets!" He felt a shiver of fear go through him. "Okay people, I'm calling in the big guns. Stand by. White Six to Thor Five. Authentication Delta-Foxtrot-Alpha-Eight-Seven-Eight. Fire mission, priority Alpha One. Over."

"Thor Five to White Six. Fire Mission, Alpha Priority One. Authentication acknowledged. Standing by. Over."

The *Omega*s opened fire, the triple volley of Gauss rounds slicing through the trees like a giant buzzsaw, sending wood chunks flying through the remaining trees. Several fragments struck the *Grasshopper* hard enough to dent armor plates.

Nathan forced himself to glance at a screen to his left, finding the numbers he needed. "Grid reference One-Three-Tango-Echo-Kilo-Two-One-Eight-Eight-Six-Three-Eight-Seven-Zero. Targets are armor, 'Mechs and a superheavy 'Mech in the open. Over."

"Acknowledged, White Six. Grid reference One-Three-Tango-Echo-Kilo-Two-One-Eight-Eight-Six-Three-Eight-Seven-Zero," the artillery controller repeated. "Targets are armor, 'Mechs and superheavy 'Mech in the open. Out." After several seconds, she said, "R, C, HE in effect, five rounds, over."

Nathan felt his stomach tighten. "R, C, HE in effect, five rounds, out."

The *Omega*s again fired their Gauss rifles as they advanced. Long-range missiles, energy beams and lighter autocannons from the rest of the Word force joined them. The trees around Nathan exploded as they absorbed the massed firepower, wood fragments scattering in every direction, covering the ground around Nathan.

"Everyone all right?" he asked.

"So far," Kidwell replied, "but we're running out of cover fast!"

"We can't face all of that!" Richey replied.

"Pick your shots!" Nathan shouted, aiming at the *Mongoose* that was now advancing. He fired and the laser bit into the light 'Mech's right arm and left nothing but a stub.

"*Mein Gott,*" Altschuler repeated. "What are *those*?"

Nathan saw smaller, four-legged 'Mechs that reminded him of spiders running ahead of the main force. Another shiver went down his spine. Reports about them were vague, but they agreed these were some sort of AI controlled 'Mech—*Revenant*s, if he remembered correctly.

"Don't worry about them," Nathan replied. "Hold your ground, pick your shots ,and keep as many trees as you can between those *Omega*s and you!" He glanced at the clock to his left. How much longer did they have to wait?

"*Splash, over,*" said Thor Five.

"Splash, out," Nathan replied on the lance channel, "Heads up! Incoming arty!"

The first round slammed into the slope 400 meters from Nathan's location, ripping apart both right-side legs of a *Revenant*, dropping the 'Mech on its side.

"White Six to Thor Five. Adjust fire," he said. "Drop one hundred, left one hundred, over."

The controller sounded almost bored. "Drop one hundred, left one hundred, out."

The Manticores and Zhukovs opened fire from the woods to Nathan's left. One of the Word tanks, a Stygian, abruptly exploded when it ran head-on into two cobalt beams that punched through the armor and found the missile ammo. Another Stygian changed direction, but a Zhukov's heavy autocannons ripped it apart.

Nathan snapped off a shot at a *Revenant*, leaving a deep scar along its side. He moved fifty meters to his right, the weight of his *Grasshopper* making the tree fragments under his feet *crack* loudly. The other members of his lance were firing, but there were so many targets...

A Word *Lightray*, supported by the *Dragonfly* and a *Griffin IIC*, charged at him. On his left, Nathan saw Altschuler open fire at the *Lightray*, but the 55-ton 'Mech avoided the *Zeus*'s fire and fired at Nathan instead.

The pulse laser found the *Grasshopper*'s right leg, melting away armor. Nathan fired back, his Clan large laser connecting with the *Lightray*, scarring it across the torso. The *Dragonfly* and *Griffin IIC* both opened fire, and the *Grasshopper*'s armor took both missile impacts and lasers hits. Missed shots shredded the trees he was using for cover.

"Splash, over."

"Splash, out!" Nathan shouted, moving to his right. The *Dragonfly* was cutting to his left, the *Griffin IIC* to the right. Two more Word 'Mechs, a *Shootist* and *Buccaneer*, were charging Altschuler's location.

The artillery arrived and the closely packed rounds hammered the Word force. The *Omega* Nathan had targeted was bracketed by several rounds, sending dirt and shrapnel flying into the air.

Nathan had enough time to shout into the radio, "White Six to Thor Five. Fire for effect!" before the *Griffin* fired all four of its missile racks and large laser at him. The missiles peppered the *Grasshopper*, but the laser missed by several meters.

The *Dragonfly* also fired, its lasers burning mostly trees, but one hit home, and Nathan lost more armor on his leg. The *Lightray* fired again, its large pulse laser and medium lasers scorching away more armor.

Nathan fired at the *Griffin*, scoring hits that dissipated armor across the Word 'Mech's torso, but the enemy kept moving. With cold certainty, Nathan knew he was in trouble.

He heard more firing from his left and right, heard Altschuler cursing in German over the radio, interspersed with the quick jabs of conversation between Kidwell and Richey as they fought. The artillery was ripping apart several Word 'Mechs, including the *Omega*, but its companion was still coming, and Nathan had to move to his left as the tree he had been standing next to ceased to exist when a Gauss round passed through it.

"Stop treating it like a museum piece and use it for what it was designed and built for—a weapon." The major's words came without warning, the memory clear down to his cold, flat tone. *"The Word won't care if you're piloting the first* Mackie. *Thus is war—things are destroyed, people die, and no one cares how old or valuable items are."*

The *Dragonfly* was also moving, looking to circle behind him. The *Lightray* opened fire again, dissolving armor across the *Grasshopper*'s chest and right arm. Nathan fired all his weapons at the *Lightray*, but scored only a single laser hit.

"Treat that Grasshopper for what it is, and worry about documenting its history after the war is over, if you're still alive."

"If you're still alive," Nathan muttered. Sweat pouring down his face, he put the *Grasshopper* into a run at the *Lightray*, crashing through several half-destroyed trees. The Word 'Mech backpedaled quickly, opening the gap between the two 'Mechs. Nathan saw the *Dragonfly* turn and run after him, intent on shooting him in the back.

The *Griffin* fired another volley of missiles, but most missed, exploding around the *Grasshopper*'s feet and the ground behind it. He fired at the *Lightray*, scoring with the large laser and a couple of the mediums. The *Lightray* backed into a tree, knocking it down, but slowing the 'Mech.

The *Dragonfly* flashed in, determined to deliver a full volley into the *Grasshopper*'s back. Nathan jammed down on the foot pedals, and the 'Mech shot into the air on streams of plasma— back toward the *Dragonfly*. The lighter 'Mech slowed, then tried changing direction, but the smashed trees all around it made the Word 'Mech stumble.

The *Grasshopper* came down on top of the *Dragonfly*, both feet slamming into the 40-ton 'Mech. Armor buckled, cracked and gave way under the pile-driver force. Inside the *Grasshopper*'s cockpit, Nathan felt the impact with his whole body, the seat harness barely holding him in his seat.

The *Dragonfly* staggered back, while Nathan landed hard on his feet, the impact leaving a slight depression. He snapped-fired his large laser at the lighter 'Mech, then charged. He slammed into the Word 'Mech, shattering more armor and knocking the *Dragonfly* down.

An incoming-missiles alert made Nathan turn right into several missiles from the *Griffin*. More armor fragmented, and Nathan knew his armor was almost gone.

Explosions ripped into the *Griffin IIC*'s back, followed by a massive explosion that ripped apart the left side of the Word 'Mech and sent the arm flying. The former Clan 'Mech staggered drunkenly, then one of the Zhukovs opened fire with both heavy cannons. The *Griffin* dropped, showering its surroundings with fragments.

The *Lightray* spun toward the tanks, only to be showered by missiles coming from Altschuler's location. Kidwell's *BattleMaster*, its armor cracked and laser-scarred but still intact, strode out of the woods behind the tanks, its PPC pointed at the *Lightray*. The Word

'Mech turned and fled. Nathan glanced around and saw other Word forces were falling back.

"Mary, status?" Nathan asked.

"Still breathing," she replied. "One *Omega* is down, artillery hammered it to pieces. Zach's *Cerberus* has a bad knee and the—"

The *BattleMaster* reeled as a high-speed round slammed into its torso, crushing armor and exposing its internals. The second *Omega* wasn't retreating but moving forward, rallying the other Word forces.

"White Six to Thor Five!" Nathan shouted. "Fire mission, priority Alpha One! Over!"

"Thor Five to White Six. Fire Mission, Alpha Priority One acknowledged. Standing by. Over."

"Grid reference One-Three-Tango-Echo-Kilo-Two-One-Six-Niner-Three-Eight-Six-Six. Targets are superheavy 'Mech and other 'Mechs in the open. Send anything you have left! Over."

"Acknowledged, White Six," the controller replied. "Grid reference One-Three-Tango-Echo-Kilo-Two-One-Six-Niner-Three-Eight-Six-Six. Targets are superheavy 'Mech and other 'Mechs in the open. Out."

On Nathan's right, Altschuler's mauled *Zeus* limped out of the trees, its right side shattered and mangled. A Manticore and both Zhukovs opened fire at the *Omega*. The massive 'Mech absorbed the fire as if it was water, then fired at Nathan.

Nathan screamed as the *Grasshopper* reeled when two Gauss rounds and a burst of autocannon shells ripped through the weakened armor, exploding the right arm, the right side, and right leg. His world spun as the 'Mech lost the battle with gravity

The last thing he heard before he lost consciousness was, "R, F, HE in effect, ten rounds, special delivery. Over."

DEADWOOD, NORTH AMERICA
TERRA
WORD OF BLAKE PROTECTORATE
25 DECEMBER 3078

Machine sounds slowly penetrated Nathan's awareness, the faint beeps acting like a beacon in the darkness. Other senses added their input. The smell of disinfectant made his nose wrinkle, touch told him he was on his back, and his mouth was desert-dry.

With effort, he opened his eyes, but all he could see was a gray blob. He closed his eyes and opened them again. The blob became a little clearer. He blinked several more times, and each time the gray became a little clearer. Finally, the blob became a ceiling. He turned his head slowly to each side and saw he was in a hotel or motel room—a couple of chairs, a chest of drawers, a tri-vid in one corner, two doors, one of which was next to a set of closed curtains.

He then noticed his right arm and leg were stiff and ached. He didn't have the strength to pull the covers off to look at himself, but he could feel the splints holding the limbs straight.

The door next to the window opened, and a woman wearing a blue jumpsuit under a field jacket came in. She was blond and tired-looking. "Good," she said when she looked at Nathan after closing the door. "You're awake. I'll let Major Wozniak know once I've checked your vitals."

"W-what happened?" Nathan rasped.

The medtech walked over to the bed, taking off the jacket as she did so. "The Coalition won. The Word has surrendered worldwide, though there are a few holdouts. You're in a Deadwood hotel we've taken over as a hospital, eighty kilometers from Devils Tower. You've got compound fractures of the right leg and arm, a major concussion, and multiple cuts and bruises across your entire body." She looked at a monitor sitting on a nightstand next to the bed. "Good. Life signs stable. Can you sit up?"

With the medtech's help, Nathan sat up far enough for her to add several more pillows behind his head. Once he settled back, she poured a cup of water. She added a straw and held it in front of his face. "Sip slowly."

As Nathan sipped, there was a knock at the door. "Enter!" the medtech called out.

The door opened and Major Wozniak stepped in. He wore a black jumpsuit under a black longcoat, and his expression was the same familiar mask. "You're awake."

The medtech handed the cup to Nathan, then turned to face the major. "Ten minutes, sir. I'll be back when your time is up."

Wozniak stepped away from the door. "Fine."

After the medtech grabbed her jacket and left, Wozniak walked over to one of the chairs and sat. "We won."

"That's what the medtech said."

Wozniak nodded. "The Devils Tower battle came down to a duel between Stone and St. Jamais. Stone walked away, St. Jamais didn't. The survivors retreated into the fortress, but we got inside, and most of them died."

"The *Omega*s?"

"Destroyed, either in battle or by the Word themselves." The major tilted his head slightly. "One of the *Omega*s was hit so hard by artillery, they can't find any piece larger than this chair."

"I don't remember what happened. The battalion?"

Wozniak shook his head. "Down to a reinforced company. Kranski didn't make it. She died surrounded by destroyed Word 'Mechs and vehicles, just like she wanted."

"I'm sorry. She and Lou deserved better."

"We all did." Wozniak leaned back and exhaled slowly. "What are you going to do? The doctors told me that it's going to take months to rehab both your leg and arm."

This time, Nathan shook his head. "I'm not going to try to regain active status. The time for soldiers is passing. It'll be gone by the time I'm ready. I'll go back to what I was doing before the war—becoming a historian."

"The *Grasshopper* is in the same condition you are, but the cockpit's intact, as are your noteputer and crystals. The 'Mech may or may not be repaired."

Nathan sipped his water. "Don't return it to combat. I think it deserves to be part of a museum display. It's served all its pilots well for three centuries. Now it can serve to remind future generations about war and what it does to us all."

"I'll pass along your suggestion to Devlin."

"What are you going to do, now that the war is over, sir?"

Wozniak was silent for several long seconds. "For now, I'll rebuild the Hammers. After that, I have unfinished business elsewhere." He stood. "I'll send your noteputer and crystals as soon as I can. For now, rest." He smiled slightly, something Nathan had never seen him do before. "That's an order, Lieutenant."

"Yes, sir."

Wozniak walked to the door. He stopped and turned toward Nathan. "Are you religious?"

"New Avalon Baptist."

He nodded. "Today's the twenty-fifth. Merry Christmas, Nathan."

"Merry Christmas, sir."

EPILOGUE:
WHERE LEGENDS COME TO REST
PHILIP A. LEE

DORCHESTER, ENGLAND
TERRA
PREFECTURE X
REPUBLIC OF THE SPHERE
25 MAY 3084

Hands shoved in his pockets, Billy Northrup wandered the streets in a daze, unsure of what to do, where to go. Rambling beat the alternative of staying home and weathering yet another argument from his uncle, but something about these streets, places he'd known since he was a child, somehow felt alien to him now, further heightening how utterly lost he felt.

Within two weeks he'd be graduating secondary school. All of his mates had *something* already lined up—college, a good job, a promising future—but he had nothing. Nothing was what his father had left him. And at this rate, nothing was what he would amount to.

It didn't help that Uncle Rupert was constantly reminding him of that. To be fair, Billy wouldn't have liked it either if his own older brother and wife died, and Billy was forced to raise their young orphaned toddler by himself. Uncle Rupert had never wanted responsibility for Billy, but he was the closest living relative Billy had left, and—fond as Uncle Rupert was of saying—he had until graduation to figure out how to get the bloody hell out of the house.

But he had no job prospects, no money to afford university, no real skills to speak of, no wealthy friends who could just hand him a job. Wherever he went from here would be on himself, by his own two hands.

"Get out!" his uncle had shouted after their last argument. "And don't come back 'til you've come up with a plan for getting out of my house!"

So, with only a handful of cash in his pocket, Billy roamed the rainy, overcast streets until the steeple of a church caught his eye. A poignant memory pricked him: his parents taking him here for Mass. Did Father Dave still preach here? He always seemed to know the right thing to say.

With nothing better to do, Billy found the rectory and knocked on the door. Twice.

No answer.

Rather than knock a third time, he shrugged, about-faced, and got halfway down the walk before he heard a door open and someone call out after him.

"Can I help you, young man?"

Father Dave—he'd barely aged a single day since Billy had last seen him. The light of recognition illuminated kindly, bespectacled eyes. "Billy? Billy Northrup?"

Even after all this time, the man remembered his *name*.

Before Billy could invent some excuse to worm his way out of a conversation, he found himself in Father Dave's office, nursing a cup of steaming black tea. And he didn't know what triggered it—maybe it was something in the tea, or just the general feeling of safety here—but his insides just spilled out, all the truth and worries piling up until he felt guilty for burdening Father Dave with so much when the priest undoubtedly had more important matters to attend to.

They talked for a little over an hour, at the end of which Father Dave wrote something down on a piece of paper and handed it over, along with a few worn bills from his wallet. "Go to this address— here's some money for a train ticket. Just take the afternoon to look around. Maybe something'll speak to you. Maybe you'll find what you're looking for. And if not, my door's always open."

Billy didn't recognize the address on the paper, but he thanked Father Dave and left the rectory, feeling like he'd left at least part of his worries back in that office.

The train took him to, of all places, the famed Bovington Tank and BattleMech Museum. He'd gone once, as a kid—after all, what young boy didn't stomp plastic 'Mechs or drive plastic tanks over their other toys?—but his father getting killed during the war had erased any desire of ever going back. After that, 'Mechs and tanks, even the pretend kind, left a sour taste in his mouth. Those giant metal machines had left him fatherless.

Yet Billy wandered into the museum anyway, even if only to duck out of the rain for a few minutes. Just inside the main entrance, he could already see a few small tanks on display beyond the ticket counter.

His first thought: *Are either of those the kind that killed my father?*

His hands shook, so he balled them into fists to steady them. Regardless of Father Dave's advice, this was the mother of all bad ideas.

A jovial middle-aged woman in a well-tailored uniform approached him. "Can I help you, young sir?"

Billy unclenched and flexed his fingers, unsure how to respond. "I, uh..."

The guide's smile broadened. "Have you been here before?"

Billy nodded sedately. "Once. Long time ago." He hesitated. Much like Father Dave, something about this woman set him at ease, and before he knew it, more words tumbled out of his mouth. "My...dad...he, uh, he was a Com Guard MechWarrior. He...he died in the war."

He did not need to specify *which* war. Everyone on the whole planet had felt the ravages of the conflict in some way, regardless of whether they supported the Word of Blake's misguided crusade or not.

"Ah, my condolences. Did you come here as a way of honoring his memory?"

Hands shoved in his pockets again, Billy absently scuffed a shoe sole from side to side on the floor while trying avoid the guide's eyes. What she said wasn't entirely true, but the guide probably didn't care about honesty, so he just went with it. "Yeah. Something like that."

"Do you know what type of BattleMech he piloted?"

Billy didn't know. In a way, he'd never *wanted* to know. But unless he opted for outright rudeness, he couldn't just shoo the woman away. She was just doing her job, after all. So he pulled a name at random, the most ridiculous and least-threatening 'Mech name he could remember:

"A *Grasshopper*, I think."

A light flickered in the guide's eyes, like he'd uttered some magical password. "Well, young sir, you are in luck. We have a special exhibit in our Star League-era collection. If you follow me, I'll show you where it is."

Billy clenched his fists again. Apprehension gripped him. Instinct told him to turn tail and scarper, but then the paper in his pocket crinkled. Father Dave had wanted him to come here for a reason.

She's just doing her job, he reminded himself.

He nodded and followed the guide into the museum's collection. The first thing he noticed upon passing through the vestibule and entering the main part of the building was just how utterly *huge* BattleMechs were. Right inside the entrance, a 100-ton *Mackie*—an MSK-5S model, according to the placard—loomed several stories above him. The first BattleMech ever built and deployed in combat.

He craned his neck to look up at it, and his hands shook, anxious about how easily this retired behemoth could crush him underfoot without its pilot realizing it had even stepped on anything. All these 'Mechs seemed even larger to him now than they had when he was younger, even though he'd grown quite a bit since that field trip. For a split second, he imagined the *Mackie* stepping off its platform and pulverizing him, erasing him from existence without a thought. Of course, the 'Mech couldn't move. Vital parts from most of these 'Mechs had been cannibalized back when Devlin Stone's Allied Coalition forces—alongside which Billy's father had fought and died—had landed in force on this planet in overwhelming numbers. The museum curators saw the writing on the wall for the defending forces, and to prevent the desperate Blakists from looting the museum's exhibits for replacement materiel, they had reduced each war machine into a shell of its former self, their parts hidden away in some secret location. Or at least that's what one of the placards he lingered on said.

Each 'Mech and tank he passed, he couldn't help wondering: *Did one of your siblings kill my father?*

One exhibit in particular sent a string of lit firecrackers down his spine and kneaded his stomach into knots just from the sight of it: a stark-white outline of angular armor, shoulder spines, and taloned

'Mech feet, a single weapon barrel protruding out of the head. This was the last surviving Word of Blake *Archangel* OmniMech on Terra. Even the silhouette filled him with a sense of dread, despite its white, "good guy" coloration.

He'd grown up fearing these things. His parents had grown up during the days of ComStar's administration of Terra, but when the Word of Blake had swooped in and drove ComStar out back in '58, everything *changed*, and not for the better. His parents had both fled Terra, only to return at the head of the Com Guard's disastrous Case White invasion in 3068. That failure had forced his mum and dad to go into hiding, and Billy'd been born not long after. Throughout his entire childhood, he worried every single day that a Word of Blake patrol would storm through Dorchester in search of ComStar spies and arrest both his parents for treason.

Even today, his friends spoke of the Blakists' unsettlingly shaped 'Mechs with a noticeable tremor in their voices.

Did you kill my father?

The plasma-rifle barrel that lent the 'Mech's head a cyclopean feel seemed to stare right back at him. *What if I did?* it seemed to answer. *What in Blake's name are you gonna do about it, you worthless frail?*

Billy swallowed. What *could* he do about it, given the chance? He was just a kid, really. What could *anyone* do against such a fearsome beast?

Several other exhibits they passed stirred up more feelings he couldn't quite put into words. Several tank-crew compartments and 'Mech cockpits were on prominent display at eye level, with cross sections visible behind lucite panels to prevent people from touching exposed wires and myomer bundles that were doubtless older than he could fathom. The lone exception: one 'Mech cockpit exhibit allowed patrons to settle down into the pilot's seat and handle the controls. Billy looked in for a few long moments, catching the odd, musty scent of old metal and cracked, sweat-stained naugahyde within, but he declined in favor of letting the little kids nearby pretend to be MechWarriors for the afternoon.

But the strangest takeaway from seeing these interiors: the jarring realization that *someone*, some brave—or foolhardy?—soul, a *real* person, had strapped into each and every one of these seats and driven or piloted their way into the jaws of probable death. His *father* had been among them.

The surreal weight of history settled on him, striking him with a dizzying wave of vertigo.

What kind of mettle did it take to do this sort of thing? Did it take nerves of steel to pull on a neurohelmet, fasten all the buckles of the safety harness, and run headlong into danger? What had spurred them to do such a thing, to risk their lives like that?

Over his shoulder and down the way, he could still spot the white shoulder spines of that damnable *Archangel*, and all the tales of Blakist atrocities, all of the news reports, the footage of battles during Stone's liberation—the reasons that Celestial-series OmniMechs like that *Archangel* were to be feared—they all came back to him in great clarity.

His father, and all of those men and women who had crewed these weapons of war, had risked their lives—and many ultimately lost them—because fighting against the Word of Blake and everything they'd stood for was *the right thing to do*. Not just some petty border conflict or a selfish grab for power or territory—the war against the Word, and ultimately for Terra, had been a great battle waged over the soul and future of the human race, and to lose such a conflict was inconceivable. Had the Blakists won, had people like his father sat back and did nothing, what would Terra— no, the whole Inner Sphere—be like now?

The thought turned his entire world upside down.

"Ah," the guide said at last, coming to a stop just ahead. "Here we are."

Billy followed her, but past one of the support beams, he saw only open space—not even a single 'Mech, just a transparent display case about three meters tall.

He turned to his companion. "I don't get it. Where's the exhibit?"

"Right here." She gestured to the case.

Billy approached with tentative steps, his mouth twisted in confusion. The case housed nothing but a rectangular metal slab, its longer side no bigger than about a meter and a half. And what was that on the metal? Handwriting? Scratches?

The large placard before the case answered most of his questions.

Lantren Corporation GHR-5H *Grasshopper* (modified)
Manufactured: 2779, Bryant, Terran Hegemony
Decommissioned: 3083, Terra, Republic of the Sphere

Written on this cockpit bulkhead are the names of the many MechWarriors that piloted this 'Mech in combat throughout a span of three centuries. The Grasshopper from which this bulkhead was taken was believed to be among the first of its kind, and it saw action in countless battles across the Inner Sphere, including the historic liberation of Terra from the Word of Blake in 3078. Though this BattleMech was surrendered to Exarch Devlin Stone's Military Materiel Redemption Program (MMRP), this bulkhead was preserved as a reminder of those who have fought and died to defend life and liberty, and it remains as a testament to their legacy of bravery, commitment, and resolve.

Billy looked up at the metal plate and tried to read all the names. Some were legible, others less so; some were written in a faded hand, some carved by a sharp object. At least one name in the list was inscribed either in Mandarin or Japanese—he could never tell them apart without context.

Tai-i Sam Tanaka, Sergeant Virgil Armstrong, Lieutenant Sigland Idelson, Sergeant Nathaniel Trivedi—each name an entire life lived, some recent, some hundreds of years ago. The full list of legible names at the bottom of the placard served as a lens into the history of those who'd fought and won and lost with this very plate mere decimeters from their heads.

The guide fell in alongside him, and just from the way she spoke, he could tell most of her speech was a memorized spiel. "The interesting thing about this bulkhead is that it's one of only a few pieces of its donor 'Mech that survived largely unscathed for the last three hundred years..."

Billy listened to her with one ear, but all he could really focus on were the names on that list. Who among them had died in combat in the cockpit this plate had been taken from? How many of these MechWarriors had been transferred to a different 'Mech, or had lived long enough to see retirement?

Had his father written his own name in a 'Mech somewhere? Had he demonstrated bravery, commitment, and resolve while fighting the Blakists? Billy wanted to think so.

His dad had done the right thing in fighting the Blakists, and that's what mattered. If his father could do the right thing, then Billy owed it to himself to do the same, to do whatever he could to prevent another scourge like the Word of Blake from rising from their ashes.

But would the Republic Armed Forces of Devlin Stone himself even accept him? Would he even meet their base requirements? And if so, could he actually muster the nerve to set foot in a BattleMech cockpit or the fighting compartment of a tank?

As his gaze refocused on the ancient names etched on that steel plate, he knew there was only one way to find out.

THIRD PRINCIPES GUARDS HQ
TIKONOV
PREFECTURE IV
REPUBLIC OF THE SPHERE
9 JULY 3090

In MechWarrior shorts and cooling vest, Billy stood at the foot of the BattleMech before him in the 'Mech bay and looked up at it, beaming. He'd piloted a half-dozen different models back at Sandhurst Military College, but this one here—this one was special.

This particular *Nyx* NX-80, fresh off the Krupp Armament Works assembly line back on Terra, was assigned to him. The other lance leaders in his company had been offered first dibs on it, but Joong and Montgomery were too attached to their own 'Mechs to cheat on them with a newer, sleeker model, so Billy got it by default. Not that he minded. After so many trainers and hand-me-downs at Sandhurst, a recent grad like him was lucky to get something so new—and just in time for today's pass-in-review for Colonel Narron.

"Got 'er all prepped and ready, Lieutenant," Billy's lead tech, Karina, said, wiping sweat from her forehead with a rag. "She's all yours. You want me to bring the gantry over?"

Billy shook his head and let his eyes trace the path upward, the silvery chain ladder leading to the 30-ton 'Mech's cockpit. "Thanks, but no thanks. Think I'd better get used to taking the long way up, yeah?"

And so he climbed, each rung reminding him that his father had taken this same sort of path years ago. He'd wormed through a similar cockpit hatch, slid into a similar command couch, latched similar harness belts into place, sat at similar controls, donned a similar neurohelmet. That anger and fear Billy had carried with him all those years ago had long faded, replaced instead by a sense of necessity and honor.

Father Dave had steered him down the right path all those years ago. The RAF had not only offered him three square meals and a place to sleep—things he'd sorely needed after Uncle Rupert had forsaken him—but military service had also given him structure and discipline. After basic training, he'd no longer felt lost. He was right where he needed to be.

Billy hadn't even taken a moment to enjoy the 'Mech's new paint-smell before his neurohelmet radio chirped on.

"Northrup," Captain Svendsen's husky voice said over the channel, "you planning to join us out here any time soon?"

"Absolutely, sir," Billy replied. "Just one last thing, and I'm oscar mike."

"Well, shake the lead out. If the colonel has to wait on us, it's your ass."

"Understood, sir. Won't take me but a minute."

From a utility pocket, he withdrew a penknife and straightened it with a soft *click*. Using short, deft strokes, he carved the knifepoint into the new 'Mech's blank canvas—the steel plate just above his head. He cut through fresh paint and scored the metal deep enough so that three hundred years from now, his name would still be legible:

3090–LT William Northrup, Jr., RAF

"This one's for you, Dad," he whispered.

With a sigh of melancholy and relief, Billy eased his throttle up and walked the *Nyx* out of the hangar to stand in formation alongside his brothers and sisters in arms.

BARTOK FARMS
OUTSIDE APOPKA, BRYANT
PREFECTURE X
REPUBLIC OF THE SPHERE
30 OCTOBER 3090

Tamara Bartok smelled smoke on the wind long before she saw it. With her hunting rifle in its saddle holster, she crossed the field on horseback, keeping the worrisome black plume in sight the whole ride. The apple grove obscured the blaze's origin from sights, so all of the worst-case scenarios gnawed at her rib cage.

A barn on fire. An exploded grain silo. Raiders.

Tamara unholstered the rifle, just in case. She'd fought too many storms, weathered too many hardships to simply let marauders come in and destroy what little progress she'd made on trying to reclaim some small measure of this planet's agrarian past.

Her heart thumped against her breastbone even after she skirted the orchard to see the lay of the empty field. Out in the middle of a half-plowed field, a mound of metal machinery lay motionless. A cloud of greasy black smoke belched forth from a removed panel on the side.

Abe, her head farmhand, had already run headlong into the mess by the time she slowed her horse enough to dismount and lend a hand. Holding a cloth over his mouth to ward off the smoke, Abe reached into the open square hole, whipped his hand out with a shake and a curse, then tried again.

A shower of sparks spat out through the hole. Abe reached in all the way up to his shoulder, ground his teeth against the heat—and a loud clank accompanied the decelerating sound of an electrical system turning itself off.

"Blasted piece of garbage," Abe muttered. His whole arm was black nearly to his shoulder from the smoke, the sleeve shredded from rooting around in the machine's interior.

"What happened?" Tamara asked.

"*Guess.*" Abe shook his head. "Same damn thing as last week. But that's what we get for buying a refurbished auto-plow."

Tamara shrugged. "It's all we could afford on such short notice." The machine breaking down again so soon was worrisome, but at least she hadn't been forced to defend her farm against raiders, with only a hunting rifle against trained killers. And on the bright side, half the field was already plowed, so even if they couldn't get the auto-plow repaired fast enough, they would still be able to plant *something* before Bryant's planting window closed for good. Still...

"Can you fix it?"

Abe grunted and pulled a spanner from this tool pouch. "Maybe. Here, help me get this panel off first."

Between them, it took about an hour and a half to remove the main access panel and then the rest of cowling, once they determined the problem had occurred deeper inside the machine. Despite the smoke having cleared, the auto-plow's innards were as black as a Blakist's soul and stank like fried electronics and melted plastic. All told, Tamara had seen worse.

Abe poked around in the works for a few minutes before giving his assessment. "Well, she's broke, that's for sure." He moved a few melted hoses around. "Compressor blew. Motivator's probably fried. But the fire mighta wrecked more stuff in the inside."

"Cheaper'n getting a new one, I guess," Tamara said.

But Abe's brow furrowed. He leaned deeper into the workings and wiped away some of the soot with his hand. "What the hell...?"

Tamara leaned in. "What'sa the matter?" If something else had broken, something too expensive to replace...

Abe beckoned her down closer to where he was looking at. He shined a small flashlight deeper into the auto-plow's guts. "Come take a gander at this."

Tamara knelt next to him and strained to see what the beam played over. "What am I looking at?"

"This here." Abe tapped a finger on a metal support strut on the inside of the machine. "Don't think I ever noticed that before."

And then she saw it. Small letters, each one laser etched into the steel surface but worn with age.

"'*Cavaletts*'?"

"Whaddaya you reckon that means? That's not any parts manufacturer I've ever heard of."

The name didn't sound familiar to Tamara either. Whatever it was, she didn't much care. There were bigger things to worry about, like raiders, or feeding the local populace. Famine could kill a community just as quickly as pirates could.

"Probably just something stamped on the scrap metal used to refurbish this," she said. "Who cares? That part's not broken." She gave Abe an encouraging smack on the shoulder. "C'mon, let's get this thing fixed. These fields ain't gonna plow themselves."

Grasshopper, in spring
arises like the Phoenix.
In fall, harvested.

–Sho-sa Saburo Atsuda, 2925

ABOUT THE AUTHORS

Kevin Killiany spent decades working in education, mental health, and family preservation/child protection/community support services before selling his first story in 2000. He has written for *Star Trek, Doctor Who, BattleTech/MechWarrior, Shadowrun*, and *The Valiant Universe Roleplaying Game. Down to Dirt*, the first of Kevin's Dirt and Stars series of young adult alternate history novels, launched in 2016 to excellent reviews; *Life on Dirt* followed in May, and the final volume of the first trilogy, *Rise from Dirt*, is coming this winter. Kevin and his wife Valerie live on the coast of North Carolina; they have four children and one grandsquiggle.

Freelance writer, novelist, and editor **Travis Heermann** is the author of seven novels, including *Death Wind* (with Jim Pinto) and *The Ronin Trilogy,* plus short fiction in *Apex Magazine, Cemetery Dance, Alembical,* and others. His freelance work in gaming realms includes contributions to the *Firefly Roleplaying Game, BattleTech, Legend of Five Rings, d20 System,* and *EVE Online.*

Darrell "FlailingDeath" Myers is a new fiction author in the *BattleTech* universe. A member of the *BattleTech* Demo Team, Darrell enjoys playing and teaching others to play the game, and is excited to contribute to the wider game universe. His other works consist of several scenarios and small unit profiles published on BattleCorps. Darrell currently lives with his family near Washington, DC.

Alan Brundage has been a sci-fi junkie for decades, avidly consuming books and other media, and honing his writing skills. He has been a *BattleTech* fan for almost as long as he can remember, and was overjoyed to publish his first BattleCorps story back in 2014. He lives with his loving partner and their two cats at the interstice of north and south Ontario, Canada, surrounded by rocks and trees, and trees and rocks, and water.

Philip A. Lee is a freelance writer and editor whose many writing contributions to the *BattleTech* universe include more than a dozen pieces of *BattleTech* short fiction and various sourcebook writing. He has also contributed fiction and sourcebook material for the *Shadowrun, Cosmic Patrol, Valiant Universe Roleplaying Game, Pathfinder, Steamcraft*, and more. He lives in Dayton, Ohio, with his wife and three cats. To learn more about his work, look for @ joechummer on Twitter and visit philipleewriting.com.

Dr. Geoff Swift got tired of his lucrative career as a materials scientist improving batteries for missiles and other defense articles, and retired in March 2017 to pursue a writing career. It pays a lot less, but at least he's his own boss, provided you don't count editors, publishers, readers, and a quartet of cats. He was introduced to (seduced by) *BattleTech* in 1991 but got sidetracked earning five degrees, including a PhD from Caltech. He got back to important things in 2001 when he refocused on *BattleTech*. His writing has appeared in over two dozen *BattleTech* products.

Writing on and off for *BattleTech* since 1993, **Chris Hussey** is the author of *Hot Spots, Chaos March, Royalty & Rogues*, and a contributor on numerous other sourcebooks. Chris has a special place in his internal structure for the *BattleTech*. He's written over a dozen stories for BattleCorps and is a published author for other game lines, with non-gaming fiction and nonfiction titles to his credit. Chris lives in the Periphery of the US (Iowa) with four kids, a wife, and a dog who feels it's his right to leave special "supply caches" around the house.

Jason Hansa is an active-duty major in the United States Army, and has deployed to both Iraq and Afghanistan. Major Hansa has also previously served in both South Korea and Germany, and is currently assigned as a doctrine developer at Fort Lee, Virginia. Jason has several science-fiction stories published on BattleCorps, including "Three Points of Pride" and "Irreplaceable," and is currently enrolled in Saint Leo University's low-residency Creative Writing graduate degree program.

Aaron Cahall is a writer, editor, and communications professional. He first climbed into a BattleMech more than twenty years ago, and was proud to join the *BattleTech* freelancing corps in 2013. In addition to his fiction work in the *BattleTech* universe, he has served as the editor of the line's recent rulebooks and sourcebooks, and provided public relations and communications assistance to the line developers. He lives in Bel Air, Maryland, with his wife Tracy and daughter Anna.

According to William H. Keith, author of the Gray Death Legion *BattleTech* novels, **Robert Jeschonek** is "a master of military mecha mayhem." Nebula Award winner Mike Resnick (*Santiago* and the *Starship* series) calls him "a towering talent." Author of *Battlenaut Crucible* and *Beware the Black Battlenaut,* Robert has written *Star Trek* and *Doctor Who* fiction, plus mind-blowing stories have appeared in *Galaxy's Edge, Escape Pod,* and many other publications. He won a Scribe Award for Best Original Novel and grand prize in Pocket Books's Strange New Worlds contest. Visit him online at www.thefictioneer.com or look him up on Facebook or Twitter.

Alex Fauth remembers when the Fourth Succession War was a forthcoming event, and has been playing *BattleTech* most of his life. When he's not pushing around tiny plastic robots, he's an academic, researcher, writer, blogger, and a few other things. He's also drawn over two thousand sprites for *MegaMek,* which he regards as "a maddening accomplishment." Alex lives in Australia, where everything can and will kill you.

Craig A. Reed, Jr.'s first *BattleTech* publishing credits were several items that appeared in the *BattleTechnology* magazine, including his first coauthored story. For the past seven years, he has written for BattleCorps, and has both writing and fact-checking credits in several *BattleTech* products and the *Valiant Universe Roleplaying Game.* In addition, he has coauthored three novels in the Outcast Ops series (available on Kindle) and is currently working on the fourth. Living in Florida after stops in Pennsylvania, England and Maryland, he keeps one eye on his writing and the other on the Weather Channel, having experienced Hurricane Charley up close and personal in 2004.

A SPLINTER OF HOPE

A BATTLETECH NOVELLA BY PHILIP A. LEE
AVAILABLE NOW

The future of the Federated Suns stands at the edge of a precipice…

Violent expansion of the Capellan Confederation and the Draconis Combine has cost recently crowned First Prince Julian Davion more than just countless strategic worlds. The war's toll claimed a mentor and close friend, and righteous vengeance burns bright.

To rally his people and preserve the future of the Federated Suns, Julian funnels the fires of justice into an ambitious yet risky campaign to retake a vital system: New Syrtis, the lost capital of the Capellan March. Success would dislodge an ancient enemy from their strategic foothold in Suns space, but failure may cost Julian the nation he inherited.

However, the Capellan people have fought dearly for their prize, and will do anything in their power to hold onto it. Will Julian's gamble save the very soul of the Federated Suns, or is the invasion of New Syrtis doomed before it can even start?

REMAGEN CRUCIS MARCH MILITIA HQ
REMAGEN, CHIRIKOF OPERATIONAL AREA
CRUCIS MARCH
FEDERATED SUNS
3 SEPTEMBER 3147

While the summit's attendees gathered, First Prince Julian Davion watched a recorded scene on the small screen in front of him: the keen edge of a *dao* sword glinted in the air, high above the neck of a kneeling elderly woman he knew all too well.

Julian hadn't set foot on New Syrtis, the Capellan March capital, in quite some time, but even the minor cosmetic changes in this footage imbued the scene with a surreal air. Though the date stamp on the footage was more than two years ago, he could ill conceive that this was the same Saso Square he had visited many, many times before.

Instead of Federated Suns BattleMechs flanking the path leading from the FedCom Civil War Monument to the Saso Statehouse, he saw Capellan Confederation 'Mechs stand sentinel while others patrolled nearby streets in search of insurrectionists. Instead of the round sword-and-sunburst iconography of House Davion gracing the Statehouse's facade in the backdrop of the footage, an all-too-familiar triangular emblem of House Liao replaced the original. Inside the stark-green Confederation insignia, an upraised arm held a curved scimitar, the blade's tip breaking out from the triangular border with hostile intent.

Below the Capellan emblem, the masked soldier held his *dao* aloft in perfect mimicry of the House Liao sigil. Below the blade, Duchess Amanda Hasek knelt in her finest courtly attire, her hands bound to either side of a block of wood. Despite the Damocles sword of a hated foe more than a meter above her neck, she struck Julian as surprisingly calm, a sinner who knows she is ultimately responsible for her own crimes.

Few members of House Davion agreed with her politics, with her rabid, outspoken loathing of the Capellan Confederation. Her decision more than forty years ago to instigate the disastrous Victoria War without then-First Prince Harrison Davion's approval had sealed her fate, and the Confederation's long-awaited reprisal against the Hasek family's homeworld was her well-deserved recompense. But this was too far.

Julian had never initially been destined to lead the Federated Suns, but the duchess had seen great potential in him and groomed him to be a contender for the throne. He owed this woman—his surrogate mother, his mentor—a good many things, including his current position as leader of the Federated Suns.

A man royal in bearing and military in garb—Daoshen Liao, Chancellor of the Capellan Confederation—rose to the platform and addressed both the accused and the crowd assembled before the square. Though Julian kept the sound muted for courtesy while waiting for the rest of the attendees to arrive, he could have quoted the Capellan's speech verbatim.

"For war crimes perpetrated against the celestial sovereignty of the Capellan Confederation," Daoshen mouthed with a smug smirk, *"I find you guilty as charged on all counts.*

"The sentence is death."

With a slow nod, the Chancellor signaled to the executioner. The *dao* descended as a curtain of silvery light reflecting off the blade. Blink, and Julian would miss it.

Something twisted inside Julian's chest, as though some part of him died along with her every time he watched the gory, decapitated form of his mother figure slump gracelessly to the platform.

He paused the playback on the Chancellor's satisfied grin, the look of a fox strutting out of a henhouse with feathers stuck between his teeth.

This was the reason for what he was about to do. For what *needed* to be done. *Revenge* was such a pedestrian word. This feeling in the First Prince's breast went far beyond mere vengeance. This was a matter of putting things right, resetting the equilibrium between the Suns and the Confederation.

But he could not make this decision lightly. Only last September had he and Daoshen's envoy—the Chancellor's younger sister, *Sang-shao* Danai Liao-Centrella—brokered an armistice between their two nations. The truce had justified itself at the time: the Confederation was cowering under the phantom threat posed by the Republic of the Sphere, while the Draconis Combine continued conquering world after Federated Suns world, including the Draconis March capital of Robinson. Soldiers of the Armed Forces of the Federated Suns retreating from New Avalon meant the Draconis Combine had captured House Davion's capital and two march capitals. The nation had spiraled into deep recession, and according to this summit of his top political and military advisors, the best economic stimulus was to retake one of the capital worlds. Like deer ticks, the Dracs were hooked too deep into New Avalon and Robinson, which left New Syrtis the easiest nut to crack. All he needed do was approve the proposed campaign.

Loath as he was to break his ceasefire with the Capellan Confederation, Julian saw a certain amount of wisdom in the action. However, every time he considered the long-term implications of breaking a pact signed by his own hand, the thought sat heavy in his guts, as though he'd swallowed a Gauss-rifle slug whole.

Julian looked out across the assembly hall. All the necessary personnel were now present. The Prince's Champion, Erik Sandoval. The Prince's Intelligence Advisor, Jennifer Dawes. MIIO Director Gary Harding. Field Marshal Anastasia Zibler. Colonels Sortek and Rhys. Everyone of consequence from the Suns' government-in exile, the AFFS, and the intelligence arms. Satisfied, he deactivated the handheld screen and called the summit to order.

"Friends and family, colleagues, and brothers and sisters-in-arms," he began, "I have decided the time has come to start rebuilding our great nation. Since my coronation as First Prince of the Federated Suns, many of you have compelled me to see virtue in an attempt to retake one of our lost capitals, to rekindle the faith and spirit of our people into a blazing pulsar for the whole galaxy to see. As a man of conscience, I have wrestled long with the matter of breaking truce with our Capellan neighbors. However, circumstances being what they are, if we are to do right by our people, now is the time to seize the initiative and restore freedom to those worlds that the Capellan Confederation snatched away from us in their bid for dominance.

"The time has come to execute a campaign for New Syrtis."

He paused to gauge reactions across the assembly. Expressions ran the gamut between unabashed patriotism to quiet condemnation. Among them, he imagined Amanda Hasek standing in cool approval of his proclamation.

This is what I would have done, he could hear her apparition say, *had I control of the Federated Suns.*

"As First Prince," he continued, "the armistice with the Capellan Confederation is mine to break. Because of this, I have decided to lead this assault personally. No one else should bear culpability for my actions."

Julian activated a podium control, and a breakdown of his invasion plan projected onto the wall screen behind him. "Ladies and gentlemen, I present Operation CERBERUS. This campaign calls for three task forces, code named Chimera, Orthus, and Hydra. The objective of Phase One is the envelopment and isolation of New Syrtis from the rest of the Confederation. Phase Two entails the assault on the march capital itself.

"Now, let's poke some holes in this, and see where we can patch them."

Julian acknowledged Harding's upraised hand, and the MIIO director rose to speak. "Your Grace, is this invasion the best allocation of our military resources? We have a standing truce with Daoshen Liao, and MI6 agents on Sian report that he spends more time jumping at Republic shadows than trying to wage further war against us. Would it not be more prudent to focus our military efforts on the Draconis Combine instead? Snatching back Robinson or New Avalon from the Dragon's clutches would strike a deeper moral victory for our people."

Julian shared a knowing glance with his champion, Erik Sandoval, before answering. "Director, we are already at war with the Combine. Coordinator Yori Kurita knows this. The Combine's warriors know this. Even now, they sit in entrenched and fortified positions, expecting—no, *daring* us to fight them. They are more than ready for us. The Confederation is not, and we can no longer squander the advantage of surprise. If we can ever hope to stand against the Combine in the future, liberating New Syrtis *now* is the key."

CERBERUS RALLY STATION
NEW DAMASCUS, CHIRIKOF OPERATIONAL AREA
CRUCIS MARCH
FEDERATED SUNS
19 SEPTEMBER 3147

From across the bargaining table inside the canvas tent, Captain Malerie Faulkner was unimpressed with this new Federated Suns liaison. It took a lot to impress soldiers of distant Clan pedigrees. This scrawny lackey, sent straight from First Prince Julian Davion himself, had to be a pencil pusher, a desk rider, not an actual warrior worthy of the title. Mal knew soldiers, and this sorry excuse for a uniform probably had a law degree, not a diploma from some MechWarrior academy or other.

She disliked lawyers. Such a dishonest, two-faced profession. She would much rather have solved negotiations the way her Clan ancestors did: put up your dukes, and the winner dictates the terms. Don't like the terms? Win the rematch. So much simpler than listening to sales pitch after sales pitch.

Thankfully her boss, Major Tallula Zheng, seemed to pay more attention. As executive officer of Tally's Talons, Mal could voice concerns about a contract, but the decision to accept terms was ultimately in Tally's court.

Tally, the battalion's golden-haired matron, gave the Davion lackey a glare that would've withered a lesser man. Mal frown-smiled to herself, slightly impressed at his resilience. But only slightly.

"No, no, no," Tally said, knifing her hands in an *x* in protest. "Our contract expired on the seventeenth. Under the terms we negotiated with your office, the Talons are now free agents, able to pursue whatever course of action we desire."

Lackey tapped his sheaf of papers atop the table to align them and straightened the sleeves of his olive-drab uniform jacket. "We understand that, Major. However, your presence here on New Damascus puts us in a precarious position. Your participation to this point required you to possess partial operational knowledge of our movements—"

"—and," Tally cut in, "our contract doesn't include a noncompete clause." She waved a hardcopy of the contract at him. "I never sign one that does. Noncompetes put a serious damper on future mercenary employment."

"Be that as it may, we are offering to extend your current contract plus an additional ten percent." With a hopeful curl to the corner of his mouth, Lackey slid a paper across the desk.

Tally shared a knowing glance with Mal. They'd acted out this charade often enough that they could do it in the middle of the night after being roused by a proximity alarm. "Faulkner, what do you think of this?" She gestured her jaw toward the new draft. "Does it look good, or should we hit up the Chancellor, see if he'll give us a better deal?"

Mal echoed her CO's nonchalant posture and made a good show of pretending to read the new contract. All the legalese was bound to be the same as the last contract: a self-righteous prick like Julian Davion lacked the necessary guile to pull off any kind of deception. People like him were known for keeping their word, even to a fault.

Mal crossed her arms and shook her head. "Twenty. We want twenty percent, or we walk."

Tally hooked a thumb Mal's way. "What she said. If you want me to take our business to the Capellans, then say so. No pay, no play."

An exasperated huff escaped Lackey's throat. He gathered up his papers and stood. "Uh, if you'll excuse me for a moment..." Without waiting for an answer, he slid a perscomm from his uniform pocket and stepped out through the tent flap.

Mal leaned closer to the tent flap as though that might help her eavesdrop on the call Lackey was obviously making out of their earshot. She caught the indecipherable muffle of Lackey's end of the conversation, but much to her irritation, that was all.

Only the Feddie's upper half reappeared through the tent flap. "My humblest of apologies, but I have something to attend to. I will return shortly."

Tally frowned once Lackey departed. "Ah, he won't be back. Shall I see if the Cappies are *actually* hiring these days? Or would you rather strike out to the Free Worlds League, hit up a province or two? The Clan Protectorate would probably hire us."

Moments later, the tent flap parted, and in strode three uniformed soldiers, the foremost a man Mal had only ever seen in photos and vids. Throughout her mercenary career, she had dealt with the occasional dignitary, noble, and celebrity. Every time she came across someone even remotely famous, the same thought struck her: these people the galaxy placed up on pedestals were mundane, ordinary folk just like her. Sans makeup or image retouching. Rough around the edges. Fame and celebrity—the mortal equivalent of godhood—were nothing but manufactured concepts.

But *this* man—

Mal's stomach seized upon seeing his countenance in person. Her brain knew he was mere flesh-and-blood, but this man, with short golden hair, arresting blue eyes, an honest, clean-shaven face, and a palpable aura of regality—he filled the tent with a kind of palpable majesty she had never before witnessed, as though his otherwise average build dwarfed the roomy space. Something about him suggested—no, *demanded*—respect, but quietly rather than by bluster.

Now *this* was a true warrior.

"Captain Sharma tells me you are considering not re-upping," First Prince Julian Davion said. Even the timbre of his voice was real and honest, unmodulated by the reverb and resonance typically saturating stately speeches given by monarchs and other interstellar politicians. "I would respectfully wish to know why."

The accusing tremble in his eyes sent a wave of guilt through Mal. "Our...our contract has expired, Your Highness. We are...merely exploring our options."

The First Prince approached the table and rapped knuckles in thought atop its fiberplast surface. "Thus far, your battalion has performed admirably as part of Task Force Hydra. My House troops are familiar with you, and you have worked well with them during combat exercises. You form a solid, cohesive force, one I will need for the days ahead."

Boots on the tabletop, Tally tipped her chair back on two legs, far enough Mal worried she'd fall backward. "Frankly, Your Highness, it's not a matter of what you need. It's a matter of payment. Are you prepared to pay us what we're worth?"

"At the risk of sounding desperate," said the First Prince, "I don't have time to scour the Inner Sphere for competent mercenary battalions on such short notice. Name your price."

Mal broke her gaze from Julian Davion long enough to wordlessly confer with her CO. Then she turned her attention back to the First Prince. "Twenty-five percent above our original contract," she said. "Plus combat bonus."

His throat contracted almost imperceptibly. Twenty-five meant a substantial amount of money, and even Mal knew the Federated Suns' coffers were running on fumes.

"Done," he said with a definitive nod. He extended a hand—bare skin, ungloved—and Tally shook it, firm and businesslike.

Mal narrowed her eyes just enough to not reveal her jealousy.

CYLLENE FOREST
TAYGETA
SIAN COMMONALITY
CAPELLAN CONFEDERATION
25 NOVEMBER 3147

The planet was lost. This much *Sang-shao* Eliza Zhao knew without a doubt, long before she had occasion to fire a single one of her *Tian-Zong*'s weapons.

Both hands clenched around her 'Mech's controls, she squinted against the actinic blue flare of an incoming PPC bolt her optics couldn't quite compensate against. The approaching black-and-gold *Prefect* wasn't aiming at her 'Mech, but the resolute steps of its defiant advance alarmed her.

Not two days before, the Enemy had come screaming down from the sky like *yaoguai* demons, combat-dropping on prepared positions in strategic places across the planet. Government buildings, spaceports, maglev transport hubs, supply depots—anything at all that could put her command off its game.

In retrospect, multiple factors had doomed their defense from the start. After the successful drive toward New Syrtis two years ago during Operation CELESTIAL REWARD, Chancellor Daoshen Liao had ordered Zhao's Dynasty Guard regiment here to Taygeta for a period of refit. Rumors of an incoming Federated Suns invasion force within the Confederation's borders goaded Zhao to put her troops on high alert, but the refit wasn't entirely complete. To worsen matters, the Dynasty Guard represented the best offensive regiment among the entire Capellan Hussars brigade. Her command could fight defensive battles when absolutely necessary, but to truly shine, they needed to go on the attack.

The advancing Republic of the Sphere troops never even gave the Guard a chance to rally and spearhead an assault into the invaders' lines. Their sheer weight forced her to make the hard choice between letting her command get pulverized between the hammer of these so-called First Dawn Guards and the regiment-plus anvil of unmarked, primer-gray mercenary BattleMechs.

What in the Chancellor's name did the *Republic* care about a relatively unimportant former Feddie world so far away from the Republic's impenetrable Fortress-wall border?

She snap-fired her own light PPCs at the target of opportunity and continued backpedaling into a stand of trees along with the rest of her augmented lance. More Dawn 'Mechs crested the rise ahead, their torsos tracking in her direction. Two flights of *Schrack*s in Republic colors shotgunned across the angry sunset in search of easy fodder along the Dynasty Guard's line of withdrawal. Two platoons of Behemoth II tanks rumbled up into view, turrets traversing for targets. Three squads of Republic-painted Taranis battlesuits emerged from beside the Behemoths.

The array of Republic troops before her only confirmed her suspicions about this invasion's outcome. Now it was merely a matter of how to conduct this defeat. It would come from no real fault of her own, but the Celestial Wisdom would not see it that way if she ordered her soldiers to pull out and head for another planet. Her duty was to ensure she and her regiment gave as good an account of themselves as possible, leaving full, off-planet retreat as the very last contingency.

In the old days of the Succession Wars, the desperation of the Capellan Confederation Armed Forces often saw units embrace "hopeless battle syndrome" and fight to the death, even in the face of insurmountable odds and guaranteed destruction. Daoshen Liao and his predecessor were far less frivolous with Capellan lives, but retreating now, when so many of her regiment and the enemy still remained operational, would be viewed as a dereliction of duty.

Though the Chancellor harbored a near-pathological fear of the Republic—an understandable sentiment, given the disaster of the Capellan Crusades nearly four decades ago—Zhao did not. Republic troops were no different than any other. With all due respect to the Celestial Wisdom, no military was truly invincible. No army lacked a weakness. As commander of a prestigious Capellan Hussars regiment, she was not about to kowtow to these invaders, not yet.

She would tear them apart, limb from limb, before ever deserting her station. For all she knew, the Strategios, CCAF High Command, could already have reinforcements en route, and abandoning her post now would doom her relief. In a fleeting moment of whimsy, Zhao imagined the familiar silhouette of *Yen-Lo-Wang* descending from orbit and landing in a cloud right before the terrified Republic troops. But Danai Liao-Centrella, Zhao's longtime friend and owner of the legendary *Centurion* BattleMech, was on Sian trying to make some sense of the tactical disaster on Marlette that had claimed the lives of countless CCAF troops.

Amusing as it would be to witness incoming Republic forces cower at the sight of a single BattleMech, Zhao knew she had to damage her enemy's war-making capacity as much as possible before she could justify retreat. The Celestial Wisdom would expect no less from her.

She adjusted her aim on the nearest target downrange, a battered Scapha hovertank, and the *Tian-Zong*'s frame shook from the tremor of a Gauss rifle discharge. Faster than a snap of the fingers, an obscenely sized hole plowed through the Scapha's glacis armor. The tank stilled.

She was about to order a strategic fighting withdrawal when a voice from her regimental command channel piped up into her neurohelmet's earpiece.

"Sheng One, this is Two," *Zhong-shao* Bogdanovich, Zhao's executive officer, transmitted from his 65-ton *Vandal* nearby, just out of her sight line. "We have received a priority-one message."

One of the dead tank's companions replied with a rotary autocannon blast. Zhao's cockpit bucked from explosive shells impacting across her 'Mech's torso. "A little busy here, Two."

"It's from Sian, sir."

Zhao's fingers loosened on her controls. The Confederation capital meant two things: orders either from CCAF High Command—or from the Celestial Wisdom himself.

Neither possibility appealed to her.

Another flight of *Schrack*s tore across the rapidly darkening sky. "Give me the short version."

Bogdanovich transmitted the official verigraphed communiqué, which displayed on Zhao's command readout. The orders came straight from the Chancellor himself:

Sang-shao, you are hereby ordered to disengage and report to New Syrtis ASAP.

Zhao clenched her jaw and fired off another salvo of Gauss-rifle fire along the encroaching tank platoon. One nickel-ferrous slug cratered the ground, kicking up a cloud of dirt clods. The other instantaneously transformed a large, majestic tree into a sawed-off stump.

The planet was already lost, but the relief a retreat order should have elicited did not come. A profound sense of hollowness inside made her feel as though obeying the Chancellor's order would still be betraying his trust in her command ability.

"All right," she replied, her voice hesitant. "Give the orders for a full fighting withdrawal from the planet."

BATTLETECH GLOSSARY

AUTOCANNON

This is a rapid-fire, auto-loading weapon. Light autocannons range from 30 to 90 millimeter (mm), and heavy autocannons may be from 80 to 120mm or more. They fire high-speed streams of high-explosive, armor-piercing shells.

BATTLEMECH

BattleMechs are the most powerful war machines ever built. First developed by Terran scientists and engineers, these huge vehicles are faster, more mobile, better-armored and more heavily armed than any twentieth-century tank. Ten to twelve meters tall and equipped with particle projection cannons, lasers, rapid-fire autocannon and missiles, they pack enough firepower to flatten anything but another BattleMech. A small fusion reactor provides virtually unlimited power, and BattleMechs can be adapted to fight in environments ranging from sun-baked deserts to subzero arctic icefields.

DROPSHIPS

Because interstellar JumpShips must avoid entering the heart of a solar system, they must "dock" in space at a considerable distance from a system's inhabited worlds. DropShips were developed for interplanetary travel. As the name implies, a DropShip is attached to hardpoints on the JumpShip's drive core, later to be dropped from the parent vessel after in-system entry. Though incapable of FTL travel, DropShips are highly maneuverable, well-armed and sufficiently aerodynamic to take off from and land on a planetary surface. The journey from the jump point to the inhabited worlds of a system usually requires a normal-space journey of several days or weeks, depending on the type of star.

FLAMER

The flamethrower is a small but time-honored anti-infantry weapon in vehicular arsenals. Whether fusion-based or fuel-based, flamers spew fire in a tight beam of bright orange that "splashes" against a target, igniting almost anything it touches.

GAUSS RIFLE

This weapon uses magnetic coils to accelerate a solid nickel-ferrous slug about the size of a football at an enemy target, inflicting massive damage through sheer kinetic impact at long range and with little heat. However, the accelerator coils and the slug's supersonic speed mean that while the Gauss rifle is smokeless and lacks the flash of an autocannon, it has a much more potent report that can shatter glass.

JUMPSHIPS

Interstellar travel is accomplished via JumpShips, first developed in the twenty-second century. These somewhat ungainly vessels consist of a long, thin drive core and a sail resembling an enormous parasol, which can extend up to a kilometer in width. The ship is named for its ability to "jump" instantaneously across vast distances of space. After making its jump, the ship cannot travel until it has recharged by gathering up more solar energy.

The JumpShip's enormous sail is constructed from a special metal that absorbs vast quantities of electromagnetic energy from the nearest star. When it has soaked up enough energy, the sail transfers it to the drive core, which converts it into a space-twisting field. An instant later, the ship arrives at the next jump point, a distance of up to thirty light-years. This field is known as hyperspace, and its discovery opened to mankind the gateway to the stars.

JumpShips never land on planets. Interplanetary travel is carried out by DropShips, vessels that are attached to the JumpShip until arrival at the jump point.

LASER

An acronym for "Light Amplification through Stimulated Emission of Radiation." When used as a weapon, the laser damages the target by concentrating extreme heat onto a small area. BattleMech lasers are designated as small, medium or large. Lasers are also available as shoulder-fired weapons operating from a portable backpack power unit. Certain range-finders and targeting equipment also employ low-level lasers.

LRM

This is an abbreviation for "Long-Range Missile," an indirect-fire missile with a high-explosive warhead.

MACHINE GUN

A small autocannon intended for anti-personnel assaults. Typically non-armor-penetrating, machine guns are often best used against infantry, as they can spray a large area with relatively inexpensive fire.

PARTICLE PROJECTION CANNON (PPC)

One of the most powerful and long-range energy weapons on the battlefield, a PPC fires a stream of charged particles that outwardly functions as a bright blue laser, but also throws off enough static discharge to resemble a bolt of manmade lightning. The kinetic and heat impact of a PPC is enough to cause the vaporization of armor and structure alike, and most PPCs have the power to kill a pilot in his machine through an armor-penetrating headshot.

SRM

This is the abbreviation for "Short-Range Missile," a direct-trajectory missile with high-explosive or armor-piercing explosive warheads. They have a range of less than one kilometer and are only reliably accurate at ranges of less than 300 meters. They are more powerful, however, than LRMs.

SUCCESSOR LORDS

After the fall of the first Star League, the remaining members of the High Council each asserted his or her right to become First Lord. Their star empires became known as the Successor States and the rulers as Successor Lords. The Clan Invasion temporarily interrupted centuries of warfare known as the Succession Wars, which first began in 2786.

BATTLETECH ERAS

The *BattleTech* universe is a living, vibrant entity that grows each year as more sourcebooks and fiction are published. A dynamic universe, its setting and characters evolve over time within a highly detailed continuity framework, bringing everything to life in a way a static game universe cannot match.

To help quickly and easily convey the timeline of the universe—and to allow a player to easily "plug in" a given novel or sourcebook—we've divided *BattleTech* into six major eras.

STAR LEAGUE
(Present–2780)

Ian Cameron, ruler of the Terran Hegemony, concludes decades of tireless effort with the creation of the Star League, a political and military alliance between all Great Houses and the Hegemony. Star League armed forces immediately launch the Reunification War, forcing the Periphery realms to join. For the next two centuries, humanity experiences a golden age across the thousand light-years of human-occupied space known as the Inner Sphere. It also sees the creation of the most powerful military in human history.

(This era also covers the centuries before the founding of the Star League in 2571, most notably the Age of War.)

SUCCESSION WARS
(2781–3049)

Every last member of First Lord Richard Cameron's family is killed during a coup launched by Stefan Amaris. Following the thirteen-year war to unseat him, the rulers of each of the five Great Houses disband the Star League. General Aleksandr Kerensky departs with eighty percent of the Star League Defense Force beyond known space and the Inner Sphere collapses into centuries of warfare known as the Succession Wars that will eventually result in a massive loss of technology across most worlds.

CLAN INVASION
(3050–3061)

A mysterious invading force strikes the coreward region of the Inner Sphere. The invaders, called the Clans, are descendants of Kerensky's SLDF troops, forged into a society dedicated to becoming the greatest fighting force in history. With vastly superior technology and warriors, the Clans conquer world after world. Eventually this outside threat will forge a new Star League, something hundreds of years of warfare failed to accomplish. In addition, the Clans will act as a catalyst for a technological renaissance.

CIVIL WAR
(3062–3067)

The Clan threat is eventually lessened with the complete destruction of a Clan. With that massive external threat apparently neutralized, internal conflicts explode around the Inner Sphere. House Liao conquers its former Commonality, the St. Ives Compact; a rebellion of military units belonging to House Kurita sparks a war with their powerful border enemy, Clan Ghost Bear; the fabulously powerful Federated Commonwealth of House Steiner and House Davion collapses into five long years of bitter civil war.

JIHAD
(3067–3080)

Following the Federated Commonwealth Civil War, the leaders of the Great Houses meet and disband the new Star League, declaring it a sham. The pseudo-religious Word of Blake—a splinter group of ComStar, the protectors and controllers of interstellar communication—launch the Jihad: an interstellar war that pits every faction against each other and even against themselves, as weapons of mass destruction are used for the first time in centuries while new and frightening technologies are also unleashed.

DARK AGE
(3081–3150)

Under the guidance of Devlin Stone, the Republic of the Sphere is born at the heart of the Inner Sphere following the Jihad. One of the more extensive periods of peace begins to break out as the 32nd century dawns. The factions, to one degree or another, embrace disarmament, and the massive armies of the Succession Wars begin to fade. However, in 3132 eighty percent of interstellar communications collapses, throwing the universe into chaos. Wars erupt almost immediately, and the factions begin rebuilding their armies.

LOOKING FOR MORE HARD HITTING BATTLETECH FICTION?

WE'LL GET YOU RIGHT BACK INTO THE BATTLE!

Catalyst Game Labs brings you the very best in *BattleTech* fiction, available at most ebook retailers, including Amazon, Apple Books, Kobo, Barnes & Noble, and more!

NOVELS

1. *Decision at Thunder Rift* by William H. Keith Jr.
2. *Mercenary's Star* by William H. Keith Jr.
3. *The Price of Glory* by William H. Keith, Jr.
4. *Warrior: En Garde* by Michael A. Stackpole
5. *Warrior: Riposte* by Michael A. Stackpole
6. *Warrior: Coupé* by Michael A. Stackpole
7. *Wolves on the Border* by Robert N. Charrette
8. *Heir to the Dragon* by Robert N. Charrette
9. *Lethal Heritage* (The Blood of Kerensky, Volume 1) by Michael A. Stackpole
10. *Blood Legacy* (The Blood of Kerensky, Volume 2) by Michael A. Stackpole
11. *Lost Destiny* (The Blood of Kerensky, Volume 3) by Michael A. Stackpole
12. *Way of the Clans* (Legend of the Jade Phoenix, Volume 1) by Robert Thurston
13. *Bloodname* (Legend of the Jade Phoenix, Volume 2) by Robert Thurston
14. *Falcon Guard* (Legend of the Jade Phoenix, Volume 3) by Robert Thurston
15. *Wolf Pack* by Robert N. Charrette
16. *Main Event* by James D. Long
17. *Natural Selection* by Michael A. Stackpole
18. *Assumption of Risk* by Michael A. Stackpole
19. *Blood of Heroes* by Andrew Keith
20. *Close Quarters* by Victor Milán
21. *Far Country* by Peter L. Rice
22. *D.R.T.* by James D. Long
23. *Tactics of Duty* by William H. Keith
24. *Bred for War* by Michael A. Stackpole
25. *I Am Jade Falcon* by Robert Thurston
26. *Highlander Gambit* by Blaine Lee Pardoe
27. *Hearts of Chaos* by Victor Milán
28. *Operation Excalibur* by William H. Keith
29. *Malicious Intent* by Michael A. Stackpole
30. *Black Dragon* by Victor Milán
31. *Impetus of War* by Blaine Lee Pardoe

32. *Double-Blind* by Loren L. Coleman
33. *Binding Force* by Loren L. Coleman
34. *Exodus Road* (Twilight of the Clans, Volume 1) by Blaine Lee Pardoe
35. *Grave Covenant* ((Twilight of the Clans, Volume 2) by Michael A. Stackpole
36. *The Hunters* (Twilight of the Clans, Volume 3) by Thomas S. Gressman
37. *Freebirth* (Twilight of the Clans, Volume 4) by Robert Thurston
38. *Sword and Fire* (Twilight of the Clans, Volume 5) by Thomas S. Gressman
39. *Shadows of War* (Twilight of the Clans, Volume 6) by Thomas S. Gressman
40. *Prince of Havoc* (Twilight of the Clans, Volume 7) by Michael A. Stackpole
41. *Falcon Rising* (Twilight of the Clans, Volume 8) by Robert Thurston
42. *Threads of Ambition* (The Capellan Solution, Book 1) by Loren L. Coleman
43. *The Killing Fields* (The Capellan Solution, Book 2) by Loren L. Coleman
44. *Dagger Point* by Thomas S. Gressman
45. *Ghost of Winter* by Stephen Kenson
46. *Roar of Honor* by Blaine Lee Pardoe
47. *By Blood Betrayed* by Blaine Lee Pardoe and Mel Odom
48. *Illusions of Victory* by Loren L. Coleman
49. *Flashpoint* by Loren L. Coleman
50. *Measure of a Hero* by Blaine Lee Pardoe
51. *Path of Glory* by Randall N. Bills
52. *Test of Vengeance* by Bryan Nystul
53. *Patriots and Tyrants* by Loren L. Coleman
54. *Call of Duty* by Blaine Lee Pardoe
55. *Initiation to War* by Robert N. Charrette
56. *The Dying Time* by Thomas S. Gressman
57. *Storms of Fate* by Loren L. Coleman
58. *Imminent Crisis* by Randall N. Bills
59. *Operation Audacity* by Blaine Lee Pardoe
60. *Endgame* by Loren L. Coleman
61. *A Bonfire of Worlds* by Steven Mohan, Jr.
62. *Isle of the Blessed* by Steven Mohan, Jr.
63. *Embers of War* by Jason Schmetzer
64. *Betrayal of Ideals* by Blaine Lee Pardoe
65. *Forever Faithful* by Blaine Lee Pardoe
66. *Kell Hounds Ascendant* by Michael A. Stackpole
67. *Redemption Rift* by Jason Schmetzer

YOUNG ADULT NOVELS

1. *The Nellus Academy Incident* by Jennifer Brozek
2. *Iron Dawn* (*Rogue Academy, Book 1*) by Jennifer Brozek
3. *Ghost Hour* (*Rogue Academy, Book 2*) by Jennifer Brozek

OMNIBUSES

1. *The Gray Death Legion Trilogy* by William H. Keith, Jr.

NOVELLAS/SHORT STORIES

1. *Lion's Roar* by Steven Mohan, Jr.
2. *Sniper* by Jason Schmetzer
3. *Eclipse* by Jason Schmetzer
4. *Hector* by Jason Schmetzer
5. *The Frost Advances (Operation Ice Storm, Part 1)* by Jason Schmetzer
6. *The Winds of Spring (Operation Ice Storm, Part 2)* by Jason Schmetzer
7. *Instrument of Destruction (Ghost Bear's Lament, Part 1)* by Steven Mohan, Jr.
8. *The Fading Call of Glory (Ghost Bear's Lament, Part 2)* by Steven Mohan, Jr.
9. *Vengeance* by Jason Schmetzer
10. *A Splinter of Hope* by Philip A. Lee
11. *The Anvil* by Blaine Lee Pardoe
12. *A Splinter of Hope/The Anvil* (omnibus)
13. *Not the Way the Smart Money Bets (Kell Hounds Ascendant #1)* by Michael A. Stackpole
14. *A Tiny Spot of Rebellion (Kell Hounds Ascendant #2)* by Michael A. Stackpole
15. *A Clever Bit of Fiction (Kell Hounds Ascendant #3)* by Michael A. Stackpole
16. *Break-Away (Proliferation Cycle #1)* by Ilsa J. Bick
17. *Prometheus Unbound (Proliferation Cycle #2)* by Herbert A. Beas II
18. *Nothing Ventured (Proliferation Cycle #3)* by Christoffer Trossen
19. *Fall Down Seven Times, Get Up Eight (Proliferation Cycle #4)* by Randall N. Bills
20. *A Dish Served Cold (Proliferation Cycle #5)* by Chris Hartford and Jason M. Hardy
21. *The Spider Dances (Proliferation Cycle #6)* by Jason Schmetzer
22. *Shell Games* by Jason Schmetzer
23. *Divided We Fall* by Blaine Lee Pardoe
24. *The Hunt for Jardine (Forgotten Worlds, Part One)* by Herbert A. Beas II

ANTHOLOGIES

1. *The Corps (BattleCorps Anthology, Volume 1)* edited by Loren. L. Coleman
2. *First Strike (BattleCorps Anthology, Volume 2)* edited by Loren L. Coleman
3. *Weapons Free (BattleCorps Anthology, Volume 3)* edited by Jason Schmetzer
4. *Onslaught: Tales from the Clan Invasion* edited by Jason Schmetzer
5. *Edge of the Storm* by Jason Schmetzer
6. *Fire for Effect (BattleCorps Anthology, Volume 4)* edited by Jason Schmetzer
7. *Chaos Born (Chaos Irregulars, Book 1)* by Kevin Killiany
8. *Chaos Formed (Chaos Irregulars, Book 2)* by Kevin Killiany
9. *Counterattack (BattleCorps Anthology, Volume 5)* edited by Jason Schmetzer
10. *Front Lines (BattleCorps Anthology Volume 6)* edited by Jason Schmetzer and Philip A. Lee
11. *Legacy* edited by John Helfers and Philip A. Lee
12. *Kill Zone (BattleCorps Anthology Volume 7)* edited by Philip A. Lee
13. *Gray Markets (A BattleCorps Anthology)*, edited by Jason Schmetzer and Philip A. Lee
14. *Slack Tide (A BattleCorps Anthology)*, edited by Jason Schmetzer and Philip A. Lee

Made in the USA
Middletown, DE
21 October 2024

62997150R00172